CRACKED DOORS

BY
P. VINCENT RIVERS

Cracked Doors © 2012 by P. Vincent Rivers
P. Vincent Rivers Publishing

ISBN: 978-0615676043

Cover Designer: MWS Designz

Printed in the United States of America

ACKNOWLEDGEMENTS

This book is dedicated to my entire circle of family and friends. Your influences have shaped the beautiful reality that is my life. Every experience good and bad has enriched my existence tremendously and shaped my voice as a writer. I hope my work makes you laugh, cry, remember, cherish, think and most of all proud. Much Love, P. Vincent.

I would like to thank a couple people in particular for their assistance and encouragement in writing this novel. Crystal Fletcher (my Nashville connection) thanks for all the phone convo's and pictures. Raquel Wright-McGowan thanks for the encouragement. You were my first fan, lol. Author Candice Dow thanks for your kind words early in my writing. It meant a lot coming from someone that had been there. My two beautiful daughters Briana and Paige, you are always the source of my motivation. My mother, dad and grandparents. . .speechless. To the Hextronians . . .to infinity and beyond. Nothing but love, homies. To the list of family and friends that gave me encouraging words along the way, thank you. It wouldn't have been possible without your support.

CRACKED DOORS

CHAPTER 1
EVAN MILES

"I can't believe I'm letting you watch me pee."

She spoke in a matter-of-fact tone. Everything was the same. The way her neck and shoulder muscles flexed as she leaned forward; the way she tucked her shiny, black, shoulder-length hair behind her ear; the way she teased me with those beautiful, brown eyes and gorgeous smile. Even the way she opened those long, athletic, chocolate legs just enough for me to see the top of what I was longing for. Everything was the same, not one single sign of discomfort. I knew her all too well. That was her way of letting me know she had taken control of her emotional rollercoaster ride and was obviously a lot closer to restoring balance to her universe than I was.

"I guess it's good that we're still comfortable around each other, huh?" I asked, as I sat on the floor in the doorway.

I tried my best to act just as comfortably as I used to. We've continued our conversations to the bathroom while the other was using the toilet a gazillion times before. Funny though, I always thought the reason I followed her there was some sort of sexual ego trip, knowing I had total access to what I considered to be the sexiest woman alive. But, as I sat there, I realized what I really missed was the wholeness I felt knowing I had someone to share my life with.

Silence as comfortable as the earth-toned walls and ocean-breeze aromatherapy candles that filled the room. Each time our eyes met, they helplessly took turns diving into one another, reliving each and every joyous, memorable, happy, and sad event that our once intertwined lives shared.

"Do you like my new perfume?" she asked with that same conniving, nonchalant manner.

She must have sensed how much I was enjoying my memories and decided she would rather have me losing a slap-boxing match with reality than dancing around in my mind with happy memories of our past. She knew how much I loved her old staple fragrance. No matter how many hundreds of thousands of bottles they sold, in my mind, she was the only woman in the world that wore Angel. She knew she was forcing me to look at her in a different light, to accept the changes in her life.

Suddenly, everything changed. Those inviting shades of olive, brown, and rust had become adequate illustrations of the dark hue of gloom that our bright love had dimmed to. The peaceful and tranquil flames from the candles were now symbols of the growing glare of rage brewing inside me. Without my control, my once reluctant and undercover glances had turned into a blatant scavenger hunt for signs of *him*.

"It's alright," I replied with a poor imitation of her nonchalant tone.

I couldn't possibly give her the satisfaction of knowing how much that change hurt me. I just smiled and gave her the blankest look I could under the circumstances. I continued my hunt. The red linen dress was not new. The shoes, earrings, bracelets were all old, even the gray cotton thongs with the ripped off tag that used to scratch the back of her waist. Old.

There was a new toe ring. It was the kind of ring that comes from the store already drenched with sentimental value. I hadn't seen her in weeks, but I could tell she wore it every day, regardless of her attire. It obviously had a story behind it, one that I did not care to know.

"I thought about you when Tiffany and I were in SexCapades the other day picking up some games."

"What made you think of me at SexCapades?" I asked, knowing damn well she really didn't think of me.

She just wanted me to know that she and her new man played sex games. That was something we had talked about doing to rekindle our passion, but never got a chance to do.

"I saw a lot of games and thought about how much fun me and you would have if we had played together."

"Oh really?"

"Yep." She paused, looked at me for a second, and then lowered her eyes. "I never realized how compatible we were until…" She paused again.

"Until what?"

"I just really miss us," she said, as she stood up from the toilet to wipe.

The sadness in those brown eyes put out my burning rage and once again warmed those beautifully rich and inviting earth tones. With the same conviction I held about never burning any scent other than ocean breeze, I also knew that part of her really meant those words.

She really does still love me, I thought to myself. "What do you miss about us?" I semi-anxiously asked, trying not to give away my excitement on the direction of our conversation.

I thought this was the moment she would finally realize how much she missed my presence in her life.

She was now standing over me with those thongs still at her ankles and her dress hiked up far enough to expose her newly developed six-pack. My mind sent emergency APB's out for every endorphin in my body to go directly to its respective arousal cell. But, my heart remained focused on the question at hand. I wanted her answer to be something related to the million and one laughs we shared; the dreams we had of our life together, complete with the 2.5 kids. I wanted her answer to be something related to how she loved me because I was the only man in her life that ever loved her enough to help her love herself. I wanted her to acknowledge the full range of my influence in her life. I wanted her to tell me that since we split, her life had not been the same and had been just as messed up as mine. I wanted to know that her days were a seesaw battle between the moments she tried not to think of me and moments she couldn't help but to think of me anyway, just like mine.

"I miss the way you eat me out," she replied, while backing away, jumping up on the sink counter, and spreading one leg all the way to the wall with the medicine cabinet and cocking the other on top of the toilet.

She leaned her back against the mirror, opened up her microwave door, and served the softest, most bittersweet entrée to the famished little bastard seated in the center of my memory. As my mind told him to eat until his appetite was satisfied, my heart already knew that meal would be the death of him.

The roadmap to her sexual fulfillment had long been etched in my brain. Hell, I was the designer, architect, and constructor of every road on that map. I knew every back road, side street, and expressway to her orgasm. As I knelt there, I traveled each and every road like we were visiting our hometown for the last time.

Ain't no way he eats the pussy like this, I thought to myself.

The way I pulled back the side lips of her vagina, made my wet tongue lay wide and flat, and massaged every muscle she had. With each lick, my travels intensified and her moans grew louder. If love wouldn't bring her back to me, then surely those three back-to-back orgasms would ooze her back into my arms.

"Why are you crying?" I asked, while kneeling there in front of her with generous helpings of her cum all over my nose and mouth. I thought to myself, *Surely she must be overwhelmed by her feelings for me.*

"I can't do Shandon like this."

She spoke with a hell of a lot more passion than she did when talking about us. The passion in her voice instantly angered me beyond control. How the hell could she be so damn flat while reminiscing over the three long years we were together? As if all the struggles we conquered as friends, all the ecstasy we created as lovers, and the bond we shared as soul mates, were not worthy enough to get a rise out of her.

"What the fuck do you mean you can't do Shandon like this? What about the way you're doing me? Do you even give a damn?" With every syllable, I felt the tide of my rage and frustration gain momentum by multiples of a million.

"I can see that you're upset. Maybe it was a mistake to come here."

This time, her nonchalant tone wasn't conniving. In my mind, it was a hopeless way of trying to protect herself from seeing and hearing my pain. It was too late for any last second river rescue. The current of my rage had broken the dam. Today, I would not be the only one drowning in my sorrow and pain.

"Naw, bitch, it wasn't *no* damn mistake! You knew exactly what the fuck you were doing! Comin' over here throwin' yo' damn pussy in my face. Talkin' about 'I miss the way you eat my pussy'," I spat, mimicking her tone. "I see your trifling ass didn't start thinking about *Shandon* until after you had busted three nuts in my mouth!" I yelled, then stood up, walked out of the bathroom, down the hall, and into the living room.

"Actually, I had been thinking of him the whole time. I never should've let you start in the first place. I apologize for that, but you gotta…"

I cut her off before she could finish.

"Erica, how the hell do I let you keep playing this damn game with my heart?"

I punched myself on the hip and turned around so she couldn't see the well of tears forming in my eyes. I was truly disappointed with myself, again. I was disappointed for letting myself get so wrapped up in her that I lost sight of who I was as a man. I even let her get under my skin enough to call her out of her name.

As I sat with my back to her, I faced myself for the first time. I realized that no matter what she was or was not feeling toward me, it wasn't enough. I realized she was no longer worth my time, tears, or love.

"You know what, Erica?"

When I turned around, surprisingly, she was not smirking like I thought she would be. Her eyes looked as if she had been crying just as long as I had: 4 months, 17 days, 8 hours, 23 minutes and counting. Still, it wasn't enough.

"You're not playing with my heart. You're playing with my head, both of them. My heart just wants to be happy, and it knows that its happiness is not with you. My problem is I keep letting my head tell me that you'll change…that one day you'll stop playing these games. Regardless of what games you play from this day forward, as far as Evan Miles is concerned, you will have to play them by yourself. I AM DONE!"

Those words were reiterated with every ounce of my aura and all nine of the sure and steady strides I made to the front door. After opening the front door, I turned towards her to see she was openly sobbing. Even though her legs were just as long as mine, it took her fifteen strides to cover the same trek from the edge of the hallway to the front door. She grabbed my hand as she was walking through the doorway and let go as she turned towards me just on the other side. She gathered herself, stopped crying, and just stared at me for a moment.

What a gorgeous woman, I thought, as she turned and walked away.

Once I returned to the bathroom, I noticed she had left her gray thongs on the bathroom floor. *But you gotta what?* I wondered, realizing I never let her finish her statement. *Oh well. At this point, I guess it doesn't matter.*

I threw the thongs in the trash, blew out the ocean breeze-scented candle, and looked forward to burning the new Glade mountain berry candle I bought earlier.

CHAPTER 2
MACHAIA {MUH-KYE-AH} JAMES

Cough! Cough! Cough! De'Mann leaned over the side of the bed and raised one hand to his mouth as he looked down, as if to find the lung he was coughing up. *Cough! Cough! Cough!* He leaned back over with the sexiest, aggravating, and totally inappropriate smirk on his face while continuing to smoke his blunt.

"Damn, girl. Stop trippin'! You might as well go on and hit this. You know you want to. Plus, that shit will be over tomorrow anyway. So, it doesn't even matter." He spoke with that strained voice smokers have when talking and holding in a mouthful of smoke at the same time.

During the eleven months after high school while sleeping in the same bed every night at his one-bedroom apartment, he smoked a blunt and talked to me with that strained voice. Never did it sound as carefree as now. He laughed out loud and looked at me, as he slowly exhaled. Every muscle in his long, slightly underweight body relaxed simultaneously. His shoulder-length locs seemed like they could reach the floor. Even his dick was limp despite the two Viagra pills missing from his secret stash he didn't think I knew about. As much as his mouth did, his eyes could never lie to me. As he turned toward me, the relief in his eyes told me that he had just released a whole lot more than just a mouthful of smoke.

Once again, he had gotten his way. It's something about the sacrifices and compromises a woman makes for her man that some dumb-asses won't ever get or attempt to try. *Why do I always give in?* I thought. Whenever he wanted to have unprotected sex, he gave me every excuse in the book.

'Girl, I just want to feel how warm it is', 'I'll pull it out before I nut', 'It makes me feel closer to you'. Even though every ounce of my gut and six shitloads of evidence told me how many females he was sexing on the side, all of those excuses worked.

When he brought a girl home and told me that we would breakup if we didn't find ways to keep our relationship alive, I pimp-slapped my own womanhood and tongue kissed him, while some strange bitch sucked his dick and rode him. Then, I cried and kissed my way through fifteen minutes of her eating me out. Against my better judgment, I even stopped using my birth control patches because he thought I was gaining too much weight. He said he couldn't have a chubby chick on his side. When I found out I was pregnant, I cried uncontrollably. I knew De'Mann's 45-minute lecture on how "we have to be smart, and I love you but this ain't the time" word for word. He only cared about himself, and he always got his way with me. My eyes filled with tears, as I began seeing myself in a new light.

"De'Mann, do you give a damn about anything other than yourself? Your child is gonna DIE tomorrow, and all you can think about is a chance to fuck without a rubber because I'm already pregnant!" My voice was strained, too. I was choking on all the emotions I had placed on the back burner while trying to be 'down for my man'.

"See, Machaia, that's the shit I'm talking about right there. If you knew you still had beef with the choice we made, why the fuck did you agree to it?" He almost said that with enough confidence to make me believe that abortion was really *our* choice.

"All I'm saying is you made up your mind without even considering all the choices. You–"

"What choices?" He yelled loud enough to wake up every dead person in a ten-mile radius. "You're so quick to start hollering about choices when you ain't doing SHIT! You sit in this motherfucker and chill all damn day. You don't clean, cook, or nothing. You just motherfuckin' chill! And then you wanna criticize me 'cause I don't feel like I can handle any more shit stressin' me out. Talking about a baby could die; what about me? I could die any given day I walk out that door, but you don't care about that. You got some damn nerve!"

For the next thirty minutes, the words of his rampage screamed at me that I wasn't 'bout shit', as he would put it, and that I was the most ungrateful woman he had ever run across in his whole life. But, the sadness in his eyes told me otherwise. His eyes pleaded with me to understand the sacrifices and struggles his soul had to make every day, as he sold shipments of drugs daily to provide for his family. He faced the constant threat of death from friends and enemies alike. Being the biggest dope dealer in Nashville, Tennessee is hard, but he did it to take care of me. The least I could do was compromise.

I passionately kissed his cheeks, wiping away his tears with my lips. Then, I laid back and spread my legs as wide as I could to welcome his unprotected penis inside my temple. *It doesn't matter. I'm already pregnant. After tomorrow, everything will be back to normal,* I thought to myself.

"I love you, baby. Don't cry. I'm down to do whatever I gotta do for us to make it. Just put it in me. I want you to feel how warm my pussy is."

It's funny how if given enough time around negativity, those sentiments become your own. Loving a drug dealer was an ugly job, but I was bitch enough to do it.

De'Mann's body had tightened to a long chain of intensity. Every muscle was rock hard, except one. The thought of what or who drew the life out of it was ever present in my mind, but he was my man. No bitch's pussy was going to be the last thing he thought of before going to sleep. So, I grabbed his limpness and began massaging.

"Machaia, not now. I'm not in the mood. You got me trippin' on tomorrow."

"Don't worry about tomorrow. I'll be fine. I just want to feel you inside of me tonight."

I kept massaging, but still limpness. It didn't make sense. We hadn't made love in almost five days.

"What's wrong, baby?" I looked him directly in the eyes, while speaking slowly and seductively to hide the curiosity in my voice.

"Just have a lot of things on my mind, that's all."

He stared directly back at me. He didn't want to, but he did. His eyes told me otherwise. Of all the fights and arguments we've had, I can't remember one being about sex. At least, they were not about the frequency of sex. After five days of abstinence, his dick should have stood up with the thought of having sex, but it didn't. I knew better. He had been messing around. Some bitch somewhere was fast asleep. My man had fucked her to that peaceful place and came home lifeless to me.

With anger and anxiety intensifying my passion, I took him into my mouth with warm, wet aggression. I didn't even know if he had washed his dick off. I sucked harder. My eyes began to well, but I continued staring into his eyes so they could tell me what he was thinking. As his limpness finally gave way to rigidity, his eyes widened.

Without speaking a word, I climbed on top of him with my anger-drenched pussy. The intensity of the moment forced me to climax hard, and moisture ran from every orifice of my body. Sweat poured from my skin, remnants of my multiple orgasms drained from my temple, and tears trickled from my eyes. I rode on.

As he reached his orgasm, the light was just bright enough for me to look in the mirror and see that smirk of satisfaction back on his face.

How lucky I am to have a man that I can love this hard. Ride or die for life. I'm down for mine.

CHAPTER 3
EVAN MILES

Liberating, isn't it? Confidently, that's what my heart kept asking me. By the minute, hour, and day, that question echoed. Through four monotonous months at the lab where I worked, a half summer of sorrow, 137 ignored phone calls from friends, 1.9 gazillion worried stares from my mother, and three "how to handle these hoes" lectures from my best friend Greg while making plans for me to move in with him in Chicago, it echoed. Through two waves of regular exams and a hellafied set of finals during my last semester of medical school, three totally insignificant dates, and one awesome night of buck wild sex with a drop-dead gorgeous lady from the gym whose eyes watered as she told me that she'd never had her pussy eaten like that, it echoed. Through it all, the question remained the same: *Liberating, isn't it?* Finally, my mind emphatically replied, *Yes, it is!*

"Let me get this straight. She waited until after she came *in your mouth* to tell you that shit?"

"Yep."

"Man, that's coldblooded. Tell me you at least got one last chance to tap that booty."

"Nah, I didn't even try to. I just walked her to the door and asked her to leave."

"ASKED? You asked her to leave? See, Evan, that's your problem. You give dem hoes entirely too much respect. Don't get me wrong. I believe you treat a lady like a lady and a trick like a trick. Damn, dawg!

You gotta make a bitch earn her place on the pedestal before you stick her ass up there. You gotta be like. . ."

Ego, pride, and pain; at some point, every living being has to fight those three demons.

I never met her, but Stacey Howard, must have been something crucial. She and Greg dated for eleven months when he first moved to Chicago. I wasn't there to measure the exact timeline, but I knew that whole 'earn a place on the pedestal' thing was related to the three milliseconds it took her to steal his heart.

Greg grew up next door to me, and his mother worked as a court transcriptionist. She would always come home and tell G and me stories of how impressing the lawyers were, especially the black ones. G's lifelong goal was to become a lawyer, and had she lived to see him finish law school, maybe that experience would have been enough to satisfy him. However, the void Ms. Mattie Gray left and the bitterness of his father deserting them when he was twelve years old drove G to place expectations on himself that no mere mortal should ever have to try to live up to.

After graduating summa cum laude from Florida A&M University's law school, Greg L. Gray, Esq. was a force that injustice everywhere would have to deal with. Then six months later, G passed the Illinois bar exam, left our hometown of Orlando, and moved into his Chicago apartment. I think he even packed a red cape.

Five weeks after he got to Chicago, he hooked up with Stacey Howard. All he talked about was how successful and beautiful she was, how sexy she walked, and how 10 out of every 12 guys in Chicago was sweating her. I was certain every time we talked that he would tell me to reserve my tuxedo. But, something life altering happened. My rights as best friend only entitled me to a watered-down generalization. On one side there was "Super G", defender of truth, justice, and the Afro-American way. On the other there was "The Double G, Baby", lover of absolutely no hoes, as he would put it. At this current point in his life, there was absolutely no doubt which side was winning the battle.

I interrupted his lecture. "Look, G, all of that is irrelevant. All I want to do when I get up there is get my residency done so I can start practicing. That's my focus. I could care less about messing with a bunch of females, man."

"Awww, fool, you trippin'. That's what you say now. Wait 'til you see these fine-ass hoes up here. Besides, your ass is still pussy whooped. You can't let the pussy whoop you! You got to whoop the pussy! BANG! BANG! BANG!"

Admittedly, he could imitate John Witherspoon damn near as well as John Witherspoon himself. I could just see him flapping his arms, with his lips poked out and head cocked to the side. We laughed uncontrollably.

"Seriously though, G, I gotta handle my business when I get up there. Those people at the hospital ain't gonna cut me no slack. I'm not gonna have time to be messing around trying to keep up with you and all your club-hopping, pussy-chasing homeboys."

"Dawg, I hear you. I'm not gonna trip on you too bad. But, hey, you have to let your hair down sooner or later. And when you do, I got you. Deal?"

"Whatever, man! I know how your 'got me' is."

"When you planning to get here?"

"I'm gonna take off from here Monday and take my time driving. I should be there Wednesday late morning or early afternoon. You gonna be home, right?"

"Make sure you make it before two o'clock in the afternoon because I have a court hearing at three."

"Another hard day fighting for the justice of Cook County jail inmates, huh?"

"Naw, bruh. I had to let that pro-bono shit go. It ain't enough money in it for The Double G, Baby! Please say the Baby," he said with the whiniest voice he could muster up.

"Your ass has been listening to too many Lil' Wayne CD's. I'll holla at'cha Monday when I hit the road. Later, fool."

"Alright, dawg. Later."

I missed talking to my best friend. Greg would never have said some idiotic crap like that. The Double G was new to me. I would have to get to know him, but I knew in my heart that he and I were destined for conflict. I just hoped Super G, complete with the red cape and all, would be capable of saving our friendship.

CHAPTER 4
MACHAIA JAMES

"Mack-uh-ha James?"

Four extra years of education and the nurse couldn't pronounce my name any better than the receptionist had done just a couple hours before. I've heard my name butchered countless times, but never did it hurt as much as now. I made eye contact and began to gather my things. As I got closer to where the nurse was standing, I noticed the expression on her face change. Each step that I moved closer to the examination room's doorway, she seemed like she was apologizing for what was about to happen, as if she already knew the toll this process would take on my spirit.

"Have you already signed the consent paperwork?"

"Yes."

"Then please step into the procedure room and change into this gown. The doctor will be with you shortly."

She handed me a blue and white hospital gown. From first appearance, you could tell it had been sterilized, purified, rectified, and sanctified over and over again. As I slowly took the robe from the nurse, I realized no sterilization process could nullify or neutralize all the blood that had been spilled on that garment. I could feel and hear the pleading of each and every baby screaming for a chance to reach their potential to be doctors, lawyers, teachers, colleagues, motivators, and soul mates.

I tightened my jaw muscles, gritted my teeth, and silenced them all. However, one voice I could not silence. I could hear the tension in De'Mann's voice rising with every second. *Baby, you gotta be strong, for us. Do what you gotta do, for us. You and me are gonna make it up out of the hood, baby. Just don't give up on us.* His voice did not have that same cockiness and confidence. Hell, it wasn't even sexy. It was desperate and growing more desperate by the moment.

As the nurse closed the door, I felt like I was being shut out from everything sacred to me. With each piece of clothing I removed, I felt like I was stripping my spirit of any piece of integrity it had. I questioned everything about myself; my womanhood, my spirituality; my very essence. My tears ran as constant as the questions bombarding me.

I love my mother. I only met her once, but as much as a twenty-seven-second-old baby could encompass, our bond was solidified for eternity. At that moment, God forged in my heart acknowledgement of my mother's beautiful example of love. She was far too young to have a child. She was far too poor to care for a child or to even get adequate prenatal care. In her fourteen-year-old wisdom, she was far too naïve to know that the grown-ass man who got her pregnant would abandon her without a trace. All she knew was that my spirit had a voice and that she loved me enough to do all she could to let that voice sing.

She hid me from her abusive father, whose only concern would have been his woes for having an extra mouth to feed. She hid me from her fearful mother, who would have tightened her jaw muscles, gritted her teeth, and kept quiet, while her husband lynched the souls of her daughter and grandbaby.

Had she had a few more years of experience, she would have known the excruciating stomach cramps were not normal. Had she had more money, her doctor would have told her working too hard, my growth, and her improper diet were placing a tremendous amount of stress on her body. If she had not been so naïve, she would have known not to trust the lies of a man who was more concerned about saving himself than sacrificing and dealing with the mess he helped create.

My mother had the strength to hold on to the only thing she could: hope. She could have easily let go and did what I was about to do to my child, but she didn't. Any earthly scale couldn't measure the legacy of my mother's love. Just days before my birth, doctors finally had a chance to examine her. They told her that going through with the delivery could possibly kill her. She held on. They told her that her baby could very likely be born with serious defects or maybe even die. She held on.

To God be the glory. In twenty-seven seconds, He gave my mother and me a bond that would last for an eternity. As nurses rushed me out of the room and doctors hopelessly tried to stop my mother from bleeding, our eyes met. The joy in her eyes told me that all the pain she went through and all the sacrifices she made were small in comparison to the happiness she felt knowing that she had given my voice a chance to sing. What the doctors and nurses interpreted as normal cries from a newborn baby was actually my first, last, and most loving serenade to the woman who in twenty-seven seconds had given me enough love to last a lifetime.

Baby, hold on! De'Mann's voice was more frantic than ever in my mind.

Then, I heard it. It started low with the opening cords of the song. Then, it grew louder with the ad-libs before the first verse. The DJ on the radio station playing over the intercom system said it was Hall and Oates' "Sara Smile", but my heart told me that God was busy forging another wonderful bond between mother and child. He was allowing me to hear my baby for the very first time. After a few melodious ad-libs, my baby began serenading me with the most beautiful voice I've ever heard.

> *Baby hair. . .with a woman's eyes.*
> *I can feel you watching in the night.*
> *All alone with me and we were waiting for the sunlight.*
> *When I feel cold, you waaarm me.*
> *AND WHEN I FEEL I CAN'T GO ON,*
> *YOU COME AND HOOOOOOLD ME!*
> *It's you and me . . .forever. . .er.er.er.*
> *Sara...smile.*

Louder and louder, more and more soulful with each bar, my daughter Sarah was giving the performance of a lifetime. I was her totally captivated audience. Even after her opening song ended, she kept on singing to me. She told me, *Hold on, for us. Be strong, for us. Do what you gotta do, for us. Make it up out of the hood, for us.*

Her voice was a gift from God. It was confident, charismatic, and intoxicating. I knew there was nothing I could do to silence an angel. The choice wasn't even mine to make. I closed my eyes, opened my heart, and followed the melody of her voice all the way out the front door of the clinic.

Love is a powerful motivator. In the span of time it took Sarah to steal my heart, the woman in me finally overcame that scared little girl that dominated my thought process. I wasn't concerned with my grandfather's criticism. I knew that was his way of trying to hide from the guilt he carried for his part in his daughter's death. I would no longer be steered by my grandmother's opinions. I knew that was her way of trying to overcompensate for not speaking out for my mother. Most of all, I didn't have to worry about whether or not De'Mann would stop loving me because I didn't do things his way. All that mattered now was that Sarah loved me unconditionally, and I loved her the same.

As frantic as De'Mann's voice spoke to me in the procedure room, it would be a lot more intense in person. The old Machaia would surely have buckled under that kind of pressure, but this time, I wasn't alone. My daughter needed me to be strong. The same way I needed my mother to be strong. The same way she needed her mother to be strong. The strength of a woman is inherited. It's passed down from generation to generation, through success and failure. The struggles and trials of the mother become the fortitude and courage of the daughter. My grandmother's fears gave my mother courage. My mother's courage gave me life. Now my life had enough substance to offer my daughter hope. Love is a powerful motivator, but unconditional love can move mountains.

As I stood outside the front of the clinic waiting for De'Mann, I realized I had to take my life into my own hands. So, I decided to catch the city bus to where he was. He had insisted on driving me to the clinic, but he couldn't stay with me because he had a business meeting at his club Pleasures, a downtown strip club that he and a partner ran as a front for his real job. I already knew he was lying before he even started speaking. With all the momentum of that ten-ton bus, I was heading towards a head-on collision with destiny. I didn't know what, but after De'Mann found out I hadn't gone through with the abortion, something major was going to happen. I needed a plan and quick. My life had changed, and his trifling ways were not part of me and Sarah's future.

The thirty-six minute bus ride from the clinic in Franklin, Tennessee, to downtown Church Street was just what I needed to gather my thoughts. As the bus drove through the neighborhood of Brentwood, I realized how beautiful this part of the city is in the spring. Large traditional styled homes lined the streets with deep green and manicured lawns, complete with white picket fences and a lifelong contract with the American dream. Clarity and calm are best friends. I never knew that before. I'm sure these people faced struggles, also, but there was a certain calm on their faces as they went about their daily business, which testified to anyone watching that they can clearly see that everything is going to be just fine.

As the bus was leaving Brentwood on Franklin Pike, we got held up just where Franklin turns into 8th Avenue. There was a mile long convoy of students leaving John Overton High School. Some were walking, while others were driving cars entirely too expensive for a high schooler to fully appreciate. Those students made left turns and were headed back up to Brentwood with that beautiful calm all over their faces. The students on buses and a few in their own vehicles made right turns heading towards Edgehill Projects. Their faces were anything but calm. Their world was full of chaos; way more than a teenager should have to deal with.

The bus continued up 8th Avenue, and I realized the road was much bumpier than Franklin. As the bus jumped and jerked its way towards Edgehill, it shook up more than just my body. My soul was stirred as I saw the thin line that divided prosperity and despair, and came to grips with which side of the road I resided. The potential to be gorgeous was there. The homes on 8th Avenue were also traditional style and the lawns were just as big. However, the level of care on this side was not the same. The worry on these peoples' faces made it evident that they were far too busy dealing with the reality of life to focus on green grass. Confusion and chaos are best friends. I've always known that.

As the bus rode into downtown, I rang the bell to let the driver know I was ready to get off on Church Street. I loved Brentwood. I looked forward to basking in the sun of that clear and calm world, but there was the reality of the thunderstorm of chaos I was getting ready to walk into.

As I approached the club, I could tell something was going on. Even though I'd never been to the club before, something just seemed odd. De'Mann didn't like me to come around. He said it was for my own good, but his eyes always told me different.

There were only three cars in the parking lot. De'Mann's white Yukon Denali had all the windows down, and anyone passing by could have total access to all twenty-thousand-dollars' worth of TVs, DVD players, 24-inch rims, and a whole assortment of gizmos. He never left his car unlocked unless his mind was elsewhere. There was his best friend Rodney's silver Range Rover, complete with all of the same toys De'Mann had plus another five thousand dollars' worth. The third car, I didn't recognize. It clearly did not belong to a person of significant means. It was an older model Toyota Camry. It used to be green, but now it was a worn mixture of green, exposed silver metal, and rust. It had two hubcaps missing and a big dent on the front passenger side door. The specialty license tag that read 'MS THANG' clearly let me know I was dealing with a silly hoe.

I was surprised the front door was still unlocked. I slipped in as quietly as possible. I could see the light coming from out of the back office down the hall. It seemed to take an eternity for me to get to the edge of the room. With each step I took towards that door, I knew I was one step closer to coming face to face with the reality of what I had been lying to myself about ever since I met De'Mann. I remembered all the times I told myself to give him another chance because all men make mistakes and told myself not to be so quick to judge him. I thought about all the times I told myself that I would have to learn to deal with things that hurt me because he was my man and I had to be down for him. All of those sacrifices and compromises I made led to this moment. The moment of truth when I would know whether or not they were all in vain, or if De'Mann really did love me and I was right for fighting for him, even with myself. When it comes to affairs of the heart, no matter how well you prepare yourself mentally for a blow that you know is coming, the hurt is always much more than you had ever imagined.

As I stood in the shadows of that dark hallway peeping into the office through the cracked door, I saw my man, his best friend, and what turned out to be two "Ms. Thangs" engaged in an all-out freak show. De'Mann was lying on his back across the length of the leather sofa, while the driver of the car was bobbing up and down on him with her mouth. I knew she was the driver because she had 'Ms. Thang' tattooed on her lower back. The other girl was squatted over De'Mann's face, while leaning forward over the far arm of the sofa in a synchronized bobbing motion on Rodney's penis. Literally, her ass was all too familiar. I would recognize it anywhere and remember it always. Two eyes, one tattooed on each cheek, with an amazing degree of detail. So much detail that they followed my every motion. As I watched that ass ride De'Mann, those eyes watched me. Ridiculed, winked, rolled at me, and haunted me. They reminded me that they had met with my eyes once before. He had been with her the whole time, ever since we had all been together that night. Probably even before then.

How could he? How could she? What kind of hoe would go out like that? If eyes are the windows to the soul, then it is no wonder why this bitch's soul looks pretty shitty, I laugh-cried to myself.

Every moan De'Mann made was another blow to my heart. While I was at the clinic alone struggling with myself, compromising myself, and giving up on our child, he was in the back office of a goddamn strip club getting sucked and fucked by two chubby, trifling-ass hoes.

Frozen, I stood there and watched the show unfold. Positions changed. Those on the bottom became those on the top, and through it all, De'Mann's moans, grunts, and screams became more excited. My eyes never watered. My heart was pounding at a frantic pace. My hands were sweating. My mouth trembled; halfway out of hurt and pain and halfway from trying to hold back the curse words I wanted to yell. I stood and watched until my heart had seen enough to move forward with conviction. Then, I closed my eyes, listened to her ask him, "Who's dick is this?" and him answer, "Yours, baby. It'll always be yours." Those sounds let my mind see enough to know to shut the fuck up when my heart led us out the front door. No cursing, no commotion, no scene. Just motivated steps forward. That situation, that day, and that man were all behind me.

I calmly walked outside and pulled out my key to De'Mann's truck. Honestly, I don't know how I made it back to the apartment. I don't remember anything about the twenty-three minutes it took me to drive home. In that short span of time, I had attempted to call my best friend Sandra in Chicago at least a hundred times to let her know I was coming. I'd called information to get the phone number for Delta, called the airline, got flight information, and even decided what I was going to wear on the flight. All of this without even paying attention to any traffic lights or turns.

When I made it back to the apartment, I was still just as stunned as I was in that hallway. I quickly gathered my things, shoving them into three suitcases, two coat bags, and a duffle bag. I took every picture we had taken together and ripped them in half, keeping the half of me. I went through the house and found anything that could remind him of me and either packed it, destroyed it, or put it in a trash bag and dumped it. Every piece of memorabilia from trips, all of my favorite foods out of the refrigerator and pantry, vanquished. I even threw away the shower curtain and bathroom decorations that I picked out. The only thing he would have to remind him of me would be his memories. Hopefully, those would soon fade, as well.

I was finishing up when my cell phone chirped. The noise let me know it was either De'Mann or Sandra. They were the only ones who ever text messaged me. I was hoping it was Sandra responding to the messages I left on her phone. Even though it was the exact same ring, something awfully familiar told me it was not her.

Baby, my meeting ran late and I think someone has stolen my truck. I'm waiting on the police to arrive now. Then Rodney will drop me off to get the Range and I'll pick you up. Love you and I'm sorry I couldn't be there, but I couldn't miss this meeting.

Words are just words. Sentiments, however, are always truth if you know how to listen to them. This was not the first time his words had lied to me. This was the first time I knew how to read the sentiments behind his words, though. When I thought I was too numb to be hurt anymore that day, the truth of his sentiments gut punched me so hard that I almost threw up. They told me how little he thought of me. More painfully, they told me how little he believed I thought of myself in order to let that happen. Time and time again, I let that happen. I thought that's what a good woman did for her man. I thought I was being strong because he needed me to be. In his mind, he was taking care of me because I couldn't take care of myself. He was. I wasn't. Not any longer.

I went into De'Mann's secret stash of money that he didn't think I knew about and took three of the $10,000 bundles, which were always wrapped in blue rubber bands. Uncle Sam may never tax him on that money, but he owed me back taxes for years of putting up with his shit. My lips trembled with anger and hurt thinking of all the sacrifices I made for him.

"That sorry-ass motherfucker ain't shit!" I finally yelled aloud.

It felt like a little piece of frustration flew out of my mouth and was projected like a heat-seeking missile through the atmosphere. It was heading straight for De'Mann to wreak havoc in his world.

"I hope your trifling ass get what you deserve!" I shouted, launching another missile.

Hell, I launched an all-out air assault. For ten minutes, the more I yelled, the more frustration missiles I launched towards him with bad intensions.

I was snapped out of my rampage by the doorbell. The cab I called to take me to the airport had arrived and reality was settling in. I was about to leave the only man I had ever known. Love bonds, however misplaced, are hard as hell to break. I already missed him. *How stupid am I to be crying over a sorry-ass nigga like him*, I thought to myself, while grabbing a pen and paper. With watery eyes, I began to write. All I could think to say was something I'd heard him say millions of times before.

De'Mann,

It is what it is, and it ain't what it ain't. Goodbye!

Not Ms. Thang ☺

I placed the diamond ring and tennis bracelet he'd bought me, along with his second cell phone I had been using, on the kitchen counter. I then rushed back to the secret money stash, took two of the $5,000 bundles, and rushed out the door. The cab driver had loaded all of my bags and was standing beside the car smoking a cigarette.

"Are you ready to go, ma'am?"

"Yes, I am," I said with a deep exhale, while firmly wiping away my already drying tears. "And could you put out that cigarette, please. I'm pregnant and don't want to breathe your secondhand smoke."

Liberation is always painful, never pleasant, but always empowering. In one afternoon, I had broken free of every shackle that had been binding my existence to a plateau of misery and self-doubt. Then I realized the strength to leave had always been there inside of me.

Two blocks away from the main entrance to our complex, I saw

Rodney's truck speeding down the street towards the apartment. A weird feeling of sadness overcame me, and my eyes watered once again. These were not tears of hurt, though. I left the last of those on the counter with the ring and tennis bracelet.

As the cab continued to the airport, I couldn't help but to think of him the whole way. De'Mann was genuinely my friend, and I felt bad for the hurt he was surely enduring. He had always told me that I was the only person in the world he felt he could trust.

Girl, wake the hell up! That ain't nothing. I heard those sentiments loud and clear. The only trust he had in me was with trusting me to bow down to whatever he wanted. Not anymore! My self-esteem was rising faster than the Boeing 747 I was now riding. Just like that plane, I sat with my nose and head held up high, speeding away from Nashville and the weakness of my past. Now, my only focus was my future in Chicago. Be it good or bad, it was my decision. I was speeding towards my future at approximately five hundred miles per hour.

CHAPTER 5
EVAN MILES

How comforting is it to know that you can count on something beyond the shadow of a doubt? It used to be the way she towered over me when she stood next to me, directing me through life's obstacles like the world's largest guardian angel. Then, it was the way she never let my acting like I had outgrown her million and one daily kisses and hugs stop her from laying them on me anyway, even in public. She made me feel like the most cherished creature on earth. No matter what time in my life, there was always something about being around my mother that gave me the courage to move forward into whatever.

"Call me when you get there."

Those were the only words out of her mouth, but her five-minute hug and kiss told me not to drive fast, don't eat too much junk on the road, stop to rest if I needed to, and all the other motherly demands she usually gave me when I left. However, this time, her eyes did not say hurry back because I'll miss you. Instead, she knew I needed to leave like a bird needs to fly. She didn't care if it was a new woman or the thrill of struggling to create my own practice; she just couldn't take the pain of seeing my misery and wanted something to end it...soon.

"Alright, alright, Deucie, I'll call you as soon as I get there, but I have to get going. I'm on a schedule. G has a case at three o'clock on Wednesday, and I gotta make it there before then. I love ya."

"Love you too, son. Drive careful."

As I drove away, I reflected on how it came to be that I call my mother by her nickname Deucie. My mother had me at an early age, and I grew up hearing people call her that. They said it was because as a child, she always said things twice. She must have outgrown that right after I was born because she only told me things once. Then, she was on me like white on rice.

My reflections made me realize how much I would miss this place. It drove me to tears. When it's really time to let go of the past, your heart has a way of reorganizing your emotions. As my heart filed away the beautiful memories of my distant past, I knew at some point I would have to deal with the file from my recent past.

By the time I merged onto the Florida Turnpike off of the 408 Expressway, that file had found a comfortable corner in the back of my mind and was a distant thought. I put my XM setting on the Groove station and began my journey. God must have created good music and thinking at the exact same moment in time. They are so intertwined. Tony Toni Toné's "Anniversary", Stevie Wonder's "All I Do", and countless other timeless classics all had been blended perfectly with my thoughts into a mega mix that just kept on going.

By the time I reached the Florida state line, I had already decided on the topic of my dissertation, knew what type of practice I wanted, and even practiced my acceptance speech for my Nobel Peace Prize. As I drove through South Georgia, the sun began to set, the Hot Buttered Soul program began to play those old familiar love songs, and all I could think of was the possibilities of what was to come. I was so excited that I started singing the songs at the top of my lungs.

They don't make songs like this anymore, I thought, while pulling off to get gas.

My structured nature always took the fun out of things. It's almost like a damn drill sergeant was standing over me and telling me what to do all the time. *Five minutes, soldier! Get a SoBe Lizard Blizzard juice, grab a bag of white cheddar cheese popcorn, and come straight back. Do you hear me, soldier!* His voice was not nearly as intimidating as usual, but was wrecking my flow. Doing something for myself felt good, so why ruin it now with structure? This experience was new, and I was determined to enjoy it to the fullest.

32

"Oh hell yeah," I said to myself, remembering the bag of weed in my glove box. My friend Dewayne left it when we had a farewell night out on the town last week. He said he had to go through hell and high water to find some Purple Haze. We never got to smoke it because he got called in to work.

"Aww sookie sookie now!" I laughed with anticipation.

If that drill sergeant was saying something, he must have come down with a sudden case of laryngitis, because I didn't hear a word he said. After purchasing my juice, popcorn, and two cognac-flavored Dutch Master cigars, I gassed up and then pulled over to the side of the parking lot to roll up two big-ass blunts. I unbuttoned my shirt and flipped my hat backwards on my baldhead. Then, I slapped that drill sergeant in the face, opened the sunroof on my Nissan Armada, cracked the windows, and prepared to lift off.

By the time I reached Atlanta, my shirt was completely off and I was barefoot. I felt entirely too good to be cooped up in a spaceship or Armada or whatever the hell I was driving. So, I decided to stay at the Embassy Suites, off of highway 285.

As I pulled into the parking lot, I noticed a decent-sized crowd at the bar across the street. Still shirtless, I pulled into the valet station, got out, and walked into the lobby with my head up and chest stuck out like I was there to collect my rent check. I was invincible; a dangerous combination of all those gym days and the brazen confidence of my current mind state. A group of sexy sistahs was breaking their necks trying to get a glimpse of me. I threw my duffle bag over my shoulder, tightened my stomach and chest muscles, and hit them with my million-dollar smile.

Once in my room, I quickly opened my laptop and began playing my Tupac music playlist that always gets me more hyped than I ever need to be. Next, I took a shower, ironed a pair of nice jeans and a shirt, then stepped out onto the balcony to smoke the second blunt. Halfway through the blunt, the metamorphosis was complete.

Somebody's daughter is gonna get it tonight, I thought to myself. After stepping into my square-toed Kenneth Cole casuals, I put on just enough Burberry Touch to cover up the smell of weed before floating across the street to the bar I noticed on the way in.

"What can I get for you, sir?"

"Let me get a double shot French Connection. Do you guys serve food here?"

"Yeah, let me get you a menu."

She smiled, handed me the menu, and took an obviously long time letting it go. *Is she sexy or what?* I asked myself, as she backed away to fix my drink. I couldn't help but to watch her the whole time. Long, dark, athletic, and the most beautiful set of lips I've ever seen. I wanted her to kiss the edge of my glass to make my drink taste better. I had been watching her so hard that by the time she came back, I hadn't even opened the menu, much less decided what to order.

"Have you decided what you would like to eat?"

I burst out laughing so hard, she joined suit without knowing what the hell we were laughing at.

"What's so funny?" she questioned in between her chuckles.

"Girl, I ain't even gonna lie. I was so busy molesting you in my mind that I forgot I was hungry. You know you bad when you make a high man forget he got the damn munchies!"

We both busted out laughing again, even harder than the first time. We laughed so loud that the people near and around the bar stopped their conversations to try and figure out what we were laughing at.

"Well, take your time and look it over while I help these gentlemen."

She introduced herself to the next group of guys with the same gorgeous smile. She made eye contact with the guy on the right and took an awfully long time handing over his menu, also. A woman is the most powerful creature on earth. The way they can manipulate a situation with ease just amazes me.

"At least you have clothes on this time," a voice came from over my right shoulder.

The voice was deep and seductively raspy. It had just enough southern drawl to let you know she took pride in preserving it. As I turned around to see what beautiful face it belonged to, I envisioned a drop-dead gorgeous southern belle, with a big, floppy white hat, a peach sundress, dimples, and holding a homemade apple pie made just for me. Boy was I wrong.

This woman was more along the lines of something out of the latest issue of Cosmo. She stood almost eye-to-eye with my six-foot, one-inch frame, and had the most beautiful dark, smooth skin I'd ever seen. Her jet-black, shoulder-length, bob-style hair and black business suit accented her complexion so wonderfully. Her slender, but strong build immediately made me think she was some sort of world-class athlete. She obviously was a woman of means. I'm no expert of fine jewelry, but if the stones in her necklace and bracelet were fake, she added enough class to them that you'd never suspect they weren't real.

"I saw you stroll your crazy ass into the lobby across the street. I thought I was gonna have to take up a collection to buy you a shirt and some shoes."

As if the Purple Haze in my system wasn't enough, she flashed just enough of that smile to send me another twelve galaxies away from earth. I couldn't do anything but laugh, partly from the effects of the weed, but mainly from the excitement of talking to her.

"No, pretty lady, you don't have to buy me any clothes. According to my mother, I already have too many."

I tried my best to articulate my words and sound somewhat debonair, but the weed and double-shot clearly had me operating at least four times below my normal level of smoothness. Again, I just laughed, partly to regain some cool points from my awkwardness.

"Well, at least let me buy you a drink then," she said, then started laughing, too.

I think the main reason for her laughter was because wherever she was trying to take me, she had good reason to believe we were well on the way to her destination of choice.

"That's cool, but I'm waiting to order my food. I don't even know what to order."

"Do you like seafood?"

"I love it!"

She turned to the bartender who had fixed my drink, raised her hand just over her shoulder, and snapped her fingers to get her attention.

"Candice, have Marvin bring a sautéed shrimp appetizer and a seafood medley special to my table right away, please. And bring him another of whatever this is he's drinking."

Then she turned back towards me, noticed my look of surprise, and gave me a 'nigga you ain't seen shit, 'cuz I can do anything' look. Again, she burst out into a comforting laugh and smiled.

"Is this your place?"

"One of them. Come over to my table and have a seat."

She grabbed my hand and led me to a remote corner of the lounge. As sexy and seductive as her smile and voice were, her hips and walk were twice as dangerous. Her grip on my hand was tight, as if to make sure I didn't bump into anything. She must have known I wasn't even thinking about looking where I was going. She knew exactly where my focus was, and her guiding me to the table was her way of saying 'enjoy the view'. If my feet ever hit the floor, I didn't have a clue of it. I was floating in outer space, and at this point, my orbit had nothing to do with the weed circulating through my system.

"Have a seat. I hope you don't mind, but I'm dying to get out of this suit. I have something a little more comfortable to wear in my office. I'm going to slip into that while you enjoy your dinner and drink. Okay?"

"K."

She gave me an extra comforting smile, then turned, spread her angel wings, and began flying across the room. I placed my head in my hands and screamed as loud and silently as possible. *Somebody, please pinch me. Please!* I thought to myself. Suddenly, the essence of sexy entered my nose and the epitome of soft graced my skin, as she seductively kissed my right cheek dangerously close to the corner of my lips. When I looked up, she didn't back away. She stayed bent over me, looking into my eyes and smiling. Her eyes were piercingly beautiful. Her smile was absolutely intoxicating. All I could think about was how I wished she would try that kiss on the cheek mess now. I know I could lick off three layers of lusciousness off her lips in a heartbeat.

"Umh umh umh, girl! You're so bea-u-ti-ful!" I slowed down my statement and put nine pounds of sincerity on each syllable. "What was that kiss for?"

"I came back because I realized I never introduced myself. When I saw your head was down, I was hoping you weren't so bored that you were falling asleep. Then, I thought of how I love waking up to a kiss, so I decided I would give you a little one on the cheek." She bit her bottom lip seductively.

"I wasn't sleep, but if I was, I would've been dreaming of you. So, you should've let me keep on snoozing," I replied with an amazing degree of honesty.

She paused, seductively bit her bottom lip again, and then hit me with another smile. "By the way, my name is Celeste Carson, but my friends call me Cee-Cee." She casually stuck out her hand to shake mine, obviously out of habit during introductions.

"Awww, girl, you're trippin'! You've already kissed me on my mouth and dangled your cleavage all in my face. We're passed that handshaking stuff."

She laughed again. "That wasn't your mouth. This is your mouth."

She slowly licked her lips, as if to add another bucket of juiciness to them, and gently kissed me directly on the lips. She used the perfect combination of upper, lower, inner, and outer lip to tell me everything I needed to know about how sensuous she is. Then she paused and remained an inch away from my face, stabbing my soul with her deep brown eyes.

"My name is Evan Mi—."

She interrupted my introduction. "I know your name, Dr. Miles." She gave me another mischievous smile. "Here comes your dinner. Enjoy your food. I'll be back shortly." Then she glided to the opposite corner of the lounge and disappeared down a back hallway.

"Here you go. Enjoy."

Candice's whole demeanor had changed. I wouldn't go so far as to say she was being cold, but she was definitely not trying to work me for a tip anymore. She was strictly business with a hint of bitterness, aggravation, or envy. I couldn't tell which one, but one of them was definitely present.

"I think I'm done drinking. You can close my tab now."

"I already did. Here's your card back. My sister took care of your tab. I don't know what you did, but you got her trippin'…for now." She made that statement with an eyebrow-raising level of conviction.

It must be envy, I told myself. *She's just mad I'm not at the bar sweatin' her anymore. Oh well and oh hell. I got the cream of the crop of that family.*

The meal was excellent. By the time I finished, Celeste still hadn't resurfaced. So, I walked back up to the bar. Before I could get a word out, Candice continued her sarcasm.

"Get used to it, buddy. She's gonna do everything on her time. Here, take this drink and sit on back down. She'll be out when she's ready."

She had none of the friendly smiles, but three times the eye contact. You could tell she was dying to elaborate. We shared an awkward stare, which lasted long enough to let me know she and her sister had some serious issues. As sure as I was that they needed some sisterly counseling, I already knew I didn't give a damn.

"Candice, you ain't trying to scare away my friend, are you?"

"Friend? Is that what you callin' 'em nowadays?"

Celeste gave Candice a 'bitch don't start with me' stare and eye roll. Candice immediately withdrew from the confrontation and left to tend the bar, but not before giving me one last 'I got some shit to tell you stare'.

"I hope you don't mind, but I made arrangements for us to go to one of my other spots. I assumed since you were obviously in the mood for drinking, you didn't have anything pressing to do in the morning." She did her best to act like she didn't already know I was going to be down for whatever.

"That's cool, and you're right. Hanging out is exactly what I had in mind."

"Good, then hang out is what we'll do, along with a few other things." She smiled and squeezed my hand, while leading me to the front door.

"Looks like Cee-Cee got her another one." Candice was talking to one of the waitresses as we passed the end of the bar. She purposely spoke loud enough for us to hear. Celeste ignored her, and so did I.

Damn she's hatin', I thought to myself.

Celeste wore a black dress that gently caressed the curves of her body, as if some famous designer had made it just for her. It hung low in the front and exposed her back and shoulders. It knew without even asking that it was a new arrival from the runways of Paris or Milan. Just like her, it was the perfect combination of sexy, elegant, mysterious, and seductive. Breathtaking with no effort, she had very little make-up, miles of legs, dabs of some lovely-smelling perfume, and a shit-load of charisma. I could see how she could charm her way into anyplace, anything, or any person's heart.

"You can't tell me that dress was just something you had hanging in your office. You must've been planning on going out or something."

She leaned over, hooked arms with me, and kissed me on the cheek again.

"You caught me. I had this delivered when I saw you earlier at the hotel."

"What did this dress have to do with seeing me?"

"You seemed like such a free spirit. I knew I would have fun hanging out with you."

"But you didn't know if I was here to meet a female or not."

"Exactly, which is why I had my 'Can't no female get with this' dress delivered."

She paused and looked at me, as if waiting for my approval of her gown. I gave it to her by way of flashing all thirty-two of my teeth. I thought I had shown her all the teeth I could, until they rolled her Bentley GT convertible around. That's when two more layers protruded from underneath my gum line. It looked like it was Millennium gray with some shiny-ass metallic coating.

The valet driver jumped out, grabbed a package and handed it to her. When she walked to the passenger side door and opened it for me, I found yet another layer of teeth to expose. She just smiled as she handed the package to me and shut the door. Then she laughed mischievously as she walked around to the driver's side and got in. I curiously opened the package to find two cigars and a generous bundle of some serious smelling weed.

"Damn, girl! What are you trying to do to me? I hope you're not some kind of female vigilante killer. Are you gonna get me fucked up, then tie me up and torture me?"

She laughed. "No, sweetie, I just admired how much you seemed to be enjoying yourself earlier and wanted to help you continue that feeling. But, that tying you up thing sounds fun, though."

She puckered up her lips, blew me a kiss, and gave me what had to be her naughty girl smirk. As she hit the button to let the convertible's roof down, I leaned my seat back and took in the warm evening air.

"Somebody pinch me. This shit can't be real. Dream girl, dream car, and some good weed. I got to be dreaming!" I exclaimed without taking my eyes off the moon.

"Trust me, baby, you might want to stay awake for this one. The reality is definitely gonna be better than fantasy."

When her radio came on, it was like a divine confirmation that we were supposed to be together. The Hot Buttered Soul program was playing, and it seemed as if I had never left my truck. I couldn't help but to laugh.

"What's so funny?"

"We must be kindred spirits or something."

"Why do you say that?"

"I was listening to this same program all the way up here from Orlando today."

"Great minds think alike, huh? I love old school music. It's 'feel good' music, isn't it?"

"Who you tellin'? That's what had me floating when I came in that hotel lobby."

"Well in your case, it's 'feel really good music'."

We both burst out laughing then enjoyed the next few songs as she continued down the road. Just before the expressway entrance, she pulled into a gas station. I let my seat up to get out and pump the gas, as she got out, swiped her card, and reached for the pump.

"Let me get that for you."

"I got it, baby. Just get back in the car and relax."

"I have to go piss anyways. Tell me what don't you do? You own businesses, drive a Bentley, and pump your own gas. Are you from Mars or somewhere? Go on and tell it. You're trying to hook me so you can take me back to your planet and run some damn experiments on me, aren't you? I know you got an extra space eye, leg, or something on your body." I tried to look serious, while playfully searching her body.

"Boy, take your crazy self in there and use the bathroom before you make me pee on myself."

She gently placed her hands on my chest and pushed me towards the store. As I walked away, I felt myself walking closer to her emotionally, spiritually, and at least five other ways. The crazy part was I wasn't even feeling the weed anymore. In the short walk to the inside of the store to the bathroom, I must have looked back at her a million times. My high escalated twelve exponents. She was looking back at me smiling each time.

Knock. Knock. "Evan, let me in real quick."

After getting to the bathroom and waiting on two stank-ass truck drivers to go before me, despite her obvious urgency, there was no way I could stop the flow of my release. I finished my leak, zipped up my pants, and opened the door.

"Man, you 'bout to make me pee on myself."

"I swear if you pull out a dick, I'm gonna kick your ass man."

We both laughed.

"Trust me, it's strickly clitly up in here right now. Some fat white girls were hoggin' up the ladies' room, and I couldn't wait."

"Well, I'll stand guard for you at the door."

"No, just stay there and keep the door locked," she replied, then hiked up her dress to expose her bare ass, squatted over the seat, and began urinating.

"I can't believe I'm letting you watch me pee."

The similarities were too obvious to ignore. That old file poked its head out of my memory closet. It was met with an immediate denial of any serious regard. I had been around other females since our break-up, but Erica was always my mind's top priority. Even when I had sex with other women, all I could ever think about was her. I wondered who she was with, what she was doing, and was she happy there. None of those thoughts crossed my mind now, though. Instead, an extreme feeling of release and joy came over me. *I'm over that bitch,* I proclaimed to myself. I stared at Celeste and tried to use my eyes to tell her how much she was helping me. I wondered if she understood.

"I hope I'm not grossing you out, but I really couldn't wait." She stared back at me as she wiped herself off.

"Trust me, you don't know how good you are right now."

My tone was not humorous. My thoughts had taken me in a more serious direction. She sensed my intensity, and as she stood up, we placed ourselves inches apart and just stared at each other for a few moments. She placed her hands on my chest, closed her eyes, and leaned in to kiss me. I watched her the whole time, never closing my eyes. I wanted to enjoy all five of my senses while kissing her.

The dimples formed in her cheeks as we backed away and she began to smile. I saw those beautiful brown eyes open back up to realize that the windows to my soul were piercingly beautiful to her, as well.

"Wow."

"Wow, what?" she asked with a huge smile.

"I guess you were right. Reality can be better than fantasy."

She laughed softly, never taking her eyes off of mine. "Not yet, but it will be," she replied, while exiting the restroom.

When we got back to her car, I realized she had already rolled up one blunt. I was on a natural high already, but I lit it and anxiously anticipated where this night would lead.

"Just the two of us…we can make it if we try…just the two of uh-uh-us…you and I." We both began singing along with the song on the radio.

I dated Erica for almost four years and never felt as in tune with her as I felt with Celeste after only an hour and forty-five minutes. We got excited about the same songs and laughed at each other's jokes. She was so down to earth. I felt like I had known her for years and we were finally rekindling our passion after years of missing each other. We smoked the blunt, enjoyed the music, and continued rekindling our obviously kindred spirits until we got to a club over in Buckhead.

"Is this another one of your clubs?" I asked, as she pulled up to the valet.

"No, this one isn't, but it's still early. I wanted to bring you here first because I know you'll enjoy the atmosphere."

"You're all about doing what I will enjoy. What do you enjoy?"

"Tonight is your night, baby. Just let me show you a good time. Trust me, I'm having fun watching you have fun." She held my hand, leaned over, and gave me a light kiss on the lips. "Do I smell like weed?"

"No."

"Good. I hate smelling like weed in public." She placed a few drops of perfume at the base of her neck just to make sure. Then, she got out the car and just like that was back in diva mode.

"Good evening, Ms. Carson. How are you this evening?"

"I'm wonderful. I won't be here long. So, please, don't put me too far out of reach."

"No problem, Ms. Carson."

Celeste shook the valet's hand, while handing him enough of a tip that he decided to park her car about five feet from where we got out and ten strides from the front door. She hooked her arm around mine and escorted me in the door, bypassing the line. The girl at the front desk not only didn't ask us for money, but she showed us to the V.I.P. section.

The club was dimly light and retro with a seventies feel to it. Old school tunes echoed off velvet-lined walls. There was a small dance floor in the middle. This was the kind of place you could get caught in the rapture of a memory and find yourself in somebody's arms with your eyes closed. The V.I.P. section was a series of private cubicles that overlooked the dance floor. Each cubicle had oversized suede sofas and giant pillows. Celeste entered the booth, kicked off her shoes, and sprawled over the sofa.

"Have them bring me a mango margarita and a double shot of Patrón. And bring him a…" She looked over at me and frowned. "What was that you were drinking?"

"A French Connection on the rocks."

"Isn't this a nice club?"

"Yeah, it has a nice vibe. I'm feeling it."

"I come here all the time to unwind." She patted the sofa next to her, motioning for me to sit there. "This is the perfect spot for a first date because it's such a relaxed atmosphere. You can talk and really vibe with someone."

"So that's why you brought me here, to vibe with me?"

"Actually, I already know that I'm diggin' you. I brought you here to help you relax. I noticed you seemed a little apprehensive. If I would've taken you straight to the other spot, I know you would have flipped out."

Curiosity immediately took me over. "Why do you say that? What type of club is it?" I'm glad she paused to answer, because it gave my imagination a few moments to run wild.

"Don't worry, we'll make it there. I have to go and check on my people, so we have to go. I just want us to get to know each other better first. It's just something about you that makes me feel comfortable."

"Oh really?" I gave her my 'don't let that apprehension shit fool you' look. "What do you think it is?"

"I can't explain it. When we saw you in the lobby, my friends and I knew you were fucked up. You thought we were looking at you because you were cute. Don't get me wrong you are definitely sexy, but we were trippin' on you because we thought you was gonna bust your ass."

I rolled over laughing, thinking how silly I must have looked.

Our vibe session ended up being several hours. Over several rounds of drinks, we shared our total histories, dreams, failures, and nightmares. I told her of my relationship with Erica and how I was headed to Chicago to complete my residency. She told me of her failed marriage with her controlling ex-husband and her struggles being a woman in the entertainment industry. I was totally engrossed in her.

She had gotten so comfortable that she was seated directly in front of me with her legs Indian style. Her dress had ridden up her thighs, and her pussy was in my clear view. It was too dim for me to see any significant details, but just knowing it was there for me to view was erotic. The epic battle of love and lust was on once again.

What an amazing woman, I thought to myself. The passion in her voice when she spoke of accomplishing her goals, and the way she described her likes and dislikes captivated me. She repositioned herself across the sofa. Forgetting she was exposed, I missed out on about one hundred peeks. Amazingly, I was much more satisfied with the conversation I got instead.

"Oh, this is my song. Let's dance!" She stood up and reached for my hands.

It was an Atlantic Star song I didn't recognize, with a captivating and beautiful melody. The words were sensuous and passionate. I knew no matter where I was or what I was doing, every time I heard it, I would travel back in time to this very moment.

As we continued dancing, her elbows rested on my shoulders and her forearms were interlocked behind my neck. She rested her face on my shoulder and her breath made the hair on the back of my neck stand up. It was apparent both of us were far more concerned about being close than keeping up with the melody of the song. We remained silent and enjoyed each other's embrace.

"Am I sexy to you?" she asked with a strangely serious look.

"Tooooo sexy," I answered with enough emphasis to elaborate how much of an influence her sexiness had on my thought process.

"I mean am I sexier to you now?" Her serious demeanor remained unchanged.

"Sexier now? I don't understand. Now as opposed to when?" Sensing that something was on her mind, my demeanor matched hers. I didn't want any misunderstandings messing up our vibe.

"As opposed to a little while ago when you were stealing peeks up my dress."

She had enough conviction in her eyes to let me know I had no chance of playing dumb. My heart rate sped up, thinking I had offended her.

"Look, if I offended you, I'm sorry, but you know you're an extremely sexy woman. You can't fault a man for being attracted to you."

"Attracted to me or my pussy?"

"Both."

"Do you know the difference between being attracted to a woman versus being attracted to her pussy?"

"Of course. When you're attracted to the pussy, all you want is sex."

"Partly, but it's deeper than that." She paused, and I stood there waiting on her to elaborate further. "It's possible that you can cherish her as a whole, but you'll never view her as an equal. It's more than just being able to fuck her. You can treat her like a princess, but at the end of the day, all she is to you is that— pussy—a warm, juicy trophy. If she doesn't know any better, a man cherishing her will fool a woman into believing she's special to him, when she's just a showpiece. I would rather be a fuck buddy. At least then everything is in perspective."

"So are you saying all you want to be is fuck buddies?"

"Are you only attracted to my pussy?"

"Trust me, if it was pussy only, it would've been on and poppin' up in the booth."

She smiled at my response and relaxed. Then she stepped back, stared directly in my eyes as she leaned forward, and reached under her dress. She took her index finger, placed it inside her vagina, pulled it out and slowly placed her finger on the edge of my lips. I used my eyes to tell her how much I was digging her as a whole. Then I opened my mouth and sucked on her finger slowly.

"We'll see what you're attracted to soon enough," she said softly with a semi-serious look. "It's time to go." She put on her shoes, fixed her dress so that it hung right, and led me out the door.

As we rode through Atlanta to Celeste's club, our vibe deepened. We hardly even spoke, instead held hands over the center console and occasionally glanced at one another. We flashed smiles, but each time our eyes met, we saw glimpses of the deep thoughts occupying both of our minds. I let my seat back, closed my eyes, and let my mind wander.

After pulling off the freeway and coming to the light at the end of the off-ramp, she looked over at me with the most gorgeous smile yet. Then she leaned over and gave me a passionate kiss. The drinks combined with our kisses had removed most of her maroon lipstick. As beautiful as her lips were when they were covered with her makeup, the natural beauty underneath gave a much deeper level of appeal.

"This is it." She announced as she pulled into a parking spot near the side entrance.

"What kind of name is FreeFalls for a club?"

"I'm in the business of creating fantasies. People have to allow themselves to free-fall in order to enjoy fully."

"But, I thought reality was better than fantasy."

She turned facing me seductively, grabbed a handful of my shirt just above the beltline, gently wrapped her other hand around the side of my neck, and pulled me toward her until our lips were nearly touching. She paused, her eyes were fixed. She was looked straight into my soul.

"You don't have to think. If you've paid attention to my actions, you'd know," she gave me a warm kiss and exited the car.

The club was tastefully decorated, but the average man would never notice. There were about twenty almost naked women walking around and another five completely naked on several stages throughout the club. All of them looked like they were handpicked out of a 'dime orchard'. Light-skinned, dark brown, tall, short, slim, and thick—all preferences were represented to the fullest.

Celeste didn't hold my hand and lead me like she did at the bar. She knew my focus was not on her figure, and she probably didn't want to face that reality. I couldn't help it. I've been to plenty of strip clubs, but these women were a zillion levels above anything I had personally witnessed.

"Nice club," I said, trying to act like the women didn't faze me.

"Yeah, they're sexy, aren't they?" She laughed. She knew exactly what I meant to say. I laughed, too, because I knew I was busted. "You're a mess!" She seemed to enjoy seeing me excited by the women. "Do you want another drink?"

"Yeah, I'll take one more."

"Do you think you can behave yourself while I go in my office and handle some business for a few?" She burst out laughing before I could respond, and I joined suit. "Sit over there. They'll bring you your drink."

She directed me to a leather loveseat just to the side of one of the rear stages. Then she gave me a noticeably slow kiss, laughed, and shook her head as she walked off.

She commanded respect as she walked through the club. Clearly, the question on everyone's mind was 'who the hell is that dude that Cee-Cee is kissing?' It didn't take long for the first interviewer to stroll over.

"What's up? Who are you, and where are you from?"

I laughed. "Damn! Just like that?"

"Just like that!"

I paused. "I'm a friend of Celeste's."

"Just a friend, huh?"

"Yep." My bland demeanor quickly discouraged her from digging any further into my business.

"I just wanted to say hello. I'll let you enjoy your drink. Take care."

Her motives became obvious when she scurried back over to a table of guys in suits and reported her findings. They looked over at me in curiosity as she informed them that she didn't learn anything.

"Are you enjoying yourself?" Celeste had snuck up on me from the side and sat in my lap.

"You're done that quick?" I asked with surprise.

"You seem disappointed. I can go back in the office for a little while longer if you'd like." She curiously waited for a response.

"These females ain't got nothing on you." My military composure made me believable enough to pass her eyeball test. "As busy as this place seems to be, I expected you to be back there crunching numbers for a while."

"I'll do the number crunching in the morning. I had to deal with a disgruntled employee issue. Plus, I knew I had to be quick with these vultures flying around. I have a little paperwork to finish but I want you to come with me."

She stood up, reached for my hand, and led me through the club. We passed the table where the guys in suits were sitting. Celeste stopped and spoke to them, briefly entertaining small talk about money and staying out of trouble. She never introduced me despite their blatant mean-mugging. She raised their curiosity to new heights when she hooked arms with me moments before cutting their chitter-chatter short. *What the hell was that all about?* I thought to myself.

"Who were those guys?" I asked.

"Those were some friends of my ex-husband." She looked like she didn't want to tell me, but my look and tone mandated the truth. "It's nothing to worry about. They were just being nosey."

"Does he live here in Atlanta?" I asked, thinking I would have to deal with a scorned ex-lover as soon as his boys told him to get to the club.

"No. Believe it or not, he lives in Chicago, also."

I didn't look at her. Instead, I kept my eyes focused down the hall as we walked, with an awkward look on my face. Once we were in the hallway leading to the back of the club, she stopped and turned to me.

"Look, he's ruined enough nights in my life. Let's not let him ruin this one for us."

She was staring at me with a look I really can't describe. I had no clue of what her look was saying to me, but I clearly understood the sentiment. The last thing I wanted to do was dwell on the depressed nights I spent on Erica. She deserved the same respect. So, I dropped my suspicions and inhibitions.

She led me into a room at the end of the hallway and closed the door behind us. Celeste immediately turned around, pinned me up against the door, and aggressively tongue-kissed me while massaging my penis through my jeans.

The room was far from an office. It looked more along the lines of a private lounge. The walls were painted a deep shade of tan. The rug was almost thick enough to lose sight of your feet. There was one oversized futon that sat low to the floor. The lamp in the corner cast just enough light to hide whatever needed to be hid and show glimpses of whatever needed to be seen.

"This ain't no damn office," I said excitedly.

"I do have some paperwork to do, but I thought this would be more comfortable."

She walked over to the control panel and turned up the volume on the speakers. The music was the same as what was playing in the main part of the club. She pushed me down on the futon, backed away, and started dancing. My mind ran wild with visions of Celeste's naked body. I jumped up and danced towards her, hoping I could help her out of that dress.

"Look at you. I see somebody is glad to be here."

I followed her eyes down to the bulge protruding out from the front of my pants.

"Boy, let me stop before I get you all worked up."

"Too late for that." I threw my shoulders back, thrust my pelvis forward, and continued dancing towards her. I thought surely it would burst through the jeans and attack her. "I-love-it-when-they-call-me-Big-Pop-pa!" I thrust my dick forward with each syllable.

"Well, you gonna have to calm Big Poppa down." She grabbed my arms and pulled them to my side. "I have to go to my office and get the paperwork. Relax. I would offer you another drink, but I can see you don't need anymore."

To someone who didn't know me, I guess it would've been a safe assumption to say I was drunk. A more accurate description of my current mind state would be total euphoria. She was right. I didn't need any more. Even after she left the room to retrieve her paperwork, I continued dancing. My bulge continued to protrude and euphoria continued to influence my thoughts and actions.

I felt Celeste reach around from the back and squeeze my chest. I was so deep into my fantasy it took me a few seconds to realize that what I was feeling was real. Her caress was much more sensuous in real life. I could feel her breasts pressing against my back. They were much softer than they were in my mind.

"Once again, you're right. Reality is better than fantasy." My eyes were closed as I concentrated on her touch.

"I couldn't tell. You seemed to be enjoying yourself pretty well without my help."

My eyes opened wide and my body tightened as I flung around to see who this strange voice belonged to.

She had a beautiful red-boned complexion, silky, long, black hair, and long eyelashes with a dark rich hazel color. They were so dreamy I feverishly gazed at them to take in as much as I could. She was a slender build. Her breasts were almost too voluptuous for such a small frame, but definitely real. Her small frame had enough curves to make a fuller figured woman contemplate surgery. She was flawless. I would have been geeked just to have a couple of drinks with her, much less have her standing in front of me topless with a pair of lace boy shorts on.

"Surprised, huh?"

"Pleasantly!" I smiled while trying to take in another week's worth of her eyes.

That response rose up out of my desire and flew out of my mouth before I had a chance to think of something more subdued to say. It had enough emphasis to tell her all she needed to know about how sexy she was to me. She smiled, and I immediately began feeling guilty. I couldn't picture Celeste's body or face in my mind. All I could envision now was this creature from heaven in front of me. "What's your name?"

She laughed. "That's a first!"

"What?"

"The first time I've come back to a private dance room and the first thing a man wants to know is my name. Usually, they're trying to figure out whether or not they can fuck."

"Oh." I stole my eyes away. "I don't know why some guys are like that."

"My name is Treasure." She smiled.

"That fits." I smiled back.

I knew it was only her stage name. Part of me wanted to know her real name, but I didn't ask because I knew it wouldn't be nearly as fitting as Treasure. After sitting me down on the futon, she began selling me a fantasy, while the DJ played a song off of Beyoncé's album.

Treasure had been dancing for about three songs, when Celeste returned. I noticed she had a spiral notebook and an ink pen in her hand. She stared at me. After a few moments, she came over and sat down on the futon next to me, before bursting out laughing.

"I told you, we would see what you're attracted to soon enough, didn't I?"

I just laughed. *Damn, busted,* I thought to myself. Celeste kept watching. My realm of consciousness fluttered back and forth from reality to fantasy.

I wanted to show Celeste that a piece of pussy couldn't deter my focus from her. So, I stared into her eyes and let mine tell her the truth about how special she'd made me feel. My eyes told her that I hoped this was the start of something special that would extend far beyond this night.

The more focus I gave to Celeste, the harder Treasure tried to sell her fantasy. Treasure was so beautiful, so sexy, so erotic, and so real. *No, don't buy that one, dawg,* my heart was instructing me. *It's not real. After tomorrow, she'll be gone!*

As momentum shifted reality to Celeste's side, Treasure turned around, bent over, and began peeling off those lace boy shorts. As juicy as I thought her breasts were, her pussy was even more. This episode obviously had excited her, as well. It showed, rather dripped. I was captivated by lust. They both noticed. Treasure smiled. Celeste didn't.

"Enjoy the show." Celeste's tone hinted that if I did, it would cost me.

She turned her back and leaned up against my shoulder in a way that I could see what she was doing. I caught a motion of her arm out the corner of my eye, as I watched Treasure spread the lips of her vagina. Celeste opened a notebook and drew a line across the top. Above the line she wrote: *What I like about you.* Each time she wrote something, she turned the page quickly. The faster she wrote, the faster I had to read because I only had fifty percent of my time to focus on her list. The other fifty percent was all Treasure's.

Treasure sat on the floor directly in front of me, cocked her legs up in the air, and spread them to the sides. She pulled out a dildo, slowly slid it into her vagina, and began masturbating. The look on her face was intense and erotic. Her dreamy eyes were locked on mine. The sounds of her happy womanhood accepting that stiff plastic crawled into my ear canal and tickled my brain until it couldn't breathe.

When I looked over to catch up on my reading, Celeste had stopped writing. She herself had experienced a free fall. Treasure was truly a gifted artist, saleswoman, fantasy dealer, and whatever else she chose to do. An official scoreboard wasn't available, but I know it was late in the fourth quarter and fantasy had a commanding lead over reality. Celeste had seen enough, or she thought I had.

"Girl, that's enough. I better get him out of here before he loses his mind." Her heavy breathing said differently. It wasn't me she was worried about losing control.

Treasure's eyes were closed, and her moans were growing frantic. She was passionately stroking herself with the full length of her tool. She was obviously moments from exploding right in front of our eyes. Never acknowledging Celeste's statement, she continued pleasing herself. She had elevated herself above whatever mind games Celeste had paid her to play.

By the time Treasure returned to our world, we were both sitting on the edge of the futon with our mouths open. She tried to get up, but her whole body was weak. So, Celeste and I stood up and helped her to her feet. That was our way of giving her a standing ovation for an amazing performance. She smiled at Celeste, kissed me on the cheek, and left the room.

It took a few moments for both of us to gather ourselves. I was glad she had gotten caught in the moment, knowing it would help my cause. I didn't know whether to thank her for allowing me to experience that or apologize for not reading the last of her list.

"Were you attracted to her as a whole or just her pussy?" I asked in a manner that suggested she couldn't tell me anything about what I was attracted to.

"I know. I'm sorry. Let's just get out of here."

"Look, I understand what you were trying to do. But, you can't set a man up to fall and then blame him for being on the ground. I like you a lot, and I hope you feel the same. In one night, you have made me feel more special than I have felt in a very long time. That has nothing to do with your pussy."

She didn't answer. She just gave me an uneasy look and a kiss on the cheek. When we left the room and headed to the main part of the club, the guys in the suits were still there. Despite all the commotion in the club, they noticed us instantly. They were obviously waiting for us.

We left out of the side door and pulled around the front to exit the parking lot, as they exited the club. They were trying to protect something. I felt it. It felt uneasy to swallow. It tasted like drama…sour drama.

The ride back to the hotel could be described as warm and uneasy, as we both sat quietly. We shared a few lukewarm stares. By the time we made it back to the hotel, I managed to swallow the uneasy vibes. *Good riddance. He was not going to ruin this night for us…me.*

Whatever digestion problems I had were instantly corrected as I followed her down the hall to the double doors that led to the penthouse. Her frame hypnotized me. It swayed from side to side and rocked away all thoughts of her ex and mine. Tonight, Celeste was mine. Hopefully, tomorrow would be the same.

As we entered the room she was mysteriously subdued, but her sensuality was noticeably evident. Sexy silence filled the room. I breathed it in. I stepped into the bathroom to flush myself of anything undigested.

When I came out, all the lights in the room were off. Her laptop had been turned on and a smooth R&B playlist was running. The sliding door was open, and a slight breeze had the white sheer curtains flapping in the doorway. Celeste was outside on the balcony enjoying the view. As I went to join her, I noticed her dress hanging over the back of the chair at the desk. *Oh my God, she's naked.* My heart skipped a beat.

When I stepped out on the balcony, she was standing with her back to me looking over the railing at the city lights. Hearing me, she looked over her shoulder at me for a moment and then turned back around. There was just enough light from the moon and city lights that I could see the outline of her silhouette. Her body seemed totally relaxed. I walked up behind her, reached around both sides of her, and grabbed the railing.

"What a gorgeous view."

"Yes, it is. I love Atlanta at this time of the year."

"Yeah, Atlanta is pretty, too."

I saw the dimple form on the side of her cheek when she smiled. She grabbed my arms, placed them around her chest, and pressed her hips and ass against my groin.

"You make me feel so sexy. I could stand out here with you all night."

I didn't say a word. I just squeezed her tighter, kissed her softly on the side of her neck, and smelled her perfume. She turned around and began undressing me.

"Are you trying to seduce me?" I asked.

"Not yet." She giggled. "I just love the way you feel when you hug me. I want to feel your skin up against mine."

She fixed her eyes on mine and continued undressing me. I didn't know what her eyes were telling me. Her light caresses told me how sexy she thought my body was. The dripping moisture from her vagina told me that she was quite ready to welcome me into the most intimate part of her world. Her squeezing of my throbbing penis said she thought we should get started right away. The silence was too beautiful to tamper with. Neither of us spoke a word. Our bodies spoke loud enough.

Her eyes were closed. They had said enough when I noticed a well of tears forming just moments before she closed them. Her breaths were deep and constant. The dripping was a constant pour. I felt her body start to tremble and her spirit lose control. She was falling fast, and I knew it. She opened her eyes, took two deep breaths, and was back in diva mode.

"I want a glass of wine." She spoke fast in an attempt to disguise how shaken she was. Then she walked into the room and plopped down in the chair at the desk where her dress was hanging.

"That sounds good to me, too." I confidently walked up behind her and leaned over to kiss her neck.

"This is Ms. Carson, in the penthouse. Can I have a bottle of wine delivered to my room?"

I could faintly hear the service person's voice reply, "Would you like the same bottle of Riesling as yesterday?"

"Yes, thanks." She tried to turn her head and the phone, not knowing if I heard the question.

I stood up before she hung up and started walking towards the bed. I've never been a good liar. I simply can't do it; at least not in a believable way. The thought of her selling me a pipedream disappointed me. The idea of her treating me, and my feelings like toys for her amusement angered me beyond mention. All the crazy questions, parading me in front of her ex's boys, and the whole Treasure scenario were all games. Once again, I was allowing a woman to run amuck with my heart and mind. I wouldn't be able to lie to her about it. Nevertheless, I tried my best anyway.

"Are you okay, baby?" I could tell she was already on to me.

"I'm straight. Are you a big wine connoisseur?"

"I wouldn't say big, but I like a nice glass every now and then to help me relax."

"Is Riesling your favorite?" My body language was clearly telling her enough of the chitchat. I wanted to know about the bottle yesterday.

"As a matter of fact, I shared a bottle here with a guest from out of town as we discussed some business."

"Here in this room? I can imagine what kind of business that was." My emotions were starting to get the best of me. "How often do you do this?"

"Do what?" She was clearly on the verge of being highly upset. I didn't care, though. I was already there, waiting on her.

"Bring strangers up to your room and walk around butt-ass naked." I had a condescending tone that called her all kinds of tramps, tricks, and hoes.

"First of all, I don't owe you any explanations. I didn't even know you yesterday! All you know is I told you that I had a glass of wine over a business meeting. You came to the conclusion that because I was feeling a vibe with you tonight, that I did this yesterday with someone else. Maybe I was wrong about you. I don't think you're nearly as cool as I thought you were."

As she lectured on, her fingers, eyes, breasts, and pussy glared directly at me.

I can't lie to others. Ironically enough, I can't ever seem to tell myself the truth. I listened to her lecture me on judging people based on things I didn't know about. I could hear myself giving Erica that same spill, almost verbatim. I invented the whole 'create a gray area and then turn it around' approach. Her story was grayer than anything ever to come out of my mouth. A person's heart is the fastest learner on earth. One taste of heartache and heartbreak, and it can smell bullshit a mile away. The problem is that real knowledge is quiet. The heart simply learns lessons, and it knows what it knows.

My mind told me that she had a life yesterday and didn't owe any loyalty to me. The lie my mind sold me was that my heart would be cool with that.

Regardless of the lessons my heart taught me in dealing with Erica, my mind told me it was possible for me to find happiness amidst bullshit. My mind told me this woman had gone out of her way to show me how special I was and that I was abusing her feelings by attacking her. I began feeling guilty for overstepping boundaries.

"Look, I'm sorry for upsetting you. After all the crap I've been through recently, I jumped to conclusions and placed other people's faults on you. I apologize." Politeness overcame my voice in an attempt to get her back to that quiet, sexy, calm place.

"Look, I really like you, but if this is how you're gonna react every time you think something is wrong, then I'd rather not be bothered." She stood in front of me still naked.

"I just jumped to conclusions, and I was wrong for that. I really do apologize. I just hope I didn't ruin everything." I reached to hug her.

"Ruin what? There you go again jumping to conclusions. You just know you 'bout to get some coochie, don't cha?" She playfully pushed me away. She couldn't help but smile.

"Yeah, just like you know you about to give me some." I gripped her waist and pulled her towards me.

This time, she didn't pull away. She grabbed my shoulders and turned me towards the bed, then aggressively pushed me on my back. Her eyes were fixed on mine as she took me into her mouth. I closed my eyes and suddenly felt her back away.

"I want you to watch me."

She waited for me to open my eyes and fix them back onto hers. Her eyes were hungry.

I've had my fair share of good head, but never an orgasm from oral sex. It's always been more metal but watching her escalated what I was feeling to a level I had never experienced before. It felt as if her mouth and tongue were directly licking the sensory nerves in my brain. It was raw, erotic, and just downright nasty. I loved it.

She grabbed my hands and placed them on the back of her head, then forced my hands to pull her deeper. I was totally lost in the moment, in the passion, in her eyes. She watched my excitement build. As my eyes widened, she watched me explode. She never took her eyes off mine and never removed her mouth from the river of excitement spewing out of me. As I released every drop of momentum I had, her eyes finally released my mind out of captivity. I leaned my head back and looked to the ceiling, desperately trying to catch my breath. I heard her in the bathroom rinsing. I knew I would always watch from now on, trying to recreate the magic I had just experienced.

"That has never...happened before!" I could hardly get my words out between breaths.

"I've never done that before either." She returned from the bathroom.

Curiously, I asked, "What made you do it this time?" I was lying in the exact same position. My mind was fully functional, but my body was still frozen in place.

"I don't know. The way you were looking at me, I could tell you were really enjoying it. So, I fed off of that. I think I was getting more excited than you were."

"I seriously doubt that!"

"Trust me…" She paused to passionately kiss my chest. "I got more out of it than you did." She gave me another kiss, while her eyes placed me back in handcuffs. "And if I didn't tonight, I will eventually."

The look in her eyes suggested those words had some serious implications. Something just didn't feel right. For some reason, her statement was hard to swallow. Her rejection of all my attempts to return her favor made it even harder to swallow. Eventually, she became quiet and drifted quickly to sleep.

Why would she go through all she that and not let me please her? Questions about her intentions and motives bounced around my head, while she lay there semi-lifeless with shallow breaths.

She had a satisfied smirk on her face. I felt played. An overwhelming feeling of disappointment came over me. My disappointment stemmed from me buying into the vibe. Even more intoxicating than the weed and liquor was the thought that I was discovering something new with somebody amazing. The night I was looking forward to revisiting every time I heard that Atlantic Starr song was simply a dressed up booty call or some sort of mind game. I could have handled that if given to me straight, but all that 'you're special' shit had me believing this was the start of something special.

Finally, my mind and hormones were satisfied and fast asleep. Suddenly, her phone started vibrating. She ignored it, and so did I. Some signs are so obvious that even an idiot like me can spot them immediately.

When I awoke the next day, Celeste was gone. "Damn, it's 12:30," I said to myself as I noticed the clock.

Usually, I'm a light sleeper but I was hung over from the alcohol, weed, excitement, and emotions of the night before. Physically, I felt refreshed but disappointment was still clogging my heart.

I noticed Celeste had left me one of her business cards. On the back, she handwrote, *Call me.* No cell phone number or email address. Nothing personal. I had scheduled myself to be back on the road at 10:00 a.m. I was late and hurt. I hurried down to my room, gathered my things, and left to go check out.

"I'm checking out of room 809 and returning the keys to the penthouse."

"Dr. Miles, Mrs. Carson has already taken care of your bill. You are all set."

"Do you know what time she left out?"

"She left about nine o'clock this morning. She was in quite a rush. As a matter of fact, are you going to see her today?" He paused to reach for something under the counter.

"Yes, I'm headed to her office right now."

"Then could you please give her this message? It came for her last night, marked urgent. She rushed off before I could give it to her."

He handed me a sealed envelope, and after stepping out of his sight, I opened it immediately.

Celeste,

I made it back to Chicago. I tried to call you late last night once my flight landed, but I got your voicemail. I figured you were still hanging out with your girls. I placed my files with all my new residents' information in the desk drawer. I didn't want to spill any wine on them (big smile). I'm supposed to meet with my new residents next week. I need you to ship that file to me A.S.A.P. because I have to decide where to place them by the end of the week.

Thanks,
J.C.

P.S.: This weekend was great. Trust me, I've grown, and I pray this is the start of us finally getting things together. I love you.

"There's something I need to get out of the penthouse for Mrs. Carson. Can I have that key back?"

"Sure, just leave it here at the desk on your way out. Have a great day." He handed me the key and I hurried to retrieve the file.

What the hell have I done? I kept asking myself that question over and over as I rushed to the room. The file was exactly where he said it was. No wine had spilled on it, but blood may later. The file was labeled *Dr. John Christopher Carson.* You know a person is important when people say their whole name, much less type it out on labels.

He was the director of the residency program at John Stroger Hospital. I was one of the residents he was referring to in his note to Celeste. I had been corresponding with his office since February. My file was there clear as day. It was complete with my application, bio sheet, curriculum vitae, and passport photo. He was here and he saw me. *Maybe he wasn't sure if it was me.*

One thing was for certain, Celeste knew exactly who I was. Playing games with my mind and feelings was one thing, but toying with my future was something I couldn't tolerate. *I can just imagine what his homeboys told him,* I told myself. Anxiety and anger overcame me as I ran across the street to the bar. I was praying Celeste was there.

When I reached the club, the front door was open, but the bar was not open for business yet. The day crew was scattered around talking. Noticing Candice sitting in a booth talking on her cell phone, I walked over to her with the whole story written all over my face.

"Is Celeste here?"

"Nope."

"Do you know where I can reach her?"

"Nope." You could tell that regardless of how much beef her and Celeste had, her loyalty was still with her sister. "Would you like for me to get a message to her?"

"If you know how to get a message to her, then you can tell me how to get a message to her!"

"Look, nigga, do you want me to give her a message or what?" Her look suggested it was too late for her to have any sympathy for me falling into Celeste's trap. She had tried to warn me last night. I understood that now.

"Just tell her that her husband left his file and needs her to get it to him as soon as possible. Me and some other residents have our applications in there."

The tables had turned. Her stares were no longer giving me clues. My looks were telling her a story. Her eyes were hungry and growing hungrier by the second. I saw the same hunger that was in Celeste's eyes last night. *These bitches are a trip,* I thought to myself as I turned to walk away.

"Does she have your number?" Candice had a concerned tone and look.

I gave her my cell phone number and instructed her to have Celeste give me a call. Her eyes continued to pry. My eyes continued telling their version of what happened, but my mouth never moved. I only needed to talk with Celeste. I needed answers.

Focus, soldier! That drill sergeant's voice was back. I welcomed his structure and vowed to follow his instructions for the rest of my journey. No more distractions. Those were proving to be much too costly.

I drove up the block, gassed up my truck, and continued my march. I had to keep this file at the forefront of my heart. I knew beyond the shadow of a doubt that this file was directly linked to my immediate future.

I turned on my Hot Buttered Soul station and prayed the beautiful combination of music and thinking could help me figure a way out of this mess before I got to Chicago and the waiting vengeance of my new boss.

CHAPTER 6
MACHAIA JAMES

"Ladies and gentlemen, the captain has turned on the Fasten Your Seatbelt sign. Please be seated and return your chairs to the upright position as we make our final descent into Chicago's Midway Airport."

I lifted the window shade and saw the late afternoon sun shining on the Chicago skyline for the first time. Something deep inside of me changed. I knew this city was even more chaotic than Nashville. At twenty thousand feet above, though, none of the city's hustle and bustle existed. There, the only things that existed were the skyline and the sky itself. It's something so beautiful about the way those buildings calmly stood there reaching upwards. As if nothing going on below them, around them, or inside them could stop them from grasping a piece of heaven. If heaven existed in this place in enough abundance for Mr. Hancock, Sears, and Chrysler to have enough, then surely there must be a little piece left for me. First impressions are enduring. Before I even set one foot on the ground, I was a native. Chicago is my home, and, at first sight, I loved it dearly.

"Ma'am, do you need information about a connecting flight?" the flight attendant asked without even looking at me. She was scurrying to get her things together. Obviously, she was as excited to be in Chicago as I was.

Without hesitation, I granted her rudeness a full pardon.

"No, thank you. This is home for me," I replied as I hurried past her.

Unable to control my emotions, I smiled wide enough for the people on the next flight landing to see. The conqueror in me was eager to begin her love affair with the Windy City, while the scared little girl inside cried tears of anxiety all the way to the baggage claim area. I called Sandra.

"Girl, I don't believe this shit!" I couldn't tell if Sandra was screaming from excitement, shock, or because she knew I could hardly hear her over the noise in the airport.

"Well, believe it, girl! I'm here. You had me scared. When I couldn't get you on the phone, I thought you were out of town or something."

"No, I wasn't out of town, but the 'or something' part might have been true." She laughed in a way that let me know she would have to fill me in on the details later. "Which airline did you come in on?"

"Delta. I'm standing in front of baggage claim looking crazy with a million bags."

"Well, bitch, take your ass back up to ticket sales and wait for me." She had an unusual tone of seriousness that I wasn't familiar with.

An uneasy feeling came over me. "It was okay for me to come, right?

"Yes," she replied, but her serious tone remained.

"Then why do you want me to meet you at ticket sales?" My nervousness cracked my voice.

"'Cuz, bitch, we 'bout to fly back to Nashville and whoop that sorry motherfucker's ass!" She burst out laughing, and so did I, but even harder than her, as my anxiety released its chokehold of me.

"Girl, you're a trip. How long before you get here?" I hurried my question while catching my breath.

She took a few seconds to catch her breath, as well. "I'm still at least twenty-five minutes away. Your ass would fly in during rush hour, but I'm doing the best I can."

"Well, take your time, girl. I'm here now, and I ain't going nowhere soon. I'll see you when you get here. I love you so much, girl."

"I love you, too, girl."

Sandra is the self-proclaimed 'craziest bitch alive' and the only person I can count on to take me seriously. At a first encounter, she comes across very snobbish, and externally, she is. However, for those chosen few who are allowed in, she's one of the most endearing creatures God ever created. I have always admired her courage. Secretly, I wished it belonged to me, and then I wouldn't have to lean on hers all the time.

Sandra left Nashville right after high school because she knew there was no future there for her. Deep down, I knew the same thing about myself. Her life in Chicago wasn't easy but she's survived. In just under three years, she turned her $1,400 life savings into a job as a paralegal at a big law firm, her own apartment, a car, and plans to attend law school. While I can't say she's the most ethical person in the world, she's always been strong enough to walk away from things that didn't sit well with her spiritually.

Change is inevitable. Sandra pulled up in a new model Mercedes Benz. I knew it belonged to her because it had a tag in the front that read CBA, her 'Craziest Bitch Alive', her calling card. I could tell it wasn't the cheapest model. I knew she couldn't afford a car like that. However, she had mentioned a new boyfriend, who was a successful businessman.

We greeted each other with the warmest embrace we've ever shared. No words, just flowing tears. She wore a pair of outlandish shades. I could tell she only picked them because they were Chanel. Diamonds glistened from every extension of her body. Her refusal to elaborate on her jewels despite my stares told me she wasn't totally comfortable with the measures she took to get them. I knew we would have plenty of time to discuss that topic later. All that mattered now was I needed my best friend desperately. Despite whatever ailments her life had, she was here. My eyes watered with happiness, sadness, relief and conviction.

She needed me right now just as much as I needed her. The tightness of her arms told me she felt the same way.

"Girl, I'm so glad to see you," I said, as we slowly let go.

"Somebody had to rescue you. You look like a damn refugee out here with all this shit."

"This is everything I own. I left a lot of the stuff he bought me."

"Trust me. You're better off without them."

She didn't look me in my eyes when she said that. Instead, her eyes were fixed into space. I knew that statement was a conviction for her as much as it was intended to be encouragement for me.

"When did you get this?" I asked, referring to her car as we shoved my bags into the trunk and backseat.

"It was a gift." No further explanations were offered.

"That's a pretty serious gift." No further comments were made.

In just a matter of moments, I knew something was not right with

Sandra. As we sat in the car, she did her best to be herself. She cracked jokes and laughed as she always did. But, the moments in between the laughs, she would quickly withdraw. Something or someone was attacking her beautiful spirit, and it seemed like the destruction was starting to take its toll.

"I feel so bad. I came and just dropped all my problems on your lap without asking how things are going for you."

"Girl, don't worry about me. I'm the CBA. Chicago ain't ready for this." She didn't even fool herself.

As we rode up north of the city to her apartment in Rogers Park, her spirit, attitude, and demeanor followed the downward flight of the setting sun.

"Girl, you're gonna kill us both trying to see with those dark-ass shades on," I said in a nonchalant manner.

She slowly removed her shades and tried her best to hide what she knew I already suspected. The result of ignorance was all over her face. Her right eye had been beaten almost shut.

"Sandra! Oh my god! Who did that to you?"

The look on her face told me that she had been trying to minimize her injuries in her mind. The shock in my voice and face could not let her do that any longer. She couldn't even respond. The tears she had been holding back finally broke free and ran uncontrollably.

I made her pull off the next exit and into the parking lot of a gas station. She put her head down on the steering wheel and began crying aloud. I got out, ran around the car, opened the driver's door, and sat beside her on the edge of her seat. I hugged her and kissed her swollen eye.

She always was the one to help pull me together. The strongest woman I knew found the strength to do what she had never done before. She displayed her weakness in front of me. She wept openly and hard. There was no reason to ask her questions now. The time would come when she would have to ask herself plenty of them.

I let her cry until her tears stopped flowing.

"My. . .boyfriend. . .Javier. . ."

She struggled to get her words out. This was not the time, and a gas station parking lot was definitely not the place. So, I interrupted her.

"Girl, listen, we can talk about this later. Right now, just let me drive you home and take care of you. Okay?"

She nodded and let me help her around to the passenger side. Soon she was dosing in and out of sleep.

Her apartment sung the same shallow song as her jewelry and car. It was a multi-level condominium, with hardwood floors, marble countertops, and every possible upgrade imaginable. It was complete with expensive-looking furniture and artwork. There were flat-screen televisions in several rooms, hi-tech phones, an intercom system, and fancy stainless steel appliances. From room to room, no expense was spared.

In the living room, there was only one picture. It was of her and Javier. It had to be taken quite a while ago since she wore a short, sassy hairstyle. She generally wore short cuts, saying they made her feel spunky and feisty. The shoulder-length hair she was hiding behind now could measure the timeline from that picture to the present. As happy as she seemed then, it was lifetimes ago. I hadn't met Javier yet, but I hated him passionately.

"Sandra, does he do this all the time?"

"We have argued before, but he usually just yells and throws stuff." She was lying, and her inability to look me in my eyes told me she knew that I knew better.

"Are you happy with him?"

"He's a good man. He takes good care of me."

I used that same response a million times when people asked me the same question about DeMann.

"You just told me at the airport that I was better off without all the shit DeMann bought me."

"I know, Chaia." She looked directly in my eyes.

That response came from somewhere deep beyond the surface layer of bruises that greeted the naked eye. Sure, she was battered and bruised, but alive. For no, that was good enough for me. This battle would take time. I was just glad to know her strong spirit was still fighting with me.

Ring. . .ring. . .ring. She jumped up to get her cell phone and looked at the number on the caller ID. She sat up straight, hoping that would mask the slump her spirit was in.

"What's up, baby?" Her posture quickly returned to its deflated form. Javier was upset. "I'm sorry, baby. I was at the airport, and my phone wasn't getting good reception. My girl Chaia had an emergency and had to leave Nashville. I had to go pick her up. She's here with me now." There was a pause as she listened to him on the other end. "Yes, she's staying here. She has nowhere else to go!"

Even in her weakened state, she was sticking up for me.

"There's nothing to talk about. She has to stay here!"

Her hands were visibly shaking, and the nervousness in her voice told me that she was not comfortable standing up to him. I could tell she felt there would be some sort of backlash from this confrontation.

Love is so courageous. She loved me more than she loved herself, placing my well-being before her safety. *I wish that motherfucker would come over here with some bullshit tonight,* I thought to myself.

She hung up the phone without saying goodbye. Javier had hung up on her, but obviously not before saying something that rattled her. She jumped up and began cleaning her already spotless home. After wiping her counters and putting away some dishes, she went into her room to touch-up her makeup.

"Girl, I'm so sorry. I sat here talking your head off all night. I know you're probably starving. There's a pretty good Italian restaurant just up the block. I'll call us in something, and we can bring it back here."

"That sounds good to me. I'm starving," I replied.

"Good, just let me put the order in so it will be ready when we get there."

As Sandra placed an order for the Sicilian Feast for four, she tried her best to sound upbeat. I'm sure it passed with the restaurant worker, but not with me. Afterwards, she placed a bottle of wine in the freezer to chill and set her dinner table for three.

"Are you expecting more company?"

"This is Javier's favorite restaurant, so he's coming over to eat dinner with us."

She gave a gallant effort to sound like that was a good thing. I didn't ask any further questions. The way she rushed to set everything and leave quickly suggested she didn't want to be home when he showed up.

When we returned with dinner, Javier was sitting in the living room with his shirt untucked and unbuttoned. His necktie, shoes, and briefcase were all on the floor beside the sofa. He was light-skinned with a low haircut and goatee. I knew right away everything in the apartment had his name all over it because you could tell he was the type of person that paid way too much attention to detail. Hell, even his fingernails were manicured. He was a gorgeous man, externally. Yet internally, he was the ugliest son-of-a-bitch I'd ever seen. His cocky, arrogant demeanor reminded me so much of DeMann that it wasn't even funny. The only difference is that I had no love for this man. I knew I would fuck him up in a minute without hesitation. My unflinching stare told him just that.

"Javier, this is my friend Machaia. Chaia, this is Javier."

He nodded and stared at me with a curious look on his face.

I walked over to him with all the confidence my anger could muster up and stuck my hand out. One good thing my grandfather taught me was to always look a man in the eye and give him a firm handshake. He said they would respect you more that way. I wasn't trying to earn respect instead I wanted Javier to know I wasn't afraid of him. My eyes and swagger told him that I was not interested in being friendly or cordial.

He stood up and continued staring me in my eyes. He was a little taller than DeMann's 6'3" frame. He positioned himself entirely too close for a casual handshake and stuck his chest out so far that it almost hit me in the chin. I knew he was trying to intimidate me. His eyes were still fixed on mine, vigorously searching for signs of fear, but they found none.

I was staring far beyond the person standing in front of me. I was eyeballing the puny little motherfucker inside of him. I saw his insecurities trembling, shaking up the very foundation he was standing on. He wasn't scared of me, though. He was scared of what affects my courage would have on his relationship with my friend. He knew that, even with her battered eye, it wouldn't take me long to help Sandra see what and who he truly was.

After Sandra set the food out, we all sat down to eat. The food was delicious, and the Italian Village Restaurant would come to be one of the many things I loved about Chicago. That's as far as the enjoyment went. The conversation consisted of Sandra trying casually to make small talk, as if her eye wasn't as swollen as the buttered garlic rolls. She still did her best to hide it behind those outlandish Chanel shades. Both Javier and I ignored all her attempts to converse. *At least he's not phony,* I thought to myself, while pondering what sounds he would make if I stabbed his ass. The only things hotter than the food were the red-hot glares of rage and hate coming from my eyes and his.

"Sandi, can you take those dark-ass shades off please? You look ridiculous at the dinner table." He spoke as if he didn't know her eye was battered.

Sandra slowly pulled her sunglasses off and immediately lowered her head in shame, as if she had let him down. I saw Javier's eyes widen. I don't think he knew the extent his rage's signature had been inscribed on her face. Deep down, I would like to believe he was shocked. He looked over at me. Surely, he was trying to gauge my reaction. I looked down because it hurt to see my friend in such a weakened state.

"Oh, now that looks a lot less ridiculous. Doesn't it, Ike?" With all the anger in my voice, you could barely tell I was being sarcastic.

When he glared over at me, I could literally see the rage brewing inside him. I saw his stomach shrink to compensate for all the flames he was breathing out of his nostrils. His shoulders broadened as he took his war stance. Even his fists balled up as they began sniffing out another eye to victimize. His eyes were fixed and ready to attack at the slightest notion of weakness. Since I showed none he diverted his attention to the one place he knew he could find weakness.

"Sandi, I need to talk to you in the bedroom."

Sandra was visibly shaking. It literally broke my heart to see her so fearing of this man.

"Right now!" He stood up to project his voice, which was loud and demanding.

"Girl, are you okay?" I asked in the most soothing tone I could, wanting her pain to end.

"I'm okay. Just let us talk alone for a few minutes."

She got up from her chair and reluctantly walked towards the bedroom. He stood at the doorway entrance waiting on her to enter. His evil eyes were fixed on me the whole time. Whatever message he was trying to relay, I didn't receive it. I was focused on Sandra, hoping she gave me permission to attack his ass. She walked on. No signs. No permission. Just nervous strides.

"Are you sure you're okay, girl?" I repeated my question, but she gave no reply.

I shifted my focus to him. His eyes were fixed on me with tremendous conviction, as if he was blaming me for what was about to happen. My eyes matched his conviction. I wanted to let him know that I, too, felt my hand was being forced. Whatever was required I was ready and willing to do.

"Just yell if you need me. I'll be right here!"

I never even looked to see if she acknowledged my statement. It was intended for him anyway. After following her through the doorway, he slammed the door shut. Immediately, I grabbed the biggest knife out of the set on the counter and stood at the door listening for any sign of commotion.

"I can't believe this shit!" He was screaming loud enough to rattle the door off the hinges. "You got some strange bitch staying here without even letting me know anything. Then on top of that, you got her nosey ass all up in our business. She's walking around my house looking at me like she wants to cut my throat!"

At least the nigga ain't dumb, I thought to myself. *You got that right on the money, motherfucker. I will cut your throat in a heartbeat for my girl.* I continued to let my thoughts talk back to him since he was not letting her get a word in.

Her muffled voice was too low for me to make out any words, but I could tell she was trying to calm him down. He fought off her attempts at peace long enough to call me a couple more bitches and call Sandra a weak ass. Her voice was strained, still trying to avoid fighting.

Suddenly, both voices stopped. When I heard a body hit the mattress, I began to panic, thinking he was choking her or something. I gripped the butcher knife as tight as I possibly could, backed a few steps away from the door, and was just about ready to charge it, when I heard him. "Suck it, baby!"

Kneeling down, I peeped through the crack between the bottom of the door and the wooden floor. I saw Javier's legs cocked open and dangling off the bed. Sandra was on her knees, her body rocking at a frantic pace. She was working hard, desperately trying to gain an elusive peace.

Moments later, I heard the sounds of him penetrating her. To the untrained ear, it would sound like her passionate moans of ecstasy. I knew better, though. I felt her pain, and it hurt more than when I went through it. I laid down in her guestroom and let my tears run constantly on her behalf, until I fell asleep.

The next morning, I awoke to the smell of someone cooking breakfast. Sandra wasn't domestic by anyone's standard. Until last night, I couldn't even imagine her conceding to a man. Obviously, things had changed.

"Smells good, girl. Since when did you start cooking?"

"Girl, you'd be surprised at some of the things I do now."

"Not anymore I wouldn't." My response slipped out without thought. I gasped for air, hoping I could suck those words back up before they caused her any more pain. It was too late.

"Don't judge me." The well of tears forming told me that she had already judged herself enough for the both of us. "You don't know how hard it's been."

"I'm sorry. You of all people know I'm not in the position to be judging anybody."

"He has a lot of good traits. That's what I fell in love with. Lately, though, things have turned for the worst ten times over. I know the bad is outweighing the good. It's just so hard to let go."

"As long as you know in your heart that it's something you have to do, then you will find the strength to let go. I'm here for you, girl."

"I know you are. Believe it or not, you being here last night helped me out a lot."

"How is that?" I was curious to hear her answer.

"He didn't want you to stay here, but there was no way in hell I was gonna put you out. I usually let him have his way, but it sparked something in me to stand up to him."

"Does he live here?"

"No. He has a condo a bit further north than here. He stays over a couple of times a week when he doesn't feel up to driving out of the city."

"What is it that makes you feel so obligated to him?"

"He's done so much to help me get on my feet. He does a lot of nice things and helps me out a lot with the bills." She stole her eyes away from me when she made that statement. She knew I wouldn't accept that as validation for her staying with a man that was beating her.

"Sandra, that doesn't give—"

"Chaia, I know!" My response resonated in her heart.

"You just don't know. I was standing at the door with a butcher knife, girl. I was about to bust the door down and slice his ass up. Then, I heard y'all in there fucking. I couldn't believe that shit."

"Girl, the relationship might be garbage, but the dick is pure gold!" She burst out laughing.

Having sex with Javier was a cop out. Her laughs were lies. The effort she was putting into selling them told me she knew. Somewhere in between his ignorance and her deflated spirit, she had lost her sense of security. At this point, a false sense of security was better than her not having one at all. After last night, it just felt good to see and hear her laughing. I accepted her lies and joined in with the same false intensity.

My new found sense of security wasn't totally honest. My personal demons had to be excised. I hadn't even told Sandra I was pregnant. Whatever burdens our lives carried, we could face them together and draw strength from one another.

Sandra finished cooking salmon croquets, scrambled eggs, hashed brown potatoes, and biscuits. It smelled delicious. It was soul food at its beautiful best. She fixed two plates and poured two glasses of orange juice. Then she sat down opposite me and started eating.

"What about Ike?" I asked with a semi-serious laugh.

"He's gone."

She smiled and winked in a manner that let me know she was talking about more than just this morning. I knew it wasn't a done deal yet, but just knowing she was letting him go was good enough for me.

"You were in here cooking for me. You must really love me."

"You know I do. And yes, I made this just for you. Plus, I took the day off so we could hang out together." She genuinely smiled, then paused and looked down before looking up at me with a serious face. "I'm so glad you're here."

A thin layer of tears covered her eyes but there was nothing sad about them. I knew difficulties lay ahead for us. But, with love and support things are surely bound to get better for her, Sarah, and me.

CHAPTER 7
EVAN MILES

My journey from Atlanta had been highly regulated by the drill sergeant. His structure and discipline helped me to make up time. It had been almost twenty-four hours since I left my number with Candice, and Celeste still hadn't contacted me. The weight of her file had grown heavier as I got closer to my destination. All I could think of was how long it would take Dr. Carson to kick me out of his residency program.

While approaching the outer edges of the Chicago area, I could see the lights of the city as it woke up. The weight of the night was being lifted off of Chicago's back, and Chicago was starting anew and refreshed. God was showing me something spectacular.

What a strong city, I thought to myself. *Strong cities make strong people.*

"Wake up, fool! I made it here early."

"Dawg, you're tripping. I just laid down about an hour ago."

"It's almost six a.m., and you're just lying down? It sounds to me like you're the one tripping."

"Whatever, man. Where you at?"

"I'm at your front door. Now, come let me in."

Heroes come in all shapes, sizes, nationalities, and ages. There is nothing physical that makes someone a hero. The only thing all heroes have in common is spiritual status. The spirit of a hero is always larger than life. Even when we were kids, there was always something about Greg that made him seem regal to me. The way his goals were always so noble. He literally wanted to save the world. While other kids were blowing their allowances on junk food and video games, Greg was skipping lunch and saving the money so he could send it to the starving children in Ethiopia. Everything he did seemed to be significant. He was larger than life to me. He was the star of the basketball team at Maynard Evans High School and best friends with a nobody. Neither he nor I ever really cared about popularity, which is why we got along so well.

What would G do? I've asked myself that question too many times to count. He always made good decisions and took the righteous stand. I didn't always do that at first, but eventually, that question and his example would help me get back on track. His spirit has been one of my life's most constant guides. That's why I was there. Everybody needs a hero. He's mine.

"What's up, boy!" His voice and eyes were still groggy, but his exaggerated handshake and embrace said he really was happy to see me. "Come in. Man, I'm gonna be real with you. I'm happy to see you, but I gotta get me some Z's. I wasn't expecting you until later. We'll have to catch up after I finish up this evening. Cool?"

"That's cool."

He led me down the hall and showed me to one of his guestrooms. "This is your room, bruh."

"I appreciate it, man. I'm good. I'm gonna get a few more things out of my truck and lay it down myself. You go ahead and get your rest. I'll catch you when you get back in. You trippin' for hanging out like that on a weeknight anyway."

"The size of the sacrifice is always relative to how much you enjoy the rewards." He flashed a mischievous grin and rolled his eyes towards the living room sofa.

On the coffee table were two empty bottles of wine, three used glasses, and two purses. On the floor beside the loveseat were two pairs of women's shoes. Greg looked back at me and laughed discreetly with exaggerated gestures. Then just before he slipped back into his bedroom, he turned towards me and gave his SuperG pose, with his chest stuck out, balled-up fists on his hips, and his legs shoulder width apart.

As great and noble as Greg seemed to be back in school, he now

74

embodied the shallowness that he despised back then. The meaningfulness that he strove for has been replaced by his thirst for material gains and his indulgence in shallow relationships. Ever since his break-up with Stacey, Greg's love life has been loveless. He was just going through the motions, in gesture, in love, and surely in life.

I was determined to help him discover a way back to himself. If Christopher Reeves could still be the Man of Steel in a wheelchair and in death, then Greg Grey could still be SuperG with a broken heart. Heroes never die.

"You're crazy." I helped him with his cover-up by shaking my head and issuing a fake laugh and fake gestures of approval. "Get some sleep. I'll catch you later when you come back."

After Greg disappeared, I gathered my things and spent a few minutes looking around his condo. The real Greg had done the decorating. Rich, warm, and inviting colors jumped off the walls and hugged you as soon as you walked in. He had piece after piece of beautiful artwork and sculptures. Some pieces were contemporary, but the bulk of his collection was African artwork, woodcarvings, and scenes from African American history. Greg had a love affair with African culture before he even started making his yearly visits. I believe back in grade school, he broke off and put a little piece of his heart in each envelope containing the twenty-five-dollar money order that he sent monthly to Ethiopian children. Greg was always dependable and faithful to a cause he believed in. That's how I knew his heart wasn't into his current practice. There's no way he would have let young Cook County cases go misrepresented for the sake of a booty call.

The next morning, I woke with the same anxiety rushing my heart's work. Greg and his two companions were gone. No purses, no shoes, no left over hairpins, not even scattered strands of hair in the bathroom sink. Nothing. Even his bed was made up. For him to be tired, he went through a lot of trouble cleaning up his mess. I knew Greg was the furthest thing from a neat freak. I saw right through his attempts to cover up his struggling demons. He didn't want anything reminding him today of yesterday's transgressions.

The meet and greet for the new residents wasn't until Friday. So, I decided to go up to the hospital a day early to look around and make sure I knew the way. Part of me wanted to know if Dr. Carson was planning to kick me out of the program. If he was anything like his mean- mugging homeboys back in Atlanta, I knew what I was in for. I would rather have it happen today and save myself the embarrassment.

I got dressed, went to my truck, and began programming the address into my navigation system. With all my focus on arriving and settling I had forgotten my cell phone in the truck. The flashing message light caught my attention. I had an unread text message: *We need to talk...Celeste.*

I checked my call history and had seven missed phone calls from a private number. No doubt Celeste was trying to get in touch with me. I called the number from the text message.

Hi. You have reached the voice mailbox for Celeste Carson. At the tone, please leave a brief message, and I'll contact you at my earliest convenience. Thank you.

Her voice had the same southern drawl. It was still sexy, deep, and raspy. It quickly sucked me in and took me down memory lane to our night together. I could feel her kissing me. My mind began pondering ways to relive that magic. *Attention!* The drill sergeant was calling my logic back to the forefront of my mind. *Stay focused, soldier! Remember what the hell you are calling for.* The anger in his voice triggered my anger, as I dwelled on the games she played and the possible consequences on my future.

If you'd like to make a call, please hang up and try your call again.

I did that several more times. Each time, I hung up without leaving a message. Finally, after almost breaking my phone from handling it so roughly, I decided to leave a message.

"Celeste, I don't know what kind of games you're playing, but you're messing around with my future, and the shit ain't cool. You're right. We do need to talk and soon." Then I hung up without saying goodbye.

I took the Eisenhower Expressway into downtown and followed my directions to the Cook County Medical Center. My mind was back in Atlanta trying to figure out what Celeste wanted to tell me. I concluded it was something about Dr. Carson and what his reaction was to the stories his homeboys reported to him.

As I pulled up, I noticed the old hospital next door to the new one. It had been abandoned, traded in for a more up-to-date version of itself. As I thought of all the lives that had been saved and lost in that building, I became nervous. Truthfully, I was scared shitless to face Dr. Carson's wrath.

What the hell am I gonna do now? I questioned myself. It's hard enough getting into a quality program as it is. I could just imagine the recommendations Dr. Carson would give when new programs called to inquire as to why I didn't work out here. I felt like I had been kicked out of my profession before I even had a chance to get in good. I felt just as abandoned as that building. Still, the things that made that building a hospital could not be changed by some corporate decision to move to a new pile of bricks next door. By the same token, the things that make me a doctor can't be changed because a simple nigga let his jealousy and anger make his decisions.

I entered the front door and walked the hallways for over an hour, like I didn't have a care in the world. I spoke to the workers and waved at the patients like I was taking a victory lap around a championship stadium. The way people responded to my greetings reinforced my confidence. I knew beyond a shadow of a doubt that I would complete the residency I came to complete.

On the way out of the front door, I stopped to notice the photos in the main lobby. There was one photo of all the department heads. Surprisingly, there were three black doctors in the picture. There was a middle-aged, distinguished-looking male doctor with a few gray hairs and glasses. There was a slightly younger bald one with 'I'm the shit' written all over his face. The third one was a middle-aged sister. You could just tell by her mile-wide smile that she absolutely loved her job. I was disappointed when I saw the names on the bottom were not listed according to the position in the photo, but rather by alphabetical order. I wanted to put a name with each face and pay those pioneers their just due when I saw them.

I skipped directly to the C's. I was looking for the only name I would recognize. There it was: Carson, John Christopher MD. *Damn, they even write this dude's whole name on a photo label. I've made the wrong guy mad.* I knew Dr. Carson was the cocky one, staring at me like I didn't have a chance in hell. His eyes glared at me off of the photo like they had been in the hotel room watching me enjoy Celeste the whole time. His spirit jumped out of that photo and charged at me in a jealous rage. I felt him. He hated my guts. As my mind bounced around all the evil he would bring my way, I considered us even. I hated his guts, too.

"That could be you, son." A voice was speaking to me from just up the hallway.

When I turned to see who it was, an older black gentleman was walking towards me. He didn't appear to be a doctor since he was dressed in shabby street clothes. He had shoulder-length locs that had more gray than beeswax. He made a few more statements about what I could do if I stayed focused. He spoke semi-proper, but with a country twist. I don't know why, but his words of encouragement sort of offended me. Why is it that black people always feel the need to 'out-status' each other? I was raised to respect my elders, but I didn't need some arbitrary old man's lecture on staying focused. Focus was my middle name. *Who is he?*

"I'm a doctor, too. I start working here next week. My name is Dr. Evan Miles." My aggravation with him caused me to add entirely too much 'what'd you got to say now, nigga' tone to my statement. I stuck my hand out to shake his.

He started laughing, while slowly extending his hand out to shake mine. "There's a lot more to being a doctor than just having a degree from medical school. Right now, you're a resident. And I know exactly who you are, Mr. Miles. I've been up all night setting up your residency rotations. I'm Dr. J.C. Carson".

I stood there frozen for a moment. It took time for my mind to grasp what had just happened. Bracing my feet, I took a firm stance and waited on him to throw the first punch, but it never came. He didn't seem angry. My temperament raced from defensive to apologetic, to curious to nervous. I felt a strong urge to apologize to him. I nervously reintroduced myself.

"I apologize for not recognizing you, Dr. Carson. I thought you were the bald doctor here." I pointed towards the young cocky doctor in the photo.

"No, that's Dr. Warren Copeland. He's the head of our infectious disease department and runs his own HIV clinic across town. He's a very talented young physician. As a matter of fact, he's from Tampa. I noticed you're from Orlando. It seems like Central Florida is a growing field for young black doctors, huh?"

"Are you familiar with the area, sir?"

He laughed. "I'm from just outside Orlando. I'm from a little town called Winter Haven. Are you in a rush, son?"

"No"

"Well, let's have a cup of coffee." He took a deep sigh and looked at me with a serious look. "I believe in being upfront and honest with people. You and I need to sit down and have a serious heart-to-heart talk."

He must be one hell of a poker player, I thought to myself. His face gave no clues whatsoever. I couldn't tell if he was going to calmly and discreetly ask me to leave town or wait for me to turn my back and sucker punch me.

I walked beside him as he led me into a private lounge across the hall from the main cafeteria. The only thing ringing louder in my ears than his footsteps was the pounding of my nervous heartbeat.

"It's always pretty quiet in here. I come here to get away and think sometimes."

"I'll have to remember that for the future." I was asking a question more than making a statement. I studied his face for a response. Nothing.

"Do you notice anything weird about me today, son?" He grabbed his clothes, just in case I was too dumb to notice.

"You're not dressed in scrubs or professional attire?"

"Exactly, and why do you think that is?"

"Because you weren't expecting to be here today."

"You're a bright one, son. That's exactly what I want to talk to you about. I was at home today landscaping my backyard, when I got called to the ER because a bus full of people overturned. What do you think would have happened if I had been home drinking and couldn't drive?" He waited for my response. I sat there quietly. "Well, son?"

I didn't answer. I just sat there like a deer caught in headlights partly because I was still surprised it was him. But, mainly because I wasn't sure what he was getting at and how much he knew.

"Did you hear me, son?" His eyes were intensely fixed on mine, as if he was trying to figure out where my mind was.

He's way too calm, I thought to myself. He didn't know anything about Celeste, I concluded. The intensity in his eyes was not accompanied by jealousy, anger, or even aggression. They were sort of familiar. Not familiar by any physical measures, but rather by a comforting feeling they gave me. The compassion in his eyes reminded me of the way my mother would look at me when she was concerned about something I was doing wrong. I felt like I was getting lectured by my parent, but I didn't quite know why.

"Do you know why I'm having this conversation with you?" He must have noticed the puzzled look on my face.

"Because you want to make sure I'm committed?"

"Son, I knew you were committed before I decided to accept you into my program. You started out poor in the projects of Mercy Drive. You wouldn't have made it this far if you weren't committed."

I was shocked that he knew so much about my past. He was a department head in a major hospital, and he took the time to research my past. He cared and it showed.

"Son, I recognized you in the hotel in Atlanta a couple of days ago. I wasn't sure if it was you, so I had my wife check with her buddy at the front desk. I was about to introduce myself to you, when I realized you were drunk or something. I didn't want to have our first encounter happen under those circumstances. So, I decided to wait until I met you here."

I didn't know whether to beg for forgiveness or explode with relief because that's all he wanted to talk about.

"Dr. Carson, I can assure you that I don't have any problems. The whole coming to Chicago and starting over was a very exciting process for me, and I just got caught up in the moment. I didn't think I would run into anyone. Of all the hotels in Atlanta, I stroll up into the one you are staying at. I feel so bad. I hope I haven't given you the wrong impression." My face automatically frowned up.

"Son, you never know who you're going to meet and when or where you're going to meet them. I respect the fact that your personal time is your personal time, but the good doctors are always ready to serve." The passion in his voice told me that his words were very much heartfelt. "I have a lot of confidence in you, and I want you to become the doctor that I know you can be. If you're going to do well here, I need to know that I can count on you to do the right things."

"I'm sorry, Dr. Carson." I lowered my head in shame.

Dr. Carson placed his hands on my shoulder and chuckled lightly. "Pick your head up, son. I'm not judging you. I've gotten caught up in enough traps to let you know the things that can stop you from being the best doctor you can be. I believe in you."

Dr. John Christopher Carson. I would use his whole name because he deserved that much respect. He sat there and shared a few stories from his past to encourage and inspire me. Dr. Carson's words were nonjudgmental, encouraging, and heartfelt. Beyond anything in my realm of control, his spirit took a father figure role in my heart. Over the course of one conversation, his compassion easily wiped away my fears of him mistreating me, only to be replaced by an even greater fear of letting him down or disappointing him any further.

"God works in mysterious ways, huh? If my wife hadn't convinced me to come down and see her last weekend, I would've never run into you like that, and we would've never had this conversation."

I felt a bond. I was inspired by his desire to see me do well. I appreciated his words. Still, no matter how uplifting his compassion, I was bound by the truth of what I had already done. I knew that as long as I carried the secret of what happened in Atlanta, the conviction of that truth would only allow us to be but so close.

"Does your wife live here in Chicago with you?" I tried my best to make my curiosity sound innocent.

"It's funny you asked that question. For the last two years, we were living in separate cities. I was in Chicago, and she lived in Atlanta. The distance was starting to take its toll on our marriage. So, just this morning, she told me that she has decided to move to Chicago permanently."

That same uneasy feeling of undigested drama that bothered me in Atlanta was quickly beginning to upset my system once again. My response to all his truths—lies. I wrapped them up in fake sincerity and presented them to him without regard for the respect his honesty deserved from me.

You didn't lie. You just didn't tell him everything. My mind was trying to rationalize my actions. *That's the same damn thing.* My usually quiet heart wasn't having any of that, and an uncomfortable feeling of shame came over me.

"Dr. Carson, I appreciate your time, but I have to get going." I couldn't even look him in the eyes.

"Have you gotten your living arrangements situated?"

"Yes, sir. My best friend is a lawyer here in Chicago. He's letting me room with him until I get on my feet."

"Sounds like he's a pretty good friend."

"He is."

"I'm glad we had this chance to talk, son. I was concerned after what I saw in Atlanta, but you have reassured my confidence in you. I know you're going to do just fine. I look forward to seeing you next week at the reception dinner."

"Likewise, sir." I stuck my hand out to shake his.

This time there was no laughter and no hesitation. He stretched out his arms and embraced me with a hug. There was nothing casual about his embrace. In my limited experience of what a father's embrace feels like, it felt sort of fatherly. There were only six residents selected to the program. I have no doubt my selection was merited by my academic achievements. For whatever reason, I was his favorite and would appreciate it always. I returned his embrace as tight as the conviction of my lies would allow me to do.

When I walked outside the building, my cell phone chirped. I had two text messages waiting. One was from Greg: *Good day n court. Where u at?* The other message was from Celeste: *Call me ASAP. Very important.*

I dialed Celeste's number, but hung up. At this point, a conversation between her and I was irrelevant. She would tell me that she loves her husband and they were going to give love another try. I would tell her that I didn't appreciate her playing games with me and my future to get back at her ex. We would agree that the best thing to do at this point is to forget the whole thing ever happened. There was no need for me to call her back Digested or not, it was over. I dialed Greg's number.

"What's up, boy? Where you at? I thought you'd be back at the house catching up on your sleep from that drive." His excitement level was far from a sleep-deprived party animal.

"No, I drove up to the hospital and took a look around."

"Well, you gotta get back to the house so we can go out tonight and celebrate." His excitement was growing.

"What are we celebrating?"

"First of all, my dawg is in town. Secondly, I settled a big case out of court today. Ya boy is 'bout to get PIZZ-AID!" His excitement finally exploded.

"Man, after last night, I thought you would want to stay home and just chill."

"Obviously, you don't know your boy very well. It's the Double G."

We burst out laughing.

Happiness and excitement are both very opportunistic creatures. I was excited about being in Chicago. I was happy my Atlanta escapade hadn't ruined my residency opportunity. Together, those two comrades chipped in and bought my first dime bag after leaving the hospital.

As fate would have it, the Double G turned out to be the kingpin of the Chicago euphoria market. He rolled me up a giant blunt of a much higher caliber vine. He told me that his client was given a seven figure out-of-court settlement, and his commission would net him close to $200,000. We met a few of his friends from work at a downtown nightclub to celebrate. His excitement was contagious. His happiness became mine. I was happy for him.

Our weekend rampage spilled into the week. He had taken me to the far corners of the city. South side, west side, downtown, and the suburbs. Night clubs, strip clubs, restaurants, and bars. We hit them all. We slept by day and flew high by night. If there were any significant events, I had no real recollection of them. I do remember ignoring several of Celeste's text messages. I couldn't take the risk of her blowing my high over something that didn't matter anymore.

By Wednesday of the next week, my binge had taken its toll on my mind, body, and spirit. Mentally, I was drained. I felt as if I was stuck in a constant state of daze. I had to concentrate hard as hell just to perform simple activities. Physically, the proof was apparent at a moment's glance. I had bags under my eyes big enough to carry potatoes. My feet dragged the ground, and my shoulders almost hung low enough to wipe away the scuff marks my feet left.

You know you're fucking up, right? The drill sergeant was starting in on me. He always told me the brutal truth whether I wanted to hear it or not. As I faced myself in the bathroom mirror, I realized what was happening. I understood the downward spiral of shallow happiness and excitement. If there were any doubts in my mind as to what the end result was, a perfect example was standing in the doorway.

"Evan, man, you better get yourself some rest. There's a martini bar downtown that has a "Wind Down Wednesday" happy hour. It's usually packed up in that joint. When I get off, we can go grab something to eat and then check it out. I know it's gonna be some fine-ass hoes up in there tonight. Is that cool wit' u?"

As beat down as I was looking, Greg should've been ten times worse. Our weekend exploits had netted him two new lovers and at least seven or eight of his self-coined S.W.H. (Sex Waiting to Happen) contacts. His eyes, shoulders, and feet resembled nothing close to the effects mine did. Greg had grown accustomed to toxic doses of euphoria. He had covered up his real feelings, thoughts, and emotions with so many levels of shallowness that the shallowness itself was kinda deep.

When I expressed to him that I didn't want to go because I needed to start getting ready for my first rotation starting Monday, he went into a passionate five-minute lecture on enjoying life to the fullest and not letting corporate America take the fun out of your life. *Don't buy that shit, son.* The drill sergeant was not about to give up his newly reinstated dominance in my consciousness. *You've got a couple of days to get yourself together. Let that fool kill his self, if he wants to. You have to take care of you.* The drill sergeant had gone through my mind and stomped out every fire the weekend's euphoria had left burning.

Rational thinking was clearly the current state of my mind's affairs. I thought about Dr. Carson's first image of me in Atlanta. I knew the last thing I wanted to do was show up Friday night resembling anything close to what he saw in that hotel lobby.

Ignoring Celeste's calls and texts became comfortable. I had no problems digesting the way I was handling the situation. As far as I was concerned, it was over. Celeste's opinion and whatever she wanted to talk about did not matter. Her moving to Chicago did raise red flags, though. There was something about that abrupt decision that was hard to digest. It just didn't make any sense to me. The way she talked about him in her stories made him out to be the world's biggest asshole. She definitely didn't make it seem like she was on the verge of going back to him.

She's up to something. This was one of those rare occasions when my mind and heart totally agreed.

CHAPTER 8
MACHAIA JAMES

"Grandma, I can't believe you gave him the address!"

"Kye, I can't believe you didn't tell me you were pregnant. This is no time for you to be running around from city to city. It's been two weeks now. You need to come on back home, baby."

Despite the countless times I told her that I'm staying in Chicago, she refused to accept it.

"Grandma, I already told you. The only reason I didn't say anything is because I didn't know what I wanted to do yet."

"Well, baby, I could've helped you figure out the best thing to do."

"That means you would've told me what to do, and it's time for me to start making my own decisions. But, Grandma, you shouldn't have told DeMann where I was."

"He already knew you were in Chicago with Sandra. He told me you were pregnant and that you asked him to send you some money, but he lost the address. So, I gave him the address."

"Well, Grandma, we can't change what's already done. Eventually, I was gonna hav'ta talk to him anyways." I made that statement with the most nonchalant tone possible to hide my uncertainty. I knew making her nervous would only produce more opinions and criticisms.

"Listen, baby, if you're not happy with him, when you return, you can move back home with me and your granddaddy. I've already told him the situation, and he knows you're coming back home."

Her smothering opinions and refusal to hear what I was saying let me know that. Two and a half weeks ago, when I was still in Nashville, that probably would have been enough to get me to move back. But, I was an entirely new creature. *Ain't no way in hell I'll ever go back to either of them.* One day she would hear my voice, but this wasn't the day. There was no need of going back and forth with her. At the moment, I was more concerned with her conversation with DeMann. I needed to know exactly what was said and what information was given.

"Grandma, when did he call you?"

"The day fo' yesterday."

"Did you give him the phone number, too?"

"No, baby. He said he already had that. He just needed the address."

DeMann was a master at manipulation. I was living proof of that. I'd never been fearful of him, but then again, I'd never been the target of his wrath either. I knew he wouldn't appreciate me taking his money. I'd seen him blow two to three times more money than what I took on a vacation. So, I didn't think $35,000 would be a big deal to him. Now, I wasn't so sure. He hated people stealing from him. That much, I did witness.

I hung up with my grandma and lay there. *He lied and said he already had the number, when I know he doesn't. That means he's not interested in talking. All he asked my grandmother for was the address. That means he wants to see me face to face.* I knew him all too well.

The next morning, I got ready and left out the door with Sandra. She had pulled a few strings and got one of the attorneys to hire me on as a receptionist in his office. Chicago in the morning was business as usual. It had been almost a week since DeMann had gotten my address from my grandmother. That was more than enough time for a motivated traveler to make it to Chicago. I could feel him. I expected DeMann to jump out at every turn. I was clearly nervous.

"Girl, what's wrong with you? I told you not to worry. Lesley is cool. He's going to be fun to work for."

"I know. I'm just nervous because it's my first day."

I hated lying to her, but under the circumstances, I thought it would be better. She had enough to worry about without my drama added on top. Her arguments with Javier had gotten worse. I'm certain my presence had a lot to do with that. Javier didn't even try to hide his feelings about my being there. Sandra was so busy in the mornings putting herself back together that she hadn't noticed my bouts with morning sickness. For the life of me, I couldn't figure out why I hadn't told her I was pregnant yet. If anyone in the world would have sympathy on my situation, it would be her. Maybe that's it. I didn't want anyone's sympathy. I needed some straight up backup. I had to come clean.

"Sandra, I got something I need to tell you." My tone suggested we needed to have a serious talk.

She turned the music down in the car and faced me with a concerned look. "What's up, Chaia?"

"The morning that I caught DeMann at the cl—"

BANG! Sandra had been so focused on what I was about to say, she wasn't paying attention to the car in front of her. Before she could look up, she had run into the back of a red Lexus convertible. She began panicking immediately.

"Oh my God! Javier is going to kill me." The distress in her voice almost made me believe she meant that literally.

Before thinking about her possible injuries or mine, all she could think about was how he was going to react. That was my first real glimpse at just how far her fear of him was embedded into her spirit.

"Sandra, are you okay? Your nose and mouth are bleeding."

She didn't hear a word I said. Her health was the last thing on her mind.

"SANDRA!" I screamed her name to break her out of her daze. She looked at me still halfway in a trance. "Are you okay?"

She nodded her head and asked me the same question.

"Ma'am, are you guys okay?" The white gentleman driver of the Lexus was checking on us. His questions and actions reflected his concern for our well-being. He didn't come across angry or aggressive. He was merely trying to make sure we were okay.

"What the fuck does it look like? I'm bleeding out the gotdamn mouth and you standing there asking me some dumb-ass questions!"

The CBA was in effect. This was surely not the first time I've seen or heard Sandra cussing someone out. However, she doesn't usually explode unless someone or something has pushed her to the limit. In this case, it was both someone and something, and neither was the accident or the gentleman standing there suffering her wrath. She just needed to vent her frustrations. She was too afraid to direct it at the person who deserved it, so she was settling for the next best thing.

Sandra jumped out of the car and began cussing the man out, as if it was his negligence that had caused her to hit him. The man just stood there and listened…for a while.

"I really don't understand why you're so mad at me. You hit me!" Then he gave a sarcastic laugh and began walking away. "What a damn idiot."

If he meant to say that under his breath, I wish he would have. Sandra heard his remark and immediately turned into a person I've never met before.

"What did you call me, cracker?"

Before he could turn around to respond, Sandra was on top of him swinging with all her might, while crying and screaming at the top of her lungs. "Motherfucker, I'll kill you" over and over again. Everyone watching was in shock, including me. By the time I was able to get her off of him, her fender bender had turned into charges ranging from assault and battery to attempted murder. Judging by the faces and finger pointing of the witnesses as they told their versions to the two officers, she was probably going to be hung in the town square immediately. Throughout the whole ordeal, Sandra just leaned up against me crying silently. Only she knew what was going through her mind.

"Excuse me, Ms. Townsend. I'm Deputy Pullen."

After getting several statements from eyewitnesses, the officer came over to get Sandra's side of the story. She just sat there rocking back and forth, leaning on me, and crying silently.

"Ma'am, several witnesses and the victim have told me that you attacked the gentleman driving the Lexus. Is that true?"

There was no answer, at least not a verbal one.

"Ms. Townsend, ma'am, if you don't give me your account of what happened, all I'll have to go by is what the others have said." He looked at me for assistance.

I tried explaining that her overreacting was really her personal issues getting the best of her.

"I understand what it's like going through tough times, but that doesn't give her the right to assault another individual. If it did, we'd have people getting attacked everywhere."

He was right. He knew it. I knew it, and the part of Sandra that was still conscious knew it, too.

"Ms. Townsend, ma'am, I'm afraid I'm going to have to ask you to come with me back to the precinct."

He was arresting her in the most polite way he could. Given the nature of her attack, the fact that he didn't place her in handcuffs was very understanding of him. I walked with Sandra to the police car, holding her in my arms for as long as the officer would let me. Then he forced me to back away, placed Sandra in the back seat, and drove my friend to jail.

After the officer gave the other driver a copy of Sandra's contact and insurance information, he looked at me with a disenfranchised look and drove away, smashed rear end and all. He was surely headed straight for his lawyer's office. *Sandra needs someone to help her, too,* I thought to myself. The only thing I could think of to help her was to notify my new boss, which was a close friend of hers. So, I got her personal belongings and the tower's card before he towed her car away. I went through the contacts in her cell phone and found Lesley's name.

"Excuse me, Mr. Manley. This is Machaia James. I'm a friend of Sandra Townsend. I was supposed to start working with you this morning."

He laughed at my formality. "Machaia, I know who you are. Sandra has told me all about you. Call me Lesley. I was looking forward to meeting you this morning. I planned for us to get to know one another over breakfast. Is something wrong? Are you going to be able to make it in today?"

The warmness in his voice told me that he was somebody I could trust. I hadn't had a lot of experience with trusting my instincts, but my gut feeling was to tell him everything.

"Sir, we had an accident on the way into the office this morning."

"Is Sandra okay?" By the way he spoke, I could tell that whatever he'd been doing had been put on hold.

"She did have some bleeding from her nose and mouth. But I think she is fine. They took her to jail."

"JAIL! What the fuck did they take her to jail for?" He was rattled and upset.

"She just lost it and attacked the other driver." My emotions finally caught up with me. Unable to help it, I started crying. My literacy crumbled as my words mutated from my cries of anxiety, anger, and concern. "I tried to tell the officer that she was just stressed from her situation at home, but all the people told him that she went crazy."

He paused a moment. He was obviously trying to calm himself down and gather his thoughts. My crying couldn't have been helping.

I gave him the information off of the ticket the officer gave Sandra. He said he had to make an appearance in court and that he would be held up for a few hours. He called the dispatcher's office and used his credit card to send me a cab. He was a good man.

"Go to the precinct and make sure they transport Sandra to a hospital. As soon as you know where they're taking here leave a message on my voicemail. I'll be there as soon as I can."

The fire this situation put in him demonstrated, without doubt, that she was a very high priority for him. She was much more of a priority than what a platonic friend should be. At least, that's what my gut told me.

By the time I arrived at the police station, whatever Lesley called and told them had obviously put the fear of God in the whole precinct. Paramedics were on the scene, and Sandra was on a stretcher being handled with the finest care by both medics and officers. After telling one of the paramedics I was her sister, he agreed to let me ride in the ambulance with her to the hospital.

On the ride over, Sandra was a lot closer to normal. The paramedic was busy asking her questions about what she was feeling and checking her vitals. In between his questions, I explained to her what I told Lesley and what he had done.

Once we got to the hospital, the doctors ran an assortment of tests on her to make sure she was okay. While they were running tests, I stepped outside and called Lesley.

"Mr. Manley, I didn't think you were going to answer the phone. I know you're in court."

"It's okay. I told them I had a family emergency and had to step outside for a moment to take this call."

"We're at John Stroger Hospital. The doctors are running a few tests just to make sure everything is cool. They said she'll probably be released shortly."

"That's great to hear! I should be finished in about thirty minutes or so.

I'll come pick you guys up and take you home." His voice was elated.

"Oh, you don't have to do that. You've done enough." I was lying. Sandra had already called Javier. He said he was on his way after he had cussed her out for wrecking his car.

"Stop trippin'! I want to. Plus, I want to see her and make sure she's alright."

"Oh, you must be a doctor, too!" My sarcasm was filled with curiosity.

"No, I'm not, but there's nothing more healing than being with loved ones."

"Loved ones, huh?"

"Yep…loved ones." I couldn't see it, but I felt his smile. It was as wide as can be. "I gotta get back inside. I'll see y'all in a few." Then he hung up the phone abruptly.

Platonic friends my ass, I thought to myself. I knew I ran the risk of having Lesley and Javier run into each other. I thought maybe Javier needed to know that somebody was willing to cherish Sandra the way she deserved to be cherished. Maybe that would get him to act right. Desperate times call for desperate measures. I rushed back upstairs and prayed Lesley wouldn't be too far behind me.

When I got to Sandra's room, Javier was already there. The look on his face darkened the room almost to the point of misery. Sandra's demeanor was back on its downward trek. No one said anything for several minutes, and the silence only amplified the tension. It seemed he was just about to boil over, when the doctor came into the room.

"Hi, I'm Dr. Carson, the director of the emergency room here at the hospital. The police chief called and asked me to personally look over your charts. You must have some very influential friends."

He laughed. We didn't. Our tension quickly choked the laughter out of his demeanor.

"Ms. Townsend, I'm happy to tell you that we were unable to find any significant injuries. The slight bleeding you had from your nose and mouth appeared to be from superficial wounds. We ran an MRI, and there was no damage to your spine or brain. All the x-rays were negative. There was evidence of some slight swelling around your right eye, but that appeared to be from a previous injury."

He looked at Sandra for a reaction. She gave none.

"I wrote you a prescription for a pain medication. It will help control any discomfort or inflammation you may have over the next few days. Are there any questions?"

"No, thank you, Doctor. Is she cleared to leave?" Javier didn't even look at Sandra to see if she had any questions.

"Yes, just sign out at the nursing station. The police department has taken care of the expenses, so we didn't need to use your insurance information. Take care." He looked at Sandra once again and then looked at me. I tried to relay a SOS signal on Sandra's behalf, but my eyes could only say so much.

After the doctor left, Javier began gathering Sandra's belongings.

"Girl, do you have any money on you?" Sandra asked.

"Yeah," I replied. "Why, you need some?"

"No, Javier drove his BMW." She paused and lowered her head. "It's a two-seater."

He had on street clothes, which meant he came from home. True or not, that's what I concluded. He always drove his SUV, but it was no coincidence that he would be in his two-seater when he knew I would need to ride with them. Clearly, he didn't want me with them. My feeling was mutual towards him.

I looked directly at Javier. "It's okay, Sandra. Lesley was on his way to pick both of us up. He said he just wanted to check on you and make sure you were okay. I'll get him to drive me back to the apartment. He must really love you. I don't know what he told the people at the police station, but he got them straight for real."

Javier and I were past the subtle shit. I was dead set on making my point to Javier without even considering how it would affect Sandra. I knew I messed up as soon as those words came off of my lips. Javier's eyes tightened and his eyebrows bowed in a dark, gruesome way. He turned to Sandra, who was looking at me in a way that told me that I had opened a door that should not have been opened.

I gently grabbed her arm and tried to apologize with my caress. "Sandra, I'll see you back at the apartment in a little bit."

"Sandra, bring your ass on!" He was talking through his teeth in a loud whisper.

"Are you gonna be okay?" She asked.

"Girl, I'll be fine. I'll see you at the house later." I smiled as sincerely as my concerns would let me. The last thing I wanted her to do was worry about me.

Thirty minutes after they left, Lesley walked in. I never met him before, but the concerned look of a 'loved one' was written all over his face. He was an average-looking man. Not ugly, but definitely not drop dead gorgeous. Right away, I knew he wasn't Sandra's type. He was tall with broad shoulders and a bit of a pot belly. He looked like he could have been an athlete before he fell in love with Chicago deep-dish pizzas. Nevertheless, his whole aura screamed integrity, respect, and class. I walked over to him at the nursing station.

"Are you Mr. Manley?"

He turned around and smiled. "You must be Machaia and I told you to call me Lesley."

When I tried to shake his hand, he playfully pushed it aside and gave me a hug. I told him that Sandra's boyfriend had come and they left together. His disappointment was blatantly obvious. My heart was comfortable. I trusted him. I wanted to tell him the whole story but it wasn't my place. Whatever she wanted him to know, should come directly from her.

"I hope it's not too much of a problem for me to get a ride home. Javier didn't have room in his car."

He laughed and motioned for me to follow him out the door. "I'm not surprised by that little trick."

"Oh, so you know him?" I tried to act like I was surprised to learn.

"It's a long story. Are you hungry? If you're going to work for me, then we should take this time to talk a bit over dinner. Is that okay with you?"

"Yeah, but I want to know all about the Javier story." I couldn't hold my curiosity any longer.

"Now I know why you and Sandra are so tight. Both of y'all is nosey as hell." He laughed and playfully nudged me on the shoulder. I couldn't help but to burst out laughing, as well.

It's so cool how friendship is transferable. Fondness, trust, and respect for a person can all be transferred to some degree from one friend to another. Sandra and Lesley have it for each other. Sandra and I have it for each other. Now, after only knowing him for a few hours, Lesley and I have it for one another. Our friendship with each other was nowhere near what had been developed with Sandra, but the basis was there for it to grow.

He must have sensed the stress I was feeling when he said he knew the perfect place to take me to dinner. We went to the House of Blues in downtown Chicago. The atmosphere was amazing. A live jazz band was playing, the food was excellent, and the contrast was night and day from anywhere I'd been before. The atmosphere of a place has everything to do with who you are with. DeMann had taken me to many nice restaurants before, but the night was always about him showing off. He was never able to just chill and enjoy the evening because he was always busy trying to make sure people were giving him his 'props'. Real class props itself.

All that mattered was that I was enjoying the music, enjoying the food, and enjoying my company. It was nothing romantic. Mentally, I was trying to plot on how to get Javier out of the picture and Lesley in. I knew he wanted the same thing.

"So how long are you gonna dodge the Javier story, man?" I was joking, but serious. I really wanted to know what happened.

"It's really not that serious. I represented a client that won a very large suit against him. When he found out Sandra and I are at the same firm and really good friends, he started trippin' on her."

"Trippin' how?" I hoped he didn't know she was getting beat and did nothing.

"You know. He was telling her not to hang around me, stopped her from calling me, and stupid stuff like that."

He was staring me in my eyes to see if I knew anything. Translated, I knew he meant that he was feeling her, but she was sending him mixed messages. She probably liked him.

"So has Javier stopped y'all from being close?"

"Sandra is my girl. I'll always lo…feel very strongly for her and do what I can to help her out. As far as Javier is concerned, I don't worry about dumb guys. Sooner or later, Sandra is going to see him for what he is and drop his ass. That's something she has to do own her own, though. Until then, she's going to keep putting up with him." The anguish in his eyes told me that day couldn't come soon enough for him. Me either.

"Well, boss man, I better get home if I'm going to be on time tomorrow."

"Listen, I'll tell you like I told Sandra. To do well in this business, you have to learn to keep the personal stuff personal and the business stuff strictly business. Right now, we're on personal time. If you ever need my help, just call. When we're at work, just help keep me on time and my office stuff straight, and we're good to go. I have a personal secretary, so you will be the office receptionist. Your job is to run errands, make sure the office supplies are taken care of, and things of that nature. I have a temp for the week. I've already paid the agency, so if you need to take a couple of days to help Sandra get things together, just let me know."

"I really appreciate that. I was looking forward to starting. It's like a new beginning for me. So, if she's doing ok, I'll come. Just let me see how she's doing when I get home."

"Sounds good. Now, let me get you back."

What an impressive man. As we walked up to his truck, I realized he had the same Range Rover as DeMann and Rodney. His was minus the toys and gizmos, just simple and classy. The way he carried himself spoke loud enough.

Lesley awakened something in me that would definitely change the type of man I was attracted to. Other than me directing him to her street, a comfortable silence and some very relaxing jazz music was conversation enough.

"This is it. I know it's better if I went up alone. They looked like they were headed for an argument when they left the hospital."

"I totally understand. Just call me if you need my help with anything."

"Okay."

"See you soon." Sincerity can't be faked.

He watched me walk to the door and get my keys out. Then, I turned to him and waved goodnight. He drove off, and I was headed upstairs into God knows what. After fumbling with my keys for a second, I walked in and was just at the door of the elevator when I heard his voice.

"Girl, you ain't been up here two weeks, and you already jumping in and out of niggas' cars."

Before I turned around, I knew who it was. I knew what his facial expression was. I even knew how his body was positioned. I didn't know was what he was about to do. When I turned around, he had a weird look on his face. I knew he was busy trying to read me, the same way I was trying to figure him out. He always played things cool until he knew how I would react.

It had only been twenty-three days since I left Nashville, but it seemed like a lifetime ago. My whole perspective on my life, myself, and my surroundings had changed. Time had altered my memory of him. I couldn't read him the way I used to. I was clueless as to what he was thinking and feeling. The thought of what he might be capable of doing scared me shitless.

I invited him up to the apartment without even thinking twice about it. I was seeking protection from Javier and Sandra's presence. I thought surely he would not react in front of them. As we rode up the three flights of stairs to Sandra's floor, he did something totally unexpected. He reached out, grabbed my hand, and smiled. As we reached the third floor, I looked over at him. His eyes were welling, his grip tightened, and he gave me the same warm smile I fell in love with when we were teenagers. His smile brought back wonderful memories of our life together. The moment was beautiful, peaceful, and very short lived.

As we approached Sandra's door, Javier was yelling at the top of his lungs.

"I bet your trifling ass be all up in that nigga's face when you at that damn office, too!" I opened the door. "And you done gave this bitch a key to my motherfucking house!"

WHAP! Javier slapped Sandra across the face as DeMann walked in behind me. She fell on the floor and started crying. Javier stood over her and drew back to hit her again.

"Nigga, I know you ain't in here puttin' yo motherfuckin' hands on my homegirl!" DeMann pushed me aside and rushed towards Javier.

The same way that friendship is transferred, protection can be transferred, as well. Even though they've known each other since they were kids, DeMann and Sandra have never been really close. He knew how much I loved her. Deep down, he feared one day she would talk me into leaving him and Nashville behind to follow her. DeMann never tried to come in between me and Sandra, though. He just kept his distance and prayed my love for her wouldn't outgrow what I felt for him. He knew that watching this man beat her was killing me inside. In his mind, Javier beating on Sandra was like beating on me, and he was having none of that.

In the first few minutes, DeMann had already beaten Javier half to death. He didn't show any signs of slowing down, as Javier hopelessly tried fighting back. I have a much better understanding of why DeMann shielded me from that side of him. He was afraid I would view him as a monster. Those people who were scared of him back in Nashville knew what he was capable of. I was bearing witness for the first time, and Javier was having it beat into him unmercifully. I couldn't see DeMann's eyes. All I could see was how Javier's eyes reacted to them. Whatever Javier saw told him that no mercy would be given tonight.

DeMann lunged forward and punched Javier, who fell backwards into the hallway wall and then the floor. DeMann then stood over him and started stomping him in the stomach and head. Sandra was frantically screaming for DeMann to stop. Javier was past the point where he could attempt any sort of retaliation. He wasn't unconscious, but he was clearly dazed and bewildered. He was on the ground moving slowly, trying to make it up on his hands and knees. DeMann punched him in the back of the head, and he fell down on his back. He wasn't even looking at DeMann. Javier was focused on the one person in the room who cared enough to try to save his life. Jesus!

"God help me!" Javier mumbled those words out of the bloody opening between his chin and nose.

"You wasn't asking for God when you was in here beatin' on my girl." DeMann spoke with a steady, rhythmic pattern to match the punches and kicks he delivered.

DeMann kept swinging and kicking for what seemed to be an eternity. His words were scrambled and started making less sense. He said something about lying to him and that he trusted somebody. He was lost in the moment. In his mind, he was punishing someone for hurting him. One thing was for sure, it had nothing to do with the man lying on the floor receiving the wrath of another's wrongdoing. True enough, Javier had a good ass whooping coming, but this was far more than any man should have to endure.

"Baby, please stop. It's over. He's done." I grabbed DeMann from the side and hugged him as tight as I could.

Eyes really are windows to the soul. Sandra's were swollen, red, watery, and bouncing all over the place. Her spirit was hurt and confused. Hurt from receiving and watching the beatings. Confused about how she felt about it all. Javier's eyes were remorseful, but had nothing to do with how he had treated Sandra. He never even glanced at her. His focus was on DeMann. He was sorry for not being able to stop DeMann from kicking his ass.

When DeMann turned to me, his eyes broke my heart. I knew my leaving would cause him pain, but seeing it in person was even more than I had imagined. He was openly sobbing, as if he was the one who had just received the beat down. I squeezed him and rubbed his back. He slowly hugged me back.

"Girl, I love you so much. I miss you."

"I missed you, too." I tried to emphasize the past tense on missed, but my eyes were dry.

Javier had made it up to his feet and was slowly moving around the living room. He hobbled in all the non-splendor of his puny little self, kept his eyes on DeMann, and his bloody mouth shut. The last thing he wanted to do was trigger DeMann's rage again. Sandra rushed to Javier to help him and console him. She had been beaten, too. She bled from the nose and mouth and was limping like her knee was injured. Javier was nowhere near as concerned about her injuries as she was for his.

"Bitch, get the fuck off me!" He carefully shrugged away from Sandra while glancing over to see DeMann's reaction.

DeMann stopped crying and looked over at him.

"Come on, baby, let's leave." I knew I had to get DeMann out of there before he really did kill Javier. "Sandra, I'm gonna walk him downstairs."

We could see the concern on each other's faces. She was worried about me being with DeMann. I was worried about her injuries. Fuck Javier.

"Then, I'm coming right back upstairs. Okay?" I shifted my attention to Javier as I made that statement.

There was no concern in my eyes for him. *You got what the fuck you deserved.* The lack of sympathy in my stare made that statement with no apologies. The blank look he returned to me was a far cry from the mean muggings he usually gave my remarks. *He's learned his lesson,* I thought to myself. *Or he's trying damn hard to make sure DeMann believes he has.* Sincere or not, I knew he would think twice before he put his hands on my girl again. That's all that mattered to me.

Me and DeMann grabbed my stuff, left out of the apartment, and began walking downstairs. We spoke no words. I knew we needed to talk. There always has to be some sort of closure. I sensed his remorse. He didn't even have to apologize. It wouldn't change my feelings anyways. Mentally, I was already preparing my responses to all the things I knew he would say. Unfortunately, I couldn't give him or that topic all of my focus. My top priority was Sandra. I told him to pull his truck around as I went back upstairs to make sure everything was settled.

"Bitch, I pay for this shit. Get your shit, and get out of my crib!"

"Javier—" He cut Sandra off before she could finish her sentence.

"Javier my ass! Just get your shit, and get the fuck out my spot!" He was yelling as if his rage was starting to take over again.

"I got DeMann downstairs pulling his truck up. Do you need me to get him to help you carry some of your stuff?" I said walking in looking at Sandra. I was really eliciting a response from Javier.

"Yeah, she's gonna need some help, 'cause she has to get the hell up outta here."

"What I was going to say before you so rudely interrupted me...." Sandra stood up straight, slowed her statements, and enunciated her words. "Javier, I never asked for these things. Most of the time you were sucking up for something trifling you had done. I don't want anything you have ever bought me. You can keep all of it and give it to the next dumb female that's stupid enough to get involved with you. I'm better off without those things, and I'm better off without you".

"Whatever! I bought you everything you wanted and then some."

"That may be true, but it doesn't mean anything if you're not willing to give me the things I really need, as well."

Javier stood there dumb-faced as he listened to Sandra tell him that she didn't want anything to do with him. He saw the seriousness in her eyes and heard the conviction in her words. When Javier and DeMann were fighting his face was bloody and his body was beaten, but his eyes never watered. Now, they poured.

Sandra continued her dissertation for several more minutes. Then, the words stopped. She had said enough. She had seen enough. It was time for action. The only rightful encore to words of conviction is action with purpose. She saw Javier for the oppressor he was. She saw the material glitz and glamour for the shackles they were. The CBA was now a free woman. After taking off her jewelry, she grabbed a few items out of her closet and dresser. Next, she grabbed a box of personal photos from the bottom drawer of her nightstand and asked me to hold them. Then she turned and started walking towards Javier.

"All of the shit you thought I was all. . ." She flung her arms in the air. ". . .in love with is yours. It's all worthless to me now. It only mattered when you mattered, and now you don't. You can't use it to hang over my head like I owe you something. I don't owe you shit! I don't want you to call me, buy me shit, or try to look me up. I'm gone, and trust me when I tell you that I'm never gonna look back. Your sorry ass ain't even worth my time." Then she took her finger out his face, turned towards the door, and began her final strut.

As she walked away from Javier, she didn't twist, switch, or tease him, and she never once looked at me. She kept her eyes and head straight forward with a stone face. I saw the painful metamorphosis of remorse to misery, beginning in Javier's eyes and spirit. His well-being was of no concern to me, though. I quickly rolled my eyes at him and followed Sandra out the door.

Once we were in the hallway, Sandra kept the same steady pace that she had walking out the door.

"Are you okay, girl?"

She didn't even turn around. She just nodded her head and kept walking.

As we exited the elevator, I looked up at Sandra. Her stone face had been melted by a constant stream of tears. I finally understood. She stayed with Javier because she really loved him. She believed he would change because she wanted him to love her the same way. She knew she had to go, but that didn't change the fact that she really did love him.

Life's lessons are never selfish. They share their wisdom with anyone who pays attention to them, whether personal lessons or not. Javier and DeMann had a lot of things in common. They were both trying to hold on to a woman they loved or thought they loved. Javier used Sandra's fear to make her feel like she owed him loyalty. DeMann manipulated my compassion to make me feel like I couldn't do anything on my own.

Whatever the method, there's nothing mutually respectful or loving about a man trying to control a woman.

After we loaded her things in the back of DeMann's truck and began pulling away, she turned and stared at her old building for half the distance up the block. I believe she hoped Javier would run after her, but he didn't. She turned around, wiped her tears away, then smiled as a new well of tears quickly formed.

I quickly turned and faced forward. I thought about how no matter how hard Sandra tried, things didn't work out. At a certain point, a woman has to come to the realization that things aren't going to work out ever. I thought that running away from Nashville was good enough, but I had to find a way to let DeMann know there would never again be an *us*.

"DeMann, I have a friend that will let me and Machaia stay for a few days. Jump on the expressway a few blocks up on the right."

"Sandra, just chill. You've been through enough changes already tonight. I'm going to take y'all to a spot where you don't have to worry about anything tonight. Just relax. I got you." He looked over at me and smiled.

I could tell he was up to something. He was trying to impress me. Had the situation been different I would have stopped him right there, told him how I felt, and sent him back to Nashville. But he was the knight in shining armor. I had no clue of where we were headed, but he was obviously excited about it. Sandra seemed to be okay, so I didn't argue with him.

"Boy, look at you acting like you know where the hell you're going. Where are you taking us?" Sandra's curiosity echoed mine.

"Girl, I told you to just chill! I got you. Let me put on something that will help y'all relax," he replied, while confidently straightening himself in his seat as he kept driving.

DeMann put on a CD that was a mix of jazz versions of popular rap songs. Passionate saxophones screamed over strong beats, while the city lights danced to the rhythm. I temporarily disconnected with what was going on around me. Sandra and Javier's fight and DeMann's hidden agenda were all afterthoughts. As we sped down the highway, I sat quietly and enjoyed the forward progression of my life.

He took the Kennedy Expressway south all the way to Congress Parkway. Then he followed the parkway east to Michigan Avenue. He never asked Sandra for any directions. He never second guessed which way to turn. To my knowledge, this was his first time in Chicago. *How does he know the city so well? How long has he been here?* The questions began rushing at me faster than the city lights from the highway. DeMann made small talk. His anxiousness always made him run his mouth. As we rode up Michigan Avenue, he pointed out some things to me as if he were some sort of tour guide. He wasn't trying to make me believe he knew all about Chicago. He wanted me to see how he could appreciate the little things. He was apologizing. He said he never really paid attention to "how beautiful buildings and shit could be." I could tell he had played this scenario in his mind before. His words were chosen. He tried to articulate his words, but he kept tripping over his southern drawl.

"This is it!" he announced.

We were facing the opposite side of the street that the hotel was on.

I followed his eyes to a statue at the beginning of the walkway to Grant Park. It was an ancient Greek or Roman warrior on his horse. His sword and elbow were pointing towards a distant star that he was about to charge. I could tell DeMann felt some sort of symmetry between that statue and him coming to Chicago. In his mind, he was that warrior. Strong, noble, and determined. He had come to rectify all that ailed the world. However, he didn't come to Chicago to notice little things or to appreciate architecture. Everything in him was focused on the very thing he took for granted...me.

This nigga ain't Greek. He ain't Roman. This nigga ain't Athenian, Spartan, Egyptian, or none of that shit. He's a dope boy from Nashville, Tennessee. That's his identity. He cannot exist outside of the small patch of universe that his street fame encompasses. Never could. Never will.

"I'm scared of you, brotherman. You got a room at the Congress Hotel. Everybody ain't able." Sandra was impressed.

"Not a room. A lakeside suite!" DeMann's eyes scanned mine for a reaction similar to Sandra's.

My face was stone. His eyes recognized the challenge and quickly danced back over to Sandra's, hoping to build momentum for a later attack.

DeMann's attempts to point things out continually poked and prodded at me, while we walked into the hotel, through the lobby, and up to his room.

"Oh my God! This is so nice!"

Sandra could hardly contain herself. She walked around touching things like she was in a museum or something. I was not all that impressed. Antique-looking furniture and accents graced the room. It looked expensive but wasn't really my cup of tea. My eyes and facial expression said so. DeMann eyes were disappointed as he turned to open the curtains.

"Oh my God!" I had heard Sandra say it, and the same statement flew out of my mouth equally as reactive and equally as excited as hers.

The view was breathtaking. Our suite overlooked an illuminated Grant Park, Buckingham Fountain, and Lake Michigan. The lights from the expressway had an epicenter. To me, it represented the very best of what my opportunities and possibilities had to offer.

I don't know how long those lights kept me captive. When I regained my focus, DeMann was the first thing that stood out. He was looking in my direction, but he was about ten or twelve blocks down memory lane. Once he realized I was looking at him, he quickly returned to the present. His hungry eyes begged for me to join him in his travels.

"Dat's some beautiful shit, ain'na?" His drawl was reaching nauseous levels.

I figured it out. The drawl wasn't what seemed weird or nauseating to me. Hell, mine was still present, as well. What made his seem out of place were the things he was talking about, or trying to talk about rather.

"The water and lights and shit is pretty as hell. And I think dat statue is da bomb. You can tell he 'bout to handle his business. Dat's me, ain'na?"

He wasn't close to being that soldier on that horse. Grant Park represented the peaceful place my heart wanted to be. That soldier, despite his origins, complemented my peaceful epicenter perfectly. DeMann, despite our history or his intentions to change, did not and he never would.

DeMann stood there smiling. It was far more humble than the confident smirks he used to give me after he had gotten his way. He was waiting on me to return his smile. A return smile from me would symbolize my willingness to accept him back in my life. In his mind, he and I were well on our way back to being us. All he needed now was the confirmation of my smile. We stared at each other and shared an awkward moment of nothing.

"Girl, I'm so sleepy." Sandra was standing by the couch in the living room area yawning and stretching her arms. "Does this thing let out to a bed?"

Sandra had perfect timing. She gave us an easy out of our stares.

"Yeah, it does. I want y'all to stay in the room. I'll crash out here." DeMann's voice was slightly deflated.

Sandra looked over at me trying to figure out whether or not she was in our way. When I began moving towards the bedroom, she caught on and began following me.

"Thank you, DeMann." Sandra's voice was both hurt and sincere. She'd been through a lot.

"Thank you so much for helping us." I spoke as flat as I could because I didn't want to send mixed messages.

"Chaia, before you go to sleep, come talk with me for a little bit." Humbleness, sincerity, and concern were all present in his voice and face.

"I'd like that." Then, I granted him a warm smile.

I followed Sandra in the room and shut the door, while his smile stayed at full mass until it was out of my sight. I felt it lingering even after the door was shut.

"Looks like he's made some serious changes." DeMann's actions and words had begun to sway Sandra's opinion of him. "Do you think you could ever give him a second chance?" Sandra's hope for DeMann meant hope for Javier.

"No."

The response was immediate. It was a natural, honest representation of what I had already concluded.

That statement hit us both very hard. We remained silent with our thoughts, while each of us gathered our nightclothes out of our bags and got ready for bed.

I began pondering what I was going to tell DeMann.

DeMann wanted two children: a boy named DeMann Jr. and a girl named Mercedes. He wanted to live outside Nashville in a house that was at least 4,500 square feet, with a gym and a home theater room. He wanted me to stay at home and take care of the kids while he worked. He planned on saving enough money to start a legitimate business and leave the drug dealing behind. However, his spending habits suggested that might be more of a challenge than he admitted to. Until three weeks ago, his dreams were my dreams, and his plans were my plans. Neither his dreams nor plans had any regard for the requirements of my heart. I hadn't fully identified what my heart was longing for, but I was certain it wasn't in Nashville, and it certainly wasn't with DeMann.

*****

"Those are my boxers!" DeMann's voice was surprised and excited.

They were my favorite around-the-house shorts. I put them on simply because they made me feel comfortable. To DeMann, they were the link he was hoping for. He thought I was signaling my willingness to go back. I wished I had put on something different.

"Yep," I replied, laughing my response, hoping to imply the pure coincidence of my choice of attire.

He cut straight to the chase. "You miss me?"

"I'll always miss you."

"Always?"

His eyes widened as my implications started to hit home. His whole demeanor changed. He was sad. He slumped back on the sofa and lowered his tone.

"What do you mean *always*?"

"I mean, you'll always have a special place in my heart." I was scared, but not saying it was out of the question.

"Always means you don't see yourself ever being with me again." The hurt in his voice presented that statement more as a sad realization than a question.

Word games are such a lonely playground. They lead you around and around with little ever being concluded or resolved. They thrive on misunderstandings and create gray areas for the tough truth to hide in. DeMann and I always took the easy way out when it came to discussing our feelings. Our relationship never had the strength to face the truth. I couldn't afford that approach any longer. It was hard, but I answered the question lingering between the lines of our word game.

"DeMann, I don't want us to be together." I paused long enough for both of us to swallow the statement. "I love you as a friend, but I know I won't be happy as your lady." I knew I was speaking from my heart. It felt so good, or at least to me, it did.

"It seems like you've thought a lot about that." He didn't even try to hide the cracking in his voice.

DeMann dealt with plenty of hardship, but he usually maintained a tough exterior. On occasion, though, his sentiments would break the surface. When his childhood friend Marc was shot to death, they broke through. When his father was sentenced to life in prison for murdering a man over money, they broke through. Time after time, when drugs seized control of his mother's mind and soul, they broke free. It was hard for me to look at him because I was the cause of his sorrow. I didn't feel guilty for being honest, but seeing his tears and emotions overwhelm him was hard. He was one of my best friends.

"DeMann, I have to try and find my happiness. But, I want you to know I will always love you." I reached out, pulled him into me, hugged him, and wiped away his tears with my lips.

"Chaia, you sure 'bout dis?" He wiped away his tears and stared at me. His eyes quickly refilled after seeing enough painful resolve in my eyes to answer his question. "It hurts so much to hear you say dat, but..." He paused, tried to regain control of his cracking voice, and wiped away the current dispatch of tears. "...I know you're telling me the truth."

We sat on the sofa in each other's arms. Our words had been honest and direct. There were no misunderstandings or gray areas. Nothing else needed to be said. We enjoyed the genuineness of our embrace for a few more minutes. As he cried, my heart hurt, but I resolved to let him struggle through the pain.

"You better go get some rest. We can finish talking tomorrow." That translated to him needing some space to get himself together.

Honestly, I needed space as well. I didn't know how much more of his pain I could witness without doing *whatever* I could to end it.

We stood up, he walked me to the bedroom door, put his hands on my belly, and said, "Believe it or not, I'm glad you didn't do it."

A genuine smile broke through his tears. I knew he was telling the truth.

"Thank you. That means more to me right now than you know." I returned his smile, then I kissed his cheek. "Goodnight, DeMann."

"Goodnight, Machaia."

Our formality solidified the words we spoke. I went into the bedroom and shut the door on that chapter of my life. With Sandra already asleep, I crawled in the bed, spooned behind her, and hugged her as I began drifting to sleep.

The next morning, I awoke to find that the roles had been reversed. Sandra had gotten up before me, crawled in behind me, and hugged me while I slept. She was just as concerned for me as I was for her. Her strength was returning to her spirit and I knew she would be okay. I was concerned about how DeMann was doing. So, I got up to go check on him.

When I walked out to the living room, my concerns escalated. DeMann was standing in the window starring out at Lake Michigan. The sofa was not let out to a bed. He'd been up all night thinking, pondering, wondering, and crying. I saw it in his eyes when he turned to face me.

I walked over, hugged him, and placed my head on his chest just like I used to. I wasn't concerned about mixed messages or his assumptions. I just wanted him to know that part of me felt just as close to him as I always had.

"Did you get some sleep?"

"A little bit." His voice was subdued and solemn.

Curiosity and concern were forming knots in my throat to the point that it was hard for me to breathe.

"What are you thinking about?"

"You and the baby," he responded without hesitation.

Despite his sorrow, he was up all night thinking about me and the baby. I had underestimated him. The selfish person I left back in Nashville was not present. DeMann had grown. The desires of his heart finally involved more than what was best for him.

We continued hugging. "I want my baby to have a good life. I want you to be happy, even if it's not wit' me." The words choked him up. "My life changed when you left Nashville, Chaia. Things that were important to me before don't seem to matter that much no more."

I stood there with my head on his chest. His heart was not used to being this exposed. I listened to his heart scream all the words I wanted to hear days, months, and years ago.

"Chaia, I'm going back today, but before I go, I want you to take a ride with me somewhere." He gripped my shoulders and pushed me back enough to look me in my eyes. His eyes were just as I envisioned, pain-filled and drowning with tears.

"Okay. Where do you want to go?"

"Just go put on something and come on." He didn't even seem disappointed that I wasn't crying. Hopefully, he saw the genuine concern in my eyes.

I rushed into the bedroom and began dressing.

We went downstairs and waited while the valet pulled DeMann's truck around. He helped me into the passenger's side, then calmly walked around and got behind the wheel. Again, he knew exactly where he was going. This time, he didn't seem anxious though. He navigated through Chicago's traffic without rushing. We rode in silence with the same jazz CD playing, while he occasionally gave me a warm smile and squeezed my hand.

I didn't have a clue where he was headed until he got off the expressway at the Midway Airport exit.

"DeMann, what are you doing?"

He didn't respond. He just kept his face forward. When I heard him sniffle, I leaned over and looked at him. Tears were falling from his eyes. He pulled up to the curb, put the truck in park, and turned to me.

"I want you to keep the truck." He finally wiped away his tears.

"But, DeMann, this is your truck!" I gasped.

"Actually, it's yours. It's always been yours. I put it in your name when I first bought it, just in case something happened to me."

"This is too much. I can't keep this truck." I was overwhelmed by his gesture. I knew how much he loved his Range Rover.

"You can and you will. Do it for the baby. Besides, I don't want you up here jumping in and out of some nigga's car." He laughed, but the tears and his cracking voice told me that he was serious.

Once he walked to the back of the truck and grabbed his bag, I got out and stood next to him on the curb. He was openly sobbing. It was hurting him very deeply, and killing me. *He's so strong.* He found the inner strength to let go of what he came to recapture--my heart.

"Girl, don't you try to shut me outta my baby's life. You hear me!" His eyes leaped from behind the wall of tears and stiffened. They demanded I take his words seriously.

"I won't." I began openly sobbing and felt like I was losing my best friend.

I was coming to the painful realization that moving on with my life meant moving away from some things I held dear. I didn't know exactly what type of relationship he and I would develop, but it would never be what it was. In certain ways, that thought inspired me. In some ways, that thought broke my heart the same way it broke his. I was not saying goodbye to a shallow man who didn't know how to love me the way I deserved to be loved. That day, I was saying goodbye to my lifelong friend, champion, and protector who I already missed dearly.

"Chaia, I wan'cha to promise me dat you gon' keep me in yo' heart somewhea. I don't care if it's in'd back or what. I just wanna know beyond the shadow ov'a doubt dat I'm in dat motherfucker somewhea." Those words had to struggle to break free. His southern drawl sounded so good.

I didn't speak. Instead, I reached out, pulled him into me, and passionately tongue kissed him. I know I was sending a mixed message. I was confused myself. I realized how much both the friend and the lover meant to me. If this really was goodbye, I wanted the most intimate salute possible. I knew if this had been anyplace other than curbside at an airport, it would have been much more intimate.

"I'll *always* love you, Chaia."

I immediately thought about how he had dissected that same word with me. *Always means you don't see yourself ever being with me again.* He was letting go. My heart needed and wanted him to do just that. I never realized my heart would break again when he finally did.

"I'll always love you, DeMann."

He turned and walked into the terminal, as I got in the truck and drove off. I stopped just outside the airport grounds and parked in a lot facing the airport. I watched at least seventeen planes take off, hoping he'd recognize his truck from the plane. I wanted him to physically see me holding on to the thought of him. I wanted him to know beyond the shadow of a doubt that he would always own a special part of my heart.

I sat in the parking lot crying intense and passionate tears. I was glad he was gone but heartbroken that he left. Both feelings equally intensified my downpour. I just let it rain out. Not wiping away any of the effects, I let the debris rot where it lay. My victorious survival cranked the truck up, my sorrows pulled my eyes towards his plane once more. Then my survival turned me around and began leading me on the long, hard journey back to my epicenter.

CHAPTER 9
EVAN MILES

"I'm Evan Miles. I'm from Orlando, Florida. I attended Florida A&M University."

I was number four of six residents that had to stand and introduce themselves. It was the first official meeting of the program, and we were having a dinner in one of the hospital's annexes, which had been converted into a conference center. The dinner plates were served during introductions, but no one ate. Everyone was too busy sizing each other up. Faculty members were eyeballing the students, establishing their role of dominance. The residents were staring down the preceptors trying to demand some semblance of respect. Family members and loved ones were just trying to figure out who was who. Every pair of eyes in the building took turns greeting each other, except two pairs--mine and hers.

After the dinner and Dr. Carson's speech, everyone mingled. Celeste stayed by Dr. Carson's side. She knew at some point in the evening I would have to speak to him. She was much more beautiful than I remembered. She had cut her shoulder-length hair to a short, spiky-looking style that suited her perfectly. She looked powerful, and her presence demanded respect. I just couldn't afford to pay her any. Other than a few head nods during dinner and waves from across the room afterwards, I stayed clear of Dr. Carson. I hoped he didn't take my avoiding him the wrong way.

"You must be Evan Miles. I'm Dr. Copeland." He came across even cockier in person.

"How are you, sir? I'm Evan Miles." He was waiting for me to say Dr., but I didn't want to give him the opportunity to pull rank the way Dr. Carson had done. He seemed surprised and disappointed.

"Dr. Carson has told me some good things about you. He's known to be a little presumptuous when it comes to handing out accolades. So, I'll hold out for now. You're going to have to earn them from me."

He offered me a bullshit laugh and a bullshit handshake. I hate phony people and certainly did not care for him. After entertaining his cocky sarcasm for several minutes, I cut him off. I could tell he didn't like that, but I didn't feel the need to impress him. My success would not come from kissing butt.

"Evan! Evan! EVAN!"

I heard him the first time. I knew it was Dr. Carson. I knew he was headed towards me. I knew who was right beside him waiting for the opportunity to look me in my eyes. I turned around to confirm my suspicions. Correct.

The fact that Dr. Carson was flagging and chasing me down was not surprising, at least not to he and I. However, two faces were absolutely shocked. One was Dr. Copeland. I felt him watching me ever since I cut him off. I figured he was Dr. Carson's star student and felt threatened by Dr. Carson's interest in me. He didn't want me to outshine him. The other face was right in front of me, close enough for me to examine thoroughly.

"Son, why are you leaving so soon?"

Her hungry eyes asked me that same question, but for an entirely different reason.

"I haven't been feeling so hot the whole evening, Dr. Carson. I decided to take it in a little early." I lowered my voice to appear under the weather.

I offered that excuse hoping he would take it as reason enough for avoiding him. She didn't, though. My nervous peaks gave me away. Playing the sick card with a world-renowned doctor might not have been so smart. He must have done a quick eyeball examination and decided I'd live. He put his arms around my shoulder, casually turned me around, and headed back inside.

"Bear with me for a few minutes. I've got some people you need to meet."

She stood there quietly waiting for her opportunity to pounce on me with an assortment of non-verbals.

"By the way, I'd like you to meet my wife, Celeste. Honey, this is Dr. Evan Miles. He's my star resident this cycle."

She looked at me with the most mismatched look I've ever seen. Her smile was very casual, but her eyes were overly intense. They were resolute. She had her mind set on something happening. She used both her hands to embrace mine and kissed me on the cheek, dangerously close to the edge of my lips. Then, she backed away.

"Hello, Dr. Miles. It's nice to meet you. From what I hear, you have a very bright future. I'm very happy for you." She kept a slight smile, and her hard stares were still trying to implement her will.

"Well, I know I have my work cut out for me. I'll do my best to stay focused and not let Chicago distract me." I gave her my version of a mismatched face and met her hard stares with my own. She knew what I was implying. "Dr. Carson, what a lovely wife you have. I can see why you were so anxious for her to move to Chicago." I turned my shoulders and shifted my attention to him. I sent that nonverbal message with so much weight that I had to tighten my jaw.

He patted me on my back. "Son, there are lot of things you don't know about me." He started chuckling. "Hell, there are a lot of things I don't know about myself. I'm a work in progress. Right, baby?" He turned to her.

The smile was gone. Her hard eyes were looking forward. "We all are works in progress. Sooner or later, we will all be what we will be." Then she paused for a second, gave a light chuckle, and just like that she was back in diva mode.

As Dr. Carson led me around the room, she followed and watched in silence. Words were not necessary. Her presence was statement enough. She made me totally forget everything I had promised myself I would remember. She wore a black dress similar to the one she had on the night we met, except it hugged her curves much closer. I couldn't help reminiscing about our evening together. Before I knew what happened, I was carefree and enjoying her presence.

I desperately tried to focus. I engaged in idle conversation just to avoid looking at her. Every time my mind would lose control of my eyes, her eyes were waiting to join me in my trips down memory lane. My mind was so flooded with thoughts of how good she made me feel that even the drill sergeant couldn't help me. He was busy gasping for air his damn self. She must have sensed what I was thinking because she hit me with a hurricane force smile. I burst out laughing. She did, as well. The white man Dr. Carson had just introduced me to started laughing, too. He must have said something semi-funny. I didn't even catch his name, much less what he said.

Get your shit together, soldier! The drill sergeant was frantically fighting the overwhelming current of my desires. He knew what trap I was falling into.

"Dr. Miles, you have quite the cheerleader in Dr. Carson. He has told me some wonderful things about you. I am very excited about your being here, and I'm looking forward to some great things." The gentleman concluded with that statement. Then he simultaneously patted me on the shoulder with one hand and shook my hand with the other before walking away.

"Of all the residents I've introduced to him, the CEO of the hospital hasn't remembered any of them by name except you. That's pretty impressive, Evan."

Dr. Carson's chest was stuck out further than mine. He acted like I had done something spectacular. He was proud of me, and I hadn't done anything yet. I didn't kid myself. The only thing the CEO knew about me was what Dr. Carson told him. The CEO being excited about me was the accomplishment of one person: Dr. John Christopher Carson. He deserved me saying his whole name. More importantly, he deserved my honesty and my best efforts to be worthy of his trust. My guilt rose up and stopped the river of desire that had been running rampant in my mind. I stiffened my eyes to match my will.

"Dr. Carson, I appreciate everything you have done to help me get established here. I just want you to know that I'm going to do my very best not to hurt you." I gasped at my own slip. "I mean, not let you down."

I don't think she knew the extent of the bond that was forming between Dr. Carson and me, but she was bearing witness to it now.

"I know you will, son." He smiled and hugged me across the shoulders.

He had a curious look on his face, as if he was wondering where my mind was. The thought of him finding out about me and Celeste bothered me to the point where I had to leave.

114

"I have to get going. I'm looking forward to getting started on Monday. I guess I'll see you at the hospital."

"You certainly will. I won'cha to be safe getting home, ya hea?" His concern was sincere. I figured out that his southern accent came across when he was speaking from the heart.

"Goodnight, Mrs. Carson." I emphasized the Mrs. and stretched my eyes just enough for her to pick up on my sentiments.

"Goodnight, Dr. Miles," she replied, then leaned in and kissed me directly on the lips.

To outsiders looking in, I'm sure it seemed like an innocent social peck. White folks do that sort of thing all the time. Black folks do it at bougie parties. So, her kiss certainly fit the bill and was nothing to raise any eyebrows over. I knew better, though.

As she backed away from kissing me, she gave me another mismatched look. This time, there was no smile. Her facial expression was blank but her eyes were intensely fixed on mine, passionately interpreting what time and circumstance wouldn't allow her to express with her lips.

I was out the door and halfway to the back of the parking lot where my truck was parked before I even took a breath. I was too scared to even inhale her smell. I couldn't trust myself around her. My will was winning the bout on points, but my desires had knockout potential. I knew the best thing was for me to stay clear of the punches, so I vowed to remain as far away from Celeste as possible. I felt comfortable in my ability to handle that, but knew I'd never be able to control her. That concern didn't have time to circulate through my thought process once. Five seconds after I got to my truck, it escalated from a concern to a full-blown problem.

"The average chick would have been hurt." Celeste had followed me out to my truck. "You didn't say goodbye to me, so I thought I'd come out here and say goodbye to you." She smiled, walked over, hid herself behind my open door, and stood with her body pressed up against mine.

As she stood there in front of me, everything about her made my desires scream *Yes!* I hoped my will had enough strength to resist her. Waiting on that command, I closed my eyes and tuned her out for as long as I could. Nothing. My will had been seduced into submission.

She pinned me against the truck door and began massaging my penis through my pants. I didn't resist. My desires ran rampant, telling me how good she smelled and how wonderful her touch felt. They told me the moisture dripping out of her panties and all over my hand was perfectly okay. She continued massaging and I continued looking away, not resisting. Suddenly, she placed both of her hands on my face and forced me to look at her seductive and confident smile. You could tell she knew she was in total control. Sadly, she was.

She pulled out my penis and started sucking it. She didn't even try to hide. She wasn't concerned about the consequences if we were discovered. She was lost in the moment, and the ecstasy in her eyes told me that she was enjoying herself just as much as I was. All that mattered to her was her pleasure. A nearby car door slammed, and she didn't even flinch. *She really doesn't give a damn.* I pulled back from her mouth and began looking around.

"Celeste, I can't and won't do this! Your husband has done so much to help me. I can't do this to him."

"You make it seem like your dick is in his mouth."

Her tone suggested that she was annoyed at her enjoyment being disrupted. Her games were not sexy to me, and did not turn me on. She was annoying me, as well.

"If that's your husband, then your mouth *is* his mouth. So, technically it is!" The irritability in my voice challenged her.

"You let me fucking worry about that shit. You betta recognize how tied up all this shit is. You ain't gonna be happy unless JC is happy. Your problem is *I* make JC happy, and he ain't gonna be happy until I'm happy. So, it would be smart for you not to do anything to fuck up that delicate balance, baby."

She turned around and lifted her dress up over her bare ass. Slowly and seductively, she spread her legs, leaned forward over my driver's seat, and looked back at me.

"Right now, I'm not happy." She slipped back into her sexy voice. Then, she reached back and used both hands to spread the lips of her vagina open. "At least, not yet I ain't."

I knew what she was implying, and given her lack of concern for getting caught, I believed her threat. Part of me wanted to tell Dr. Carson, but I didn't want him to associate me with that kind of disappointment. Feeling manipulated, anger overcame me. I thrust hard into the place she so brazenly invited me. My intent was to make sure she didn't enjoy a second of it. I rammed her savagely, as hard as my anger could thrust. My grip around her neck and shoulders became dangerously close to being too tight.

"Bitch! Is-yo-ass-hap-py-now!" With each syllable, I pulled backwards on her shoulders and neck.

I kept mashing with hard aggression. She loved every bit of it. She thrust into me just as hard. Her moans grew so loud she had to bite my blazer lying in the passenger's seat. My anger had turned into uncontrolled eroticism. I was fucking the shit out of her and loving it, too. For the first time I witnessed a woman squirt the way a man's does. It vigorously ejected itself while I continued thrusting. Seeing and hearing that made me reach my orgasm. As I backed away and began shooting sperm on the ground, she quickly knelt in front of me and savored all that had not fallen. Our eyes intensely relayed messages of how much.

After she stood up, she leaned on the side of the truck until her legs regained their strength. I nervously zipped up my pants. She laughed, surely at my insecurities.

"Dr. Miles, I must say that your future is even brighter than I expected. Your talents run deep...very deep." She laughed at her own implication. "There's much work for you to do here in Chicago."

"Celeste, we can't let ourselves get caught up in..."

"Shhh!" She placed her index finger over my lips. "Remember, only happy thoughts."

She gave me a funny look, smiled, then walked off. Disappointment quickly filled the huge void left by the fading erotic euphoria.

Sex without love is simply a power struggle. In this particular case, there was not much of a struggle at all. Her will whooped my will's ass. Hands down. The power she felt over me was as much responsible for her orgasm as our intense sex. What troubled me most was why she chose me. She could have gotten damn near any man in America to fall under her spell, most of them willingly. *Why me?* I knew the answer revolved around her relationship with Dr. Carson and what she thought he saw in me. Whatever games she was playing with Dr. Carson, the fact that I was a participant was heartbreaking. Something told me she would use the same facts to break his heart later.

I knew we were lucky not to be caught. Recklessness does not go unpunished for long. That realization came to me with a great deal of conviction. God don't like ugly.

CHAPTER 10
MACHAIA JAMES

"I can't believe he just gave you a damn Range Rover!" Sandra was still shocked three days after DeMann left.

I tried to downplay the gift as I continued driving. I still hadn't gotten over the fact that he was gone for good.

"That ain't all he wanted to give you. I saw the way he was looking at you," she said jokingly. She was doing her best to make me laugh. It hadn't work over the last couple of days in the hotel suite and it wasn't working now.

DeMann paid for the hotel room through the week, and we had one more day left before check out. Sandra and I both needed the time to regroup. DeMann called every day. Our friendship was off to a wonderful start. We shared our dreams, and he still included me in his future. I knew I didn't want that, but part of me still found comfort in his thoughts. Selfishly, I wasn't quite ready to let that go. If I couldn't be with him in the physical form, then running across his mind from time to time seemed like a reasonable compromise.

Sandra had not heard from Javier. She wouldn't admit it, but part of her was really bothered. I was a little concerned, as well. I didn't give a damn about Javier. I just wanted to make sure he wasn't planning some kind of retaliation.

Thoughts of Javier still ran rampant in her heart and mind. I could tell by her solemn reaction every time his name came up.

"I think I'm pregnant."

I couldn't believe my ears. I almost lost control of the truck as I turned towards her. She was looked out of the passenger window, staring into space. Clearly, she was hurting.

"My period is almost three weeks late, and I'm never late."

"Does Javier know?"

"No, he doesn't. I realized I was late the week you called and said you were coming. I was waiting for a good time to talk to him about it, but we kept getting into arguments. Then when the accident happened, everything just exploded. The emergency room doctor told me there were indications that I might be. He wasn't sure, but I said no and asked him not to say anything that day in the hospital."

"If you are, have you decided if you want to go through with it or not?"

"Chaia, I haven't even decided what I'm gonna do with my damn self, much less a damn baby," she snapped.

I was asking questions she wasn't ready to answer. I knew her position all too well.

"I'm pregnant, too. I was supposed to have an abortion the morning I caught DeMann and Rodney at the club." I hoped my revelation would help take her mind off her situation. It seemed to work.

"Oh my God, Chaia! Why didn't you tell me?"

"Probably for the same reasons you didn't tell me you thought you were pregnant. I just didn't know what to think about the whole thing myself. I'm going to have her."

She immediately bounced out of her slump and began really talking.

"Her! How do you know it's a girl?"

I told her the story of the song and how I felt Sarah singing to me. It was powerful reliving the whole thing. Sandra was moved to tears. She knew my history with my mother. She knew how much I cherished the very thought of her. In my mind and spirit, the sacrifice she made for me validated my place in the world. Someone loved me that much, and now, I could give that same love to my child. Motherhood is the most empowering experience a woman will ever go through. Sarah wasn't even born yet, and I was already drawing strength from her.

I don't know which way Sandra was leaning in terms of going through with the pregnancy or not. After listening to me talk about Sarah, I could tell she was reevaluating her position. Her demeanor was not as depressed as it was before. She was still quietly staring into space, but she seemed to be enjoying whatever was occupying her mind. She was smiling, and occasionally, she chuckled lightly. I let her enjoy those thoughts without any interference.

"Are you gonna stay in the truck? I just have to run in for a few items. It shouldn't take too long."

I spoke fast and got out of the truck while still talking. Not wanting anything to steal her joy, I wanted her to stay behind. There's no such thing as running in and out of Wal-Mart, and I knew I would be at least thirty to forty-five minutes. She needed that time to start mapping out what was going to make her happy. From the look of her face, she'd already found a small piece of it. Her joy lifted my spirits.

As I walked around the store, I reminisced on the beautiful view out of our room. I looked forward to having that kind of peace in my life permanently. I knew a view like that was not likely, but to have a small piece of universe to call my own would be just as rewarding. We had one day of regrouping left on our lease at the Congress Hotel, and then it would be time for us to get on with the business of life. I hoped Sandra's moment of joy would spark those kinds of thoughts for her, as well.

After grabbing the few items I needed and heading out the store's exit, I stopped and grabbed an Apartment Guide, knowing we would need it soon.

"Girl, I got us an apart—" I stopped mid-sentence when I realized she was talking on her cell phone.

"I'm looking forward to it, too. I'll call you back a little later, okay? Bye."

"Who or what got you cheesing like that?" I dressed my question up in excitement, not wanting my concern ruining her high.

"That was Lesley. He invited us to stay with him for as long as we needed. I told him we were gonna chill out in the room one more day before we came." Her smile grew even wider.

What is she thinking? Lesley was cool and all, but the last thing we needed to do was start shacking up with another nigga.

"Sandra, I have some money. We can get an apartment with no

problem." My tone was ten percent angry, thirty percent disheartened, and sixty percent concerned.

"I'm not going back to Javier. I thought you would want me to do this!"

"Sandra, it's not about what I want, what Javier wants, or what Lesley wants. You have to decide what the hell you want!"

"Right now, this is what I want. Lesley has a huge house. We'll each have our own room. You already know how cool Lesley is. It's gonna be fine. Just trust me, girl."

We both knew she was lying. It's definitely not what she really wanted. She quickly broke eye contact and started rummaging through the bags I brought back. She wasn't interested in the contents; she just couldn't stand the heat from my unsympathetic stares.

All afternoon and evening, I contemplated looking for my own place. I was disappointed in her decision, and she knew it. Although there was a gap growing between us, it hadn't developed nearly enough for me to walk away from her. We were a team. I decided to hang on with her a little while longer.

*****

The next morning, we woke and began packing our stuff to check out. While we gathered our things, she made several comments about how less stressful things would be at Lesley's place. She saw this as an opportunity to get to know Lesley better without Javier's interference. Her actions sung an entirely different song, though. Regardless of what words came out of her mouth, her actions told me that she was reluctant about what she was doing.

"You want me to save this Apartment Guide or throw it away?" I hoped she understood what I was really asking her.

"Apartment Guide? Girl, wait 'til you see Javier's—" Her real thoughts intruded on her words. "I mean Lesley's house. An apartment is gonna be the last thing on your mind."

Sadly, she didn't have a clue what I was implying. I hoped she was only playing dumb to avoid facing the hard truth.

We checked out and drove up north to Lesley's house in North Brook.

His home was absolutely amazing. You couldn't see it from the road. Tall hedges lined the iron-gate. A cobblestone driveway curved through a large manicured lawn. It was a two-story home that sprawled across what had to be five acres of land. It was contemporary style, with bricks that were various shades of tan and brown. The house was a perfect representation of the man—classy, elegant, and tremendously successful.

"Damn, man, you living like this?" My mouth hung open as I walked inside of his house.

The inside was even more breathtaking than the outside. Marble, hardwood floors, granite countertops, beautiful furniture, and tasteful artwork reinforced every statement the exterior made.

"It's alright. I like it." He was trying to be humble. It didn't last long. He burst out laughing. Understandably so, he knew his house was tight. "Let me show y'all to your rooms."

He led us down a hall between the kitchen and the side of the family room. He opened the first door on the right.

"Machaia, this is your room." Sandra and I walked in. He stood in the doorway, while we looked around.

"See, girl! And you was talking about a damn apartment." The room was very nice, but the fact that she couldn't see the value of having your own place bothered me.

I walked into the private bathroom instead of looking at Sandra. I couldn't respond the way I wanted to, and I didn't want to seem ungrateful. "Thank you so much, Lesley, for letting us stay."

"No problem. I'm happy to have you. Sandra, let me show you your room."

After I placed my stuff down, we all walked up the hall to the last room on the left. The room was tastefully decorated with a private bathroom, as well. It had a beautiful set of French doors that led out to the lanai and pool area.

"Oh my God. This is so nice. Thank you so much, Lesley." She sat her things down and gave him a hug.

We followed him out the French doors to the pool area.

"That's my room through those doors over there." I found it pretty peculiar that he would mention that before he pointed out anything about his lanai and pool.

We toured the rest of the house, and it was a dream home in every sense of the word. The backyard was reminiscent of a royal courtyard, complete with fountains, ponds, sculpted trees, hammocks, and a couple of sitting areas.

We got comfortable and spent the rest of our Sunday afternoon just hanging out at the house. Good company can make up for a bad situation. We laughed, ate, played a card game, and watched *Boomerang and The Wood* in his theater room as he and Sandra took turns leaning and laying on each other like lovebirds.

"Look at y'all! All hugged up and lovey dovey."

Lesley smiled wide as hell. He was excited by that thought. Sandra was behind him with a much less excited look. She knew I was being sarcastic.

"I would stay and watch another movie with y'all, but I'm full as hell from all that food I ate. That 'itis' is starting to kick in." I really wasn't that tired, but I wanted to give them a chance to talk alone.

"Wait a minute, girl. I'm tired, too." Sandra waited for Lesley to rise up off of her chest.

Lesley's face showed disappointment. I don't know what he was expecting to happen, but I could tell it didn't involve Sandra going to sleep. Her mind was somewhere else, and wherever it was, Lesley wasn't there. She didn't even look at him when he asked her if she needed anything else. She stood up and stretched out her arms to hug him.

"No, I'm good. Thank you so much…Lesley, for helping us out."

As he was leaning over to hug her, I saw her face as she made that statement. I'm certain I saw her almost say Javier's name before she caught herself and finished her sentence.

"You okay, girl?" I hugged her as we walked down the hallway.

"Yeah, I'm good. I'm just tired as hell."

I didn't care if she lied to me just as long as she told herself the truth.

We walked down the hall together and moved forward into our individual worlds of solitude to gather our thoughts.

I went in my room, showered, and laid in the bed for at least an hour and a half thinking about my relationship with DeMann. It was the first day DeMann and I hadn't talked since he left. I didn't want to admit it to myself, but I was bothered by what he might be doing. How long would it be before he put another woman in my shoes? Questions stripped away at my security until I felt naked and alone without my man.

He's not your man anymore. You've got to save that place in your heart for someone else. Detaching myself from DeMann emotionally was proving to be a lot more difficult than leaving him physically. Some bonds just can't be broken overnight.

I got up, slipped into my robe and went to get a drink from the kitchen. I looked through the living room onto the lanai, and saw the light on in Sandra's room. The curtains blew from the open French doors. I thought maybe she was sitting out on the lanai enjoying the cool night air, so I walked over to the open door. Just as I got to the doorway, I heard her say Lesley's name. She spoke in a passionate tone and between heavy breathing. I peeked through the curtains and saw Lesley on his knees beside the bed, passionately performing oral sex.

He spread her legs open, caressed her thighs, sucked, licked, and kissed all over from her navel to her toes. His moans were just as passionate as hers. I could tell he was paying extra attention to all details. Surely, he had been dreaming of this day for a long time, and finally it had arrived.

I was shocked. *Why would she be fucking Lesley when I know she's not feeling him like that?* That question preceded the concern and troubled me deeply.

"Turn the lights off," Sandra instructed Lesley as he stood up and began taking off his pajama pants.

Her voice was calm and suppressed. One thing I knew for sure, Sandra loved to keep the lights on. For her to ask him to turn the lights off was basically her way of admitting to herself that she didn't expect to receive any enjoyment out of the experience. Whatever they were, she was going through with it for the wrong reasons.

As I walked away, I tuned out the sounds of the make-believe love she was selling him. I tuned out the sounds of him naively buying it.

Between her father's drinking and gambling demons and her mother's vanity as a result of being known throughout Nashville for her beauty, Sandra never felt loved at home. Of all the stories she told me about her home life, I can only remember a few being pleasant memories. Love, comfort, acceptance, happiness, and most notably security were all luxuries that were not afforded to her. I figured out a long time ago that Sandra used her joking and crazy nature to cover up her hurt and pain. But, of all her attributes, she never found a way to make herself feel secure.

The way a person deals with relationships is as much a learned behavior as speaking. Sandra's mother never demonstrated to Sandra how to love a man and demand love in return. She definitely never exemplified security. As beautiful as her mother was, she was never satisfied with her looks. *How do I look? Is my make-up okay? Sandra, you look a hot mess. You need to fix yourself up more. Girl, you ain't ever gonna get a man looking like that!* I've personally heard those questions and statements come out of Sandra's mother's mouth enough to make me question myself sometimes. I can only imagine how much more demeaning and convicting those questions and criticisms were behind closed doors.

To the same degree that her genes passed down to Sandra her physical attributes and beauty, Sandra's mother's questions and criticisms passed down her insecurities and self-doubt. The only way Sandra was ever taught to deal with those voids was through a man's validation. Somewhere deep inside of her very essence, Sandra accepted her mother's example as protocol. She didn't trust herself. She found false security with Javier, and now, she had begun the process all over again with Lesley.

I knew what lie ahead for Sandra. As long as she looked outside of herself for security, she was headed down a path of self-destruction. No matter how great a guy Lesley may have been, her heart was not with him. Mine wouldn't allow me to be comfortable with the lie they were starting to live.

I went back to my room and fell asleep thinking about what I could do to get her off that path. *What if she never wakes the hell up?* My soul began painfully contemplating how long it could allow me to travel down that path with her before I sacrificed too much.

CHAPTER 11
EVAN MILES

"Are you shittin' me? A woman that bad shouldn't have to force anybody to sex her." Greg stood in his bedroom doorway, ridiculing me, while I stood at the front doorway watching Celeste walk to her car.

Fittingly, her black Dodge Durango was a far cry from the silver Bentley. She was creeping. The less attention she drew the better. She seemed far more comfortable than I felt.

By nature, guilt is a delayed reaction. It never hits you until after the damage is done. I was two months into my residency and three visits into an affair with the last woman on earth I should have been involved with. Initially, I held true to my pact to avoid her. I didn't answer her calls. I didn't attend two drug company sponsored dinners because I knew she'd probably come with Dr. Carson. I did everything I could until two weeks ago, out of the blue, she showed up at my front door. The guilt that scarred my soul only existed as a mere afterthought.

"Man, you must be out of your damn mind. All she wants to do is fuck with no strings attached. What's the damn problem?"

"You just don't understand. It really ain't about the sex. She just wants to manipulate and control shit. Plus, I already told you, she's married to the program director at the hospital."

"What a man don't know won't hurt him." His tone suddenly turned much more solemn than the sarcastic one he had while ridiculing me.

I had heard Greg make that statement several times since I'd been in Chicago. Each time it sent him down some solitary, solemn road. Whatever it is that he thinks about in those instances, I can tell he wishes he wasn't forced to confront those thoughts. Curious silence filled the room. I ransacked my mind trying to imagine what his thoughts were and how I could help him get past them. *Maybe guilt isn't so forgetful after all.*

"Bump this! Man, it's Friday night. We need to hang out! I know this tight club that I haven't taken you to yet. It's gonna be some fine-ass hoes up in that joint!"

His gestures and movements tried to exclaim his excitement, but his eyes told the truth.

"Man, is that all you think about?" I asked, trying to bait him into a conversation about his sorrows.

"Nah, fool! The Double G Baby thinks about a whole lot more than just hoes. I'm concerned with the hoes' friends, too." He burst out laughing.

I needed to escape as much as he did. The guilt of my affair and pressures from the program were starting to strangle me. Another world seemed like the perfect place to be, real or not.

We smoked a blunt, took two shots of Hennessey VSOP, and got dressed. By the time we walked out the door, there was no trace of trouble anywhere in either of our lives.

"Dawg, let's go get these bitches!" Sadly, there wasn't even an afterthought to my decree.

"That's what I'm talking about, boy! You 'bout to become the Double E Baby!"

"Please say the BABY!" I burst out laughing before I even finished my statement. "Nah, nigga. It may take two G's for you, but my game is too tight to double up. These hoes might overdose or something. I am The E, Motherfucker!" I stuck my head out the window and yelled at the top of my lungs, as if I was trying to introduce myself to all of Chicago. The burdens that were weighing my heart down were nonexistent. The only real thing I felt was the uplifting embrace of clouds of happiness and excitement. I didn't want to ever *not* feel like this.

Greg drove us to Bottoms Up, a strip club on the south side of town. I could tell he was at least a semi-regular patron of this club. He parked, walked up to the front door, and stood off to the side of the main entrance where a small line of anxious men were waiting to get in. The doorman immediately came over to where we were standing. He then walked us inside the front door, and a brother with an expensive looking suit broke his conversation and walked over to us.

"What's up, man? Ain't seen you in a minute!" The brother gripped Greg's hand and gave him a pound on the back as he spoke.

"I've been grinding, dude. Tryin' to make a dollar outta fifteen cents." Greg used an overly exaggerated street accent, and his smile was wide enough to let everybody watching know that he was lying about anything related to financial struggles.

"It's more like trying to turn two mill into four. You ain't gotta lie to kick it, at least not in *my* club you don't."

They both laughed.

"Evan, this is my homeboy Ty. Ty, this is my boy E. We're just trying to hang out and have a good time." His gestures were just as overly exaggerated as his street accent.

"Well, y'all are in for a treat. I got some new girls working tonight. I got ya hooked up in the back." He walked over to one of the waitresses, pointed at us, and gave her some instructions.

"Where you know that dude from?" I was starting to be amazed at the spectrum of people in Greg's circle of friends.

"He was a client of mine." Instantly, the street accent and gestures were gone.

Greg has never been one to pretend. He was always sure of himself, and it showed in the way he interacted with people. All the years that I've known Greg, I never once associated him with the word phony. Until that night, the very thought of him pretending to be something or someone he's not seemed highly unlikely, if not utterly impossible.

"Damn, dawg. Do you stay cool with all your clients like that?" A hint of sarcasm gave away my curiosity and concerns.

"Some of them." He looked at me and smirked in a way that suggested he didn't think I would understand the truth. Maybe he was right.

Before I could even respond, he turned to speak to a dancer that he knew, and just that quick he was gone. Not in any physical nature of course. He was gone in the sense that in a split second, he had separated himself and thoughts from anything that contradicted his enjoyment. He paid me no attention. His companion paid me no attention. I looked around the entire club. No one was paying me any attention.

You can't blame them. You haven't even been paying attention to yourself. The drill sergeant's voice didn't have the same intensity it usually had. In fact, it sounded like he was on the verge of ignoring me, as well.

Control is life's biggest hoax. At any instance, life can make you feel like you've gained or lost it. After me and Erica split, I thought depression spiraled my life out of control. Coming to Chicago, I thought I'd gained it back. I spent my whole life either fighting to gain or struggling to keep control.

Life isn't about control, though. It's simply about the momentum of thoughts and actions. What you continually think becomes how you feel; what you continually feel becomes what you do; what you continually do becomes who you are. Up until recently, my life's momentum had me moving in a positive direction. It led me to working out; it led me to focus on my future; and it led me out of depression. However, since I first encountered Celeste, my momentum had slowly turned about. I don't work out nearly as much as I could. I've even noticed my gut coming back. I'm not as focused as I need to be at the hospital. My guilt barely even lets me greet Dr. Carson. The momentum of my thoughts and actions are slowly turning me into a person that I don't like; The E, Motherfucker. Deep down, I was not happy with myself.

"Dawg, where's the bathroom?" I slowly turned and headed in the direction Greg pointed to. I wanted to splash some water on my face to wake myself up in more than one way.

"E!" Greg yelled at me from where I left him. I turned to see what he wanted. "Come back to the VIP room! I'll be there chilling!"

He reached through the group of dancers gathered around him and pointed to the area he wanted me to meet him. I laughed, nodded my head, and continued on my mission even more focused on my awakening.

If you allow yourself to get comfortable with this shit, you'll be just as gone as he is. The drill sergeant's voice was back to normal intensity. He had already gotten refocused.

Outta the frying pan and into the fire. A new voice introduced itself to me. Oddly, it didn't feel new. It seemed familiar. It was too warm and comfortable for me to consider it a stranger in any way. *You're always jumping from one extreme to the next,* the voice continued.

My new internal friend seemed to have a profound understanding of me. It dissected all my flaws, fears, and fantasies. It evaluated all my convictions and beliefs. It laid them all out in front of my plain view, and I saw how they fit together. As I stood in the bathroom mirror, for the first time in my life, I saw myself as a whole. I realized I always viewed myself in fragments. All I ever saw of myself was whatever was at the forefront of my consciousness at the time. If I was scared, I saw my fears. If I was disappointed, I saw my flaws. If I was mad, I saw my convictions and beliefs. Whenever all of those things freed my mind to wander, I saw my fantasies. Until then, I had never seen the entire scope all at once.

You are a beautiful man. As the voice concluded its dissertation, I realized whose voice it was. It was Evan Clifford Miles. It was my true voice. It represented a perfect balance between the drill sergeant's convictions and the influences of fear, anger, disappointment, happiness, or whatever emotion was currently overwhelming my consciousness. Regardless of how frayed the outer extremes were, overall, I was a balanced and beautiful man. I left the bathroom without even having to splash my face with water.

"I've *got* to be the jazziest motherfucker of all time!" Greg yelled at me as soon as I entered the area his friend had reserved for us.

He never flinched when he made that statement. He never glanced around to see who heard. As far as I could tell, he didn't care. Nothing about his aura was contradictory to that statement. He really did believe he was the jazziest motherfucker of all time.

Greg was rich. No matter how much he tried to play it down, his reputation as a spender and that black-on-black Mercedes S550 parked at the front door announced it to the entire club. The dancers flocked to him at every opportunity. The brother who greeted us at the door was busy directing and instructing.

"Ty asked me to come over and say hello to you." A female in classy lingerie began smiling and talking to Greg.

She had to be the most gorgeous girl in a million mile radius. Her smooth caramel complexion and light brown hair were so unique. Her smile, her curves, her movements, everything about her made me want to just shut the hell up and watch. I didn't want to miss anything. I don't know if Greg's decree on being the jazziest motherfucker included women or not. If it did, then the gap from his jaw dropping was a good indicator that he was seriously rethinking his ranking. He didn't say anything for an awkwardly long time. Finally, she broke the ice.

"My name is Privilege." Greg kept staring. "You've been treated to a dance. Would you like it now?" she asked nervously while smiling.

She couldn't tell what was on Greg's mind, and neither could I. Still, she started dancing before she even finished asking the question.

Music and moments can be such a wonderful couple. Together, they can create a special blend of magic. The song "Fortunate" by Maxwell played as Privilege danced. Being on the outside looking in, I had a better view than Greg and Privilege. They were caught up in the moment. They never knew what hit them. I saw the whole thing happen in my plain sight. She smiled, caressed, and grinded, while Greg watched in amazement. Their eyes never left one another's. She stripped away a lot more than just clothes. Sexy isn't even the best way to describe it. It was much more than physical. Greg didn't even grope and rub on her like he usual. It seemed like her spirit straddled his heart like she was performing a lap dance for his emotions. The music embraced the moment with passion and sincerity. As Maxwell declared all the things their eyes said. Greg never had the spirit of a woman introduce itself to him this way. Privilege never had it drawn out of her in this manner. The only word I can think of that even comes close to encompassing the entire scope of their interaction is: endearing.

"Did you like your dance?" She held her face noticeably close to his. She smiled.

Greg returned the most genuine smile I've seen on him since coming to Chicago.

"Would you like another dance?" She started dancing again.

Greg looked over at me and then turned his head back towards her. "Yes, but not here." He had a serious look on his face as he stood up, grabbed her hand, and led her out of the booth we were seated in. He never gave her a chance to consent.

Since my arrival to Chicago, Greg had taken me to too many strip clubs to count. The routine was the same: a VIP booth, gorgeous girls, Greg and I side by side enjoying the show. When Privilege walked into our booth, Greg's reaction let me know this night would be different. As Greg led Privilege out of the VIP area, he handed some money to a dancer and pointed in my direction. He and Privilege then went down a back hallway, undoubtedly to enjoy a much more intimate dance.

There's no substitute for substance. Anything physical about a woman, anything material about her lifestyle is black and white. Her full color spectrum can only be viewed through her substance. Either it's there or it's not. A television is either black and white or color. It's never both. Once you've looked at a color set, anything black and white seems too bland to bear. I sat through three songs of the pale substitute Greg had sent my way before excusing myself to go to a restroom that I didn't really have to use.

Once I reached the back hallway, I was surprised to see Greg standing there. He was leaning up against the wall outside the dancers' locker room, waiting patiently. Too patiently. His mind seemed far away. He was deep in thought. He paid no attention to the half-naked strippers passing in and out of the doorway where he stood. He barely even noticed me. He wasn't waiting on a private dance. He wasn't waiting on an opportunity to rub, caress, and kiss her. The expression on his face showed that he seemed quite comfortable and content with doing exactly what he was doing, which was patiently waiting on her.

"Dawg, you okay?" He didn't respond or even look up for that matter. "GREG!" I yelled. Finally, he looked at me.

"Huh?" He smiled and laughed softly.

At first, I thought he was laughing at me having to yell at him to get his attention. Then, I realized I still didn't have it fully. His laughs were remnants of the place I pulled his mind from. After seeing his thoughts torment him earlier, it was refreshing to see. I was just glad to know that happiness was possible for my friend, even if it only existed as a thought for the time being. I didn't want to interrupt his enjoyment any more than I already had. So, I decided to go back to our booth and waste time until he was ready to go.

*****

"Evan, you ready to go?" Greg returned with a smile.

"Yeah, whenever you are." I returned his smile, even though I didn't know what it meant.

"She's getting dressed. We're ready to get out of here."

It's so amazing how the smallest thing can make a big statement. His statement seemed casual enough, except for one word: WE'RE. He didn't say I'M. He didn't say SHE'S. He made eye contact and without hesitation said WE'RE. I didn't know what they had planned. It had to be more than just a physical thing, or he would've said he was trying to go fuck. I've heard him make that statement in a similar scenario before. It had to be more than some sort of *business arrangement*, or he would've said she was trying to get paid. I've seen strippers aggravate the hell out of him by pressuring him to spend money on dances or *whatever*. One thing for sure, whatever they were getting ready to do, it was mutual. From the onset of their interaction, Greg saw himself and her as a WE.

My thoughts were curious. I raised my eyebrows to let him know I sensed something out of the ordinary. As I turned and walked away, he smiled back and continued waiting patiently.

After about ten minutes, Greg and Privilege met me in the front lobby. She wore a simple pair of jeans, a pair of black stylish heels, and a black silk top with her shoulders out. Her hair was pulled back into a ponytail, and she had taken off all her makeup except for a lovely shade of peachy brown lipstick. Dressed down, she was even more gorgeous. She wasn't a stripper anymore. She left that world in the dressing room. This was not a strip club anymore. This was the place my best friend had found something special. Exactly what that something special was would have to be discovered. But, in the most unlikely of places and under the most unlikely circumstances, he had definitely found something special. From the outside looking in, if their chemistry seemed that real to me, I could only imagine what they were feeling themselves.

"I see ya, boy!" Greg's friend Ty shouted from a short distance away. He thought he was seeing the Double G, Baby heading out the door with an easy piece of pussy.

"Nah, man, we're just going to chill and get something to eat."

There was that word again: WE'RE. The WE left out the door holding hands and smiling at each other, while I trailed closely behind bearing witness to the magic.

"I want to play something for you." Greg looked over at Privilege as he scrolled through his CD collection.

She was seated in the passenger seat eager to hear his selection. I kept quiet but my curiosity was just as eager as hers. When the song came on, my jaw dropped. It was "Sunshine" by Alexander O'Neal. *DAMN!* I quietly screamed to myself. He definitely knew the words. He sung that song to Beverly Singleton at the school talent show in 11th grade. Beverly was his high school sweetheart. No one knew Greg could sing except me and his mother who died at work six months before the show, from a massive heart attack. He serenaded Ms. Mattie just as much as he did Beverly. It was a special night for him, and I couldn't help but to relive the moment in my mind as the song played.

She touched me with a smile that glows. I can't go a day without my sunshine. She warms me with her heart of gold. I can't go a day without my sunshine.

There was not a dry eye in the whole auditorium. I could still see the tears running from his eyes as he accepted his first place trophy. In retrospect, Beverly was an insignificant recipient of a significant display of emotions. For Greg, that song was his heartfelt and tearful thanks for Ms. Mattie being strong for him, for all her sacrifices, for all her stories and encouragement. He was thanking his mother for all her love.

"That was so nice." Privilege smiled at Greg while rubbing his hand and forearm.

"I really like that song and wanted to enjoy it with you." He looked over at her briefly, smiled, then turned and continued driving down the expressway.

There was no explanation of why it was special. I couldn't see his eyes, but from over his shoulders, I noticed him tightening his jaw muscles.

"You alright, dawg?"

"I'm good, man," he replied without looking back.

I saw him tighten his grip on the steering wheel. She must have sensed something, too, because she interlocked her fingers with his.

Greg was definitely feeling much more pain than he was showing. I could almost feel his tension.

The same way that night of the talent show was the breaking point of the pain he carried from his mother's death, this night was the breaking point for whatever burdens Stacey Howard had left on his heart. He was not focused on the road. He was focused on freedom. He saw something in this woman that gave him hope. He tightened his grip on the steering wheel, tightened his grip on Privilege's hand, and kept pushing forward, while I closed my eyes and said a silent prayer for my friend to be free from the pain.

We stopped at a late-night pizza parlor downtown. Greg was much more relaxed, but I could still sense a serious resolve under his laughs. All the signs were there for genuine attraction. There was plenty of eye contact, good conversation, and more hand holding than I'd ever seen from Greg.

He told her a little bit about his past and how he ended up in Chicago.

"My real name is Loverne Shaw, but everyone calls me Lovie. I'm a twenty-five-year-old Psychology major at the University of Chicago. I'm from New York, but I've been in Chicago for seven years."

After a little more about her, she told us financial struggles caused her to drop out of school for a semester, and she started dancing to get back on her feet. She was beautiful, intriguing, charismatic, passionate, and seemingly sincere. From first encounter, my impression of her was that she is definitely a keeper.

*****

The next morning when I woke up, I heard *SportsCenter* playing on the television in the family room. That was Greg's routine, whenever he didn't have work to do. After having pizza, the three of us came back to the house together. I was happy for Greg's newly found source of happiness, but I was concerned they were moving too fast. I went out to the family room to access the damage.

As I came down the hallway, I saw the top of Greg's head rested on the left armrest.

"Wuzzup, fool?" I greeted him as I walked around the couch into the room.

"Nothing to it. Just watching the highlights." He looked at me with the biggest smile I had seen from him since we were kids.

I noticed he was sprawled out over a blanket and pillow that had been worked deep down into the crevices of the couch. *He slept on the couch,* I thought to myself.

"Yes, I did." He reacted to the statement I thought I had whispered to myself.

"What's up with that? I thought the way y'all was all hugged up last night that you was gonna tear that up, for sure."

"Nah, it ain't even like that. I wasn't trying to hit it. I just wanted to chill with her." He wasn't trying to hold back a laugh or anything. He was serious.

"Damn, bruh, this sounds like it could be something serious."

He lay on his side, closed his eyes, and inhaled deeply. Then, in sequence, he opened his heart, mind, and eyes. Slowly, he released that breath and comfortably spoke the word YES.

Still something in his eyes bothered me. As confident as his response and gestures were, his eyes still held a deep, dark secret. Something was keeping them from expressing the same happy confidence as the rest of him.

"You sure you don't want to ride with me?" Lovie came out of Greg's room wearing one of his FAMU t-shirts, a pair of his gym shorts, and some slide-on Nike sandals.

"Nah, you go ahead. I've got a few things to go over, and then I'll be ready to chill later when you get back." He stood up and began walking her to the front door.

She leaned over towards him and slightly puckered her lips to kiss him. Greg smiled and pulled her in for a hug instead. After everything magical that had happened between them, I didn't understand why he wouldn't at least give her a little peck. Curiosity and concern escalated within me.

"I'll see you later, Evan." She smiled and waved at me. Then she turned back towards Greg.

"Okay. I think the way y'all are going I'll be seeing a lot of you." I laughed, fishing for a reaction.

"We'll see." She stared into Greg's eyes with a warm smile. She was fishing as well.

"Yes, we will." Greg smiled and stared into Lovie's eyes.

Then, without any noticeable hesitation, he handed the woman who he wouldn't kiss the keys to his one-hundred-thousand-dollar car for her to drive to a home that he had never been to. I was thoroughly confused.

"Dawg, you must really like her." I couldn't hide the curiosity in my voice even if I tried.

He stood silent in the doorway, watching as she drove away. Then he turned towards me. "She's a good girl. I want to help her."

There was a thin layer of water forming over his eyes that he didn't try to hide. He just smiled, walked back towards the kitchen, and went to the refrigerator to grab something to drink. By the time he turned around to face me again, tears were trickling down his face as he laughed to himself. He knew he was doing the right thing.

"So all of that last night was about you wanting to help her?"

"No. It was about us becoming friends. Friends help each other, right?" The tears were drying up, but the conviction was still present in the way he spoke.

"So, the Double G wasn't trying to get some pussy?" I tried my best to put a humorous spin on a serious question.

"The Double G done got enough pussy to know that pussy ain't everything." His response seemed as natural as his breathing.

"DAMN! I bet Iceberg Slim is turning over in his grave hearing you talk like that."

"That motherfucker can turn over a million times. At the end of all his turning, he's still gonna be dead. I'm alive. I gotta live."

Who said that heroes have to have good timing? Forget the clocks and calendars. I was just happy to finally get a chance to see and talk to my hero. I've been in Chicago for six months now. When I came looking for him, I found him battered and worn. He had been victimized by some sort of Chicagoan version of Kryptonite and submerged under the will of his arch nemesis. I've always known what he was capable of. I don't know if Chicago ever got a chance to witness his powers, but as sure as he stood now, they would have their chance. Super G is back!

Greg still had major battles to fight, but at least now he had purpose. That same purpose had just left, driving his car. I sensed the presence of it in the conviction of his tears, in the comfort of his 'yes', and in the natural ease of him denying his impulses for sex.

We carried our conversation into his bedroom. As we talked, he took Lovie's jeans and blouse and hung them on a hanger in his closet. He had opened his heart and was preparing a permanent home for his purpose. Perfect timing. My hero found his strength in just enough time to make his most daring rescue yet: himself. Saving Lovie, the world, and me would be a piece of cake.

I was far from just. The conviction of my affair with Celeste could no longer hide behind fading memory and erotic pleasures. What's right is right. What's wrong is wrong. The bright light from Super G's presence lit up my whole consciousness. I could clearly see which side of the justice fence I was on. I knew there were changes I had to make.

CHAPTER 12
MACHAIA JAMES

"Machaia, could you come into my office for a second, please?" Lesley always talked very professional when we are at work. I liked that about him.

When I walked into the office, I noticed he had a strange look on his face. So, I knew whatever he wanted to talk about was a serious matter.

"Could you shut the door please?" he asked, still wearing the strange look.

"Is everything okay?" I was starting to get worried.

"We're pregnant!" He strained to keep himself from yelling at the top of his lungs.

The excitement on his face and the passion in his voice exploded from deep within him. A smile as wide as the room told the whole story. He was ecstatic about Sandra having his child.

He stood up, walked from behind his desk, and hugged me tightly. Then he released me and stared into my eyes. He was looking for my blessing. He wanted me to be just as happy as he was. He knew my happiness was a direct indicator to how Sandra felt about the situation.

Can he really be that naïve? I avoided eye contact and kept a straight face for as long as I could. Part of me was hoping that would be enough to raise questions inside of him. It was too late, though. His spirits were soaring about twenty stratospheres higher than the realm of reality. I didn't want it to, but it did anyway. I stared right back into those useless eyes of his and smiled. He saw what he wanted to see. I granted what I wanted to withhold. Immediately, our spirits took off, traveling at amazing speeds in opposite directions.

Lesley's excitement put a sour taste in my mouth, as if I was the one who initiated the lie he was so eager to live. I knew what Sandra was doing, and it hurt me. From now on, every time I saw her, every day I worked with him, every day I was around them together at home, I would know the truth. I would be just as guilty of lying to him as she was. My best friend's world was spinning out of control in a direction that hurt me to even think about. Our relationship was at a major crossroad.

For the rest of the afternoon, I contemplated what to do. I ran the scenario around in my mind and tried to find a way to believe what she was doing was right. Nothing. She was lying. She was wrong. She knew it. I knew it. Lesley was too high to even know the possibility existed. By the time we began preparing to leave the office for the weekend, worry had consumed me. My biggest concern was what would happen to me and Sandra's friendship once I told her how I felt about the whole thing. Worry turned into damn near panic as I prepared myself for the inevitable confrontation.

I didn't go straight to the house. Instead, I drove around for two hours to think. The possibilities stung me more than the October cold. I knew Sandra didn't take criticism and contempt very well.

I was so caught up in how Sandra would respond to my contempt that I forgot they were HER lies. She created this mess. That realization quickly turned my panic and concern into disappointment and anger. *She should be riding around wondering how I'm going to respond. She should be somewhere feeling like shit for what she's doing to Lesley. Her trifling ass is probably somewhere with a good man's credit card buying gifts for a sorry nigga's baby.*

Those thoughts angered me to tears. I turned the truck around and headed straight for the house. I couldn't get there fast enough. I needed to say what was on my heart just as much as she needed to hear it.

By the time I made it to the house, Lesley had been home long enough to thank every lucky star in the sky for the third time. Unnoticed, I stood by the doorway for a moment to watch and listen. Lesley was barely breathing as he shared his views of their future together. I thought it was weird he hardly mentioned the baby. Sandra was watching with a noticeably blank look on her face. He didn't notice, though. Occasionally, she mustered up enough strength to put on a fake smile. She was offering her acceptance of another man's validation.

A woman that can't validate herself inherently accepts inferiority by letting a man do it for her. There is a procession of steps that occur when she officially accepts that lower level of existence. First, she has to be introduced to the man's view of her. Then, she has to reexamine her views of herself. The painful part of the process begins when she realizes some of the wonderful views she has of herself differ from what he sees. Views from an inferior source are inferior. The woman absolutely has to take a back seat to the views from the superior provider. The most crushing part is when she finally reaches inside of her own heart and squeezes out any room for those wonderful things she hoped for herself. As Lesley continued rambling on, I could see on Sandra's face when each step began and ended. It was a sad and painful process to watch indeed.

"I hear that congratulations are in order!"

Sandra turned towards me as I entered the room. She wiped the pain off her smile and haphazardly threw it at me.

I didn't make that statement with anything near the sarcasm I originally intended to. That harsh cold front had been partly converted to sympathy by the warmth of unconditional love. I couldn't stand to see her hurting.

"Yeah, it's pretty exciting, ain't it? I finally see what you were going through." She shrugged her shoulders and grabbed her belly as she spoke, while displaying the dumbest dumb-assed look on her face.

I can't believe this bitch is gonna stand here and act like I didn't know about her ass being pregnant. That fiery thought resonated from deep within me. *Hurting or not, what she is doing is trifling as hell.* She continued looking at me with a ridiculous look on her face.

"Yeah, it is. I wish I could enjoy it more, but suddenly, I feel sick to my stomach."

I grabbed my stomach and screwed up my face like it was my pregnancy bothering me. I stared at Sandra, waiting for her eyes to meet mine. Then, I rolled my eyes away. I wanted her to know for sure what was really turning my stomach. She glanced at me for a split second and then lowered her head. She knew.

Once in my room, I locked the door, kicked off my shoes, and threw my clothes on the floor. I jumped in the bed and covered both me and Sarah with my arms in a protective way. Slowly, my anxiety and fears were tranquilized by the comfortable rhythm of our synchronized heartbeats. I fell into an easy sleep.

"Are you okay, girl?" I felt Sandra's hand gently stroking my forehead and hair.

Sandra always did that when she was concerned about me. I never told her how much I loved it when she did that. *She's not worried about me. She's trying to seduce my heart into supporting her deceit.*

I closed my eyes and tuned out the feel of her touch. The angry and contemptuous sides of my consciousness would not allow me to enjoy it. "Girl, I'm alright."

"You rushed out of the kitchen like your stomach was hurting. I was concerned that something was wrong."

It seemed like she really didn't know what was bothering me.

"Sandra, how could you tell Lesley that you're pregnant with his baby?" I sat up in the bed so I could look directly in her eyes.

"Because it is! What are you asking me?"

"That's bullshit. You told me before we moved in here that you were pregnant."

"I told you that I *thought* I was pregnant. But, I wasn't."

"And you are now?"

"Yep." She couldn't even look me in the eyes.

"How far along are you?" I spoke with a very condescending tone.

"I don't know yet."

"The doctor confirmed that you were pregnant, but he didn't tell you how far along you are? Sandra, stop bullshitting!" I felt my face growing hot as my convictions turned into anger.

"Damn, Chaia! After all I've been through, I thought you would be happy for me. Girl, please…I need you to be happy for me."

Happiness wasn't what she really expected. Hell, she wasn't even happy for herself. What she really wanted was for me to tell her she was doing the right thing. That lying to Lesley was the best option.

"Do you love him?"

I already knew the answer to that question. I just wanted to see what flew out of her mouth.

"No, but..." She repositioned herself, and looked me directly in the eyes. "...I respect him, and I know I will grow to love him."

Her words were filled with sincerity. Her eyes were filled with tears. I believed both of them, but she was still wrong.

"Sandra, whether it's due to respect for him now or love for him later, eventually you're gonna have to tell him the truth."

"Chaia, this is Lesley's baby!"

I could tell Sandra was telling the truth. At least she was telling her biased version of it. Whatever the reason, she really felt she was having Lesley's baby. I realized there would be no reasoning on her part. There really is no middle ground between truth and lies. I didn't press Sandra any further about the situation. I didn't give her my blessing in any form. There were no warm and understanding looks. She wasn't willing to compromise and neither was I.

For the next few weeks, we didn't speak. We barely even looked at one another. Without words, we waged a war of wills. She wanted me to accept her lie. I wanted her to free us both from its bondage.

*****

Between DeMann's bribery, my grandmother's pleas, and the heartache from fighting with Sandra, I was quite certain I would be going home for Thanksgiving. DeMann was putting the final touches on his bribe to get me there.

"Machaia, sweetie, are you ready?" Lesley asked through the cracked door of my room.

He always spoke to me very polite. I guess it was his way of trying to compensate for Sandra's coldness.

"Yes, I just finished up my makeup. I'm ready now." I walked out into the hallway and looked at Lesley.

"Wow! You look amazing!" His smile said it before his words, but it still was nice to hear.

"Why, thank you, Lesley." I couldn't help but to smile as I walked up the hallway.

That nice compliment from him set the tone for Sandra and me. I walked out into the foyer as Sandra came down the hallway from the master bedroom. She moved from my side of the house a couple of weeks after we moved in.

She was gorgeous. Her face was plump. Her body had swollen just as much as mine. Despite it all, she was radiant. She had on a black designer maternity dress with a lovely pair of heels. She'd always been very stylish. Something else she picked up from her mother. I guess *kept* women always have to look nice.

We were going to the firm's Thanksgiving dinner. Lesley was to be officially announced as partner, so the evening was about celebrating accomplishments and progress. Since I was his secretary, I had to go for professional reasons. Sandra had become his fiancée, so she had to go for personal reasons. It was a very big night for Lesley. The least we could do was put our differences to the side and help him enjoy it.

"You look very nice, Sandra." My words were laced with anxiousness. Part of me was yearning to speak to her. I missed her. We smiled at each other and leaned in to hug.

It's hard waging spiritual warfare with someone you love. It drains your soul. We held each other tightly. Despite our differences, despite the convictions, judgments, and blames we placed on each other, anything we felt stemmed from genuine love.

"You look amazing, too."

When we finally released one another, I saw she was just as teary eyed and choked up as I was.

Lesley had a limousine drive us to the ballroom. Once inside the limo, we held hands as we exploded into chit chat. Lesley sat back smiling and laughing. He was happy to see us talking again. We held hands all the way to the ballroom. We were lifelong, loving, caring, and mutually respectful friends.

"Your table is this way, Mr. Manley." A hostess greeted us at the door and escorted us to the table reserved for Lesley.

Leslie stepped between Sandra and me and extended his elbows for us. His pride was evident to everyone in the room. Every eye in the room seemed to be locked on us.

"Not bad for a man stuck with two whales." Sandra waved at a few people she knew as we walked to the front of the room.

"If this is what you call stuck, then don't ever release me, okay?" Lesley stared into her eyes, kissed her, and gave a sincere chuckle.

"Don't worry, baby. I've sentenced you to life. You're gonna be stuck with us forever."

Sandra stared into Lesley's eyes and smiled. Then, she glanced at me to gauge my reaction. Perpetuating the lie to the fullest, my smile was wide, bright, and false.

"This is your table, Mr. Manley."

Lesley pulled out each of our seats. The table had six settings. I assumed that was standard.

"Machaia, just to let you know, I invited three of my friends to have dinner with us." Lesley stared at me weirdly, as if he was looking for my approval.

"Don't worry, girl. I already checked him out."

"Him?" I asked curiously. "I thought you said there were three friends."

"There are. My friend Chris is coming with his wife Iris."

"And?" I knew he and Sandra were trying to play matchmaker.

"I invited my friend Donald to dinner, also." Seeing the nervousness in my eyes, he looked over at Sandra.

"Wait 'til you see him, girl. He's fine as hell and he's a lawyer!" She threw that reasoning at me like the correct sum of an easy math equation.

The part of Sandra that stemmed from her mother's influence had officially taken over. The insecurities and doubt had all manifested into an age-cured need for validation. I realized why she had been so stubborn. She needed my validation. She had to have it. The cease-fire had not changed my convictions. After a few moments of awkward silence and stares, Lesley's friends arrived.

"Machaia, this is my friend and fellow partner."

"Hello, I'm Donald Randolph. It's nice to meet you."

What kinda dude reintroduces himself after someone just introduced his ass? I was on alert, ready to yell foul at the first sign of bullshit.

"And this is my friend Chris, his son Body..." Lesley paused. "What happened to Iris?"

"She couldn't make it, so I brought Boadea here." He playfully nudged his son as they took their seats.

"Actually, it's pronounced *Bow-dee* but don't worry, Big L, if you can't get my name right."

They were seated and we made light conversation. Sandra was trying to figure out what I was thinking.

"Are you okay, girl?" Sandra asked with a concerned look on her face.

"I'm good." My glance was quicker than my response.

"Let's dance, baby!" Sandra stood up and pulled Lesley towards the dance floor.

That's right. Put on that CBA mask and run, bitch! I thought to myself. All sides of me were still on red alert, ready for an instant strike. The wonderful music from the live jazz band couldn't even help my mood. That tension and Donald's attempts to rap had me totally on edge. *What the hell kinda nigga tries to holla at a pregnant bitch that came to a dinner by herself?*

"Maybe a nice dance will help you relax." Donald reached for my hand. He was smiling like my attempts to ignore him were more funny than disrespectful.

The band began playing their rendition of R. Kelly's "Step In the Name of Love". The music took over the room. Couples, young and old, black and white, were all dancing and having the time of their lives. I was missing a great party. I grabbed Donald's hand and was determined to enjoy the rest of it.

"I'm sorry about being standoffish. I just—"

Donald cut my statement off before I could finish it. "Woman, you don't owe me any explanations. Let's just dance." He briefly glanced at me, chuckled softy, and led me to the dance floor.

We danced over the second half of R. Kelly's tonic and then glided through four more songs. After the second song, I was enjoying myself just as much as anyone else.

"See, girl, you just needed to get out and dance!" Sandra yelled out. She and Lesley were right beside Donald and me the whole time.

Shock and anger knocked me out of the trance the music and dancing had me in. Just that quick, I dropped my guard. All those voices that were on red alert were lullabied to sleep by the Pied Piper of R&B. I frolicked across the battlefield drunk with enjoyment.

"Well, Chaia, did you have a good time?" Lesley sat opposite me and Sandra in the limo. On the way back home, he made small talk to compensate for the cold silence between her and me.

"It was very nice. Congratulations again on making partner."

"Next week is Thanksgiving. What are we gonna do?"

We! What the hell does he mean WE? I immediately became angry at Lesley's question. WE represented all that were on board with the lie.

"*I'M* going home!" That statement came across with enough conviction to raise every eyebrow in the car.

Lesley's eyebrows were raised because he was finally starting to wonder what the tension between Sandra and me was all about. Sandra's eyebrows were raised because she realized the validation she thought she gained on the dance floor was still a long way coming.

She was curious about how my new resolve would affect our war and our friendship. She was wondering if I was going to come back. My eyebrows were raised because I was wondering the same things.

The largest amount of love can find room to exist in the smallest of places. For the next three days, we remained steadfast in our bunkers. Our curiosity and concerns were evident. We wanted to save our friendship. Battles had been fought. War had been waged. There was no room for weakness now. There would be no retreat. Both of our survivals depended on the war continuing. Neither of us could exist in our current state without victory. My war waged on, dedicated to liberating her from the shallow shell she was trapped in. Her war waged on, relentlessly clinging to the last bit of false security she could hide behind and oblivious to any harm she was inflicting on her loved ones. Our battlefield was filled with corpses of dead emotions and wounded memories. There in the middle of it all, dead center of the battle was a small space where love remained.

*****

Lesley was supposed to drop me off at the airport on his way to the office. Oddly, he had something come up so Sandra drove me. He was attempting to intercede on our war.

"So, what are your plans?" Sandra reached over and tenderly touched my arm.

She could barely drive straight as she looked over at me. Her eyes told me that the only thing she feared more than losing our war was losing our friendship. I looked through those windows and saw her exposed soul begging for any signal from mine that everything would be all right.

"I don't exactly know, Sandra. I'll call you in a couple of days and we can talk." I stared into her eyes as I reluctantly used my right hand to release her embrace from my left wrist.

I knew she loved me, and I hoped she knew I loved her. My heart was rejoicing at the resiliency of our love. I leaned over, kissed the side of her face, and smiled.

"I love you, girl."

That's all I said. That was enough. Then I got out of the car and continued waging war on behalf of her, me, and our two babies.

CHAPTER 13
EVAN MILES

E, you wanna come n get smthn 2 eat w/us? Greg's accent even came through on text messages.

Two and a half months had passed, and he and Lovie had grown very close. A month after they met she officially moved in. She would come downtown to his office a few times a week for lunch. He would invite me to go with them, saying he needed me there in order to stop her from 'working his nerves'. I knew he really needed me there to save him from overdosing on the excitement spewing from his heart and spirit. None of the excitement he had been getting high on before stemmed from either of those two noble origins. I was maintaining a sustained high off of a secondhand contact, so I always took him up on his invites. Getting high off of some good stuff sadly became my way of detoxing my system from the evil I was inhaling with Celeste.

"Dawg! Since she changed her major to pre-law, she's just using me for my brain. She don't really love me." Greg started laughing and reached across his chair to hug Lovie.

The way he embraced her told me that he didn't believe that for a second. The smile he always flashed whenever he said it told me that he was more than a willing participant in the whole process. Lovie playfully pushed him away and continued telling me about her excitement over her new major. She was so passionate about what she wanted to do. It was strikingly familiar to me. *Damn, she kinda sounds like Ms. Mattie. I* thought to myself. I could tell Greg saw those same similarities. I saw it in the way he interacted with her. He was happy. He was comfortable. He was in love.

My phone chirped with a text message. *I thought we were doing lunch ~ DC.*

I had to meet my female friend for lunch. I typed my response as quickly as I could to prevent the lie from hurting as bad.

With each keystroke, guilt and shame banished all the wonderful feelings I had from watching Greg and Lovie. I had been telling Dr. Carson I was dating to detour him from thinking I was fucking his wife. I knew that was the furthest thing from his mind, but I lied to him anyway hoping I could fool myself.

"I have to go. Dr. Carson just asked me to do him a favor." I offered Greg and Lovie that lie with the most comfort I could fake.

Silently, I gasped. The shame of lying to a loved one was stinging me from two sides. Guilt and shame had seized dictatorship over me. I rushed off to find a suitable place for them to beat me to death.

Stop by my office before you leave today. I have something important to talk to you about ~ DC.

. I had successfully completed my rotation with Dr. Sinclair on Wednesday. Next, I was due to start my infectious disease rotation with Dr. Copeland. Dr. Carson seemed a little determined to make sure we met.

"J.C. wants to talk to me bad. Is there anything I need to know?" I left that message on Celeste's voicemail and hoped she picked up on the urgency.

Being around Greg and Lovie had inspired me to start backing away from Celeste. I had denied her three previous attempts to come by and ignored countless text and voicemail messages. Now, my heart pounded as I contemplated what the ramification of those actions forced her to do or say.

While on my way to Dr. Carson's office, the vision of me standing in front of him and looking into his heartbroken, disappointed eyes clouded my view of the road. My day of reckoning had come. My heart pounded.

"What's up, Doc? You wanted to see me?" It was hard to sound normal. I walked through his office door and did my best to conceal my anxiety.

Immediately, he broke into a smile as wide as an adoring father. He walked behind me, shut the door, and gave me a hug. His warm embrace quickly erased any fears.

"Dr. Sinclair had some very good things to say about you today." I smiled and let him continue gloating. "She said you were one of the brightest residents she's had in years. She was very impressed."

He paused and stared at me oddly for a few seconds.

"Have you given any thought about a specialty?" His slightly mischievous smile told me that he had.

"Dr. Copeland called me today and said he isn't going to be able to take you on as a resident right now. He has some obligations away from the hospital that are going to have him traveling a lot over the next few months."

That news didn't surprise me. I could tell Dr. Copeland was bothered by how much of an active role Dr. Carson was taking in my rotations. He thought I was getting things handed to me on a silver platter. Whenever our paths crossed, he made smart-ass comments. He wanted me to know that he was not impressed. That he would make me earn his respect. He wanted me to know he was higher up the totem pole than I was, and he deserved to be there. No matter what I accomplished as a physician, my dishonesty with Dr. Carson nullified any respect my skills would eventually earn me.

"So, I worked a few things out. How would you like to do your next rotation with me?" His expression told me how he felt about the whole thing. He was elated.

"Would I have to start now?" I was already contemplating different angles to get out of it.

"Well, yeah, I only could clear about three weeks out of my touring." His face saddened as he realized there may be a conflict.

The disappointment in his shoulders amplified my anxiety. I saw the inevitable question forming in his heart. *Why doesn't he like being around me?* Eventually, that question would enter his mind, his heart would yearn for the answer, and his spirit would be unsettled until he knew the truth.

"I'm sorry, Dr. Carson..." I paused for a moment. "I can't do your rotation with you. I really need a break and need to go home and check on my mother." I looked him in the eyes, while trying hard to sound sincere.

He bought it, but his spirit seemed reluctant, though. The first cancer cell was formed. The fact that I was the carcinogen broke my heart, as I watched the beginning of the end of our bond.

After leaving his office, I immediately made arrangements for an early flight out of town and hopefully away from the sting of conviction I felt when in his presence.

CHAPTER 14
MACHAIA JAMES

"Oh, look at you, baby!" my grandmother screamed, as I walked out of the terminal to the airport curbside.

"Hey, babygirl." My grandfather hugged me and walked around from the driver's side to begin loading my luggage in the trunk.

They've really missed me. I could tell by the way they interacted with me as we drove home. My grandmother made a couple of mentions of some good "positions" she could hook me up with. She was still dead set on me staying. My grandfather didn't try to hide his emotions. He hugged and kissed me at least a million times in the first few hours I was at the house. I felt validated. God uses validation to confirm doubts, answer questions, and order steps. I felt my heart become more resolved as I realized his plan for my life was in progress.

The next morning, a soft touch and a wonderful aroma subtly awakened me. I opened my eyes to yet another nice surprise.

"These are for you." DeMann handed me a bouquet of beautiful flowers and smiled as wide as I had ever seen him.

"Thank you. They're nice." I inhaled deeply.

My grandparents stood in my bedroom doorway. I was starting to sense their and DeMann's collaboration in changing my mind about Chicago. DeMann reluctantly gave in to my grandmother's request for him to leave the room so I could get dressed. I think I actually saw her hold his hand out the corner of my eyes. *Ain't they some slick asses.*

DeMann had a whole day planned for us. My grandparents' eagerness for me to go along with it suggested they were probably co-conspirators.

I was convinced by his impromptu trip to Chicago that DeMann missed me. Seeing him in Chicago made him seem so Nashville, but seeing him in Nashville forced me to view him in a new light.

DeMann's biggest change was very evident. He had on a brand-new pair of white Air Force Ones. His jeans and shirt were new. I could tell he had just gotten his locks re-twisted and hairline edged. Even his jewelry looked like he had just gotten it cleaned and shined. DeMann had gone all out trying to look his best. The DeMann that I knew thought too highly of himself to go all out to impress anybody. *He loves me and wants to make sure I know it.*

Just as he did in Chicago, DeMann anxiously drove me around from place to place. He had so much he wanted to show me, so much love to prove. He took me to a botanical garden out in the country. He even tried to take me horseback riding, but I reminded him that I was pregnant.

"Oh snap! I guess I can't set my baby up like that, huh?" His accent even seemed different. "Well, we got two and a half hours before my big surprise." He could barely contain himself.

"Boy, what do you have up yo' sleeve?"

"You'll see! Just calm down and relax." He was talking more to himself than me.

It seemed like I left Nashville yesterday. Physically, everything was the same, but my home seemed much more comfortable to me than it was before. My bed was cozier. My grandparents were more loving. DeMann was more appreciative. It was a wonderful contrast to the uneasy feeling I had in Chicago watching Sandra and Lesley.

Whatever DeMann's surprise was, it couldn't come soon enough. He took me to the nail shop I used to go to. We got hot paraffin waxes together, while he stuttered through what he'd been up to since he returned from Chicago. Then he took me to Monell's Restaurant on North 6th Avenue, where I stumbled through what had been going on in Chicago. The excitement was so contagious.

"Let's get outta here and go for a ride."

"Where you wanna ride to?" I could barely get my words out.

He burst into a humungous grin. He loved the fact that I was just as excited as he was.

"You'll see. Just calm down and relax." This time, he was definitely talking more to me than himself.

He was quiet as he drove, but not in a distant way. He looked at me and smiled every other second. He held my hand, and even that seemed more comfortable than before.

After driving us to the Opryland Gaylord, DeMann looked over at me to gauge my reaction. It wasn't hard for him to figure it out. My eyes were watering before he pulled into the parking lot. When I was a little girl, my grandmother took me there every year. She said when my mother was a little girl she brought her there, too. My grandmother told me that if she could've, my mother would have stayed there forever. In my heart and mind, she did.

Strips of beautiful all-white lights streamed down from the tall ceilings. They looked like lit-up highways that angels used to travel from heaven to earth. Whenever I went there during the holidays, the feeling of my mother's presence was strong. While watching some little girls enjoying the lights, I saw my mother in each of them. I knew Sarah would enjoy it the same way, and I couldn't wait to bring her for the first time. I could envision my mother's spirit traveling down from heaven on those highways. She would be so happy to see her grandbaby. I rejoiced in her happiness. The warmness of their spirits as it hugged and embraced me. Tonight, just as every other time I left this place, I cried.

"You okay?" DeMann tightened his embrace, pulled me to him, and kissed my temple.

He already knew the answer. He just wanted me to know he was being considerate. He knew what this place meant for me. When we were in high school, he would bring me there every year, also. He's a very sentimental man, which was one of the qualities I fell in love with.

I submerged myself further into his embrace and further into the memory of what he was to me back then. I looked up into his eyes as we continued walking back to his truck. We didn't say a word. We just enjoyed the comfort of each other: a comfortable stare, a comfortable smile, and a comfortable tongue kiss. Comfortable really is a persuasive temptation.

*****

157

"Where are you going?" I asked when he got off of I-65 southbound at the Wedgewood Avenue exit. "I thought we were going back to your place."

"We are. I know how you like looking at the Christmas lights on the houses in Brentwood. So, I decided to take the scenic route. Dat alright wit' you?"

He flashed a wide, confident grin. He was proud he knew me so well. I couldn't help but to return his smile.

DeMann drove up Wedgewood for a couple of blocks and stopped in the turning lane to go left onto Franklin Pike. I glanced right and stared up the block where Franklin turns into 8th Avenue. My mind instinctively drifted back to the time I was riding the bus. Again, I noticed the worlds of difference. The lights, the people, the whole holiday feeling were only a few blocks apart physically. Spiritually, they may as well have been on different planets. There I was halfway in between both worlds at the exact same spot when I first noticed the difference. On the bus ride, the contrast between them was much more depressing than the way it felt today. That day, my glass was half empty. Today, it was half full. The difference is totally related to which way your momentum is taking you. DeMann and I shared another comfortable smile. He made a couple of turns then turned onto a beautiful street where every house seemed to be part of some sort of winter wonderland.

"Damn, girl! Close yo' mouth. These people gonna think you plottin' to break in they shit." His joke broke me out of my trance.

His laugh erupted from his heart and burst out of his lungs. Then he pulled into the driveway of the biggest house on the street. It was beautifully decorated. A huge Christmas tree adorned the living room window. *This must be where the Governor lives.* I hoped DeMann would hurry and make his U-turn. Instead, he pulled in and shut the truck's engine off.

"Boy, you know they gonna come out and shoot yo' crazy ass for parking in their yard!" I burst into a loud, playful laugh. Hey, if he didn't care about getting caught, I shouldn't either.

"Nah, we ain't gotta worry 'bout no mess like that here." His statement didn't have the humorous tone I expected.

My curiosity grew. "Why not?"

He reached into the center console and pulled out my keychain. It had the dolphin ornament I brought back from our first cruise. Every key had the same old dusty hue I remembered, except one. There was one bright, shiny, brand-new key. He extended the keychain to me.

"What's this, DeMann?" My lip started to tremble.

"It's our home, baby." He was definitely not joking. "I got it for us and the baby." He didn't even flash his cocky little smirk.

He got out of the truck, walked around, opened my door, and helped me out. I was so shocked that I was sure he would have to carry me part of the way through the front door.

When I entered, I was again shocked. DeMann had to have paid someone to decorate the interior. The walls and ceilings of the foyer were all highly glossed wood planks with soft recessed lights. Contemporary wood, leather, and stainless steel made me feel like I was back in some downtown Chicago flat. So much detail surrounded me that I couldn't take it all in.

He escorted me through the rest of the house. He had stories about what he had done to each room. He had a room decorated for Sarah. He even had her name carved on a wood jewelry box sitting on the armoire. It was perfect. I followed him back out to the front. He turned around at the counter that separated the kitchen and family room and pulled me close to him.

"So, this is the big surprise? You got a new house." I backed my face away from his shoulder to look him in the eyes.

"Stop playing. You know what this is. This is *our* house."

"Oh really!" I smiled wide enough to grant him my approval.

"And no, this is not the *BIG* surprise!" His words had to battle with his smile for freedom from his lips.

He backed away from me, drew a serious look on his face, and reached into his pocket. When he removed his balled up hand, I already knew what he was about to do. He knelt down in front of me on both knees. He reached around my waist, pulled me to him, and pushed up my sweater to expose my pregnant stomach. He kissed and smiled at Sarah and spoke her name. Then he looked up at me with tears in his eyes and spoke with ten times the passion I envisioned.

"Machaia James, will you marry me?"

My jaw dropped open. I could tell he spent a serious grip on the ring. It was easily the most beautiful piece of jewelry I had ever seen. It was big enough and bright enough to make anyone close catch the gazillion rays of sunlight reflecting from it.

The image of DeMann blurred in my eyes as a thick coat of water formed over my pupils. I knew exactly what he was. He was sorry for not doing right by me. He was sincere in his intentions.

"Yes," I replied, swallowing the lump in my throat.

DeMann's emotions erupted. He stood up, hugged me tightly, and started crying. Then he passionately kissed me, placed his hands on my cheeks, and stared into my eyes for a few moments. "I thought I lost you forever." His eyes were intense and piercing, as if he was searching for the part of me that never left him.

"Forever has a whole new meaning right now, baby." My statement came without thought from somewhere deep inside of me. It seemed more like I was talking to myself than him.

Immediately, DeMann started detailing his plans for us. Never once did he stop and ask for my opinion. His plan for our life was finalized. My acceptance of his proposal was all he required.

My opinions, wishes, desires, and wants were all unnecessary side items. Once again, he had gotten his way with me. Just then, that old familiar uncomfortable feeling came back to me. For about an hour, DeMann's excitement would not stop running his mouth. He ran hot bath and squeezed me for forty-five minutes while we soaked. After the tub, we relaxed in the bedroom. I sat back and listened to him continue to detail *our* future.

He had the closets sectioned out and had divided the drawers in the chest. All my clothes, shoes, and accessories were there. Then it hit me. Obviously, he went through the dumpsters, found my belongings, and kept them. I stood in the middle of my walk-in closet amazed.

"I couldn't let us stay in that dumpster. It was like I threw away my life. I had to get it back. I had to get you back." His face was balled up. His eyes were swollen and ran uncontrollably. He was butt ass naked, physically and emotionally. "I can't lose you."

DeMann went to the top drawer and pulled out a wooden box. When he opened it my tennis bracelet, rings, necklaces, and earrings were clean and neatly placed in the box. He had gone through a great deal to protect the thought of me. To him, I never left.

"Do you still love me?"

I couldn't see his eyes, but the tenderness in his voice yearned for an answer. He reached around from behind me and embraced me as we spooned in the bed.

"I said yes, didn't I?" For some reason, that seemed like an easier answer than a simple yes.

"I want to hear you say it." DeMann spoke slow and seductively as he leaned closer to me and tried to penetrate me from behind.

"I see what you want." I pinched my legs together as hard as I could to prevent him from getting in.

"You still didn't answer the question." His continued efforts to penetrate me with his rock-hard penis told me that hearing those words wasn't his highest priority. I almost felt relieved.

DeMann kept trying to penetrate me. I was glad he stopped asking me about how I felt about him. I couldn't answer his question even if I wanted to. Something was not right. My heart was troubled by the decision I made. *Isn't this what you wanted? What are you waiting for?* My mind tried to rationalize the situation. Still, my heart was troubled. Instead of turning around and asking DeMann the tough questions my heart needed answered, I did what I usually did -- went along. I relaxed my muscles, lifted my leg, and let him in.

"Damn, baby, this shit is so wet and warm. If pregnant pussy is this good, I'ma hav'ta keep you knocked up." DeMann's voice had a disgusting amount of excitement.

"It's all yours, baby." I don't know where that empty response came from, but hearing it come from my lips hurt me even more than DeMann's words.

With that decree, DeMann's excitement grew by leaps and bounds. I heard and felt it on his breath as it hit the back of my neck. I felt it in his grip as it tightened around my waist. I felt it in the thrust of his pelvis as his dick drove deeper and deeper inside me. It seemed like an eternity since he'd been inside of me, but I can't remember it ever feeling this hard. Sadly, his excitement seemed to be purely physical. All the passion that was in his voice when he proposed was gone. I felt his eyes watching me submit to his will. I felt that old familiar smirk forming on his lips. I didn't feel like we were making love. I felt like he was getting some good, pregnant pussy. As his body grew more excited, mine grew more lifeless. He never noticed.

My mind shifted to our heart-wrenching goodbye at the airport in Chicago. I remembered how passionate and sincere it was. As hard as walking away from him was that day, my heart's resolve never wavered. Now, with each thrust, he thought he was getting closer to the place in my heart where he was before. With each breath I felt on my neck, squeeze of my waist, each gush of semen I felt spew from him, I became sure that place did not exist anymore.

"Do you feel that?" His voice was excited but a lot more subdued.

"Feel what?" I wasn't even curious about what he was feeling.

"I can feel her heart beating."

DeMann's penis was still inside of me, and he could feel Sarah's presence. My heart began racing as I realized what was happening.

Spirits are so porous. They can be penetrated so easily. Mine was the epitome of that. I had let so many things penetrate my spirit that should have been blocked. The overbearing grip of DeMann's selfish spirit had held me down far too long. Sarah's spirit hadn't even had the chance to breathe yet. I couldn't subject her to that. He was her father and deserved to play a role, but I be damned if I let him sell her the same bullshit he sold me for so long. He would have to earn her love. I jumped up to prevent him from stealing anymore of her presence.

"What's wrong?" He actually sounded concerned.

"Nothing. I didn't want you to hurt her." My response came without thought, but I meant it in a way that I knew he couldn't comprehend.

"Girl, you trippin'." He laughed as he crawled out the opposite side of the bed. "If you wasn't worried about me hurting her while we were fucking, why you so worried about her getting hurt with me just laying in it?" He became flustered.

"DeMann…" At a loss of words, I paused. He interrupted me before I could continue.

"I done bought this big ass house and you in hea' tightening up yo' legs like you don't wanna give me no pussy? Girl, you 'bout to be my wife, and that is my baby in 'dere." He pointed at my stomach. "If we gon' be a family, then y'all gonna hav'ta get used to me."

His accent aggravated me again. In his abundance of ignorance, he was absolutely right. *IF* we were going to be a family, Sarah and I both would have to get used to his selfish ways. She would be taken for granted. She would be brushed off, just like I would. She would have to learn to tuck her real feelings and emotions away, just like I did. She would suffer the pain of all those actions, just like I did and would. Without thought, I got up, walked into the closet, and put my clothes back on.

"Girl, what are you doing?" DeMann walked over to the closet slightly concerned.

"DeMann, you need to take me home." I didn't say it with nearly the emphasis I should have. My heart was reluctant of conflict.

"I've already done that. Home is where your ass is at right now." He was a mixture of concern, frustration, and aggravation.

"DeMann, I think we're moving too fast. So much stuff has happened and so much has changed. We need to take our time and make sure this is what we want to do." I spoke softly, but I looked him directly in the eyes as I made that statement.

Even though my fearful heart toned down my words, my eyes represented the conviction of the place deep within me where those words originated. I saw his eyes widen as he realized my challenge. He chuckled to himself lightly, then turned around and began walking back to the bed.

"We ain't going nowhere tonight! Chaia, you need to stop trippin' and come lay down."

He didn't even have the decency to face me as he issued that directive. I felt so disrespected that my eyes began to water. Conviction and resolve stiffened every muscle in my body.

It's time to go! Ms. Machaia James, the conqueror, was spoke to me for the first time. *It's time to get your shit and get the hell away from here.*

I walked out of the closet into the bedroom. DeMann had turned the lights off and was in bed. *He can't have gone to sleep that fast.* I assumed he was lying with his back turned, ignoring me. He assumed he would get his way.

"Nigga, I asked you to take me home. Now you gonna just lay your ass down like I ain't said ONE MOTHERFUCKIN' WORD!" Ms. James' swagger and attitude were at full throttle. My voice was loud and forceful.

DeMann turned around in the bed. There was just enough light coming from the closet that I could see the stunned look on his face. He'd never heard me go off on him that way. It was long overdue.

"Who in the hell do you think you're talking to like that?" He turned the light on and rose up on his elbow. His face was confused and scared.

"Obviously, nobody 'cause you ain't heard shit I said! You don't give a damn about what I think or say. All you care about is your damn self. You…"

Ms. James was kicking ass and taking names. DeMann laid motionless for a few seconds. That was a few seconds too long. Ms. James didn't have time for any games. There was a lifetime worth of mess she had to clean up. She was off to a wonderful start.

I gathered my things and walked out the front door. My friend Stacey lived about a thirty-minute walk from his house. So I started my march. I breathed in the crisp air and enjoyed the beautiful homes. The lights seemed much prettier to me now. With each step, I felt more energized, freer, and more determined to never turn around.

DeMann pulled up slowly as I walked down the sidewalk. He rolled down the passenger window and called my name.

"Chaia, get in the truck! You gonna get sick out hea' in this weather!" Humbleness and genuine concern were in his voice.

"DeMann, I'm going home!" I wasn't exactly sure what I was referring to, but I knew it was more than my grandparents' house.

"I know, baby! Just let me take you there safely. We got the baby to think about."

I stopped, turned, and stared at him from the sidewalk where I was standing. As mad as I was, I didn't want to catch a cold and risk making my baby sick. After a few seconds of the meanest 'nigga don't try me no more' stare I could muster up, I got in the truck.

"Are you cold?" He turned up the heat. He made sure my seatbelt was fastened and that I had plenty of leg room.

I see your ass ain't lying down like a damn knot on a log no more. The attention did little to curb Ms. James' attitude. I sat still and kept quiet as he drove. The silence was awkward, peaceful, and necessary.

We rode in silence until he pulled in front of my grandparents' home and shut the truck off.

"Chaia, if this is gonna work, you can't be running to your grandmama's house every time we have a disagreement."

Ms. James stood dead center of the battlefield with her sword out ready to hack a bitch in half.

"DeMann, I don't want to marry you." I let my cold eyes relay how much I meant those words. I saw his spirit buckle.

"Chaia, you just need to cool off. We'll talk tomorrow."

"DeMann, I've already cooled off. I've already thought about it, and there is nothing between you and me. I hope you want to be a part of your daughter's life, but you and I will not be together." Ms. James did not let up.

DeMann's eyes started to tear and I saw his bottom lip tremble.

"I bet this is about that nigga in the Range Rover. As soon as a nigga throw some damn money in your face, your nose is wide open. I bet you up there fuckin' that nigga?"

Any sympathy his pain gathered from me, his ignorance quickly dispelled. He knew that Lesley and Sandra were together. He tried desperately to hurt me. He didn't realize I already was.

"DeMann, this is not about any other guy. I'm not dating anyone. I'm not having sex either. I mean damn! I'm seven months pregnant. What kind of chick do you think I am?" My tone was calm, cool, and collected. "We have a lot more to think about than just ourselves now, DeMann." I rubbed my belly just in case his emotions didn't allow him to comprehend.

"And taking my daughter away from her daddy is what's best for Sarah?" He added a bit of sarcasm to his tone. He thought he finally had a valid point.

"First of all, I'm not taking her away from you. You will always be her father. I'm just not going to be your wife. If our child can't grow up in a happy home, that's not the best for her."

"So, you saying you won't be happy in that house I bought?" He rolled up his lips to suggest that he knew better than me saying I couldn't.

"DeMann, it's never been about the things you buy. What's my biggest problem with our relationship? What is my biggest problem with you? What do I want most for myself out of life? Tell me." I paused and looked at him for a few seconds. Silence. "Exactly! You never cared enough about me to find out. Your idea of happiness is just that; YOUR idea. It has nothing to do with mine. I have to find my own happiness, and that's what I intend to do."

I reached over and grabbed his hand. Anger and remorse were splitting him down to his very core. His anger was pulling him back. His remorse pushed him forward, frantically trying to rectify itself. He made no attempt to embrace my hand. His eyes yearned for another chance.

As I exited the truck, I heard him gasp. I turned around to face him. He couldn't speak. His eyes yelled all the words anyway, but his lips never parted.

"Goodbye, DeMann." I granted him a warm smile and a loving stare. Then shut the door behind me.

There was no desire for a last kiss or anything like the airport episode. *What's done is done. It really is over.* I had to gasp myself.

*****

"Well, baby?" My grandmother was waiting for me to tell her about DeMann's proposal. "DeMann is a nice young man. I'm happy for you, baby. I want y'all to–"

"Grandma, I told him no!" I cut her off before she started rambling. Disappointment scarred her face almost immediately.

"No? Baby, are you sure?" She slowed down her words and asked the question more to herself.

"Grandma, he doesn't love me the way I deserve to be loved, and if I stay with him, I will be miserable for the rest of my life. Is that what you want for me?" I tilted my head and stared at her.

Comfort has to be balanced with conviction. Without conviction, everything and anything can seem comfortable. My mind and spirit dove into DeMann's pipe dreams headfirst, but the convictions of my heart would not let me fall for the okie doke. What I thought was comfort was not even close to comfortable. It was just plain old settling.

For the rest of the weekend, I battled with my grandparents, DeMann, and myself trying to perfect a balancing act.

Something about Sunday morning greeted me with warmth and dare I say, comfort. DeMann agreed to take me to the airport. I knew he wanted one last ditch effort to persuade me to stay. Our conversations over the weekend had ranged from sharing shallow laughs as we joked about being 'just friends' and Sarah's future to him hanging up the phone in my face because those laughs weren't enough to keep me from 'ruining his life'. Even now, he's still all about himself. Despite DeMann's selfish efforts and despite my grandmother's condescending nature, I had the strangest feeling that something special would happen.

"You ready to go?" DeMann stood in the doorway of my bedroom.

"Yeah, I did all my packing last night. I just need to put away my make-up bag."

"Damn, you packed last night. You can't wait to get away from here, huh?" He chuckled lightly as he helped me. By the way he snatched my bag, I knew the thought of me being anxious to leave him was far from humorous.

Nine times out of ten, subliminal messages are not nearly as subliminal as people think they are. The notion of an unnoticeable message doesn't make sense to me. The goal of any message is to be received. Subliminal or not, I received all the messages DeMann was sending me. 'I miss you. I want you back. I love you.' He sent those messages with all the shallow laughs and fake politeness. He was still hoping they would win me over. Those expressions were only surface level, though. I knew deep down underneath he was the same selfish nigga that ran me off in the first place.

Both of my grandparents were emotional. They didn't take my move seriously, until then. I knew they felt like they were losing me, but that was the furthest thing from the truth. I was finding myself.

I said my goodbyes, promised to call, turned, and confidently walked out the door. As I passed through the doorway, I glanced over at DeMann. *Bring yo' ass, nigga.* He received that subliminal message with no problem.

"Sandra gon' be there to pick you up?" DeMann tried to ask the question in a polite, calm manner. His noticeably tight grip on the steering wheel hinted about his real emotional state.

"Yeah." That's all I said. I could tell he was hoping for a little more dialogue, but I thought quiet thoughts were much safer.

He tried to maintain his composure for a few minutes by making small talk and asking questions about the things I had to do when I got back. Each time, I gave short answers. I watched his emotions boil inside of him.

As tight as he was gripping that steering wheel, I thought he was going to rip it out of the console at any moment. He began shifting in his seat more and more. All the while, his toned down conversation was his best effort to mask his anger. His shallow questions continued. My empty responses persisted, until finally they had irked his last nerve.

"You really just gonna sit there and act like this ain't shit to you?" He released his death grip on the steering wheel. I knew he was finally ready to let his words do the talking. He tried to keep his tone under control.

"At this point, DeMann, it really doesn't matter how you see it, or I see it. It is what it is." I took my time. I was amazed at how much I sounded like him.

"Are you fucking mocking me?" His calm flew out of the window. "I'm in this motherfucker hurtin', and yo' ass over dere making goddamn jokes!"

DeMann ranted and raved for damn near ever. He cursed me for being selfish. He criticized me for not considering him. He scorned me for not holding on to our love. He finished his rampage and faced the road as he drove. The finality of the moment became undeniable as we rode in hurtful silence. I watched him the whole time. I wasn't afraid of eye contact. I was in absolute awe of him. I was speechless. He said everything he wanted to say. At the end of it all, he didn't say anything. The war was over. I won.

"DeMann…" I paused and waited for him to gather enough courage to face me. It took a few minutes and me calling his name twice more before he did. "Despite what you think, I love you. I always have and always will. I wanted you to love me back so bad–"

He interrupted my statement. "Chaia, I do love you!" He tried to return to the polite tone.

I stretched my eyes and leaned my head to the side to get his attention.

"There's a whole lot that both of us need to learn about love. You need to learn that love is respectful, love has priorities, and love is never selfish…"

He interrupted me again. "Chaia, that's bullshit! You know I love you. I ain't never disrespected you, put my hands on you, or nothing. I put everything to the side and got our family a nice home to live in. That shows you right there what my priority is. After all the stuff I done bought you, I know you ain't calling me selfish!" His tone was getting the best of him.

168

Before he interrupted me, I was getting ready to add that love is not shallow and that it can't survive off of empty words and promises. I decided to save my breath with those two. He clearly wasn't ready for that yet.

"DeMann, how the hell can you say you respect me when you were running around town fucking all those trifling-ass bitches behind my back? Have you ever even thought about how fucking stupid that makes me feel! That hoe you and Rodney had up in the club was the same bitch you brought home." My voice buckled as those words escaped. "And don't even try to act like you weren't fucking her the whole time!" My emotions and tone were starting to get the best of me, as well.

"See, you letting these hating-ass bitches 'round here put that bullshit in your head."

"Naw, nigga! I ain't talking 'bout what somebody told me. I'm talking about what I've seen with my own eyes!"

He knew there was a strong possibility I busted him before. Guilt forced his eyes to come clean.

"As far as your family being your priority, you showed me where we stood with you that day. When I was battling with myself about going along with your decision to kill our baby, you left me alone to go through it by myself. And for what? So you could lay up in the backroom with Rodney and stick your face and dick in some dirty-ass ghetto hoe's pussy! What was your priority then, nigga? Was I your priority when you went out, did that kinda shit, then came home to stick your dirty-ass dick in my mouth?"

My emotions had overwhelmed both of us. Both of our eyes flooded. It was the first time I forced him to see the pain he caused me. He didn't say anything. I took a moment to catch my breath and gather my emotions.

"DeMann, I don't care what you buy. You have a selfish heart. You feel you have the power and authority to treat me any kind of way you want. When I trusted you with my heart, you hurt me. I can't trust you with it anymore." I managed to tone my anger down to a wounded resolve.

Crystal clear hi-definition doesn't automatically make a picture beautiful. Sometimes it allows you to see the ugliest of details. There was a time in my life when I thought DeMann was the most beautiful person in the world. Looking at our relationship through fuzzy smoke screens distorted my perception. There was no going back.

"I have to go." I was talking about more than just catching my flight. I got out of the car, stepped up on the curb, and waited for DeMann to get my suitcase.

When he came from the rear of the truck, finality was written all over him. He openly wept. His shoulders hung so low that he was almost dragging the luggage. His face balled up in a way I had never seen. He kept yelling my name at the top of his lungs. People turned around to see what the commotion was all about.

DeMann's outburst was his best and final attempt to distort my perception of him, our relationship, and our future. I had all of the information I needed to fully evaluate the situation. I studied the origins of his pain. Those origins were still selfish in nature. I dissected the intentions of his outbreak. They were selfish, as well. I critically evaluated all the information provided by the details. I was searching for any valid, pertinent, or necessary affect I should allow his outburst to have on my decision to leave. There were none to be found.

One thing I did find lurking between the details was a heartfelt sympathy for him. This was not totally his fault. I was also to blame for the dynamics of our relationship. I helped to create them in the first place. I walked up to him, caressed the side of his face, and tried to soothe his pain with my empathy. That was all I had to offer.

"DeMann, I want you to know that I love you. I'm not mad at you. If I was mad at you for not loving me the way I wanted and needed to be loved, then I would have to be mad at myself for the same reason." My heart was cold and numb. I hoped the way I touched and looked at him was enough to relay my sincerity.

He tried his best, but his cries mutilated every word he tried to speak. I stood there, continued caressing him, stared into his eyes, and waited for his spirit to stand up and face mine. It never did.

"Goodbye, DeMann." I hugged him, kissed his cheek, and turned to walk away.

"GOTDAMN YOU, CHAIA!" He gathered himself enough to yell at me as I walked off.

He was hurt. He didn't know what to do with his pain. It was devouring him, eating him alive. I didn't even turn around to physically see the damage the storm was causing.

I took a deep breath and then turned around to look out the door of the terminal. DeMann was still there. He didn't notice me looking because he was arguing with the patrol officer that was trying to get him to move his truck. I turned back around quickly before he saw me looking. I knew that would only prompt another outbreak. He would have thought I was second guessing myself.

With each step forward I felt my future embracing me. I let that beautiful energy navigate me through the terminal. It commanded all my thoughts, hopes, and dreams. My new foundation was a beautiful rock named me. I was my future. I was embracing myself.

Once on the plane, I struggled to put my bags in the overhead.

"Ma'am, can I help you with that?" An older white gentleman seated in the window seat offered assistance.

"Yes, please. Thank you so much." I smiled hard. I knew it wasn't that big, but it seemed so symbolic of how things would be working for me now.

I looked at the seat number and noticed I was one row off. I shifted my focus to the black gentleman seated there. Before I could get a chance to notice him, his spirit blindsided mine in a very undeniable way.

"Would you prefer the window or aisle?" His warm smile penetrated way beyond my comfort level.

"I'll keep the aisle. Lord knows I could use the extra space." I gripped my seven-month stomach and sighed.

"Awww, I know you ain't complaining about a blessing like that. I bet you would carry it three more times if that's what you had to do for that baby." He continued smiling at me, driving himself deeper into my core.

"Let me make it through the first nine months first! I might not make it through that."

We laughed, but the windows of our souls pierced one another's in such a way that he knew he was absolutely right about the kind of woman I am.

The effects of his introduction were growing pale in comparison to the connection I felt forming now. We made small talk. Our conversation was just formality. It was the outer cover of the book. The pages within were being transcribed as we spoke. He walked into my life and read my mind.

He heard all the thoughts my heart whispered only to me. He sent a little piece of his spirit into mine and evaluated everything written there. His spirit agreed with everything mine had to say.

We continued our small talk for about half the flight, before I started drifting to sleep. He motioned for me to lean on his shoulder. Before I could think about me not knowing him from Sam, I was already leaning.

I don't even know his name.

CHAPTER 15
EVAN MILLS

"Welcome to Orlando." The attendant at the terminal gate greeted each passenger as they went by.

She didn't know me. She didn't know I was home. Orlando knew me and I knew Orlando. Comfortably, I navigated myself through Orlando International Airport. From the gate, to the monorail, to the terminal, I moved with ease. I didn't have to think about what I was doing or where I was going. Most importantly, I didn't have to think about where I had just come from. There were no noticeable outward signs of the troubled spirit I was hiding from the world.

"What's up, boy?" My cousin, Dre, came to the airport to pick me up. "Man, I know you and Greg up there tearin' them hoes up!" He looked at me with an expectant look on his face. He was waiting for me to tell him something amazing.

"Man, I'm just up there working hard." That was the best I could do.

"Whatever, dude. I know better than that. When Greg came home, he told us about them hoes up in Chicago. What's the real deal, fool?" His look turned from amazed to downright ignorant. At least in my eyes it did.

Millimeters or miles, the measure of a man is totally related to the scale he allows himself to be measured by. All Dre knew was millimeters. Even in their infinite minuteness, they excited him. He had no clue what a mile was. No clue at all. I didn't fully understand myself, but I did know it was a hell of a lot more than a goddamn millimeter. I had already spent too much of my life measuring myself by that inferior scale. There was so much more about me that I could be proud of aside from how many women I fucked.

"Boy, you crazy. What have you been up to, besides chasin' pussy?" I didn't think about my statement and I wasn't trying to make a point. My mind had naturally shifted from where his was.

"Nigga, you trippin'. What else is there?" He made that statement with an exaggerated amount of attitude.

Translated, he was a millimeter. He was not a centimeter, inch, yard, or any other intermediate unit. He couldn't even be considered a fraction of a mile. He was simply a millimeter. I can't say that he was happy to be one, he just didn't know what a mile was. His life's journey hadn't taken him that far. Mine had. Millimeters did not interest me to any degree at all. I stared out of the window as he drove and let the conversation fade to black. My mind had bigger scales to master.

You got some damn nerve. Evan Clifford Miles was too much of a man to let me get away with that hypocrisy without being heard from.

Conviction is a persistent motherfucker. The real me was not happy with my actions not in Chicago and not here either. Conviction had followed me home. I felt its presence on the plane, but I ignored it and focused on the clouds. Then, Dre's shallowness forced me to bear witness to the painful image I had of myself. No matter what I did to run away, hide, ignore, play down, or deny it, conviction persisted. This would not be a comfortable visit home. It would not be a comfortable return to Chicago. Nothing would ever be comfortable until I rid myself of that guilt.

"I'm fucking a good man's wife." The wimp in me uttered his horrible confession. The words actually stumbled from my lips.

"You alright, boy?" Dre's voice had a believable amount of sincerity.

He was trying to show me he had some depth, but it was too late. The damage was already done. He had already shown me exactly what I didn't want to see—myself.

"Yeah. I was just thinking out loud." I couldn't even turn around and look at him.

My eyes watered as I realized that not facing Dre wouldn't stop me from facing myself. Conviction was starting to seize total control. Dre made a couple more attempts to talk before he figured out I was ignoring him. He finally shut up and left me to my thoughts. I wished he wouldn't have done that.

"Call me later if you trying to do something." We reached Meadowbrook Middle School where my mom taught. Dre waited for me to get out of the car.

"Will do! Thanks for picking me up, man." I tried to act as if I was my normal self.

He smiled, dapped me up, and drove off. He didn't have a clue what I was hiding.

As I walked towards my mother's classroom, I tried to minimize any indication of the turmoil. I dried my eyes, straightened my posture and checked my tone. I reached deep inside, pushed back my burdens, and lifted my spirits. As I approached the room door, I put the final touches on my facade.

"Hey, baby! Come in for a second. I want to introduce you to my class." Her smile was almost too broad to get through the doorway. She looked at me for a second then hugged me tightly. "Class, this is my son I was telling you about, Dr. Evan Miles." She was so proud. "Do you have anything you want to say to them, baby?"

I smiled back at her, almost forgetting what I was feeling just minutes ago. I glanced over at her often as I gave her class my usual spiel about taking their future seriously. She loved it and I loved that she loved it. The presence of true love is the most healing power on earth.

"I have a few kids coming for tutoring at four, so come back at about five-thirty." She held my hand as she walked me to the end of the hallway where her class was.

"No problem. I'm going to make a couple of stops, then I'll just be at the house."

She stared at me until I met her eyes, then smiled and paused. "Baby, whatever it is that's bothering you, you'll get through it. I love you." She said it with so much passion and conviction that I knew it was useless to deny I was troubled.

How do mothers know? She looked past the fake peace I presented her with and saw all of the turmoil. Tears of joy and pain clouded my vision as I drove out of the parking lot.

I spent about three hours visiting my old job and a couple of my homeboys. I brushed off the pain and covered it up with the same face I'd presented my mom. They were all so happy to see me. Their smiles, their hugs, all of their excited questions about my residency, all made me feel . . . normal.

R u home?

When the text came through, I was taken back as I looked at the number.

I'd deleted Erica's name and number before I left Orange County. I had been so consumed by my dilemma with Celeste and focusing on my residency that I hadn't thought of her in months. Truthfully, the thought of her was refreshingly easy.

Yeah, made it in this morning.

U wasn't even gonna call. Do u hate me that much?

Wasn't bout u. Had to fix me.

I want to c u. Let's do dinner.

Can't. Gotta pick up mom in 45 min.

Later?

Me and mom gonna spend time. Just call me. U got the #.

Yeah, I got your # ☺!

She's chasing me, anxious to see me, I thought. After all she'd put me through, to have her chasing me made me feel powerful. I continued driving towards my mother's school. The wind felt great as it blew through the finger-length locs. I started growing them the day I left Orlando. I drove for about five minutes then sent her one more text.

Shandon gonna let u out? I hoped she would pick up on the sarcasm.

Who? ☺. Her response came back super-fast. It seemed like she sent it before I had even asked the question. She was hoping to be able to point that out.

My thoughts of Erica back in Chicago were all related to what was she doing with him—concerts, movies, weekend getaways, and lots of sex. I went from being tortured by them, to being jealous, to toleration, to honestly not even giving a damn. She had seen a weak version of me and I wanted to prove that person didn't exist anymore. I didn't want to get back together with her. But, I definitely wanted to find time to show her the new and improved Evan Miles. I flexed my muscles in the rear view mirror as I drove. Then, I burst out laughing. Partly because I realized how silly I was behaving, partly because I felt good about getting over my heartbreak, and partly to keep from crying about the conflicts and convictions about what I was doing to Dr. Carson.

"I'm glad to see that you're feeling a little better." My mom heard me coming up the hall and peeked out to find me acting silly as I walked towards her room.

"It was good seeing some of my old friends and coworkers."

"You must have talked to Erica." She didn't even wait to see my reaction before she turned around.

How in the world do mothers know so much? I thought.

"Here, help me carry this crate to the car. I have to grade all of these papers over the holiday weekend."

"Deucie, I don't like it when you put so much stress on yourself like that. I'll be glad when I'm done, so you can stop working."

"Baby, if we don't teach our kids, who will?" She loved what she did. Teaching was her passion.

"I still don't like it."

"Me either baby. But, what can you do when a job has to be done? Enough about that. So, who all did you go see besides Erica?"

"I didn't go see her. We just sent a couple of messages back and forth."

"Baby, that ain't nothing new. You and that girl been sending messages back and forth for a while now."

"No, I meant through our phone."

"I knew what you meant, but that isn't the only way to send somebody a message." She looked at me and smiled.

My mother and I spent the rest of the afternoon together. She held my hand as we walked through the grocery store and rubbed my back as I loaded the groceries in the car. She smiled the widest of smiles every time our eyes met. She was happy to have her baby home and I was glad to be there. Her spirit crept into mine and began soothing all the troubled areas. I love her so much.

What'cha doing? Erica's anxiousness was present in her texts.

Me and mom just done eating. Just chillin'. Wuzup?

Cum outside ;))).

The mere thought of us playing those word games again used to excite me beyond measure. Now that we were, I didn't feel like I thought I would.

As I walked outside, I saw her smiling through the windshield of a brand new Lexus. I knew it was hers. It was white with white leather interior—just like the one I promised to buy her one day. A totally different viewpoint on the origins of her anxiousness slapped my dumb ass in the face. She just wanted to make sure I saw her. The thought occurred to me that to the same degree I wanted to show her I had gotten over her, she wanted to show me I could still kiss her ass anyway. The thought of her playing games with me was more of a nuisance than anything painful. The power behind the games was gone. The emotions were gone.

"Oh my God, I love your hair!" Erica hadn't seen me since I started growing locs. "It's so good to see you."

She nervously ran her fingers through my hair. I could tell she was waiting for a hug so I initiated the contact.

She's never squeezed me this tight. "I missed you, too," I responded to what she was really saying.

"I was coming back from Yolanda's house and decided to swing by and say hello in person. I hope you don't mind." Her speech was rushed and anxious.

"It's cool. It's good to see you." Without the emotions, my words seemed matter-of-fact. I thought how much I sounded like she did before I left. I wondered if she noticed.

"I can't tell. You acting like you didn't even wanna see me." Yep, she did. "You wanna go to Goff's?" It seemed my hesitancy made her try harder. She wanted to go to our favorite ice cream shop. *She's trying to be sentimental.* I couldn't help but smile.

"Sounds good. Let me go let my mom know."

I went in the house and told my mother where I was headed. Her answer was unspoken, but my own questions bombarded me as I rushed out of the house. *What am I doing? Am I falling prey to her once again?* They electrocuted my body as I sat in her new car. *Where did she get this kind of money?*

As we drove to the ice cream shop and ordered, we made small talk about what we've been up to. The questions continued their onslaught. They oozed in between the lines of my monotone words. As we pulled back into my mom's driveway, another legion of questions was forming when I noticed something funny. When I noticed my mom looking out the window to see who was pulling in, the nature of my questions changed. While we rode to Orange Blossom Trail and back, I never once questioned myself. All my questions were about her. I questioned who she was with, what she did, her happiness, and her motives. Never once, away from my mom's presence, did I question myself. The presence of true love makes you question yourself.

I looked over at Erica. I focused my thoughts, stared squarely into her eyes, and saw her lack of love. Once I realized what I saw, there was only one thing left to be said.

"I'm not supposed to be here." My truth had a swagger that was undeniable.

"What do you mean?" That was the last thing she expected to hear.

"I'm not supposed to be here with you."

"Damn! We can't even be friends?" She balled her face up. She was out of her comfort zone.

"I'm not saying that. It just can't be anything serious between us." Listening to myself, I wondered if the lack of emotion is what used to cause her to sound so matter-of-fact.

"Evan, I'm not trying to get back with you. I'm still dating Shandon."

Eight-and-a-half months prior that remark would have been a devastating. Emotions lived then. They were gone now.

"Then why were you so anxious to see me and spend time with me?" That question came from the most instinctual place of my heart. I asked it with so much fervor that she didn't try to deny her anxiousness.

"You want the truth?" She looked at me with a seductive smirk.

I looked at her with a face that had to have screamed 'what the fuck are you talking about?' but she must have mistaken the look for curiosity. She leaned back, arched her butt up, and slid her skirt up to her waist.

"I miss the way you used to eat my stuff."

Familiar is very comfortable. The faded jean skirt wasn't new. The tight white tank top wasn't new. The muscle definition in her arms and legs looked as good as ever, but they weren't new either. She still sprayed her skin with the only bottle of Angel ever made. Even the smell of Aqua-Marine lotion in the pink bottle that only Walmart sold wasn't new. The way her eyes seemed to get browner in the dark. The way her smile made her intentions seem so innocent. They were all familiar. They seemed just like old times. But, this didn't feel like anything that had ever been present between us.

My reaction was delayed. I stared at her for a few moments. My hesitation must have given her the impression that I was contemplating obliging her wish. And I was. She spread her legs as wide as the driver's door and center console would allow and I saw that she wasn't wearing any panties. My eyes expressed the instinctual excitement of my desires and both sets of her lips formed an all too familiar smirk. Both sets of them. But the sting of conviction persisted. What she thought was a moment of weakness was actually a moment of reckoning.

I can't love a woman who doesn't make me question myself. Evan Clifford Miles issued a grown man decree. Without love, I would never question myself. Without questions, I'd never challenge myself. If I never challenge myself, I will never grow.

"Why do you want to do this?" I looked her in her eyes as I asked the question. I was questioning myself twice as much as I was questioning her.

She was speechless. She slowly gyrated her hips in an unrewarded attempt to distract me. It was painfully obvious that she didn't have anything meaningful to say. She stared back at me for a few minutes and then sat up.

"Erica, I don't know what I feel for you, but I know it's not this." That was the most honest thing I could say.

Conviction is such a flexible guardian. My mind was captivated once again by her charms, but my conviction would be having none of that. It backed away from my emotions and desires and focused its power on physical manifestations. My penis fell limp and my eyes wandered from her. There would be nothing pleasurable.

"I'm not supposed to be here." I began fumbling at the door, trying to find the door handle. She knew I meant it.

It took just a few seconds for her emotional state to race from shocked, to angry, to sad. The lights from the console illuminated her face just enough for me to see her expressions. I saw each emotion form. They all came and went before she could even speak.

"Do you really hate me?" She finally found a question worth asking.

I turned from the door and faced her. She was leaning forward, her forearms draped over the steering wheel with her head bowed on them. She wasn't even looking at me. How could she ask me a question like that and not even look at me?

"I don't hate you, I just love me. And I'm not supposed to be here." She still didn't look up.

My heart was satisfied that I heard myself, but my eyes were disappointed because they didn't get a chance to tell her what they had to say. She wasn't allowing me the opportunity to properly say goodbye. Nevertheless, it had to be said. I said it in a way that she didn't even have to look up to notice.

Dong!

When the door chime rang and the lights came on, I was expecting them and was still startled. She jerked her head up and looked at me.

"Bye, Erica." My body easily followed my heart and soul out the door.

Even though she looked up, she still didn't speak. In a funny kind of way, I respected that. *At least she wasn't pretending.*

She turned on her headlights, watched me walk to the door, and waited for me to go inside. I always used to do that when I took her home. She never did it for me in return until now. I smiled, as I walked inside. *That's her way of saying I'll miss you.* It was nice to receive those sentiments. *I'll miss you, too.* My heart and soul collaborated for one final decree. My body mailed it out for them with a final wave and smile before I closed the door.

"You alright, baby?" My mom was sitting in the den. She had fallen asleep watching the evening news and grading papers. She asked that question as if she already knew I had just had a serious event in my life. I did and she knew it. She was barely even awake and she could tell.

"I'm fine. I was just outside talking with Erica for a bit." She opened her eyes and stared at me. She was evaluating whether or not I was telling her the truth about being ok. Our eyes locked just long enough for her to get the reassurance she needed.

"I'm glad you two got the chance to talk, baby." Her eyes stayed fixed on mine.

"I'm glad, too." I couldn't help but let out a deep breath and a smile. The release felt good to both of us and we both chuckled. Both of our spirits were satisfied with the results of my examination.

"Good night, baby. I'm so glad you're home." She reached up, embraced the side of my face, and smiled.

Just like that, the conversation was over. She was happy to see me starting to love myself more.

It was a beautiful Thanksgiving. "I'm so glad you're home, baby." She embraced my face, looked me in the eyes, and said that so many times over the weekend that I lost count. I knew she meant more than just physically being here. She was happy about where I was in life. Her happiness gave me reassurance that I was heading in the right direction. While, I spent the weekend stuffing my face with good food, my spirit ate up the love she lavished me with.

I reread a brief text conversation I had with Dr. Carson earlier.

DC: What time does your flight arrive tomorrow?
Me: Noon. Y? Do u need me to come in?
DC: No. I'm going to pick you up. We need to talk.
Me: Smthn up? U need me to call?
DC: No. We will talk tomorrow. Delta, right?
Me: Yes.

I was totally creeped out. The abbreviations and slang he used to type text messages had designed mine. Why was he so formal now? What does he want to talk to me about so badly that he has to pick me up? I knew that ignoring Celeste would make her mad. *What has she told him?* Thoughts ran rampant in my mind. Guilt and shame had been sent to help me finish packing, and escort me back home. I fell asleep with them both bearing down on me. The next day, they would follow me back.

"Baby, I'm so proud of you." It was a far cry from the last time I left her to go to Chicago. She knew I was ok. I knew I wasn't, but, looking at her, I knew I would be.

She stood in the driveway smiling at me.

"E, we better hit it if you gonna make that flight." Dre had come to drive me back to the airport so that my mom wouldn't have to miss church.

"Yeah, you right." I turned to give my mom a hug. "I love you and I'll call you later to let you know I made it."

"Ok, baby. It was so good having you home." She didn't give me the safety lecture or her normal caution about eating right. She didn't even give me her 'I'll miss you' look. She really did feel good about where I was. My confidence in myself multiplied ten times as I backed away and got in the car.

Our ride to the airport was marred with Dre's explanation on how I messed up by not trying to have sex with his girlfriend's cousin over the weekend.

182

He really didn't get it. Just as before, he went into his breakdown of what I should've done according to his minute reasoning. And, just as before, I tuned him out, focused out the window, and thought about my own journey, one mile at a time.

"Alright man, but I'm tellin' you. You slipped on that one, homeboy." He reached over to dap my hand as I gathered my things to get out of the car.

"Yeah, I hear ya." That statement was the best I could do to entertain his conversation. Me not looking at him was my attempt to let him know that he really didn't have a clue. I knew he wouldn't get it, but part of me just wanted to make him think about it. I told him bye and walked off without even trying to explain.

I checked my bag at the curbside and rushed into the airport. The line at the security checkpoint was backed up, from all the holiday travelers. I knew I cut it extremely close as I arrived at my gate.

"But, it's right there. The plane hasn't left. It's still docked at the terminal and everything. All you have to do is let me board." I spoke in the most polite voice possible under the circumstances.

"Sir, I'm sorry, but passengers have already boarded. I can place you on standby for the next flight, but I'll warn you, it's oversold as well."

"How long before that flight?"

"It departs at 1:30 in the afternoon."

"I have to wait in this airport for five hours because y'all gave my seat to someone else?"

"The snow storm in Chicago has delayed flights. I apologize, but all the flights into the city are overbooked and the standby lists are full."

"So, if I can't get on the one-thirty flight, when is the next one after that?"

"Quarter after seven, but there's no guarantee that you could get on that one either."

"Ma'am, there has to be something better you can do." I kept my cool. I really couldn't blame her for my not making my flight. She must have appreciated that, seeing that she had been fussed at by the three passengers before me in line. She punched a couple of buttons and worked magic for me. She smiled and lowered her voice.

"Tell you what. I've confirmed you on a connector flight through Nashville. They have flights into Chicago almost every hour. I put you on flight 926 from Orlando to Nashville at 9:45 a.m. and confirmed a seat on flight 713 from Nashville to Chicago Midway at 3:15 p.m., arriving in Chicago at 4:45 p.m. You'll have a few hours layover in Nashville, but at least you have seat confirmation." She looked up at me and smiled.

"You are my hero!" I had to calm myself down. The thought of not having to sit in the airport for twelve hours was enough to make me want to scream. "How much do I owe for the switch?"

"You already paid it when you were nice to me."

As my plane flew hundreds of miles per hour over cities, fields, rivers, and mountains, my spirit soared at the same speed out of my past, over my struggles and into my future. I witnessed it all out of the view of my window, mile after mile after mile. By the time I landed in Nashville, I was so accustomed to the clouds that, mentally, I was still there. I walked around the airport smiling and staring at people so hard that I knew they must have thought I was high or something.

"Damn, now that's love." I mumbled to myself when I noticed a pregnant lady kissing her man goodbye outside at the curbside.

Even from upstairs, I could see the love she had for him in her expression. It was in the way she caressed his face and looked directly into his eyes. He seemed like a knucklehead. I could tell he was battling with himself over whether to cherish her embrace or keep up his tough guy routine. As she walked away from him, I witnessed his emotions explode. I couldn't tell if he was cursing her out or begging her to stay. She was conflicted herself. Even when he wasn't looking, she kept glancing back as if she wasn't really sure she wanted to leave.

DC: I'll be there.

Dr. Carson's reply to my text about my new arrival time had finally come through.

Guilt and shame hadn't gotten the hook up at the Orlando airport. They were a flight or two behind, but they had finally caught up to me. They quickly grasped me in a way that let me know that they would not be denied today.

Affairs of the heart are never uncomplicated. Clean cuts are still kind of jagged. Easy decisions are hard to make. Dead emotions find a way to keep breathing. I was just as stuck as the woman at curbside. I didn't want to go in either direction. The emotions that elevated my spirit to the clouds were quickly killed by the reality on the ground. Down here, the grass is just as green as it is from thirty-five thousand feet. The difference is that now I realize the real world exists beneath that dreamy layer of green. I wandered around the airport aimlessly for the rest of my layover, reading the departure lists. Subconsciously, I was looking for another destination. I wanted to go somewhere where I could breathe easier.

I boarded my plane and sat gazing out of the window. A plane pulled in to the terminal next to us and I could see people in its windows gazing just like me. Their faces looked just as torn as mine.

The noise from someone struggling with their bags startled me from my thoughts. I turned around and saw the pregnant woman from the curbside trying to get her bag in the overhead compartment. A guy in the row ahead of me helped her before I could get up. Her smile made him do it. She was intoxicating. She looked at the number on the rows and then stepped over to my row. I didn't help her, so the least I could do was offer her a choice of the seat.

"Would you prefer the window or the aisle?" My smile tried to tell her what an impression she was making.

"I'll keep the aisle. Lord knows I could use the extra space." She gripped her stomach and moaned.

"Aww, I know you ain't complaining about a blessing like that. I bet you would carry it three more times, if that's what you had to do for that baby." Instinctively, my remarks had a very 'non-surface level' purpose.

"Let me make it through the first nine months first! I might not make it through that." She looked over at me with a huge smile and warm eyes that suggested her comfort sitting next to me was more than just having the aisle seat.

Her smile told me that I nailed the very essence of who she was. Her spirit didn't even flinch. Neither did mine. They both dove head first into a very endearing encounter. Our laughs were instinctual and our connection was undeniable. When I noticed that she was falling asleep, I braced my arm, propped my shoulder up, and motioned for her to lean on me. Without any hesitation, she did.

I watched her drift off to sleep. She needed a shoulder to lean on and in a very short period of time, I was it. I didn't feel awkward, at all.

Something about this encounter seemed very natural. The peaceful look on her face, as she slept on my shoulder was all the reward I needed. *I'm doing the right thing.* Evan Clifford Miles was satisfied with my actions.

"You better wake up. We're about to land." I softly shook her.

She opened her eyes and smiled. "I was out like a rock." She slowly sat up.

Part of me wanted her to lie back on my shoulder.

"By the way, my name is Evan Miles. I didn't get a chance to introduce myself before you started snoring all loud in a brother's ear." My smile told her that I really didn't mind and we both laughed out loud.

"My name is Machaia James." She smiled and extended her hand.

My happy emotions were supposed to be eaten alive by the real world as soon as I touched down. Instead, my emotions joyfully expressed themselves as I helped Machaia off the plane. We enjoyed a pleasant conversation as we walked to baggage claim.

"Do you have someone picking you up?"

"Yeah. My girlfriend just sent me a text. She'll be pulling up out front for me shortly."

"Well, my ride is out front, too. I'll help you carry your bags out to the curbside."

"That's very nice of you. Thank you."

"My pleasure."

I've never had a problem defining my attraction to a woman. I wasn't trying to make a love connection with her; she was pregnant with another man's child. And I could tell by the way she was so torn at the Nashville airport that she still had feelings for the knucklehead. I respected that also. Yet, something was happening. For some reason, and by some method, our spirits made an impression on each other. I could tell it was mutual. I knew she had been through a lot today and the last thing I wanted to do was make her feel uncomfortable by being too pushy, so I decided not to ask for her information. I'd let her decide if she wanted to make a new friend.

"There she is over there." Machaia pointed to a beautiful black Mercedes. I pulled the luggage to the car and began loading her bags in the trunk. I was already thinking of non-pushy ways of asking for her number. She was taking entirely too long.

"Evan!"

Someone was yelling my name, from over my shoulder. Even with all of the noise in the terminal, I could make out her voice easily. I didn't have to turn around to confirm, but I did anyway. Celeste was standing there with a smug look on her face.

The formality in the text messages, the insistence on picking me up, all made perfect sense now. Celeste texted me from Dr. Carson's phone. She'd made sure I saw her. I had been ignoring her calls and avoiding her visits for over a month. I thought she would let the whole situation fade to black, but I was wrong. She had gotten her way.

The problem wasn't that I saw her. My feelings and convictions would direct me the same way they did when I decided not to deal with her anymore. The problem today was that Machaia saw her too. *What did this mess seem like to her?* That question was at the forefront of my mind.

"Hi, I'm Celeste." She stuck out her hand to shake Machaia's. Despite what her words said, the look on Celeste's face was anything but friendly.

"Hello, I'm Machaia. This is my friend Sandra. I met—"

"Sweetie, I pulled up the car when I saw you. We need to go. There's something important we need to do." She gave me an overly exaggerated smirk and looked over at Machaia.

As I finished putting her bags in the trunk, Machaia and her friend made funny faces at each other. The kind of faces girlfriends make at each other when they realize that a guy is full of shit. Before it had time to build up immunity to bullshit our connection had been infected by a virus.

Celeste walked back over to her car. She drove her Bentley. The flashiness coincided with her tight wool dress and knee-high boots. Her clothes, her car, and her attitude all demanded attention. Her intent was to be seen and her plan worked. And seated front and center, was a new woman with a special soul and a negative image of me. The vibe between Machaia and I was already dead. It was written all over her face.

"Well, it was nice meeting you." I tried to use my expression to say all the things that would've sounded trifling coming out of my mouth.

"It was nice meeting you, too." There was no longing in her eyes, no disappointment in her expression. She was blank. My attempts to reconnect had fallen on deaf ears and a hard heart. The look in her face screamed two words: *Negro, please.* I stood there for an awkward amount of time with an anxious demeanor. I was hoping that our pleasant encounter on the plane would trump Celeste showing up. I wanted her to want my contact information. She said nothing and continued staring back at me with a gorgeous poker face.

"Dude, you better get over there before your girl comes over here tripping."

Machaia's friend had just a little too much attitude for my comfort. Machaia and I glanced over at Celeste. She stood outside her driver's door yelling obscenities with her body language and stares.

I wanted to respond that she was not my girl and that we weren't together. I wanted to let Machaia know that there was nothing between us, but the way Celeste presented herself left no doubt that we were *something*. To deny it altogether would have made me seem like a player, a liar, or both. I had a strange desire to tell Machaia the truth. *She's your boss's wife and you are fucking her.* The brutally honest version of me whispered the truth in my ear so I could preview what it sounded like. This was definitely one of those situations when the truth was better off unspoken.

Time to move out soldier. The drill sergeant was taking charge. *About face!* The command was clear. It even made sense. I was supposed to turn around and walk away. She's pregnant and she still loves the knucklehead. Celeste had ruined any chance I had of changing that. Executing a clear command should have been easy, but it wasn't. I looked in her eyes one last time, looking for any reason not to leave. Nothing. I turned and walked away.

As Celeste pulled away from the terminal, Machaia's friend was still fumbling with all the junk in her trunk. I glanced over at Machaia. She was seated on the passenger side, staring back at me. Her eyes were screaming everything I was hoping they would have said just a few minutes ago. Sadly, it was too late. I had already accepted the fact that she was not for me.

Celeste drove for about ten minutes before I even spoke. Evan Miles was a man of few words and profound sentiment.

"Celeste, you know and I know that this has to stop. Why do you keep trying me like this?" She looked at me in a strangely familiar way.

It was the way she looked at me at her bar and the glance she gave me in the truck stop bathroom. It's the same one that sold me the pipe dream back in Atlanta. It was warm, inviting, and intoxicating. I had gotten so caught up in what her look was saying that I almost didn't notice its contrast to the words coming out of her mouth.

"'Cause this ain't over 'til I say it's over!" There was a significant degree of coldness in her voice. It seemed more orchestrated than angry, almost business-like. It was the kind of cold that let me know it was just the tip of a massive iceberg.

You're only as great as the things you stand for. Another one of Evan Miles' profound sentiments choked me. I actually had to cough it out of my lips. My champion had found a cause worth fighting for. The victory was a foregone conclusion. Celeste looked over at me with a confused look on her face.

"Well, *it* ain't an *it* unless I *let* it be." Those words charged out of my heart, ready for whatever battle lie waiting. My resolve met hers head on. I felt strong enough to move an iceberg.

She drove straight to Greg's house without saying anything else. I could feel part of her didn't want to give up on whatever it was she had planned. I felt that all over the tone of the quietness. Despite that, the ride felt like a victory lap around the world. *Doing the right thing is far more satisfying than giving in to a bad temptation.* I didn't cough that sentiment up, but it choked me just the same.

"I'll be seeing you around, baby." She flashed a confident smile as she watched me grab my bag out of the backseat. Her resolve conceded this battle, but vowed that the war was far from over.

"I look forward to seeing you around as well, Mrs. Carson." I over-formalized her name, staring courageously into her eyes to make sure she got my point.

At that moment, she saw me in a new light. She knew she was in for a dogfight. I got out of her car without pause. By the time I made it to the front door, the satisfying power of my decision ignited every muscle in my body. I felt confidence burning at every nerve ending.

I opened the door and walked forward into the foyer and into a new era in my relationship with Celeste.

"Greg!" He was draped over the edge of the couch, his body positioned in a lifeless posture. He slowly lifted his head.

"Damn, E. When you got back?" My heart's panic eased, he wasn't dead.

"Just now. What's up with you, man? I thought you were in New York." I walked over to get a closer look at him.

He was high. I saw it in his dazed eyes, even though I didn't smell weed. My fears escalated. I began eyeballing the area around him twice as hard as I had examined him. My mind ran through each detail, recalling each item's origin. My heart and spirit purposely lagged behind. Neither of the two wanted to see what my mind knew would be found.

A small metal canister lay just to the side of a small pouch of white powder. Its presence made it seem like the largest thing in the room.

The power of a hero exists only in the hearts of his fans. Despite Greg's state, I knew Super G would return. It was my charge to take care of his house until he got back. I cleaned Greg up and put him in bed. Then, I called his office and told his secretary to let the firm know he was sick. I cleaned up the table and living room. Through it all, I kept his canister with me. If he wanted it, he would have to ask me for it and answer my questions.

I took a hot shower, grabbed a bottle of wine off Greg's wine rack, and went back to my room. *Whew, bout time*, Evan Clifford Miles was relieved to be able to dump his armor on the floor. No more battles would be fought that night.

I tuned my satellite radio to the Smoove Grooves station and laid down to relax. Happy emotions were in charge. Tomorrow's battles would bring pain, but, tonight, my emotions decided to party like there was no tomorrow. Just before my complete submission to the will of the house, I noticed something wonderful. In the corner of the party, nestled amongst the emotion, was a beautiful question. It walked into the party cool as could be, on the coat tails of the happy emotions it evoked. *What's up with Machaia?*

CHAPTER 16
MACHAIA JAMES

"You better wake up. We're about to land." A warm feeling from deep inside of me burst its way to my surface and erupted into a smile so wide that I felt the inside of my cheeks showing.

"I was out like a rock." I gently pressed against his chest, as I slowly leaned up. *Damn, he must work out!* Ms. James yelled so loud, I thought he might have actually heard her. I had to grit my teeth together to keep the rest of her comments from blurting out.

"By the way, my name is Evan Miles. I never got a chance to introduce myself before you started snoring all loud in a brother's ear." His smile was beautifully honest. It told me right away that he was holding back some comments as well. I smiled back at him with that same level of truth.

"My name is Machaia James." I smiled and extended my hand to shake his. Our eyes locked.

Without me asking, he stood up, got our bags, and headed out the plane. Without hesitation or words, I followed his lead. In my mind, we were actually holding hands. We walked together towards the baggage claim. Our conversation seemed so natural. From the start, it went in a very heartfelt direction.

All the formalities of chitter chatter had been waived. His attraction pulled at me from so many different directions. He was handsome, smart, funny, kind, and fine. Ever so softly, the blessing crept into my heart and introduced itself. I was caught up in the package it came in I almost didn't notice it. True friendship is the best blessing in the world. It strolled into my core and enhanced that troubled placed immediately. Blessings really are subtle beings. *Maybe that's why I haven't recognized most of them until too late.*

"Do you have someone picking you up?" He gave me a warm and concerned look, as he asked that question. My convictions granted me the right to consider him caring. Trustworthiness was the final test. My convictions held that right, waiting for more proof.

"Yeah. My girlfriend just sent me a text. She'll be pulling up out front for me shortly." I couldn't help but hope this would be one time Sandra took her time.

"Well, my ride is out front too. I'll help you carry your bags out to the curbside."

"That's very nice of you. Thank you."

"My pleasure." Definitely trustworthy! We walked outside and looked for our rides.

"There she is over there." I waved at Sandra to pull the car up. He gathered the luggage, carried it to the car and began loading it in the trunk.

"Evan!"

A woman was calling for him from the forward curbside. I could tell by his reaction that he was surprised to see her. I could tell by the look on her face as she marched up, that she was surprised to see me.

"Hi, I'm Celeste." She looked me up and down, as if she was searching for a weak point to strike.

"Hello, I'm Machaia. This is my friend Sandra. I met—"

"Sweetie, I pulled up the car when I saw you." She cut me off mid-sentence and rolled her eyes. "We need to go. There's something important we need to do." Her message was loud and clear: Back the hell off.

She was trying too hard. Everything about her was exaggerated—her eye contact, her tone. Even her funky ass walk back to her Bentley was overdone to the n'th degree. She wanted to make sure I understood that Evan was her man. As nice as I thought he was, I had to understand that he was taken. I was disappointed. I had already put a down payment on the pipe dream. I could tell Sandra was looking for some clarification. My expression was just as puzzled as hers. The only thing I was sure about was that he was taken. *She called him sweetie.* Ms. James made sure I didn't let that fact hide behind my desires.

"Well, it was nice meeting you." I could tell he was stalling. He looked at me as if he wanted me to say something. I wanted to, but I didn't know what the hell to say.

"It was nice meeting you, too." That was the best I could do under the circumstances.

Obviously, this encounter was not romantic in nature for him. I guess I shouldn't have expected it to be in the first place. I was seven months pregnant. *What kind of guy would try to pick up a pregnant chick anyway?* Reality reached back and slapped me in the face.

There was something about Evan that resonated with me. I definitely didn't want this to be the last time I saw him, but I didn't know how to tell him that and still be respectful of his relationship. I waited, hoping that he had the words. He didn't. He stood there for a second looking at me with the same blank look I had on my face.

"Dude, you better get over there before your girl comes over here trippin'. Don't make me have to whoop that bitch's ass." Sandra didn't actually say the last part, but I could tell it was on the tip of her tongue. She didn't know what was going on, but her girlfriend sensors detected some bullshit. Her eyes were already cursing Evan out. She continued as Evan walked away.

"Girl, you know he wasn't right. He about to mess up my Jimmie Choo boots." Evan accidentally set my bag on Sandra's shoes. Why someone would leave a thousand dollar pair of shoes in the trunk of her car for months baffled me.

This was the first time I had been in Sandra's car in months. I noticed a good deal of her belongings stuffed into every possible space. It was much more than just shoes. She had clothes, coats, bags, and papers. Then it hit me. These weren't things that she put in the trunk and left there, they were things that she never brought in the house in the first place. For whatever reason, she was reluctant to fully move into Lesley's home.

"Sandra, why is all this stuff still in your trunk?" The question was out of my mouth before I could think. I tried to make it sound innocent and curious, but my tone gave me away.

Sandra didn't look at me. She paused to let me know that she heard my question, but she never answered it. It's never simple for a woman to remain true to her heart. Despite the drama of the woman showing up, something deep within me felt like I was making a big mistake by letting Evan just walk away.

I saw him looking at me as his girlfriend drove by. She shot me a unit as well. I didn't look at her and I wasn't listening to Sandra talking to me through the trunk. I'd already let both of those distracters draw too much attention from what I really wanted to focus on.

Our eyes connected for a brief moment. They synched and instantly my heart was moved. Sandra's opinion didn't matter. His girlfriend's insecurities didn't matter. All that mattered was that Evan and I felt something.

"Whooo!" Sandra sighed as she plopped in the driver's seat.

"I see why you tired. That's a whole helluva lot of baggage you toting around." I briefly stared at her with a semi-serious look. I was checking to see if she would acknowledge that I wasn't talking about the stuff she shuffled in the trunk. She didn't.

"Tell me, what was that bullshit all about? What the hell you and ole' boy talking bout on a plane that got y'all all googly-eyed?"

I was asking that same question. I was actually excited about talking about the experience with Sandra.

"Girl, it—"

"It don't matter. Good riddance. That nigga' ain't hittin' on bout shit anyway!" She cut me off. Sandra answered her own question before even thinking to hear my response. Excitement quickly escaped me. Left in its place was contempt.

"What the hell you say that for?" Her negativity had annoyed me.

"Come on, girl. I know you can tell that nigga' is sorry as hell." She balled up her face, as if the thought that I could be that naïve disgusted her. "He had on a fake-ass, wanna-be expensive suit. He trying to act all chivalrous with yo' ass while he chin checkin' a dumb, rich bitch. Girl, that nigga' is all about games! I can see that from a mile away."

Sandra rambled on for a while about what she could tell down in her gut about what kind of man "he" was. She had sized Evan up just that quickly. "Why wear a cheap knock-off, when you can by a 'real' quality suit? His girlfriend don't even respect his ass enough to wait in the car before she walk up, mean muggin' people."

Her logic even had a backup angle. She had really put some thought

194

into what kind of man "he" was. By the time she finished her tirade, she wasn't even looking at me. She gazed out of the window, as she faced herself.

"Sandra, Evan didn't even have a suit on." I was disgusted with her naïveté.

Sandra looked at me dazed and confused. She was asking herself some hard questions, the kind of questions that turn a girl into a woman.

Being naïve doesn't excuse ignorance. Whether she knew better or not, Sandra's criteria for measuring a man's value was ignorant. She wouldn't and couldn't understand the connection Evan and I had made. I didn't even want to discuss it with her anymore. Even if he had on a knock-off suit, I was captured by his warmth, inner-beauty, caring, and that fine ass chest. I burst into a big smile.

"What the hell you over there cheesing about?"

Sandra sat across from me with her ignorant self, asking me about something that was very non-ignorant. There was no way to avoid the conversation we were about to have. "Sandra, what do you want from a man?" The smile was gone. The tolerance was gone. I wanted her to answer the question seriously.

"All I need a man to have is the three goods: good dick, good job, and good enough sense to know when to leave me the hell alone!" The CBA mask was firmly in place. There would be no serious conversation today.

"Well, if that's all you need to be good about a man, then you're leaving room for a whole bunch of bad shit to tag along for the ride." I wasn't in the mood to humor her evasiveness. I turned, faced the window, and thought about all the good things I was looking for.

Sandra didn't say a word. Even if she had, I wasn't paying her any attention. We drove in silence all the way home. I could tell she was thinking. We pulled into the garage and popped the trunk to get my things.

"Whenever you're ready, I'll help you bring some of this stuff inside." Honestly, I didn't know what I was talking about or what I was offering to help her with. I did know it wasn't about her damn Jimmy Choo's.

"I'll let you know, girl. Right now, I just want to go inside and lay down." The hard work of fighting with the truth had worn on her. She acknowledged my implication. Then we smiled, hugged, and went inside.

"Chaia, welcome home. How was your holiday?" Lesley was noticeably bubbly.

"It . . .was good. How was yours?" I stretched my neck and words out. I was curious about what had him so excited.

"It was great!" He turned to Sandra. "Baby, you gotta' go get dressed. I took something out for you to wear."

"Lesley, what's going on? I'm really tired." She scrunched her brows together trying to show him how tired she was.

"Baby, not now. Just get dressed." Even with a pleasant tone, some statements can hurt. He wasn't concerned about how she was feeling.

She wasn't on her knees sucking his dick, with a black eye. Nevertheless, she was bowed before a man and beneath herself. Sandra was once again in a relationship that forced her to put her heart's desires aside in exchange for a man's validation.

"Okay, baby, just let me throw it on real quick!" Her excitement sounded almost sincere. Lesley never once considered it was fake.

"Chaia, you should come, too. Donald Randolph, from dinner the other week, will be there." He put a small sample of *his* excitement on a saucer and offered it to me. Even if it did appeal to me, witnessing him suffocate Sandra with it took away any attraction it could've had.

"Nah. I'm mo' tired than *she* is." I over exaggerated the word and pointed at Sandra walking up the side stairway. I looked over at him to see the dumb-ass look on his face when he realized that he just forced himself on her.

Before he had a chance to acknowledge me, I noticed him do something surprising. He smirked. It was small, very subtle, but definitely a smirk. He knew what the hell he was doing. He looked over at me and gave me the dumb face I thought he would.

"Well, suit yourself, Ms. James." He had a relieved look in his eyes, as if he didn't want me to go in the first place.

He only called me that when had his 'thinking cap' on. He paced back and forth across the office, called everybody Mister and Misses, and used exact words like "precisely" and "as it stands." Usually, he was trying to outthink another lawyer on different angles to argue. That same exactness was all over him. I could tell he felt he was making a point. This nigga was playing mind games with my best friend.

"Baby, I love this outfit! How much time do I have?" Sandra was yelling from the top of the stairs in her good bra and panties, hair already pinned up. *How this chick gonna be comfortable enough to walk around the house half-naked, but scared to bring some shoes out the trunk?* One thing was certain, Sandra willingly bought into whatever it was Lesley was selling. *That bitch ain't even wash her dirty ass!* Ms. James was so judgmental.

"By the way, Ms. James, DeMann left you a few messages on the voicemail." He almost couldn't hide the smirk now. *Now this motherfucker tryin' to play mind games with me!* Not only was he up to something, but he knew I knew it. It didn't seem to bother him at all. He didn't even try to hide the smirk as he turned to walk away.

"Chaia…" *Sniffle cry* "I love…" *Choke* "…you." I almost couldn't make out what he was saying. "Why you giving up on us, Chaia?" DeMann cried through his entire voice message.

I'm not giving up on us. I'm giving me a chance. My heart stuck that message in a bottle and threw it out to sea. One day, his heart would get it and understand.

DeMann seemed so far away. Physically, I knew it was the exact same distance as before, but today, the distance seemed greater. He was much farther away than two states south. He was at least two galaxies away from where my heart stood.

I envisioned the world of Nashville all around him, and I realized that I was the one who had traveled. I couldn't breathe for a minute as I thought about how far. I was heading at light speed towards something beautiful. The lure of it melted all urges to slow down; every part of me couldn't wait to get there. I don't know why exactly, but the thought of Evan popped into my head and made me smile.

"Baby, fix me one, too."

My thoughts were disturbed by Sandra yelling out of the car at Lesley as he left the car and ran back into the house. I looked out of the room window at them.

"Sandra, don't even play like that. You ain't drinking anything with my baby in your belly."

"Oh shit, I forgot." It's weird, but I really believe in that moment she did.

Despite what they say about high blood pressure being the silent killer, sadness is the quietest and most subtle way to die. Sandra didn't know I was watching her from my room. Her face was so solemn. It was miles away from the mask she wore for Lesley. Her shoulders drooped as if they couldn't wait to rest the weight they had been bearing. She leaned her head on the window and stared out into space. After a few moments, I saw her reach up and wipe her eyes. I always wonder what people do when they think no one is watching. Painfully, now I know what my best friend does when she thinks no one is watching her. She cries. Her sadness was subtly and quietly killing her.

"Alright, baby, let's roll!" Lesley came running back out of the house with a drink in his hand.

In the second it took me to glance over at Lesley and then back to her, Sandra put the mask back on. Her face was cheery, her shoulders pronounced. Her eyes lit up enough that I noticed them from over the garden. They shined uncomfortably bright—the way stage lights blind you from seeing the commotion going on backstage. Sandra was busy performing, but backstage was chaos. There, in the center of the commotion, sadness was straddled over her heart strangling the life out of it. I watched her drive off, wondering what version of her would return.

What matters to you? The questions I bombarded Sandra with earlier still lingered. I acknowledged them all and braced myself for their raid. *Bring it!* Ms. James was standing on my right with her game face on. She had taken off her shoes, earrings, and the rest of her jewelry and wiped her face with Vaseline. She was ready to scrap. *You'll make it through.* My beautiful spirit was on my left with a glow that suggested she had some kind of superpower.

As I fell asleep, I felt proud of my life as a whole. Even with all the regrets and hard lessons I was still proud. Just as I was leaving the conscious I saw a beautiful image of the very attractive thought of Evan Miles. He waved and blew a kiss at me.

The next morning, I woke to the smell of breakfast. I was starting to think that Sandra's newfound love of cooking had to do with her trying to buy into "a woman's role."

"Good morning, Ms. James." Sandra was trying to mimic Lesley. We laughed at her imitation.

"Girl, don't play. I ain't got time for you or Lesley." I meant that on so many different levels. "So, what was he all excited about going last night?"

"We went to a party one of his buddies threw on the west side. It was fun. We danced all night."

"Tired as you were, I'm surprised you even went." I didn't try to hide the undertone of my question.

"Girl, I was fine. Donald asked about you. Chaia, you should call him. He's really a good guy." She softened the tone of her words to emphasize how good a guy she thought he was.

She rushed those sentiments out before I could direct the conversation any further. I could tell she didn't like where I was headed.

"Well, I ain't like you. I'm gonna need a man to have more than just the three goods." I took it there anyway.

Just as quickly as we called the cease-fire, we cancelled it. The war was back on and I had thrown the first blow.

"Chaia, you are not my judge!" Sandra yelled at the top of her lungs.

Her eyes were teary, and she didn't hide them. She opened the windows to her soul and let me see how wounded it was. It was full of pain and sorrow. She cried out loud as she told me that she knew she had made mistakes and tearfully admitted that she had things to work on. I stood there and witnessed it all. My spirit wept. This was exactly the kind of pain it didn't want to cause.

I walked over and hugged her so tight I strained to get my words out.

"Sandra, I just want you to be happy." She stayed in my embrace long enough for me to know that she believed me.

War is never an easy thing. I knew it wasn't over, but I dreaded the thought of future battles. I was scared that one of them would leave a permanent scar on our friendship. Nevertheless, I was committed to being honest with her and myself.

CHAPTER 17
EVAN MILLS

The television was off, the newspaper was untouched, and there was no fresh coffee in the pot. Greg had rushed out once again. It had been nearly a week since I found him on the couch. He's avoiding me. Sooner or later, he'll have to face that I know about his addiction. Little did he know, I was dreading that moment just as much as he.

I dwelled on Greg's addiction all the way to the hospital. The drill sergeant was commanding as usual. He was trying to get me focused on the road ahead of me. By the time I got to the hospital, his determined guidance had completed its mission. Greg's problems had taken their proper place in the backseat of my consciousness. I was still very aware of them, but they could not be the focus today.

This was the day of my biggest presentation. I had been working on this project for a month. Dr. Carson usually presided over the forums and resident presentations, but he was still out of town at a conference. Today, Dr. Copeland was in charge. He'd always made it clear that he didn't like the way Dr. Carson had 'spoon fed' me. He thought I had received special treatment. He didn't have any firsthand knowledge of how hard I work to be good. I knew he saw this as an opportunity to make sure I paid my dues, so I expected and prepared myself for the worst. He and I walked into the conference room at nearly the same time from opposite sides of the room. I placed everything nonmedical in the back of my mind and got my game face ready.

Presence has a greatness that is unmistakable. My fellow residents and the other attending physicians greeted me with genuine smiles. They were happy to see me. My humor had brightened their moods and my personality had hugged them. My sincerity had drawn on theirs. My smile made them smile. My presence occupied the whole room.

Dr. Copeland's presence didn't even put up a fight. It limited itself to the space that his physical being occupied and never once tried to come outside of that boundary. I was watching him and his reactions the entire time and still almost forgot he was here. *Nobody even knows he's on the picture out in the lobby.* The thought hit me like the answer to a riddle. He's jealous of my presence. People that know him didn't even notice the picture until he told them to look.

"My name is Dr. Evan Miles and I'll be presenting on the efficacy of inhaled antibiotics in pediatric cystic fibrosis patients." My presence had engulfed so much of the room that I felt like I was presenting to myself.

By the time I was done, there couldn't have been much doubt left in Dr. Copeland's mind about the quality of my presentation. I fielded every question he had for me with ease. I could tell he was convinced of my ability by the way he wouldn't look me in the eyes as I was closing up my presentation. He knew I was gloating and he knew I had good reason to. *This kid is going to be a great doctor.* The thought circled the room and introduced itself to everyone present. They all were forced to recognize it, including Dr. Copeland.

"I must admit that wasn't bad, Mr. Miles." Dr. Copeland was trying his best to be Dr. Carson. He wasn't even close.

"Thanks, Dr. Copeland. Your opinion means a lot to me." I looked him directly in the eyes for an uncomfortably long time. I wanted him to know that was a political lie.

I rode the wave of my splendor for the rest of the presentations. I continued riding it the rest of the afternoon and early evening as me and the other residents went out for dinner to celebrate the end of the rotation. By the time I pulled into Greg's driveway, I had been riding that wave so long that I forgot the ground even existed.

Opening the garage door, Greg's car parked in the driveway was a crash course in reality. I would finally get to see him face to face. My feeling of achievement and pride was quickly consumed by anxiety. In a way, I was relieved because at least now I knew what had been destroying my hero. Super G's kryptonite had been exposed. All I had to do now was help him get rid of it and everything would return to normal. I had been looking forward to and dreading this encounter since Sunday, when I found him on the couch. I knew he was dreading it as well. I paused at the front door, took a deep breath, and prepared myself mentally for a tough conversation. I opened the door and strode in. I was ready to conquer a demon.

When I walked into the house, Greg and Lovie were sitting at the nook table eating sushi and laughing.

"Now use these two fingers to pinch against the bottom like this." Greg was trying to show Lovie how to eat with chopsticks. He was laughing and relaxed. There was no sign of anxiety, concern, or even reluctance. He was acting as if he didn't even know I knew he was a powder head.

I don't know the overall rankings of my emotions. I do know anger and contempt were battling for the top spot. *How can this motherfucker just sit there and act like ain't nothing happen?* I couldn't believe it was actually the drill sergeant cursing. I was starting to lose my cool. Contempt was in my heart, assembling an army of hurtful words to attack him with. Anger was taking over my body, separating my lips to allow that army out. Just at the moment of attack, the inevitable happened. Anger and contempt gave way to the champion of all emotions. Love conquered them all. I held back on all the hurtful things I wanted to say. I realized my desire for reckoning was a far less authority than respect for his dignity.

In that moment of clarity, I saw my friend and my hero in a way I hadn't in a while. The cape was still dirty and the colorful suit was even dingier, but the crest was still pronounced and the uniform still stood for something. Super G stood before me with his fatigued muscles flexed, hard as ever. He was struggling to hold up his honor. He was raggedy, battered, and worn. He needed help. The last thing he needed was a self-righteous friend adding another ton of guilt to his load.

"You two look like you're having fun." That seemed like the lightest thing I could offer.

"Yeah, we just chilling and tripping out." Greg leaned in as Lovie threw her arm around his shoulder.

Immediately, the not-so-serious attitude he was taking to his problem pissed me off. *Damn, nigga, at least act shamed.* I watched him laughing and his laughs were genuine and his smiles were bright. He really was happy with her. Maybe she could love away all those layers of pain Greg was buried under. It seemed she had wiped clear at least two or three of them already. Despite his flaws, my friend deserved love, even if it took me biting my tongue for him to experience it. I did just that.

"Man, you wanna play Pluck?" Greg was taking nonchalance to a new level. Pluck was a three-person version of spades. We always played it as kids.

"Yeah that sounds cool. Let me cha—"

"You ate? I got you a couple of slices of Geno's." Greg cut me off before I could finish telling him I'll change clothes. He seemed anxious.

He seemed determined to steer my mind away from where he feared it was. I could tell the thought of me looking at him in that way had been ravishing his mind all afternoon. The hard truth is that my mind was on him and his problem constantly. No matter where he tried to steer my thoughts, the center of them remained steadfastly focused on him.

I changed clothes, ate the pizza, sat down to the table with them, and began playing cards. He avoided all but the necessary eye contact and even those instances were cut short. He was much more aggressive with conversation. Every open opportunity and even some closed ones, he poured on the stories and jokes. If he couldn't steer my thoughts away, it seemed he was trying to do the next best thing; just run them the hell over.

"Pluck, pluck, pluck. . .pluck, pluck. . .pluck, pluck!" He was doing his best to imitate the song I made up for when I'm winning.

"Greg, please!" Lovie was starting to get agitated. I don't know if she knows about his problem or not, but even she seemed to notice that he was determined not to let either of us talk.

"Uh oh, don't get me started on you." Greg bucked his eyes open as far as he could and made a funny face. He shrugged up his shoulders in a silly manner and stared at Lovie until she burst out into laugher.

"Boy, you so silly." To Greg's credit, her smile was beautiful enough to warm the coldest thought instantly. After running from my cold stares all night, her warmth must have seemed like heaven to him. He dove in headfirst.

"I love you so much, baby." Greg was on the verge of tears. Lovie's face stiffened as she realized how emotional he had gotten.

"I love you, too, baby." She leaned over and kissed him as she spoke.

I hope she doesn't know. If she does, then she's enabling him. That would change my opinion of her drastically. Greg definitely knows about his problem. He was content pretending and Lovie seemed ready and willing to play along. The games for me stopped at Pluck.

I finished playing cards and told them I was going to bed. Greg never stopped joking. Lovie never stopped laughing with him, even when I could tell she was irritated. I never once laughed; wasn't shit funny to me. I got up and went to bed. *It's only a matter of time before I have to leave.* Evan Miles' life was pulling me in another direction. I fell asleep thinking about all the things I would have to get together to get my own place.

For the next few days, Greg's strategy didn't change. He was gone early every morning and out late every evening. Whenever our paths did cross, he slid out of striking distance on the fastest joke or story he could manage.

It consumed me to the point where I struggled to focus at work. My Infectious Disease rotation with Dr. Copeland was off to an uneventful first two days. The next morning was the first day I went with him to his HIV clinic on the north side. This was, without a doubt, his specialty. If there was any place he could make a point to me, this was it. I reviewed all my notes and journals on HIV. I wanted to be ready for his best shot.

The next morning, as I drove to Dr. Copeland's clinic, I played *Zoom* by the Commodores, just like I used to do back at school. I banned anything related to Greg or Celeste from my mind and went over my HIV notes in my head. Occasionally, I glanced out the window at potential condo buildings I could lease.

The clinic was very classy and discrete. It was located in the corner unit of a shaded block of brownstones converted to offices. A small, classy sign read 'Positive Influences, Extended Care Center'. It seemed more like a private spa than a medical clinic. His clinic was utilized mainly by upscale HIV positive people. I walked into the front lobby and introduced myself to the receptionist.

"Hi, I'm Dr. Evan Miles. I'm Dr. Copeland's resident." That actually felt natural to say.

"Hello, Dr. Miles. I'm Maria Rivera, Dr. Copeland's office manager. He told us to expect you. He wanted us to let you know he's consulting on a patient in ICU and running late. He had us order you some breakfast. He thought you'd enjoy something from Panera Bread." The young Spanish woman walked from behind the reception desk and shook my hand.

"That sounds good to me." I tried to sound and act as professional as she did.

She escorted me on a quick tour of the clinic and introduced me to all the staff. Everything about the clinic, from the staff to the facility, was classy and professional. She gave me a brief overview of the services they provide. The medical care was only a small portion of it. The clinic covered everything from private testing and counseling to support groups. It even had a small private pharmacy. It was impressive, to say the least.

Almost immediately, I had a newfound respect for Dr. Copeland. His clinic was amazing. He'd even remembered how much I liked the Panera Bread breakfast sandwiches we have at our monthly presentations. *Maybe old Dr. Copeland ain't so bad after all.* I actually mumbled the words to myself, as I sat in the staff lounge and ate breakfast.

"Oh, by the way, Dr. Copeland left a list of patient charts for you to review until he arrives." One of his nurses came into the doorway to tell me that.

"Thank you. I'll be starting with them right away." I tried to sound as smart as a mouthful of food would allow.

I felt a little intimidated by the operation as a whole. But, I was determined to show Dr. Copeland I was comfortable working in a great clinical environment. I quickly finished my breakfast, straightened my tie, adjusted my slacks, and buttoned my smock. *It's time to shine.* Evan Miles had his game face on.

I sat at Dr. Copeland's desk and began reviewing the charts. I made mental notes of things I wanted to teach the patients about nutrition and exercise. From Dr. Copeland's notes, I didn't think he was emphasizing it enough. I already felt like I was making a difference and I hadn't seen one patient yet. Then came the bomb.

I knew there would be times when my career challenged me emotionally. I envisioned scenarios of death, horrible diagnosis and negative test results. I knew I would have to be strong enough to deal with patients and family members in a professional way. I prepared myself mentally for those moments. I'd rehearsed them in my mind and heart countless times. But, I wasn't nearly ready or strong enough for this.

After I went through the charts he left for me, I began reading over the list of Dr. Copeland's current patients. Line sixteen floored me like a sucker punch: Grey, Gregory L. There were fifteen other names before his, but his may as well have been first on the list. It stood out and looked like it wasn't supposed to be there. The font size and type and the line spacing just didn't seem like the correct way for his name to appear on this list. No way would be the correct way. Even before I opened the actual chart and confirmed it was him, I knew it in my heart. That ugly ass font and off-centered line spacing had done their jobs. They'd told me that my best friend was HIV positive.

I spent the rest of the morning aimlessly flipping through charts. I did my best to interact with Dr. Copeland once he arrived. He seemed very excited to be working with me. It didn't take him long to realize something was bothering me.

"Evan, do you need to leave?" He sounded genuinely concerned.

"I appreciate the concern Dr. Copeland, but I'll be okay. I just got some bad news this morning before you arrived." There was no use in me trying to play it off. I was shocked, scared, worried, and hurt. I couldn't hide it if I wanted to. It showed in every movement I made and every word I spoke. It felt like it was my name on the list.

"Well, there's not much more for you to do today anyway, so go ahead and leave. Tomorrow, we'll start looking at some of the new antiviral regimens." He looked away and didn't give me a chance to respond. I don't think I could have responded anyway. I gathered all my things except my thoughts. They were all over the place.

My image of Dr. Copeland was forever changed. There were plenty of things he could have had me do, but he didn't. Today, he placed my personal concerns over all else. My words were not able to express my gratitude fully, but hopefully, the relief in my eyes said it better. I thanked him again and left.

When I walked in the door, Greg was sitting on the couch. He was staring at the television entirely too hard to be paying attention to a commercial. I could tell he was in deep thought. He had on his lucky tie. It was still tied, as if he was about to walk into a courtroom any second now. His tie is usually the first thing that comes off when he walks through the door. He wasn't comfortable. Neither was I.

"Greg, what's up, man?" I tried to ease the tension.

"You tell me. You were the one that had to ask a question. What's up?"

He was nervous. I could tell he was still embarrassed about me finding him on the couch.

"Greg, I know you're HIV positive."

The weight of that statement fell and crushed us both. I'd been carrying that sentiment around for hours. Unloading it still didn't relieve its burden from me. Greg's face was frozen. It seemed almost like he had just received that information for the first time.

How can my soul be the judge of his? Evan Miles would be definitely holding me to a higher standard of self-evaluation. Once the conversation began, my whole approach to it evolved. I wasn't concerned with any form of reckoning. Greg didn't owe me any explanations. In fact, I owed him. I owed him the support our friendship demanded.

I listened to him explain how he'd fallen in love with Stacey Howard. She was also a lawyer. They'd met at the courthouse and spent a lot of time together over lunches and time in the law library. He told me how she captivated him instantly. He said he bought into her with everything he possessed and had talked about getting married and starting a family. He said after six months of dating, they decided that they would get rid of condoms. Even now, his face lit up with the thoughts of her and I couldn't help but feel his love for her. The brief moment of joy was quickly subdued as his face continued the story before his words could.

His tears flowed as he told me about how he discovered he had HIV. He didn't look at me as he spoke. He wasn't focused on my reception of his words; he seemed to be purging himself. I looked down and noticed that he was even clinching his fists as he talked.

"Man, you think you know somebody…" He shook his head from side to side like he still didn't fully believe the truth and didn't want to. "She was fucking this NBA nigga the whole time. Some nigga that play for the Portland Trailblazers. They been fucking since college. She sat her ass in my face every day talking about how she loved me, how much I meant to her, and all that shit. Knowing damn well that she was still fuck buddies with that nigga. All he had to say was 'come suck my dick for me' and what do her ass do?" He flung his arms in a way that let me know it all still didn't make sense to him, then squeezed his chest so tight that I thought he was hurting himself. "She'd lie to me so she can sneak out and go fuck and suck this nigga up!"

"Damn, G. That's messed up." I knew he hadn't gotten everything he needed to out.

"That's why I can respect strippers and hoes. At least they straight up with you. They don't be in your face selling you a motherfucking pipe dream. That's why that's all I fuck with now." I know he meant 'fuck with' on a broader term, but the thought alarmed me greatly.

"But, if they straight up with you, then you gotta be straight up with them."

"Man, fuck these hoes!"

"Greg, I know you ain't serious. You have HIV." I lowered my voice and slowed my speech. I wanted my statement to resonate with him. It shook loose the foundation of his anger.

"I mean it ain't like that. I put on two condoms and make them hoes feel like I'm scared of them jacking me up. I ain't trying to give nobody nothing." He was looking away from me again.

"So what's up with Lovie? I can tell by the way you sleep on the couch whenever she stays over that you not having sex with her."

He paused everything for a moment, even breathing. Then he took a deep breath, looked me directly in the eyes, and prepared to say something that it was clear he wanted me to hear.

"I want the best for her. She's different from the rest of these bitches. She don't be trying to play a brother."

"But if you don't tell her what's up with you, then you're playing her. You don't think that's just as fucked up?"

"I keep it at friends with her. I just like hanging out with her. She makes me feel good, you know?" He looked at me, searching for support and loyalty again. I couldn't offer any now.

"Greg, if you let that girl fall in love with you and you don't tell her what's up, you're dead wrong!" Even though I tried to calm my tone, it still seemed like I yelled that statement.

My compassion stood by while my convicted words helped shame almost choke him to death. He knew he was wrong the whole time. The tears were enough proof of that. At that very moment, I realized what shame was really doing to G.

"Listen, Greg, you can't change what's already done, but you can change the things you're going to do." My posture and demeanor changed just as much as my tone.

"I know. I just. . ."

I waited a few moments, but he couldn't finish his statement. Shame hadn't fully released its chokehold on him. After a couple of minutes, he stopped trying.

Just like that, the conversation was over. He hardly ever spoke during my tirade, but he gave me more understanding in one afternoon than I had gained in the whole seven months I'd been living in Chicago.

Over the next two weeks, that understanding grew. We talked and we hung out. We came home from clubs alone. For Greg, I did my best to help him, encourage him, and not convict him. For me, Greg did his best not to deserve conviction.

Helping Greg focus on getting his life back in order was carrying over into my residency. I was well ahead of all my projects and research for Dr. Copeland. I had written and rehearsed every presentation I had coming up over the next few weeks. I dove into everything with a keen sense of purpose. I was able to tune into whatever needed to be tuned into and tune out everything that needed to be tuned out, Celeste especially.

I hadn't talked to her in weeks. With the exception of a couple of her slick attempts to text me through Dr. Carson's phone, she hadn't tried to contact me. There were no pop up visits to Greg's house and she didn't accompany Dr. Carson to a dinner we had. Nothing. I concluded that she finally was starting to get the picture. By the time the day of my next presentation came, I was on cruise control. I was relaxed, confident, and worry-free.

I walked into the conference room with even more confidence than the last presentation. Dr. Carson and Dr. Copeland both were sitting in the back of the room. I saw Dr. Copeland look at me and then lean over to say something to Dr. Carson. It had to be about how well I was performing on his rotation. My confidence escalated about five exponents of a hundred. I didn't even bother introducing myself. Hell, these motherfuckers know my name.

"Today, I'll be presenting on the relevance of direct thrombin inhibitors in the treatment of post-cardiac arrest patients."

I wasn't scanning the room to make sure my audience understood my topic. I wasn't even checking the body language of the attending physicians for approval of my presentation. My confidence allowed me to take all of that for granted. I was scanning the audience for someone who didn't seem convinced of my greatness. I scanned the whole room. There was one face that met those criteria.

Dr. Carson was paying very close attention with an unusually cold face. Usually, he's the one person in the room I could count on for the approving nods, curious grunts, and warm eyes that tell me I'm doing pretty well. Today, there was none of that. I wasn't quite sure what the cold face was suggesting, but it certainly wasn't giving off a positive vibe.

The confidence from the last presentation forum was gone and the confidence from today was crumbling fast. I prayed that it wasn't as evident to everyone else as it was to me. I stumbled through the rest of my presentation and sat quietly for the break at the halfway point of the presentations. I waited as long as I could to see if Dr. Carson was going to leave at the break as he sometimes does. He didn't. We were in the conference room almost alone and he didn't even look up at me. I got up and tried to ease by him without speaking.

"Mr. Miles, I need to see you after the presentations are done." He wasn't even looking at me when he spoke. He was thumbing through a stack of papers. "Do I have your presentation outline here?" He was strictly business today. *Somebody has made him mad.* I thought to myself.

"Yes, I gave it to Dr. Copeland on Monday." I waited to see if he would look up and acknowledge me. He didn't. "Dr. Carson, I thought you were out of town on conference. That's why I haven't called since I made it back." I offered my excuse in case my not calling had offended him. He stopped what he was doing and gave me a funny look.

"Well apparently, *I've* been text messaging *you.*" My gut fell to the floor. I knew exactly what he was implying. "Just make sure you see me today when the presentations are over." He looked back down at his papers and continued thumbing.

Pride and confidence were replaced instantly with shame and guilt. Those two executioners were destined to finally have their way with me. My presentation was a lifetime ago. This moment had a life of its own. I left the conference room and went to the residents' lounge to catch my breath. *What could I tell him?* Nothing. *How could I face him?* I couldn't. I knew I'd have to find the way and strength to do both, but it wouldn't be this day. I needed time to think.

Before the break was over, I was already in the parking lot. By the time

Dr. Carson realized that I wasn't coming back, I was probably damn near home. I knew I couldn't avoid him forever. If I could just make it to the end of my lifetime without having to face him, that would make things so much better.

I avoided going to his office, calling him, or even text messaging for several awkward days. I was desperately trying to outrun shame and guilt. *What do I do?* The cancer of that question plagued my mind, body, and soul. The drill sergeant had no answers and Evan Miles was quiet. The only voice I could detect was the shameless cry of the weakling Erica used to dominate. Even it could only muster up two words: *Just hide.* For now, that directive would have to do.

CHAPTER 18
MACHAIA JAMES

"I really don't do reality shows, but that one caught me." Donald was describing how he had gotten caught up in *The Contender*, a boxing reality show on TV.

According to Sandra and Lesley, he'd been asking about me ever since the night of the party. He always made it a point to come by or call Lesley's office to invite me to lunch. Usually, I made up excuses to say no. That day, I was in the mood for some good conversation. I had been doing a lot of thinking lately and was really looking forward to bouncing some thoughts around. I'd learned that he was a self-made man from very humble beginnings. I respected that about him tremendously.

In all of our brief encounters, he seemed intelligent, well rounded, and relatively sane as far as all my senses could tell. I thought he'd be the perfect person to talk with about issues like 'following your heart' and 'starting out on your own'. Instead, we talked about The Contender. Neither the meal nor the conversation satisfied my appetite. He wasn't able to pick up on any of my leads. Even if he had, I doubt seriously that he would've changed the topic anyway.

It had been several months since I first met him that night at Lesley's dinner. Donald was sweet, charming and funny, in a goofy kind of way. I adore those qualities in a man. But, just having them isn't enough. I didn't feel drawn to him. For whatever reason, a connection wasn't there.

Well at least the nigga ain't half-bad to look at. Ms. James always has a fresh two cents to throw in. Donald's toned physique poked at his suit as he walked a couple of steps ahead of me to open the door to the hallway. He was walking me back to Lesley's office in the Civil Law department before he went back up three floors to his office in Corporate Law.

"You don't have to walk me all the way back." In my attempt to rush my statement out in between his words, I may have stiffened my tone a little too much.

He looked at me as if he finally understood that I couldn't give a good goddamn about The Contender.

"You sure? I don't mind." I'd never really blatantly brushed him off before. I usually would entertain him until he decides to leave me alone. I could tell he felt a little dissed.

"Yes, I'm sure. I have to use the restroom and get me a cup of coffee. So, I guess I'll just see you around." I issued that statement carefully and with much more tact than the last one. I also started walking before he could respond just in case he offered to get it for me. I didn't have to use the rest room and I don't drink coffee, but I was fully prepared to fake both, if need be. The softer tone must have eased his mind. He smiled, said goodbye, and walked off.

When I walked back into the office, Lesley was standing in the hallway beside the copier staring at me with a curious look on his face.

"And what are you over there smirking about?" I asked him. He was getting to be just as annoying as Donald.

"Looks like you and Donald had a nice lunch together." He gave me his 'I knew you would' face. I didn't even feel like trying to explain to him how wrong he was.

"Donald is a very nice guy, but he's not my type."

"Women kill me with that crap. A woman will jump on any type of man that will give them what they are looking for." Minus the big words, he spoke in that precise manner he uses when he's debating cases. I could tell he really believed that.

"So, are you being yourself with Sandra or are you just giving her what you *think* she's looking for?" As fast as I asked it, it seemed like that question just came out of nowhere. It didn't. It had been floating around my heart for some time, just waiting on an opportunity like this.

"You say that as if you don't believe I know." His precise tone continued. He was ready for a debate and so was I. I let him begin.

"Sandra is looking for peace. She wants to feel safe and secure. She hasn't had that in her life . . ."

I listened to him explain what Sandra was looking for. He sounded emotional and appeared sincere. He made some very good points about her insecurities. It sounded and felt like a well-rehearsed opening statement.

"All of that is very true, but I thought we were talking about the type of *man* Sandra was looking for." I felt myself getting emotional already. "Do you know how the way she grew up makes her see men? Do you know the way it makes her see herself? Do you know the type of man she needs to balance her flaws? Do you know what her flaws are?" My eyes began to water and I stumbled over some of my words. "Do you know what type of man she needs to create the kind of family she prays for every night? Do you even know what kind of family she dreams of? Do you know what any of her dreams are? What type of man would be a good compliment to those?" I could tell by the look on his face, he was clueless. "Lesley, if you don't know who she really is, then you can't possibly know what she really needs from a man. You're not giving her what she wants. You're just handing her what you want her to have."

My statement wasn't rehearsed; it was from the heart. I asked him all the questions that Sandra should have. I questioned him to see how much he knew about her. If he really loved her he would've known that type of stuff. He didn't. I paused to let him reply.

Silence.

The debate was over. Case closed. *She probably tried to ask his ass that shit and he was too busy talking about some dumb bullshit like The Contender.* I struggled to keep Ms. James' thoughts in my mind.

Ever since the night he made Sandra go to that party, I've been skeptical of everything Lesley says and does. He likes manipulating people. I do believe he has genuine feelings for Sandra, but his nature preys on hers. Lions love lambs. How else would they know how powerful they were? He doesn't know Sandra the way I do. What he doesn't know is that beneath all that self-doubt, she is far from a lamb. She is a lioness, a hungry one at that. One day, she'll break free of the chains that trap her. When she does, he's going to have one hell of a fight on his hands.

"Well, if there's nothing left you need me to do, I guess I'll head home, Mr. Manley." I can tell it bothers him when I mock his formality.

Reality will never be as beautiful as make-believe. Knowing what's behind a person's mask stops you from ever seeing them the way you did before you knew. It takes a brave spirit to remove its masks and reveal its true self to the world.

As I drove home, I observed the faces of every other driver I could. *How many of them were wearing masks?* I wondered to myself. *How many weren't confident enough to live life as themselves?* Instead, frightened into a make-believe reality, they presented themselves the way they thought others wanted them to.

Everyone I knew was guilty— Sandra, Lesley, DeMann, my grandparents, even myself. I went over my conversation with Lesley's in my mind. The same way Sandra validates herself through men, Lesley validates himself by manipulating others. It's the same validation DeMann got by controlling me and that my grandparents got by forcing their opinions on my life. I couldn't think of one person who seemed real to me.

Then I thought of one—Evan Miles.

Despite the drama with the chick at the airport, he seemed real. His eyes never told lies the way DeMann's does. At least, none that I could detect. Our conversation was fulfilling and our smiles happened naturally. I really would have loved to talk to him again, but he was involved with someone. The reality of our interaction probably never would've been as beautiful as the dreams that ran rampant in my mind before his girlfriend showed up. But, at least our friendship would've been real. I knew I'd never see him again, but the image of his beautiful and brave spirit standing there unmasked would be my gauge for all other encounters I had with men.

When I made it to the house, I walked straight to my room. Sandra was sitting in the family room watching a movie and laughing. I wasn't in the mood. I had observed every mask between downtown and home. The thought of getting up close and personal with one more wasn't appealing at all. I took my shoes off and plopped down on the bed. After just a few minutes, Sandra cracked the door open.

"Chaia, you had a couple of messages on the recorder." She gave me a mischievous grin that let me know who one of the messages were from.

I checked the machine. Just as I thought, the first one was from Donald Randolph. He was calling to ask me out to dinner.

Oh, hell to the nawl! I love it when I can actually let Ms. James scream out loud. I had already heard enough about The Contender to last a lifetime.

The second message was from my grandmother, asking me to give her a call. I knew she just wanted to inquire about me and DeMann. *Damn, she's nosey.* Ms. James had stripped down to her bra and panties and gotten very comfortable.

Even though I knew it was impossible, I couldn't help but wish that there had been one from Evan. Since I couldn't call him, I dialed my grandmother's number.

"Baby, you need to call DeMann. He called here all hysterical, asking for the number to the house, but I didn't give it to him." *Now, her ass wanna be discreet!* I almost burst out laughing.

"Did he say what he wanted?"

"No, he just said that he didn't have time to talk and wanted the number to the house. But, I didn't give it to him." I knew she felt bad about giving him the address to Sandra's old apartment.

"Ok, I'll call him and see what he wanted. How are you doing?"

"I'm ok, baby, but you should go ahead and call him. He sounded like he needed you. You know it's been kinda hard on him since you left." Her concerned almost sounded genuine.

In all of the years I've known and dated DeMann, my grandmother had only expressed concern for him once. That was now. *They're up to something again.* My bullshit detectors were on full alert. I hung up and dialed his cell number.

"Who dis?" I almost didn't recognize the voice with all the noise in the background.

"Rodney?"

"Dis Chaia?" The background noise was horrible. I could hardly make out anything he was saying.

"Rodney, where is DeMann?" I yelled loudly. Partially, to make sure he heard me and partially to let him know I wasn't game for any b.s.

"Look man, I can't talk right now where I'm at. I'mma give DeMann this number and he'll call you back tonight." He hung up the phone. He'd created a million questions and answered none.

That was the first time I talked to Rodney since the day I saw him and DeMann at the club. Instantly, my suspicions began to flare. *He probably at that club up to no good and had Rodney answer his phone for him.*

I know how quick Rodney and DeMann are to lie for each other. I've listened to DeMann tell Rodney's baby mama too many lies about when and where they were hanging out to think differently. The thought of them trying to make a fool of me again pissed me off even more. "If he can call me back tonight, then obviously he ain't dead. Other than that, I couldn't care less." I spoke those words to myself and then, mentally, I hung up the phone on Rodney first.

My mood was destroyed. The relaxation that I was about to enjoy was over before it began. I put on my favorite 'unwind' album of all time, Toni Tony Tone's *Sons of Soul* and tried to relax anyway. I lay on my side rubbing my belly and listened to "Slow Wine," "Lay Your Head on My Pillow" and "Anniversary". All I could think about was how this negro was trying me again. I was officially heated. I got up, turned off the music, and went out front where Sandra was.

Lesley had made it home and they were both on the couch, laughing at the same movie Sandra was watching earlier. It was some movie about pineapple weed with the goofy looking white boy from *Knocked Up*. I sat down and tried to watch it with them. It didn't seem nearly as funny as their laughs made it out to be.

"This mess ain't *even* that funny." I actually felt myself almost boiling over.

"Chaia, you wouldn't know funny if it came in here dressed up like a good man trying to date you." I could tell Lesley was still bothered by the conversation we had at work. They both laughed at his joke. Needless to say, I wasn't amused in the slightest.

"Lesley, let's not talk about what people don't know." My serious demeanor suggested to Sandra that I was trying to make a point. Lesley's shocked face confirmed it.

Up until now, anything that Lesley and I talked about at work, stayed at work. That was an unspoken understanding. We'd had numerous conversations about their relationship at work before and they'd never left the office. We had developed a comfort level that allowed us to speak freely. I knew he never intended for our conversation today about what Sandra wants to follow him home. Honestly, I didn't even think it was that big of a deal since most men don't understand their women. But, the intensity in the way I threw it out there made it seem like a 'must know' item. Sandra's curiosity, or concern, was very evident.

"Lesley, is there something you need to tell me?" She had a half-crooked smile on her face as she asked him that question. She must have thought it was some kind of inside joke.

"Shit, he needs to be asking you the same question!" I dealt out two hands of pure conviction with that statement. Then, I called her half-crooked smile and raised her one mean ass unit.

Lesley knew I wasn't joking about him, so he took my statement about Sandra a lot more seriously than she took my stab at him. He gave her a very concerned look. The movie kept playing, but wasn't shit funny to nobody now. I walked out the room before they could get through eyeballing each other and turn their contempt to me. My conscious made me feel bad about calling them out as soon as I made the comments. I knew my irritation with DeMann was the cause of all this crap. But, in a weird way, I kind of felt like I was helping them.

I went into the kitchen and fixed a glass of water. By the time I came back out to the family room, they were laying across each other laughing at the movie again. They had both put on their masks and 'pretended' the problem away. Hard questions were not visibly present in the room, but I knew they were there, deep down in both of their hearts. I could easily detect their presence in the cracking of those fake laughs.

Ring . . .ring . . .ring. A little over an hour later, I was in my room and still not fully calmed down. *Ring. . .ring.* I glanced over at the caller ID just before I picked up the phone: *Correction Corp. of America, Metro.* Everything about the way I was feeling changed in the time it took to read that ID.

C.C.A. The fact that a jail is part of a corporation, says it all. This is serious business. DeMann had been arrested before, but he'd never panicked like this. I knew this was going to be very bad. I answered the call.

"Hello." I could hear the concern in my own voice.

"Chaia." He paused. I couldn't tell if he didn't know what to say or if his emotions were keeping him from talking. "I messed up." It was both.

DeMann struggled to speak as he explained that he had been busted in a sting operation involving him and four other guys. He said there was a shootout and an officer had been killed. Even though he was not the triggerman, he was being charged with murder. Also charged with violating

219

his parole, he was denied bail. His trial was Thursday—three days from now. He wanted me to come.

How could I go? I couldn't witness that. Before, I had a chance to let those thoughts fester. A recorded message interrupted us.

"You have fifteen seconds remaining." It came just two seconds after the one that cut DeMann off, saying sixty seconds left.

Find a way. My spirit was sure that I needed to be there. I hurried my goodbyes and promised him that I would get back to Nashville before his trial.

Once again, DeMann's presence was larger than life to me. This time, it was in the saddest of ways.

I walked back out front to tell Sandra the news. She and Lesley were gone. They probably went somewhere to get away from me. I'd been so ugly to them earlier. I knew I didn't deserve it, but I needed their support and understanding now. I went into my room and turned on my laptop. Through watered eyes and blurry vision, I found and bought a ticket for the next evening at 7:10 pm. Whether they understood or not didn't matter; I had to go.

About an hour later, I heard them coming back into the house. I went out front again to tell Sandra the news. Only the hall light was on. Everything else was turned off, including any connection to them I had pushed them away, along with DeMann and my grandparents. For the first time that I could remember, I really needed someone to talk to and didn't have anybody. I went back into my room and fell asleep with a deserved sense of solitude.

The next morning, both of them were gone by the time I awoke. Lesley always goes in early, but Sandra had taken maternity leave a month ago at Lesley's request. She usually sits at home bored, cooking, and wishing she was at work. Today, she was gone as well. They had escaped into the world as fast as they'd retreated to their room last night. I knew they were avoiding me.

When I got to the work, I walked straight to Lesley's office. Tracey, his personal secretary is usually very distant with me. I think she was concerned that I would replace her once I got a little more experience. Today, she was warm and inviting.

"Machaia, Mr. Manley wants to see you." She was happy about

something. I knocked on his door and went in.

"Ms. James, come in and have a seat." He was sitting at his desk, leaning back with a semi-serious look on his face. "I don't know if you realize it, but you've been here over ninety days and your benefits with the firm are active. I went ahead and scheduled you for maternity leave starting now." He had his precise and articulate thing going on big time.

"Lesley, I—" He cut me off before I could get my apology started.

"I thought we would be able to separate personal matters from business matters, but I feel, lately, those lines have been blurred. Therefore, when you return from maternity leave, I've found a spot for you upstairs in the Corporate Law office." He paused and waited for my reply with a poker face.

I knew he was playing games with me. He knew I knew it, too. The last place I wanted to work was upstairs in the Corporate Law office with Donald. I also knew that he didn't have to find me a place at all. He could've come up with something and fired me altogether. He didn't and before all else, I thanked him for that.

"Thank you so much, Lesley. I really thank you for everything you've done for me since I came to Chicago." I didn't even try to play the articulate game with him. He was holding all the power chips. "Well, I guess I'll see you back at the house." He jumped at the word 'house.' He stretched his eyes and scrunched his mouth in a way that suggested he was contemplating making a change in that area as well. I held my composure and gathered my things while Tracey gloated. I said goodbye to both of them and left the office.

It took everything within me to hold my smile together as we made our final eye contact. I felt that mask already melting as soon as I started to turn away. I felt like my world was coming apart. DeMann, Sandra, Lesley, and my job were all too much for a seven-month pregnant woman to bear. I walked straight and tall through the main lobby and out to my truck. I greeted the young lady at the information booth and the nice security man at the main entrance. I gave no visible clues that, internally, I was in turmoil.

By the time I made it to the truck, panic and anxiety had nearly taken over my entire existence. The questions they created were flying through my mind so fast that I barely had enough time to breathe. *Where do I go now? What do I do? What will happen?* Their target was my epicenter; my very core was under attack. *You will survive.* My spirit looked me in the eyes and was not fazed at all.

As I turned around to back out of my parking space, I noticed my apartment guide still lying in the back seat, perfectly positioned for me to notice it. It seemed like a movie that I had already deduced the ending of. The next scene would be me finding a wonderful apartment in the perfectly positioned guide. Following that would be several scenes of my life coming back together. By the time I made it onto the freeway driving home, I had already replayed the happy ending scene five times.

Once I got back to the house, I spent the rest of the morning and the majority of the afternoon apartment shopping over the phone and computer. *Ain't nothing better than having your own shit anyway.*

By the time I heard Sandra returning through the front door, I had already taken six virtual tours and arranged four walkthroughs for next week. I was nearly finished packing my weekend bag for my trip back to Nashville when she opened the room door.

"Are you leaving?" The surprise on her face told me that she wasn't expecting or hoping to find me packing to leave.

"Yeah, I have to." I let that blank response linger and mislead her for a moment.

"What do you mean you *have* to?" She rolled her neck like she just wasn't having it. "You think I would let him kick my pregnant best friend out on the streets?" She knew her words spoke volumes.

I didn't know to what extent her and Lesley had words about me being here, but it was clear whatever she said was for me, not against me. In the midst of our personal war with each other, my best friend had my back. Regardless of her own situation, wasn't nobody gonna do her girl wrong. She protected our friendship like it was the most cherished thing in her life. And it was. I think it was the only thing she knew was true. Living a lie is much harder when you know what truth is.

"Sandra, I have to go home because DeMann has been arrested and his sentencing is Thursday. But, I am moving into my own place after the holidays." Her face froze.

Both statements hit her hard. She asked a few concerned questions about DeMann and listened attentively as I explained the little bit I knew. She fidgeted as I continued packing. Her worried eyes seemed concerned with far more than just DeMann's legal issues. She knew this wasn't my final goodbye, but watching me pack to leave must have made it seem real to her.

"You want me to drive you to the airport?"

"Honestly, I was looking forward to the quiet time to think and clear my head. But, I'm cutting it close on time and you dropping me off would save me the time it takes to park. I could just check-in curbside and go straight to the gate."

"Well, tell you what. You can have the best of both worlds. I'll drive; you think. We don't have to say a word to each other at all. Hell, you can even sit in the back like Ms. Daisy or something and I'll be Morgan Freeman." We both broke out laughing at the thought of that.

"You look bout like a chauffeur. Where you been dressed like that?" She looked over into the mirror at herself. Sandra had on a worn cotton sweat suit. Her hair was pulled back into a simple ponytail and she didn't have on any makeup.

"Girl, its warm, comfortable, and the only thing in my closet that still fits my big ass!" We laughed. I totally understood the shrinking number of options in both of our closets. Something told me that, even if she had more options, she would've chose something comfortable to her. That was a wonderful sign.

Just as she suggested, she drove while I sat on the passenger side and gazed out of the window. We shared a couple of brief glances and smiles and very few words. I could tell by the way her eyes were always there waiting to meet mine that she was concerned about me. I was concerned for myself. So much was happening so fast. My thoughts could hardly keep pace.

In the nearly forty minutes it took for us to get over to O'Hare, my mind raced over everything from my living arrangements, what was going to happen to DeMann, how all of this stress was affecting Sarah, to things like how would it be working with Donald Randolph. Of course, I didn't have any answers for any of it. I needed more time to sort things out. But, there was one thing I was able to conclude on the way to the airport. The war between me and my best friend was over. I still couldn't watch her live a lie, so my plans to move out were still concrete in my heart. However, the love and support she showed me in my times of need demanded that I never view her as anything other than an ally. Between us, love is all there ever was or will be. The war wasn't over; it never existed.

"Please call me and let me know what happens."

"I will." We hugged and said goodbye. Our warm embrace said everything that we didn't in the car.

The flight to Nashville seemed shorter than it usually does. Life always moves ten times faster than it's expected to. I knew that DeMann and I needed to work on our friendship. In approximately two months, I would give birth to our first child. I envisioned us coming together for constructive conversations about Sarah. I knew that she would steal his heart the first time he laid eyes on her and held her in his arms. Before now, the image of that moment used to warm my heart. Now, it aches my soul because I know there is a strong possibility that it will never happen.

By the time I landed and made it to my grandparents' home, it was far past visiting time at C.C.A. It was even too late for him to call me. My grandmother said that he had called too many times to count. He needed me desperately and I had no way of letting him know I was here for him. My soul ached even more.

The next morning, I was the first person in line at the jail for visitation. The security officer took my ID and information and went to have DeMann brought to the visitation area. He came back out after a very brief moment.

"Ma'am, this inmate is actually already down here. He's meeting with his lawyer right now. I'll let the inmate know you're here and, as soon as he's done with his lawyer, we can send you in."

That was the first time that I heard DeMann referred to as an inmate. It seemed like making 'inmate' his official name was part of the sentence or something. It stung me much more than I had anticipated. I don't know why, but I felt a little relief knowing that DeMann knew I was here. I sat down and waited for them to come back and get me.

After another brief moment, the same guard came back and told me that DeMann and his lawyer requested that I join them. He asked me to follow him down the hall to a small room where a female officer was waiting. She frisked me and searched through my clothes. Then, I followed her out of the room and into a medium-sized room with about twenty cubicles around the edges. Each cubicle had a thick glass barrier that separated the visitors from the inmates.

I scanned the room, looking for DeMann. I almost didn't recognize him standing up on the other side of the glass looking at me with a shaved head. They had already forced him to cut off his locs. As I got closer, I could see the expression on his face. His heart was weeping. He'd already been in jail too long. I could see the bruises on his face from where he'd been hit. My heart hit the floor. I could only imagine what life was like in prison with a "cop killer" title on your back.

DeMann's lawyer was a short, stocky black man with a grim face and a gold tooth outline around one of his side teeth. If we had met under other circumstances, I would've thought he was a drug dealer too. He introduced himself as Mr. Neismith and asked me to sit down so he could finish talking with DeMann. I could tell he started over from the beginning of his spiel. It seemed like he was trying to sell something. I braced myself to hear what he had to say. The harsh words were already written all over DeMann's face. Whatever he was selling wasn't good.

He explained that DeMann was facing several felony charges. The most serious was first-degree homicide of a law enforcement officer. He said it carried a possible death sentence and, given DeMann's previous felony charge of armed trafficking, the state prosecutors would definitely seek the death penalty.

He said that the only eyewitnesses besides the other two defendants were the other officers who were involved in the shootout. They were all lining up to testify against DeMann. I had no doubt that they had something to do with his facial bruises. He said that the most damaging piece of evidence to DeMann's case was the forensic test that proved DeMann did fire his gun during the shootout after he made a statement that he didn't shoot it at all. He said the autopsy of the dead officer would confirm whose gun fired the fatal shot. But regardless of whether or not it was DeMann's gun, the fact that he fired a weapon in the first place hurt him tremendously. Then he looked DeMann in the eyes and suggested that rather than go to trial, he take a plea deal that would ensure he get sentenced to life in prison and save him from the death penalty. I almost passed out.

"Ah shit! Man, you telling me that the only choice I have is between life in prison or death?" I don't know how far Mr. Neismith got in his explanation before I arrived, but his suggestion was just sinking in for DeMann. As he leaned back in his chair and placed his hands over his face, I could sense his spirit caving in.

I've known DeMann damn near his whole life. If only he could've seen what selling drugs was really costing him. He was fully aware of the damages to others and he couldn't care less. He was aware of the risks like jail and death but he'd never taken them seriously. Until now.

If only he knew that the reason he didn't care was because he'd already paid the ultimate cost. I knew him before all of this. Selling drugs had stolen all the substance of his beautiful spirit. At the point when all the substance is gone, all that's left is an empty, materialistic shell. He'd attached his self-worth to the only thing he had left—his money. It really was the root of all his evils. Now, he stood face to face with its consequences.

DeMann could hardly speak when he told Mr. Neismith that he would agree to the plea and asked him to leave. "I'll call you in the morning before they bring me to the courthouse. I need to talk to my girl alone now."

I felt a definite sense of detachment when I heard him refer to me as his girl, but that was the last thing in the world I would hit him with now. I'd let him think whatever he needed to comfort him.

Mr. Neismith briefly went over a few particulars for the arraignment the next morning and left. To come to the table with those terms and leave with a sale, Mr. Neismith was one hell of a salesman indeed.

Once he left, DeMann and I faced each other and let the tears flow. I wasn't crying because I was scared of what would happen to him. We both knew he would be able to take care of himself physically. I cried because I knew my child's father was a much better person than what his life had reduced him to. Regardless of what they referred to him as, DeMann Crowley was much more than just a damn inmate. Right then, I made a silent vow to make sure his daughter knew that about him.

"Chaia, listen to me." He gathered himself the best he could. "They confiscated everything I had. The house, the cars, everything is gone. All I got left to leave you is a package that Rodney has for me." He was falling apart as he spoke. "I want you to take that and make sure my daughter is alright." He paused. I knew he wanted to elaborate more, but was scared he was being recorded. "I'm so glad that you didn't have that abortion. I'm sorry for all the trifling shit I did to you, you deserved better than that. I know you gonna end up with another dude eventually. Just make sure he treats you better than I did and that he loves my daughter. If anybody starts tripping on you, call Rodney and he'll get that shit straight." He made it seem like he had chosen the death penalty instead of a life sentence. To him, maybe they were both the same.

He didn't give me a chance to talk. He gave me a few more directives, made sure I was coming to the courthouse, and then stood up and started to walk away.

"DeMann!" I didn't know what to say, but I felt I needed to say something. I wanted him to know that someone would be thinking of him. Someone would miss him. "I'm gonna bring her to see you and I'll tell her what a good person you are."

He broke down. He was trying to get out of my sight before he did, but what I said broke him down. He sat back down.

"Do you still love me?" I nodded as we both reached towards the glass.

"And I always will." I knew I didn't love him in the way he meant, but whatever comfort I could pass through the glass was a worthy compromise. We shared a few more quiet moments as he gathered himself to walk away. I blew him a kiss and left.

*****

The next morning, I went to the downtown courthouse in the Justice A. Birch Building on 2nd Avenue North. I entered the courtroom and saw Rodney sitting in the middle of the room. I went and sat down beside him. He was barely holding himself together. As I looked around, I saw the sad faces of family members and loved ones everywhere. This is the last place you want to see someone you love.

I watched several cases go before the judge. He seemed unbiased, impartial, and frighteningly unmerciful. In five cases, he sent five young men to jail. To me, it seemed he was warming up for the main event.

When they brought DeMann in through the side door, he was wearing shackles on his hands and feet. The look on his face was heartbreaking. I immediately felt overwhelmed. This was going to be much harder than I thought. He searched the room for me and I stood up so he could see me. I saw the relief in his eyes once we made eye contact. Me and Rodney were the only ones there for him.

"The People of the State of Tennessee versus Demon Crowley." The bailiff mispronounced his name in a horrible way. *That motherfucker did*

227

that on purpose. Even Ms. James was aware that this process wasn't set up in DeMann's favor.

They made him stand up while the judge read off the charges he faced. DeMann stood tall and strong, as I knew he would. That's why he wanted me here; so he would have the strength to face them. The judge then acknowledged that a plea agreement had been made and looked at DeMann with the same unmerciful eyes that had looked at the last five young men.

"Mr. Crowley, do you enter this plea agreement of sound mind and of your own free will?"

"Yes, sir." I had never heard DeMann speak with such a defeated tone before. My already welling eyes began to overflow.

"Mr. Crowley, for the felony charge of armed distribution of a controlled substance you are sentenced to seventeen years in a state penitentiary. This sentence is to be served in continuum with eight years of a suspended sentence for violation of parole." DeMann still appeared strong. "For the felony charge of homicide in the second degree of a law enforcement officer, you are hereby sentenced to life in a state penitentiary beginning immediately at Riverbend Maximum Security Prison. Do you understand your sentences?" All DeMann could do was nod his head and mumble the word 'yeah'.

Bam!

The judge banged his gavel down and life for DeMann, me, and Sarah was officially changed forever.

My head began to spin. If it was affecting me that way, I could only imagine how it was affecting DeMann. Wounded, defeated, and vulnerable, he responded just as I thought he would. The only way his fearful spirit knew how to respond to anything that challenged it to change—he looked to me. I was his strength the whole time. I stood up so he could see me as they escorted him back out of the courtroom. Emotionlessly, he watched me the whole time. He would have to be his own strength now, just as I would have to be mine and Sarah's.

I walked out of the courtroom numb and deflated. I had lost a friend. My daughter had lost a chance for a meaningful relationship with her father before she even had a chance to breath. I cried for her as well.

When we walked out to the parking lot Rodney asked me to walk with him to his truck. As he drove me towards mine he reached in the backseat and handed me a Hello Kitty backpack.

"This is for you and the baby. It's the whole 125. It's all there". He made it seem like he was handing it to DeMann himself. In his heart and mind he was.

I didn't know what to say. I had never seen money like that much less had it handed to me. I thought of what that money costs DeMann and it seemed like such a puny amount in comparison. My thoughts ranged from burning it to all the things it would do for Sarah. I gathered all those thoughts, thanked Rodney for being there to support DeMann and left the truck. I pulled into my grandparents' driveway and couldn't even remember the drive home. I was still numb.

Riverbend Maximum Security State Penitentiary
7475 Cockrill Bend Blvd.
Nashville, TN 37209-1048 (for inmate correspondence).

Damn, they don't even get to use the real zip code. I thought to myself as I navigated the internet home page. I used my laptop to visit the prison's website once I got back to my grandparents' house. I learned that this was the prison where they filmed *The Green Mile*, but that was nothing prestigious to me. They offered vocational training in printing, commercial cleaning, residential construction, cabinet making, and computer information systems. None of these applied to DeMann; he'd never get an opportunity to use those skills. He was there for the rest of his life.

You're not in there with him, what about your life? As tough as it was, I knew I had to move on. I felt like I was abandoning him, leaving my dear friend stranded on a deserted island. I had to, or I'd perish with him. I spent the rest of the day, all night, and the next morning crying, reflecting, and reminiscing about better days between me and DeMann. Then I wiped my eyes, packed my things, gathered my emotions, and left to go back home.

Once I got back to Chicago, I did my best to resume life as it was before. Even though DeMann had not played a significant role in my life there, things seemed different. I constantly thought of him. The backpack full of opportunity only produced more thoughts of DeMann. I almost felt guilty taking it. It felt as if I was accepting this as a suitable replacement for him. He placed his self-worth in money, but I always had a higher image of him. He was much more than a bag full of money. He was my friend and my heart ached for him. I prayed that the pain would subside. I knew eventually I would get used to the thought of him in that place, but, right now, it was just too new. The look on of his face as he was led out of the courtroom hurt to remember and I couldn't get it out of my head.

Since we were both on maternity leave, Sandra dragged me out shopping, almost daily, for baby items. She called herself cheering me up because she thought I was depressed. I totally agreed.

"Ooh, girl, look at these!" Sandra was showing me some bedding sets for a baby boy.

"Those are cute. Now that you know it's a boy, have you decided on a name?"

"Lesley wants to name him Lesley Jr." I lost my breath.

"Sandra, how far are you going to take this?" I was hoping she'd pretended she didn't know what I was talking about.

"Chaia, being a father is about much more than where the sperm may or may not have come from."

"Sandra, that's all well and good as long as Lesley knows the truth and decides to be the father regardless. But, he thinks he *is* the father. You lied to him and now you are gonna have to lie to your baby as well. Do you really want your baby growing up believing a lie?" She didn't have a response, at least not one she was willing to say aloud. "Look, I'm not your judge, but I am your friend and I know you're a better person than that. I can't watch you live like that. I'm moving into my own place in January after I have Sarah." We both fell silent for a moment. She quickly threw on her CBA mask and tried to joke her way out of that conversation. I let her, but I could sense how much those words hurt her.

As we were going through the baby section of Philemon's Basement, we saw a man tickling his wife as she pushed their child in a stroller. She playfully tried to tickle him back with one hand and then they shared a beautiful kiss. They paid no attention to anything around them. I didn't notice anything but them.

Now that's what the hell I'm talking 'bout. Even Ms. James' crass ass could appreciate that kind of honesty. My mind drifted off into a wonderful daydream where Evan Miles and I shared a moment just like that. I don't know why, but he always comes to mind with thoughts and dreams of that nature.

230

"Girl, so are you gonna come or what? I promise not to try to hook you up. We both are as big as whales anyway. Just come. It'll be fun to get out of the house!" Sandra was trying her best to convince me to go to the Christmas party for Lesley's firm.

"I don't know girl. I don't like the way any of my maternity dresses look on me."

"Well, then guess what section we are going to next." She was obviously not going to take no for an answer.

She was such an amazingly strong woman. I wondered if she realized that about herself. No one will ever fully know the hardships she'd had to endure. I was her best friend and I only remotely had a clue. Through them all, Sandra was still Sandra. Sure, she had her moments when the burdens got heavy, but she always bounced back to Sandra. I admired her resilience tremendously. Her strength has been just as much of a blessing to me as it has been to her. I knew in my heart that one day she would be just fine.

*****

On the night of the party, everything seemed to be perfect. The party was being held in The Signature Room restaurant, at the top of the John Hancock building. It was my first time being there. It was breathtaking. I even loved the maternity dress Sandra helped me pick out. It was a black velvet dress that looked as elegant as anything I've ever owned. It was gorgeous, just like me. Nothing could ruin my evening, not even Donald Randolph's aggravating ass.

Everything was pleasant and everyone was nice. Lesley was being especially nice since he'd learned that I was moving out. I guess I couldn't blame him. I wouldn't want someone questioning my perfectly placed lies at every turn either. Tonight we all gave each other passes. Sandra deserved to pursue her happiness however she saw fit to do so, even if I didn't agree with it. Lesley deserved to enjoy the company of the mother of his child, even if he manipulated his way through it. Sarah and I deserved everything that our future had in store.

Thoughts of that future led me to ease my way out of the party up to the observatory. I stood outside on that balcony and lost myself in the lights of the city. This was the first time that I saw Chicago like this since that first day on the plane. Only this time, I felt like a significant part of the beauty.

P. Vincent Rivers

This place held a very special significance in my life. This is where I found myself. Chicago was my home. I pretended that I saw the light on in my apartment. I couldn't wait to get there and I knew it wouldn't be long.

CHAPTER 19
EVAN MILES

I take life entirely too seriously. A chorus of every voice I'd learn to trust sang that song in total harmony. It didn't take away from the seriousness of the scenarios I'd created for myself. But still, I couldn't stop laughing. I was so high that I had just tried to text message somebody from my house phone. The mere thought of it tickled me to the point of choking. I finished smoking my blunt and went to sleep thinking about everything except what I should've been dealing with.

For nearly two weeks, the fear of facing Dr. Carson dominated my entire consciousness. I knew I couldn't let it dominate my life forever; I had to overcome the fear of facing him at some point. Today was the day. If this really was gonna kill me, then my death would be now, on my own terms.

For every step I took closer to Dr. Carson's office, ten excuses popped into my mind as to why I should turn the hell around. I could only think of one reason to keep going forward; he deserved that much from me. The drill sergeant was silent and so was Evan Miles. Both of those voices were scared shitless, just like the rest of me. As hard as walking up the hallway was, actually knocking on the door was ten times as challenging.

"Come in." He didn't even ask who it was, he already knew. I could tell by the way he had already stopped doing whatever he was doing by the time I entered the room.

"How are you, Dr. Carson?" He just nodded with a solemn look on his face. "I guess we need to talk," I continued.

"You guess?" He almost started laughing. "It's been nearly a week and a half since I asked you to come talk to me. I didn't think you were going to come."

"I guess I didn't know what to say."

"Well, you can start by telling me everything that happened."

I started at the beginning. I told him about how Celeste and I met in Atlanta. How she saw me at the restaurant and introduced herself. The fact that he saw me walk into the hotel lobby high as the ozone had to somewhat validate my helpless approach. Leaving out any detail that hinted at how much I enjoyed her company that night, I told him the whole story. I told him that she had gotten one of the dancers to give me a private dance in a back room, but didn't go into any details other than that. I couldn't think of any credible way to water that down.

"Was her name Treasure?" His question interrupted me. I could sense that he thought he was on to something.

"Yeah." The fact that he knew who it was immediately told me that he was. "Do you know her?" He grimaced and I realized I wasn't the only one guilt and shame was working on. He turned his chair around and stared out of the window. "Dr. Carson, what's going on?" I still felt myself trying to sound helpless in all of this.

"I need for you to finish telling me everything that happened." He spun his chair around and looked me directly in the eyes.

His eyes were already watering. Agony was written all over his face. It was pain I didn't want to be the cause of. I tearfully told the rest of the story. I told him about what happened at the hotel when we got back and about the times we got together in Chicago. I knew he was mad at her as well. Their confrontation was also inevitable.

I didn't know what all she would say, so I wanted him to hear everything from me first. The part about the parking lot made him jump out of his seat and slap his stack of papers all over the office. I thought for sure I would be the next thing he slapped. I watered down and summarized the rest of my story. He sat down and breathed heavily as he stared out of the window.

"Me and Cee Cee have been married for twelve years. When we met, she was a twenty-six year old dancer. I had just turned forty and my buddies took me to a strip club called Nikki's VIP in Atlanta. She was one of the dancers there that night. She took my breath away." He paused briefly as if the memory of her that night took it away again. "I invited her out that night, after she got off. She took off the rest of the night and made me feel the same way you said she made you feel." A lump formed in my throat. "I went back to see her the next night and went back to Atlanta nearly every weekend for six months. I couldn't get enough of her. She said that I was the first person she danced for and then dated because her goal was to keep dancing strictly business. She was extremely conflicted about dating me. She thought that I would never be able to trust her or love her fully, but we enjoyed each other's company too much to stop." A slight chuckle crept out between the sobs and sighs. "After about a year, we decided to get married and I helped her open her own club." She lived down there and I lived up here. For a doctor, that was perfect. When I was here, I could focus on my work and not have a wife at home that I was neglecting."

I could tell by the way he stalled that this part of the story was hard for him to recount.

"I met Treasure about a year-and-a-half ago. I had flown to Atlanta for the weekend and went to the club to pick Celeste up for dinner. She was still in a meeting with some promoters in the back office. Treasure walked up and offered a dance. I never wanted to mix business with pleasure so I don't know what made me say yes. I guess I didn't think it was a big deal. Cee Cee always offered to get the girls to dance for me whenever I had to wait for her. Treasure triggered something in me that was uncontrollable. Before I knew it, I was flying her ass up here to be with me during the week. Of course, that bullshit blew up in my face in no time." I could see the remorse in his eyes. "When Celeste found out, she was devastated. She yelled and cried in a way that I had never seen her do. She kept asking me how I would feel if I came to work and found out that one of my employees had been 'busting nuts in her mouth.'" He gasped. I didn't detail that in my story, but I knew he had married that statement with an image of my orgasm in her mouth.

He stopped talking, braced his elbows on the desk, and placed his face in the palms of his hands. I stood there, frozen. Despite a strong notion to slip out of the door, I felt an overwhelming urge to try to comfort him in some way.

"Dr. Carson, I feel so bad. I'm so sorry." That was the only thing I could think of.

"Are you, son?" He'd called me 'son' too many ways to count. This time, there was nothing fatherly or friendly about it. "Dr. Miles, all I hear are great things about your development. Professionally, your residency is not in jeopardy. Honestly, I'm too embarrassed by this to make an issue of it. Personally, however, I don't think I'll ever be able to look past this."

He looked right through me in a very uncaring manner. My professional career had been spared at the sacrifice of the closest thing to a father I'd ever known. I wanted so badly to reverse that trade. Guilt and shame made room for regret to join the execution. They all led me out the office and down the corridor to a significantly emptier life. I'd fucked up a good thing. That regret was branded into the walls of my heart by the sound of him crying as I left.

Celeste was entirely too smart to do some of the things she did. She knew better than using his cell phone to text me. She wanted to get caught eventually. She wanted to devastate him through me. I was her tool for a cruel vengeance. She saw how he responded to me in Atlanta and sensed the protective nature he had towards me. She noticed the personal, hands on approach he took towards my residency. The closer she witnessed him and I grow, the more pain she knew she could inflict. I had often wondered why me. Now I knew.

I was simply a pawn in a much bigger scheme of deceit. I was meaningless and stupidly cooperative. I ached in my soul. For the rest of the day, I was a shell of myself. The presence I usually command was noticeably missing. No one seemed to respond to me. It was just as well I was too hurt to respond to them as well. I left to go home.

"Dawg, you alright?" Greg was bothered by my silence.

"Yeah, I'm good. Just thinking that's all."

"About ole boy again? Man, it's over; just be glad you ain't lose your residency. That chick was trying to mess you up big time! You talk to her yet?"

"No, there's really nothing left to say."

We were on our way to meet one of Greg's lawyer friends. The firm was sending her to Japan for a year and she wanted Greg to help her sublease her apartment. It was in a beautiful apartment building called Museum Tower. It was located a short walking distance from Grant Park, at the intersection of Lakeshore Drive and Prairie Avenue.

"Dang, this joint is phat. Why is she having problems leasing?"

"She's not. She just found out about having to go to Japan two days ago. The firm wants her there within the next week and she wasn't going to have time to interview people, so she asked me to do it for her."

"She trusts your crazy ass? That ain't saying much for her."

"Trust me, she has good reason to. . ." He flashed a silly grin as he dialed her phone number. "Hey, I'm downstairs. I'll be up in a minute. You decent? I have my homeboy with me."

Since he found out that I knew about his HIV status, Greg had abstained from sex. At least as far as he let me know, he did. I thought he was taking time to get his mind right before he decided to date again. I hoped I was jumping to conclusions about him sleeping with this woman.

"Hey, Greg!" She seemed excited to see Greg.

"What's up, Tan? This is my good friend, Evan Miles. Evan, this is my colleague, Tania Owens.

We exchanged greetings. She had a pleasant personality and a cute face, but I thought her style was way too homely for Greg to be seriously interested. I knew him all too well. Their interaction was strictly physical. My question was, *When?* I searched their playful and flirty interaction for clues as she went over how she wanted him to handle the lease.

What is it about sex that makes people do things they know they shouldn't? I couldn't tell if their flirting was something new or old. One thing was for certain, Greg was inviting it now. It seemed his situation was the farthest thing from his mind. Currently, she was his drug of choice and he dove into the thought of her fully. Whatever consequences came with the territory, he seemed prepared to accept. But was she?

"Does she know about you?" I came straight out and asked him as we were leaving the building. He immediately got uncomfortable.

"Man, what the hell? You think I just go around telling every hoe I meet 'Hey, baby how you doing? I got HIV.'" He tried to use sarcasm to cover up his annoyance with my question.

"Nah, I don't expect you to do that. But, you going around leading them on like *you* don't know better."

He immediately got quiet. I assumed he had nothing good to say.

If you don't know what to expect from a person, it's hard to trust and believe in their words and actions. Neither of us knew what to expect from the other from day to day. I knew Greg's heart, but I didn't trust him to listen to it. He knew my intentions to help, but he didn't trust my convictions to not judge him. I allowed the conversation to fade to black. We weren't ready for that discussion yet. I knew I had to give us some space verbally, mentally, as well as physically. I needed my own place.

"How much is she charging for rent?" He thought about it for a second before he comprehended what I was implying.

"If you're sure that's what you want to do, I can make it work for you." He turned to look me in my eyes. He wanted to know if I was serious.

"Yeah, I think that would be cool." My eyes didn't waiver nearly as much as my words. I watered them down for political reasons. "But, I don't want any favors." I could tell by the building that I couldn't afford it without the favor.

"Like I said, I'll make it work for you." He laughed, seeing right through that lie and willing to help me anyway.

For the rest of the drive home, we both remained silent. We were going over everything in our heads. A lot had been said, and even more had been implied. Despite the silence, we both bobbed our heads to the music and sang the lyrics we knew. Our friendship would survive.

When we pulled up to the house, Celeste was parked at the curb, waiting. Greg looked over at me and smirked.

"Just in case you and ole boy's wife got to throwing stones at each other, please don't throw them towards my glass house."

Right is right, wrong is wrong. He made a very valid point. I conceded him that point and got out of the car.

I walked over to Celeste's car, got in, and looked at her. This was the first time I had physically seen her in weeks. She was absolutely gorgeous. I had made her a monster in my mind. For weeks and months, I had trained myself to strip her of all attraction; that was my best defense. Today, those defenses were gone. I didn't need them anymore. They had been replaced by the power of a much more efficient defender—knowledge.

There were no more shameful secrets to hide and no more selfish lust to ignore. Those bombs had already exploded and done their damage. All that was left now was the aftermath and the knowledge of what went wrong. I saw right through her beauty.

The shame, regret, and fear that usually distorted my perception of our affair were nonfactors. I looked at her and could only see what I knew to be true. Me and this woman being together was wrong. The pain I witnessed on Dr. Carson's face branded that truth in my core. I couldn't touch her again, even if I wanted to.

"I'm sure you know by now that my husband found out about us." I don't know why I paid attention to it then, but that was the first time I could ever remember her referring to Dr. Carson as her husband. *Careful, soldier. She's still playing games!* The drill sergeant was preparing me for battle. I braced myself, sharpened my knowledge, and ran onto the battlefield.

"Celeste, did you use me on purpose to get him back for cheating with Treasure?" We both knew the answer to that question was yes, but she had a confused and hurt look on her face that suggested it wasn't that simple.

"Evan, I don't know if you've ever fully given yourself to a woman before, but sometimes love hurts so bad . . ." She struggled to hold her face together. "I've been in the backseat of my husband's heart for years. I've always felt like his research, his patients, his students all came before me. He always said I was crazy for thinking that, but I thought that at some point he would care enough to indulge my heart even if he didn't agree. Instead, he gave the attention I was looking for to another woman. I gave him my best and it wasn't good enough. I felt worthless and stupid." She stared out the window and fidgeted with her hands. "He talked about you so much. That day when he saw you in Atlanta, he was so worried about you. He wanted to come check on you, but he didn't because he didn't want you to feel awkward around him. I could tell you were very special to him and I was jealous in a way. I guess I thought that if I could make you fall in love with me, it would make me feel better about all the things he placed before me. So, I pursued you." She finally looked over at me.

"Did it help you feel better about things?"

"Not in the way I was expecting. That night, Evan, you made me feel appreciated. I hadn't felt that way in so long. I could feel you noticing me in different ways. It made me feel so good I was scared to let that feeling go. Even when I came to Chicago and saw how close you two were getting to be, I couldn't let you go. I knew it was selfish, but I told myself that I had earned it."

"So what will you do now that it's over?"

"I just came to tell you that I'm truly sorry for my part in this and to let you know that I'll be moving back to Atlanta very shortly."

"Will you and Dr. Carson be able to work it out?"

"At this point, I doubt it. Our marriage has taken some serious blows."

"Do you still love him?"

"I'm in the process of redefining what love is to me. Until then, all I can say is that I love me."

She never answered the question. But when she encouraged me to talk to him, I knew she did. It made me feel worse. I had destroyed a home. It may not have been the ideal happy home, but it was blessed with the presence of genuine love. I helped sink the ship before they had a chance to right it. Guilt and shame were once again choking me to death. I coughed up a heartfelt apology in return. This wasn't all her fault. Celeste drove off crying. A foolish game had concluded with absolutely no winners.

When I walked back inside, Greg was sitting on the sofa ignoring the television. He was anxious to see what happened with Celeste.

"Man, I keep telling you that you're too nice to these bitches! You shoulda brought that hoe in here and knocked that ass out the box one last time." That wasn't the substance I was looking for. "If it was me, I woulda—"

"You woulda gave her HIV! That's all your silly ass woulda done!" My face balled up as soon as those words flew out my mouth. They stung my lips on the way out; I could only imagine how they felt to him.

"Dawg, you don't have to keep throwing mud at me. I ain't got nothing to do with the dirt you did." He paused before he spoke and used a low and calm tone. I could tell he was deeply hurt. I was already feeling guilty for blasting him like that. That guilt jumped onboard with the shit load I was already carrying.

"Greg, you right. I'm sorry, dawg. Straight up, man, I feel like shit for what I did to that dude. Dr. Carson is one of the best teachers and friends I've met in a long time. It's bad enough I messed around with her in Atlanta. But even after we got to Chicago and I knew she was his wife, I still kept fucking her. If you could've seen his face, you'd understand. The *last* thing I shoulda did was fuck her again today, so when you said that, I just snapped. But, sometimes, it seems like you don't take your shit serious." He stared back at me with a numb look on his face. It took a couple of moments for him to respond.

"When I found out I was positive, I'm not gonna lie, I sat in here and cried for days. I didn't go to work for about a week. I even contemplated suicide. I felt like my life would never be normal again. Hell, in a way I felt like it was already over. I just stopped caring. I was mad as hell at the whole world. By the time I found out, me and Stacey had been broken up for about two months. I had already done fucked two hoes. I told them to get checked out and both of them were negative so I got all excited. I thought maybe I had a false positive result or something. So, I went and got retested." He had broken down in silent tears as he spoke. "I don't know why, but when that second test came back positive again, it hurt more than the first one. I think, the first time, I was too numb to feel anything. The second time, I felt like I had a chance to get my life back, like the death sentence was overturned or something. It hurt bad, man. I had to do something to get that pain off me and keep living." He buried his face in his hands and wept.

I didn't know what to say. Even if I did, the same guilt and shame that was killing him would have choked my words as well. Earlier, when I got out of Celeste's car, all I wanted to do was go to my room, turn on some music, and be alone. Now, I couldn't leave even if I wanted to. I wanted to stay in the living room with him.

I wanted to be around him because each breath that escaped his guilt and shame gave me hope that I would survive as well. We struggled to express a few more regrets to each other before the pain forced us apart. I went to my room and turned on my music. It didn't ease a thing. I fell asleep afraid that guilt and shame wouldn't allow me to open my eyes again.

*****

The next morning, Greg seemed to be back to normal. He didn't rush out of the house to avoid having to face me. He was watching Sports Center.

"Man, I can't believe I forgot the game was on last night. Damn, I missed it!" Less than seven hours after damn near breaking down, it seemed like he didn't have a clue.

"Last night was a necessary evil." I threw him one to see if he noticed it.

"Yeah, but based on those highlights, I missed a good ass game. Just like you gonna miss a good ass party tonight. The firm's Christmas party is always a good time. C'mon and go with me. It'll be way better than that bourgeois hospital's party." He didn't have a clue, or at least he didn't let on that he did.

Greg had ignored and denied his pain so long that it had caused him to go numb. I could tell from how he reacted to things, that he doesn't feel anything anymore. If that's what ignoring the pain does to you, I didn't want any part of it. I wanted to confront it, deal with it, and overcome it. I left the house without entertaining his offer. I was determined not to ignore my situation. I didn't have a clue as to how to handle it, but sweeping it under the rug and pretending it didn't exist wasn't an option for me.

By the time I made it to work at Dr. Copeland's clinic, I had signed a contract with myself to face any and every problem head-on. I went straight to work on my assignments and didn't talk much with anyone. I was too busy thinking of ways to carry my momentum into my personal life.

"You okay, Evan?" I didn't even second-guess his sincerity. Dr. Copeland was turning out to be a good friend. "Are you going to the party tonight? Everybody's going to be there." He sounded really excited about it. "I just got off the phone with Dr. Carson. He said he RSVP'd for he and his wife. He told me to tell you to make sure you come because he wants to talk to you." He didn't know it, but he'd just made up my mind for me.

Dr. Carson and Celeste together would've been too much to bear. I didn't know what else he wanted to talk to me about, but it couldn't have been good. I wasn't trying to avoid it, but I definitely didn't want to fight that battle until I was fully prepared. Initially, I decided to just stay home, but something compelled me to go to Greg's party. It seemed like a much better scenario than sitting at home alone with my guilt and shame.

*****

"Aww sookie, sookie now! Look at'cha boy! Dawg, you clean." Greg had seen me in a suit entirely too many times to be overreacting like that. He was overhyping the evening. He wanted me to be just as excited as he was.

He was trying to sell me a dime bag of excitement and euphoria, but, tonight, I wasn't buying. I had seen what it had done to him. I didn't want any part of it or the blunt he rolled and smoked out on the balcony before we left.

Progress is measured by the most personal of all standards—your own damn satisfaction. I wasn't satisfied with where I was spiritually. I felt like I was moving backwards and I needed to change course. I couldn't find anything exciting about us doing the same things at the same type places. Greg's high antics seemed so aggravating to me I knew I wouldn't be able to hang out with him for long tonight.

"Greg, I'm gonna drive my truck. I probably will cut out a little early just to show my face at the hospital's joint. I don't want to hear anybody's mouth next week, you know." I hoped he would buy that lie with no problem.

"Whatever, man. You trippin'. It's gonna be some fine ass hoes at this joint, trust me!" After second thought, I really didn't care if he bought it or not. I just needed to be able to get away from him. I followed him downtown to the John Hancock Center.

Greg's party was just as bourgeois as what I thought the hospital's party would be. It was held at the Signature Room Lounge on the 96th floor, a floor above the restaurant. Everything seemed overly beautiful. The tables were decorated with expensive looking ornaments and flowers and all the guests had on expensive looking suits and dresses. It seemed more like show and tell than a party. I immediately felt distant from everything going on there.

At least here, I can breathe. Evan Miles was gasping for air. I didn't have to confront any angry, jealous husbands that I happened to be very fond of. I mingled a little, but mostly stayed to myself and watched Greg work the room. I could tell he had done a very good job of keeping his condition a secret. No one acted as if they knew, including him. He gave at least four young ladies his business card. I would have assumed they were business connections, but he was cheesing entirely too hard for anything professional in nature. It seemed he was satisfied with his progress, but I knew better. His dissatisfaction was killing him. His laughs served only to keep him from crying in everybody's faces. It hurt to even watch.

I walked over to the window and looked. It seemed like I could see the entire city. It was tastefully beautiful. There was nothing overdone or over exaggerated about it. Chicago is beautiful just the way it is—cold, harsh, engulfing, honest, and true. The good and bad together make a wonderful place. *Your mistakes are not your future.* Evan Miles put his arms around my shoulders and gazed out over the city with me. *Your future is out there and it will be whatever you make it.* That thought comforted my spirit. I decided to brave the cold and go downstairs to the observatory skywalk to look out. I wanted to feel closer to my dreams.

As I walked out onto the skywalk, the cold air made me start coughing. Oddly, each cough made me feel better. It seemed like I was coughing up bullshit, getting it out of my system for good. There's something so purifying about Chicago's cold air. The bitterness filters out anything false. Only truth can withstand that type of cold.

"Bless you." A woman was wrapped up several feet away, enjoying the view. Her voice sounded so lonely.

"I see you're enjoying the party about as much as I am." She laughed at my assumption as she looked over at me and smiled.

I froze in place and it had nothing to do with the cold. It was Machaia. I couldn't believe it. Her face had been in my mind so much that I had to stare at her for a moment to make sure I wasn't dreaming her up again. A million laughs, a million smiles, and endless memories all ran through my mind as if they had already happened. I don't know if she was envisioning the same things I was, but the look on her face said one thing with absolute certainty: she was just as happy to see me.

"Oh, my God. Evan! What are you doing here?" She reached over and hugged me. She said my name so naturally. It seemed like she'd been calling it forever.

"I came to the party with the friend that I told you I was living with." Excitement had stolen my breath more than the cold air.

"The crazy one?"

"Yep, he's a lawyer with this firm. Who you here with?"

"My girlfriend from the airport. Her boyfriend is a lawyer at this firm too. Small world ain't it?" We both smiled at that wonderful fact.

What is it about a person that makes them The One? We sat out on the skywalk overlooking the beautiful city of Chicago. It was like a scene out of a fairy tale. It was romantic, perfectly scripted, and unforgettable. It was the perfect setting to fall in love at first sight, but I didn't believe in love at first sight. Luckily for me, God did.

I'd been praying for a good woman, yet I hadn't even really defined to myself what I thought a good woman was. Even if I had, I didn't know if she would fit that criteria anyway. As we stood outside talking, what God showed me in her was much more than a physical attraction and it had nothing to do with a list of 'haves' and 'have nots.' It didn't follow any logical reasoning. All I knew was that despite her being pregnant and despite the fact that this was only the second time we had talked, she was beautiful in a way that I couldn't help being drawn to. I knew it would take a little time for my fearful heart to follow those wonderful thoughts into the unknown, but there was no way I would let myself just drive off again.

We sat out on the balcony talking, laughing, and sharing a moment that I would never forget. Eventually, we went back inside and spent a little more time sitting at a table in the corner of the room, enjoying each other's company. Greg came over and I introduced him. When he saw that she was pregnant, he gave me a crazy look that asked, "What the hell are you doing?" I didn't entertain his "simpleness". He'd never understand anyway. Her friend from the airport came over. Once she realized who I was, that same look she gave me at the airport came over her face and waited for me to realize that she still wasn't very fond of me.

"You wanna get out of here and go somewhere else?" I felt like asking her that same question on so many levels.

"Yes." She was reaching for my hand before she even spoke. I helped her up and we left. Neither of us even said bye to our friends. We just sent them text messages as we pulled out of the parking lot.

I drove us around downtown for a while, enjoying the city sites. We laughed about how different the city looked from the 94th floor of the John Hancock Building. She thought it was prettier from up there, but she preferred seeing it this way. She said she felt more alive down here amongst the hustle and bustle. I totally agreed.

We spent a few hours riding, stopping for hot lattes, and talking. I acknowledged life in the hustle and bustle of Chicago was a very thrilling feeling, but it was a totally different feeling from the thrill I felt from being in her presence. Whatever I was feeling seemed much more encompassing than that. It added more meaning to my words. It gave more conviction to what I was feeling. I was feeling her something serious. I watched her talk and I listened to her laugh. With all sincerity, they screamed that she was feeling me too. She directed me to her home. I dropped her off and within five minutes of driving off, we were on the phone.

"What are you up to tomorrow?"

"I have a Lamaze class tomorrow morning. After that, I'm free."

"What time is your Lamaze class?"

"Why you gonna come help wheel my fat ass in?"

"If you want me to come, I'd like that." She couldn't believe that I really wanted to go. I couldn't believe how much I really did.

"Okay. It starts at ten. I'll call you at eight o'clock *sharp* to give you the directions." She burst out into a very pleased laugh. We shared a couple more jokes and said goodnight.

The next morning, we met at a community building near downtown. I could tell by her voice over the phone that she hadn't gotten a lot of sleep either. I spent the whole night trying to make sense out of what I was feeling. The only thing that made sense was that I wanted to spend my time with her. Our eyes met and looked past the sleepless night we both had. We were both anxious to meet again. This thing we were feeling was absolutely mutual.

Only six couples showed up for the class. I can tell by the size of the room and extra mats that there should've been several more. The couples spread out in a very comfortable spacing. I focused on what the coach said the male partners should do. I wanted to support Machaia. I didn't think I would be in the delivery room or anything like that, but I was compelled to do as much as I could to help her be ready. We got into our positions and proceeded to do just that.

As we went through the class, I noticed everything about her. Her gray sweatpants and pink and gray Nikes were new. She'd bought them just for this class, I could tell. Eventually, they'd become worn. They'd be stretched and bent to the curvature of her body and motions. They'd get used to her and she'd get used to them. They would undoubtedly become her favorite. She'd cherish them and she'd cherish me the same way.

What's new today will get better with time. I dwelled on that thought for the rest of the day as we walked through a couple of stores she wanted to shop at. Sunday, we got together and went to a movie and out to dinner. We talked, laughed, nearly cried, ate, smiled, and laughed some more.

She told me about what happened with the knucklehead. She'd been through a lot and seemed so strong to me. I told her about my past relationships. I even gave her a very watered down version of me and

Celeste's affair.

We listened and watched each other as we spoke. We weren't looking for flaws. They were powerless against the momentum of our bonding anyway. We listened to each other's stories, searching between each line for a way to enhance the ending. We talked after I had dropped her off at her house and during my drive home. I fell asleep that night still dwelling on the notion of things getting better with her in time. It had evolved from just a thought to a full-fledged belief.

*****

Monday greeted me with the same bittersweet kiss. I had presentations to make, reports to prepare, and patients to treat. They didn't have any weight today. My consciousness picked them up and flung them in the "already defeated" bin. Problems weren't really problems at all.

I'm a doctor. I felt like that more than ever before. I felt like the perfect blend of swagger and humility, knowledge and curiosity, eagerness and restraint. I went to the hospital and walked into the residents' lounge with that same balance. I felt my confidence guiding every encounter I had with my colleagues.

"Evan, could you please come with me? We need to talk." Dr. Carson had walked into the room and was already walking back out the door before he even finished his question. He was not going to be avoided like before. I followed him back to his office. We didn't speak in the hallway. There was no interaction at all. I still felt balanced, but I sensed an encounter that could possibly change that.

When I walked into his office and saw Celeste sitting there, my heart nearly jumped out of my chest. My mind ran wild with the possibilities of what she's told him. He looked me directly in the eyes as he walked around his desk and sat down. His face gave me no clues. I didn't even look at her.

"Evan, we want you to know that we've decided to work it out." Celeste broke out into a warm smile. I was still on guard, waiting for the bottom to fall out of this meeting. I just stared at them until Dr. Carson started explaining why they wanted to talk to me.

He gave me a filtered summary of what happened between them. They held hands and occasionally glanced and smiled at one another with teary eyes. I could tell by the way that they squeezed each other's hand that they had resolved some painful issues.

"Evan, I believe what happened between you and my wife had more to do with a break down in our marriage than anything you did." His watery eyes stiffened. "That doesn't mean I don't recognize what you did was wrong. As a man, I have to tell you that fact will always haunt me to some degree. But, what I'm trying to say, son, is that I forgive you." He paused between some of his words. It seemed like his heart needed more time to add an extra layer of truth to them. "I don't know exactly what will happen between us, but I do know that I've grown fond of you and that still means something to me."

It took a few moments for what he was saying to sink in. Part of me felt like I didn't deserve forgiveness. He walked over and hugged me with tears in his eyes. Those tears were from both love and pain. Regardless of what I thought I deserved, he offered it to me anyway. It brought me to tears as I acknowledged my sins against him and apologized for making them. He squeezed me harder.

Dr. Carson was the closest thing to a father that I'd ever had. What a wonderful example he was. His love for his wife was bigger than that for himself. He had enough love for me that he swallowed a lot more than a man usually would in order to maintain our friendship. I returned his embrace and forever welcomed whatever presence he was willing to have In my life.

As Dr. Carson was hugging me, Celeste and I finally had a moment of direct eye contact. Our affair was over. I could tell by the way we hung on to the moment for a few extra seconds. We both wanted to make sure the other understood. Whatever circumstances and emotions created, the affair was over. I knew our interactions would always be awkward. Our history couldn't be changed. Dr. Carson and I were family now. The presence of unconditional love defined us as such. The respect and boundaries of that bond would always have to be maintained.

"Are you going home for the break?" Despite his still watery eyes, Dr. Carson had gathered himself enough to offer that question with a smile. It lightened up the interaction immensely.

"I'm going home for Christmas, but I'll be back before New Year's. I'm moving into my own place."

"From the stories you tell me about your roommate that sounds like a good thing. Where are you moving to?" I reached into my overcoat and gave him a card I took out of Greg's lawyer friend's building.

Museum Tower
1400 S. Prairie Ave./Lakeshore Dr.

"I know this place and I know how much we pay you. Can you afford this?" He gave a curious laugh. His eyes weren't laughing though, he really was concerned.

"I'm pretty sure I'll have a roommate." He looked at me with puzzlement on his face.

"A female?" He asked like he already knew it was. Me showing all ninety-seven of my teeth must have given it away. They both looked even more curious after I told them yes it was a female.

Machaia moving in with me was just a thought. It had crossed my mind a few times over the weekend, but I wouldn't dare ask her now; it was entirely too soon. The thought of it really felt good to me. I thought it was a great idea. She told me that she really needed to get out of the house she was staying in. This was a two-bedroom place, so she could have her own room for her and her baby. And it was much more convenient to her job than where she was staying now. Everything about it made perfect sense, except the fact that we had basically just met.

*****

Over the next week-and-a-half, before I went home for Christmas, Machaia and I hung out almost every night. We went to dinners, we caught movies, and I helped her shop for baby items. Sometimes she drove over to Greg's place and left her truck while I drove us, but mostly I went and picked her up from the lawyer's house. The nights we didn't hang out, we talked on the phone more than we would have if we did get together. We never discussed becoming a couple; we just enjoyed each other's company. There was no pressure or any over thinking the situation. The more time we spent together, the thought of us moving in together felt more comfortable to me.

During my five-day trip home for Christmas, we talked for hours each day. I was convinced that this was something I wanted to do. I mentioned to her that I was moving into my own place. I told her that it was a two-bedroom unit near downtown. She said she was happy for me and that she couldn't wait to see it. If she did catch on to what I was implying, she didn't act like it. It was still too early so I didn't ask her that question. For the rest of my visit home, I tinkered between asking her and not asking her.

*****

"You're gonna what?" Greg was beside himself. "Man, you crazy as hell. You don't even know that chick. How you gonna just move in with her *and* her newborn baby? E, that's crazy, man. You gotta rethink that shit, big time." I decided to run the idea by Greg before I asked Machaia. I knew his reaction before he even gave it. I just wanted to hear his argument.

"I have thought it over and I think it's a good idea."

"For her! Dawg, I'm telling you, that hood rat is just throwing some pregnant pussy at you, trying to get a nigga to take care of her and her baby."

"Greg, you trippin! Me and her ain't even thinking 'bout sex."

"You ain't even got the pussy and you moving this bitch into your crib?" He smacked his lips and sighed loudly, like he was frustrated with me. "E, trust me, dawg. That bitch found out you're a doctor and lit the fuck up. She's after your money. Please believe it. If your dumb ass wanna go out like that, then fine. It ain't nothing else I can tell you." He looked at me as if I was the dumbest person on earth.

There was nothing else I could tell him. Greg had enough knowledge and insight to have a much better perspective of women; he simply didn't want to know any better. It seemed he preferred living in ignorance. He chose to ignore all that his experiences had taught him about love and ignored all of Super G's pleas for growth and change. It was easier for him to pretend that all women 'ain't shit.' That way, he wouldn't be wrong for disrespecting them the way he did. He was dead wrong and absolutely content being so.

Not me, I knew better. I had been through enough rainy days to know what sunshine looked and felt like. There was something special about what was forming between me and Machaia. The last thing I was gonna do was let a bitter, ignorant nigga mess it up. I had learned a valuable lesson;

affairs of the heart are better off determined within my own heart. I regretted even asking him.

Machaia and I had decided to spend New Year's Eve together in my new apartment. Her due date was the next week and being pregnant was getting on her last nerve. She was always uncomfortable and never slept well. Even so, she was always happy to see me and wanted to spend as much time with me as she could. Some things can't be pretended or ignored—I was falling for her. I went out of my way to make her New Year's Eve perfect. Blackened fish, a pot of homemade zuppa tuscana, microwave popcorn, *Boomerang*, *Jason's Lyric* and *The Five Heartbeats* all made for a very unconventional New Year's Eve. It was just the way she liked it, which made it just as I wished . . .perfect.

"Evan, this was a really nice night. Thank you so much."

"What time is it?" I already knew it was 2:00 a.m. "Wow, I didn't know it was that late. Your friends are still probably out. You should just sleep here and let me take you home in the morning."

"You had this whole thing planned out, didn't you?" Her smile told me she was happy that I did.

"I already got the guest room set up and everything." I burst out laughing.

She got up and followed me to the guestroom. It was very tastefully decorated. Greg's friend had wonderful taste. I had washed the linens and made the bed. The lights were off and my favorite Ocean Breeze candle was burning. Shadows of an abstract sculpture sitting on the nightstand were projected over the ceiling and walls. They looked like a protective cage. She was safe to sleep, dream, and love. I prayed that was how she felt.

"I'll let you get set for bed. I put a clean t-shirt on the bed for you. Just call me if you need anything."

I wished her Happy New Year again, kissed her lips, and left for my room. Our eyes hung onto one another's, as I closed the door. She was happy to be here. I saw that in her expressions. I saved the image of those happy expressions in my mind. I lay in my bed and scanned them over and over again. Her expressions were genuine, honest, and excited. They were perfect imitations of mine.

"Evan, are you sleep?" She crept into my room holding the candle on a hand towel.

"Nah, just laying here thinking. What's up?" She walked over and placed the candle on my dresser.

"Do you mind if I sleep in here with you?" She was already climbing into the bed before she finished asking the question.

Just like that, we were official. She was wearing the t-shirt I bought her, her make-up was off, her pregnant belly was sticking out, and her hair was combed back. She was comfortable and showed no reservations to climbing in bed with me. She got under the covers, backed up to me, placed my arms around her, and took a deep breath.

"This feels good." She squeezed my arms against her body. It took me a few seconds to realize that it wasn't just my heart I heard talking, but that she had actually spoken those exact words too. I squeezed her back and we fell asleep, smiling and laughing from the inside out.

*****

The next morning, we woke and had little to say. The hugs and deep breaths as we continued to lay in bed for a while said enough. We made small talk as we gathered her things and took them to the car. We stopped for hot lattes, as we drove back to her house.

"You know, I'll probably have to get a roommate to stay in that condo." I threw that statement out very nonchalantly, as she was preparing to get out of the truck.

"Why? Is it too expensive? It looks like a pretty pricey spot."

"Nah, it's not too bad. Greg got me a good hook-up on it. I could do it by myself, but it would be much more comfortable with a good roommate." I knew she had a good idea of just how many ways I meant that.

"Sounds like a good deal for somebody looking for a new place. I'm sure you'll have plenty of people interested in moving into a nice apartment like that."

"That's just it. I don't want just anybody being my roommate. I need a really good roommate." I could tell by the way she widened her eyes that she understood what I was asking her.

"Well, I know a young lady that might be interested in something like that. I'll talk to her about it and get back to you." Her wide smile suggested that the young lady was very interested. I burst into a big smile as well.

I drove off in the best mood I could remember being in for long time. Everything seemed good today. It was my turn to pull call duty at the hospital. The fact that it was always miraculously the residents turn to pull call duty on the holidays seemed cool today. I almost felt like I should pay for being that happy. Happiness should always require some sort of sacrifice, so it could be cherished properly.

I had been in the hospital for about six hours and I still riding my natural high when Susan from the front desk came to give me a message. .

"Dr. Miles, you have a visitor at the front desk." She peeked into the residents' lounge to tell me that.

"Okay, I'll be there in a second."

I knew it wasn't Dr. Carson. He would've just come back himself. I didn't think it was Greg either. He would've texted me before he just showed up at the ER. The nurse didn't make it seem like an emergency, but I rushed out front anyway. I was curious who it was.

"Hello, Evan." It was Sandra, Machaia's friend.

"Hey, what's up? Is everything okay?" I was frightened and confused.

"Yeah, everything is cool. I was wondering if you had a moment. I needed to talk to you"

"Yeah, sure." I pointed and escorted her to an empty part of the reception room so we could talk.

"Things between you and Chaia seemed to have gotten pretty serious, pretty fast."

"Yeah, I guess they have. I like her a lot."

"*Like*! The things you two are talking about seem much more than just *like*. I don't know what your deal is, but I just want to let you know that Chaia has been through a lot of shit and I hope you ain't just trying to play games with her."

"Sandra, that's your best friend. I respect you questioning me on this. Trust me, it's not as much as I've questioned myself. Honestly, this doesn't make total sense to me either, but, there is a connection between us that makes all the thinking and rethinking irrelevant. Right now, all I can tell you is that I genuinely want her in my life."

"'Right now.'" She looked at me crossly, a manner similar to when Celeste showed up at the airport.

"What more is there?"

"There's tomorrow and the day after that and the day after that!"

I started laughing. She didn't. She was seriously checking me. I stopped laughing and answered her seriously.

"Sandra, what I'm trying to say is that Machaia has become a priority to me. I care about what happens to her and I care about how she feels. I'm not just playing games. I've been a part of and witnessed enough of those in my lifetime to know that's not what I want for myself. Just judge me by my actions. If you see something that ain't right, call me on it. Deal?"

She stared at me with a stern look on her face. After a moment, she gave me an agreeable smile. She must have found the reassurance she was looking for. "Girl, you wasn't playing. You came way up to my job to chin check me." I was joking, but the thought of it made me realize how important this was to her.

"Dude, you give yourself entirely too much credit. I didn't come all the way to this hospital just for you." She burst into a huge grin. "She's upstairs in Labor and Delivery, giving birth. We passed damn near a hundred hospitals on the way here, but she wanted to come to the hospital where you were at."

I don't remember what she said after that. My whole focus had shifted from everything other than Machaia. I rushed up to the L & D unit on the third floor. It would be too easy to disregard the coincidence of my feeling so good today and her being here. Nothing worthwhile is ever easy. It wasn't a coincidence and I didn't pretend it was.

By the time I made it upstairs, Machaia's OB/GYN had arrived and was examining her. I let Machaia know that I would be back to check on her later. She lit up when she saw me and I tried to make it as evident as possible that she'd had the same effect on me. I went back downstairs and anxiously finished out the remaining four hours of my shift. By the time I made it back upstairs, her daughter had already been born. The baby had been cleaned and brought back to Machaia.

I cracked the door to the room open and peeked in. Machaia was staring at her baby and crying. They were undoubtedly tears of joy. I'd never witnessed a mother hold her child for the first time before. It truly is one of life's miracles. Witnessing God in the process of forming that kind of bond between two strangers is the most powerful thing I've ever seen.

My practice was forever changed. I realized that a good doctor must allow God his space to perform the surgeries on the things I'd never be able to nip, cut, or sew. I saw him wrapping that little girl in her mother's love. I immediately placed myself in that baby's place and wondered how my mother held me and what she said. I decided not to interrupt the moment. There was important work being done. I backed away before Machaia noticed me, closed the door, and went back out to the lobby.

"Did you see her?" Sandra almost seemed excited about me going to see Machaia.

"She was crying 'cause she was so happy. I know she's probably thinking about her mom. I didn't want to bother her right now. I'll give her a little time to spend with Sarah, then come back and check on her."

Sandra seemed surprised at my sentiment. She seemed shocked that I knew all about Machaia's birth and how her mom died. She hugged me and said that she thought it was a good idea to wait before she went back herself. I went back downstairs and volunteered to help out a little while longer. That was the only way I could keep myself from running back upstairs.

By the time I came back to Machaia's room, Sandra was getting ready to go. It seemed like she would be delivering herself in any second now. Both of them were teary-eyed. I could tell they had some emotional words before I came in. Sandra got up, kissed the baby, hugged me, and left smiling. I took her seat beside the bed.

"Sandra told me you came up earlier."

"Yeah, I thought you needed some mother-daughter time, so I left you alone."

"Thank you. I appreciate that. I don't even know what to say. She's so beautiful."

"You both are." Even with her wide smile, she looked like she was about to tear up again.

"You want to hold her?"

She handed Sarah over to me. There was so much I didn't know. I didn't know how to act fatherly; I'd never had an example growing up. I didn't know what to say, what to do, or what I was supposed to be feeling. I didn't even know if I had the right to feel anything in the first place. I felt pretty comfortable with how Machaia felt about me, but I didn't know if her baby was off limits for me to feel connected to.

Despite my confusion, my feelings took off in a very deliberate direction. Whatever bond existed between Machaia and I was readily transferred to Sarah. As I sat there playing with her, her beautiful light brown eyes melted me. She had a father. Through no fault of hers, he couldn't be here, but I was a willing substitute. I was willing to share with her, love her, and absolutely willing to shield her from anything that may come. God hadn't put his tools down yet. The second bond was just about complete.

"You sure you want something like that in your apartment?"

Until Machaia laughed that question to me, I had almost forgotten she was in the room.

"You can't just accept a child into an apartment. You have to accept it into your heart and life." That statement felt as profound as it sounded to me saying it.

"And you're saying that you're willing to do that?" She almost sounded defensive, protective.

"Machaia, listen. I won't pretend that this isn't freaking me out just as much as it is you. I keep telling myself that this can't be real, but, the more I think about it, the more I realize that meeting you was the realest thing to happen to me since I came to Chicago. I'm not saying that we're ready to go get married or anything. We can take things slowly and let it be what its gonna be. I know for sure, that the very least we'll be is very good friends. You moving in with me is a good move for both of us. There's no pressure and it doesn't mean that I expect you to commit yourself to me. Just take your time and think about it before you make your decision." I tried to scale back what I was saying. I was sure that if I told her what I was really feeling, it would've freaked her out.

"Evan, I made my decision as soon as you asked me." She reached over and placed her hand over the hand I was using to rub Sarah's head.

Through my relationships, life has taught me that I don't know everything. Everything I thought I knew for sure, I learned I really didn't know at all. There was no real sense in even trying to know. Everything in life changes daily. The only constant is love. It's the rock I learned to lean on when life's winds of change come roaring through. In the wake of those storms, I learned that happiness is simply a choice to overcome struggle. I'd already decided.

"I have to go back downstairs to grab my things." I stood up and passed Sarah back to Machaia.

"How long before you get off?"

"I'm already off. You want me to come back up?"

"I wanna see you, but I'd rather you to go to the apartment and get everything ready. I told Sandra that you would be coming to pick up our things. We're gonna be coming home tomorrow."

For there to be so much sentiment in that statement, if felt comfortably good hearing the words roll off her lips.

I left the room. I did come back to check on her before I left; I couldn't help it. When I peeked in the room, they were both sleep. I walked over and stared at them for a moment. As good as I felt coming into the hospital this morning, I left feeling infinitely better. Chicago finally felt like home.

CHAPTER 20
MACHAIA JAMES

"Oh my God. Evan! What are you doing here?" I almost yelled his name. This was only the second time I've ever seen him and I felt like I had run into a long lost friend. I reached over and hugged him.

"I came to the party with my friend that I told you I was living with." He was so excited he could hardly speak.

"The crazy one?" He seemed shocked that I remembered our conversation. If he only knew how much I had thought of him, he'd really trip out.

"Yep, he's a lawyer with this firm. Who you here with?"

"My girlfriend from the airport. Her boyfriend is a lawyer at this firm too. Small world, ain't it?" After the way things played out at the airport, I decided to keep my expectations to a reasonable low. I didn't know if the stuck up, rich girl was here with him or not.

It didn't take me long to figure out she wasn't. We talked and talked. Everything about him seemed to be the way I imagined him to be. He was funny, smart, respectful, and seemingly honest. He told me that the woman at the airport was married and that he had made a mistake in being involved with her. The pain he felt was evident when he told me.

We left the party and rode around while we continued talking. All the reservations I had about him from the airport were quickly disappearing and being replaced with confidence. I believed he was a good guy. It came across in his conversation, his manners, and the most beautiful smile in the world. We were just scratching the surface of getting to know one another and I already felt like I couldn't get enough of him. He even agreed to meet me at my lamaze class the next morning. I couldn't believe he was willing to do that. I couldn't believe I felt comfortable letting him. An incredible feeling of happiness and excitement comforted me for the rest of the evening.

"Good morning." He looked and sounded like he'd had a rough night.

"Good morning to you, sir. I bet you're asking yourself 'what have I gotten myself into, huh?"

"Please. I'm gonna go in here and get my breathing on." He joked and took several over exaggerated deep breaths, trying to show me how he was gonna do it inside. "Oooh, I'm 'bout to kill myself out here sucking in this hawk. I feel my lungs freezing as we speak."

I had actually breathed in some cold air myself, laughing at his crazy butt, but that beautiful smile warmed it over before it even had a chance to sting good.

I couldn't believe he actually showed up. Hell, I can't believe he walked out onto that skywalk last night. Part of me believes he really did walk right out of my dreams. I thought he was joking about wanting to come to my Lamaze class, but I could tell by his excitement and demeanor, he really did.

This was one hell of a first date. I believed he was one hell of a man. The instructor directed me to sit in front of him. He had to help me hold my stomach while I practiced my breathing technique. I felt unbelievably comfortable in his arms.

"I ain't playin'. I think that fool is in labor for real. Look at them big ass veins in her forehead. You can't pretend strain like that. She's either in labor or shitting."

He kept making jokes about how hard the lady next to us was practicing her breathing. He had me rolling. Laughs and smiles were bursting out of me from the inside out.

The instructor explained that the class was designed to reduce the fears of delivery. With Evan here, that had already started to happen. When does faith in a person begin? In regards to me and him, it doesn't matter. Discussing it is a moot point. Whenever it began for us, one thing is certain. My faith in him had arrived.

We had about two weeks before Evan went home for Christmas. We spent every moment we could together. It wasn't something we planned or even decided to do, it just happened like that. Morning calls to say hello, lunch get-togethers downtown, dinners, movies, and late night calls to say goodnight—they all just happened. The more time we spent together, the more time I wanted to spend with him. It was a very natural progression.

"The One! Girl, you ain't known this man but two weeks. What in the hell makes you think that he is *The One*? What does he do?"

"He's a doctor." I was proud of him for accomplishing the things he had. The fact that her mind associated being The One with what he does for a living told me everything I needed to know about her advice.

"That knock-off suit wearing nigga ain't no damn doctor. He just running game on you, girl. Please don't fall for that bullshit, Chaia. I'm telling you, I've seen his type before. He'll sell you whatever pipe dream he thinks you wanna hear—"

"In order to what?" I interrupted her foolishness. "To get some pussy?" I grabbed my belly and she could tell she struck a nerve. She waived her arms like 'I've already warned you, we'll see' and eased away.

A conversation that started about a man possibly being the one for me ended up being about him wearing knock-off suits and lying. Her perspective and opinions were born from her own experiences. Surface-level bullshit experiences were all she'd ever known.

Up until now, DeMann was all I've ever known. Lies, lies, lies, and more lies. Her relationships with men and my relationship with DeMann were all built on lies to some extent. Lies we told ourselves. DeMann didn't love me. I told myself that lie and used it as an excuse to accept his bullshit for far too long. His selfish ass probably couldn't even spell love; he was just comfortable having someone that he could control.

Sandra was still caught up in her web of lies. She had wiggled around in them enough to get comfortable there. From whoever to Javier, to Lesley to whoever; she jumped from one web to the next, creating relationships built on lies. She told herself every lie imaginable, hoping that one would turn out to be truth. What I knew to be true was the opposite—the lies she thought she could live with were steadily becoming the death of her.

*****

"Everything is prepared just as you wished, my lady. What time will you be arriving for dinner madam?" Evan was trying to sound like an English butler. His fake accent was hilarious.

"Thank you for all you've done, fine gentleman. I shall arrive whenever the hell I get there." My accent was just as ridiculous and my response cracked us both up.

Our laughs couldn't hide the anxiousness we both seemed to have. This was the first time I'd see him since he came back from visiting his mother for Christmas and I couldn't wait.

There were so many details in the little things. He'd paid attention to so much of what I had said. He remembered my favorite movies, and had made notes of all the things I said I usually had pregnant cravings for. He'd even rubbed my feet while we watched the movies. It was all there, all the comforts of home. Evan was a single, attractive doctor. He could've been a million and one places celebrating New Year's Eve, but he seemed ecstatic to be spending it catering to me. He'd even gotten the guest room ready for me and bought a large maternity t-shirt that read "Chicago's Finest in the Making" with an arrow pointing to my stomach. The attention he paid to the little details spoke volumes. The most honest of all it said was that he cared.

"Do you need anything else?" He was still looking for other ways to please me.

"No, thank you. I think you've done enough. Thank you for everything."

He leaned over, kissed me on the lips, and wished me goodnight. We had kissed before, but they were quick pecks as I was getting out of his truck. Never in public and never with enough length for me to feel what I felt in that moment. I'd just kissed the softest lips that God had ever made. I could feel the gentleness of his spirit, the tenderness in his heart, and his caring touch. I melted on the inside and had to disguise my gasp for air on the outside. He left the room without saying anything else. I tried to thank him once again, but I couldn't get the words out.

I got comfortable and changed into the t-shirt. I lay in the bed, watching the candle flame burning. It flickered in perfect unison to the one he lit in my heart. It only took a few minutes for his presence to summons mine.

"Evan, are you sleep?" I didn't even try to talk myself out of going to his room.

"Nah, just laying here thinking. What's up?"

I was done pretending that this wasn't happening. For whatever reason, God saw fit for us to feel this way for each other. It was obvious to us both. We had been trying to make ugly sense out of something that was senselessly beautiful. I walked over and placed the candle on the dresser.

"Do you mind if I sleep in here with you?" He was already scooting over to make room for me as I walked towards the bed.

No one will understand, including us. Sandra will judge, my grandparents will judge, and I hated to think about how DeMann would react. But, they would all have to get used to us. They would have to learn to be as comfortable with him as I was in his arms. I knew that wouldn't be an easy transition, but that fact seemed so trivial, right now. Despite my back hurting and all the other discomforts of being pregnant, I felt good in his arms.

The same comfort that caressed me and eased my pain as I fell asleep, kissed me as I woke. I was still speechless, but so was he. We joked a little as he drove me home and we laughed much harder than the jokes required. It seemed we were both bubbling on the inside. As he dropped me off at Lesley's, he subtly asked me to move in with him. He'd made slight hints at that thought before, but I played dumb.

I was intrigued by the thought, but I wanted to make sure he really was serious and not just caught up in the moment. I wasn't even sure if I thought it was a good idea yet. I had Sarah to think about. She was due within the next week or so and I needed to make sure everything for her was as stable as could be. It was too close to my due date for me to be making any drastic changes now anyway. Still, the thought was intoxicating. I couldn't help but to burst out laughing as I joked with him that I would think about it. If only he knew I'd been seriously considering it ever since he first started hinting.

"Are you okay, girl?" Sandra looked at me with a puzzled look as she asked me that question. She stopped what she was doing and started walking towards me.

After Evan dropped me off, I was sitting at the kitchen table talking to her as she was putting some black-eyed peas in the crock pot, for New Year's Day dinner. I'd been feeling pains in my back and pressure building since the night before at Evan's house. I knew exactly what was happening.

"Take me to Stroger Hospital. I think I'm going into labor."

All of the signs were there. The lower back pains, the pressure in my pelvic area—everything I was taught to notice was happening. I was scared. All of the Lamaze classes, all of the planning, and all of the dreaming of motherhood were supposed to have prepared me for this moment. I hoped they had. The only thing outside of my training that I could think of was getting to Stroger Hospital. I knew Evan was there and that he'd take care of me.

By the time I made it to the hospital and got admitted into the Labor and Delivery unit, my doctor had left several messages for me to call her. She had a trillion and one questions. I had a trillion and two answers. She wanted to know everything I was experiencing. I told her. She wanted to know if I had any questions. I asked them. She also wanted to know why I chose to come to this hospital and not the one we had planned on. I told her that I had recently moved to an apartment downtown and that this would be the most convenient hospital for me. She understood. I didn't, but I still felt very good about the decision. She left instructions with the nurse to call her when I dilated to seven centimeters. She said that if my water had not broken by then, she'd break it to help progress my delivery. She also said I was in for a long day. I closed my eyes, worked on my breathing, and tried not to think of the pain.

Ain't nothing but pressure. Ms. James was trying to get her game face on. I requested to not receive an epidural. Sandra thought I was crazy. I agreed, but I believed motherhood had to be earned. My mother earned hers. I'd earn mine. My doctor came and stuck a long pin inside of me. I didn't even know she'd broken my water until it felt like I pissed all over myself.

"Everything ok in here?" Evan had come upstairs to check on me. I wasn't able to talk with him, but his presence was very comforting.

The pressure built up to a point that I thought I was splitting in half. I opened my legs wide and my heart wider to let my blessings flow. I breathe hard and squeezed harder.

"Sarah Gayle Crowley!" I yelled her name as she came out. Sarah Gayle Crowley. I never had the problem of having to decide a name. Gayle was my mother's name. DeMann earned his respect. His name would forever be bonded to his child and I'd make sure she knew the beautiful things about him that I knew.

They handed her to me. Sarah Gayle Crowley was here. I felt so strong when she was in my arms. She'd never be too heavy for me to hold. Our eyes met for the first time and I couldn't see her clearly at first because my eyes wouldn't stop tearing. They had wrapped her in a blanket, but I had wrapped her in love well before they did that, just like my mother did me. Sarah was in my arms and my mother was here with us. My heart exploded and emptied its contents all over them both. There was no way I could hold all that love in. I cried hysterically. It felt so wonderful. Sandra, my doctor, and the nurses all tried to help me stop, but I didn't want to stop. Eventually, they all left me alone and I let my emotions spew until I fell asleep.

When I woke, Sandra was sitting next to the bed watching over me.

"Girl, how do you feel?" She was holding Sarah. She had been crying.

Part of me knew they were tears of joy. Of all people, she knew how much Sarah meant to me. Sadly, I also knew some of those tears came from a more convicting source. She would soon be holding her baby. The world she must be envisioning for her child had to be a lot different than the one she was preparing.

"I feel beautiful." That was the best way I could describe it. I know I didn't look it, but I've never felt so beautiful in my life. Sandra looked at me and smiled, while her eyes began to well. "Pretty soon you will to." I reached over and rubbed her pregnant stomach. I was referring to much more than just becoming a mom.

Our eyes met and held on to each other while we talked. I saw the effects of war all over her face. I heard the tone of resolve in her words. More importantly, I saw hope and strength in her eyes. She wanted better for herself and her baby. She would be ok. That's all that mattered to me.

She handed Sarah back to me and stood to leave, just as Evan came back into the room. Sandra kissed me on the forehead and mouthed the words 'I think he's a good guy'. Not that I required it, but her reassurance was nice to have. I mouthed the words 'I know' back at her. We laughed silently, as she turned greeted Evan and left.

"Sandra told me you came up earlier." He came and sat down next to the bed.

"Yeah, I thought you needed some mother-daughter time, so I left you alone."

"Thank you. I appreciate that. I don't even know what to say. She's so beautiful."

"You both are." He looked at me in a way that no man ever has. He made me feel the way no man ever has. I believed it would only get better. My eyes welled with happiness.

My trust in him had been warranted. I don't know why God does what he does and it's really not for me to know; I can only accept his will. For whatever reason, and in a very brief time span, I loved this man. I didn't tell him, though. I still battled with trying to make sense of it for my own rationale. My mind told me it was like Sandra running to Lesley, but my heart told me that our interaction was based on truth. I wasn't running towards anything, I was simply following my heart. It was leading me to that beautifully warm place at my heart's epicenter. Evan was there with my spirit and Ms. James waiting on my arrival. He was nothing like Lesley. Our interaction wasn't shallow. Me and Evan were not a lie and I can live with that. I can live with him and I told him just that.

The End

www.ingramcontent.com/pod-product-compliance
Lightning Source LLC
Chambersburg PA
CBHW021956170626
46808CB00001B/181